Praise for *Pavel & I*

"[*Pavel & I*] spools out moodily in post-World War II Berlin ... The novel is grotesque, sometimes funny, and completely chilling, a wonderful re-creation of the Europe of 1946. Dan Vyleta is a name to watch."

—*Cleveland Plain Dealer*

"Impressive ... There is a lot to admire about *Pavel & I* ... Like most mysteries, literary and cinematic, this one grows complex nearly to the point of irritation; but unlike most, this one is entirely logical, and every dead body is accounted for ... Readers in search of a good story will find one here."

—*Denver Post*

"A tremendous first novel that will gather accolades like shards of broken glass littering the once-fashionable Kurfurstendamm. *Pavel & I* is not to be missed."

—*I Love a Mystery*

"Vyleta pens an intricately creative tale pillared by a historical framework that illuminates and strengthens the story. His characters are multifaceted. A few are barbarians, but most are wonderfully complicated: simultaneously concerned with the well-being of others while never straying from the need for self-preservation. This novel charges through a frigid winter and an equally chilling political adventure."

—*Booklist*

Pavel & I

A Novel

DAN VYLETA

BLOOMSBURY

NEW YORK · BERLIN · LONDON · SYDNEY

Published by Bloomsbury USA, New York

All papers used by Bloomsbury USA are natural, recyclable
products made from wood grown in well-managed forests.
The manufacturing processes conform to the environmental
regulations of the country of origin.

LIBRARY OF CONGRESS CATALOGING-IN-PUBLICATION DATA HAS BEEN APPLIED FOR.

ISBN: 978-1-59691-451-3 (hardcover)

First U.S. edition published by Bloomsbury USA in 2008
This paperback edition published in 2012

Paperback ISBN: 978-1-60819-807-8

1 3 5 7 9 10 8 6 4 2

Typeset by Westchester Book Group
Printed in the United States of America by Quad/Graphics,
Fairfield, Pennsylvania

For Chantal, and for Rick. You read me first.

I was in the habit of observing the ways of the *faubourg*, its residents and their characters. *[. . .]* Observation had already become deeply ingrained in me, it took hold of the soul without neglecting the body, or rather, it seized on external details so well that it immediately moved beyond them, it gave me the ability to live the life of a person upon whom I had trained my sights by allowing me to substitute myself for him, like the dervish in 1001 Nights who stole people's bodies and souls after pronouncing certain words over them.

Honoré de Balzac,
'Facino Cane'

It is a striking and generally observed characteristic of the conduct of paranoiacs that they endow small, negligible details in the behaviour of others with enormous significance; they interpret these details and find in them grounds for far-reaching conclusions.

Sigmund Freud,
The Psychopathology of Everyday Life

Part One

The Midget

1

18 December 1946

The boy was always around him then. Time and again he had to shoo him away into his room, only to see him re-emerge a few moments later, chewing at his lip with crooked teeth, and fussing. They did not speak. The boy tried to now and again, in German, or else in that flat-vowelled English he had, but Pavel never answered with more than a gesture until the boy, too, took to this language of signs and trained his face to betray his purpose. It was during this time that the pain in his kidneys grew worst. They sat in him like stones, cold against his skin. He would trace their outlines gingerly, lying face down upon his bed. Every half-hour or so they bid him get up, his kidneys, walked him over to the corner and pushed him to his knees in front of his chamber pot's blood-flecked rim. At first he'd had qualms about exposing himself before the child and had tried to shield his nudity with the flat of his hand. Now it did not matter to him, and he even felt grateful when the boy drew near and stood over him, a hand upon his shoulder, and watched him squeeze crimson drops from his organ. Afterwards he would help him up, unbend those stiffened knees; time and again he had to walk them supple across the hardwood floor. Upon every turn, his image in the looking glass, loathsome to him now with its hollow cheeks and stained overcoat, a woollen hat drawn low into his brow. And behind him, watching, the boy with the crooked teeth, running grubby fingernails across the window's frost-lined glass and etching his name, always his name, *Anders*.

There was no noise to the night, no means of telling the time. He did not have a watch, had not owned a watch for a long time now. His kidneys were his only timekeepers, that and the interval it took for the frost to eat into the boy's name and obscure it. Pavel longed for liquor but had none. Perhaps in the morning he would send the boy to find him some. He had cigarettes, of course, but dared not smoke them. Cigarettes were the only currency left to the city, would buy him coals tomorrow, could buy him company if he should seek it, six Luckies for a sympathetic lap, and less if all he required were the services of a pair of German lips, cold-chapped and bare of lipstick that cost more than the sex. Once or twice that night he would bend to prise a pack from under the corner of his mattress, and sniff at the tobacco through layers of wrapping for minutes at a time, the boy's eyes upon him, crooked teeth dug deep into his childish lip. Then his kidneys would bid him kneel again before his blood-encrusted idol, his manhood between fingers that had long lost all sensation. 'God,' he cursed once, and meant nothing by it. Behind him, the boy moved his right hand in deliberate provocation, touched chin, belly and both sides of the chest. 'Amen,' he said, hardly a whisper, and for the first time in their month-long acquaintance Pavel had the urge to lash out at him, though truth be told he loved that boy. Then the phone rang, rang shrill in the half-lit room, and before he even had time to wonder that the line was working again, he answered it mechanically, giving his number, one palm against the icy window, melting yet another hole into Anders' frostbitten name.

———·———

It was the winter of '46, Berlin, the city trussed up into twenty pieces like a turkey on Thanksgiving dinner, eight to the Russians and word had it not a woman there who had not been raped. A winter of death, people freezing in their unheated flats, impoverished, hungry, scraping together something less than a living from the crumbs that fell from their occupiers' tables. And yet, amongst the misery, the first stirrings of recovery: a nightclub in Schöneberg, a working man's brothel in Wedding; some bars around Zoogarten and in the December air the reek of the monkey cage. Small-time businesses, American customers, local staff. It was in one of these that Boyd White was standing, one eye out onto the street, where snow was trying to bury his car. He shielded the phone with his girth, his collar turned high over neck and chin, counting off the rings under his breath. Pavel picked up after the third.

'Your kidneys keeping you awake?' Boyd asked and listened to the lie that answered.

'Glad you're feeling better. Listen, Pavel, I need help. Are you alone?

'The boy? Send him away.

'What do you mean you can't?

'I'll be there in ten. Make sure the downstairs door is unlocked. I'll have my hands full.

'Let's say I'm bringing some laundry.

'Laundry, Pavel. A man's gotta wash.

'Ten minutes, Pavel. Just wait in your place. And get rid of the boy.'

He rang off and asked the barkeep what sort of booze they were serving.

'Potato vodka. Chocolate liqueur. French brandy, but it's watered down and costs a fortune.'

'You tell that to all your customers?'

'Why not? My boss is an *Arschloch*.'

Boyd shrugged and bought a half-bottle of vodka. He paid with some food coupons and whatever was left of a pack of cigarettes. They shared one, he and the barkeep, watching the snow through the dirty windows.

5

'That your car?' the barman asked enviously.

'Sure,' said Boyd. 'If someone asks, I was never here.' He put another half-dozen cigarettes on the counter. 'You hear me?'

'Hear who?'

'Thatta boy.'

Boyd threw the butt of his cigarette onto the floor and made his way out into the cold. He walked over to the car, opened the back. Inside lay a trunk, the kind one uses for overseas travel, brass on the corners and two belts to hold it shut. Boyd ran a hand along its base, testing for wet. Then he got in, turned the ignition, and set off for Pavel's place. A ten-minute drive on ice-slick roads and all the while his lips were moving, rehearsing the words he would have to speak. Trying them on for size.

———·———

'I swear to God I never saw him coming. I mean, Jesus Christ, who drives around looking out for a fucking midget? All I know is I was driving through one of the Russian sectors, a quart of rye for company, and then I hit him, hit *something*, and felt it dragging under the car. I get out and it's snowing hard, my breath showing in the air and not a soul out. Some godforsaken alleyway, a handful of bathroom windows sticking out of the ruins, frost-blinkered glass, and not a light to be seen. At first I think it's my tail lights that are tinting the snow, but when I get my flashlight from out of the glove box, I see it for what it is, a path of red starting ten yards back and leading right up to my rear fender. So I grab under, feeling spooked, you know, figuring I hit a dog or something, and what is it I touch? Two hundred dollars' worth of cashmere wool, that's what, warm and soggy with somebody's dying. It takes me a while to drag him out, he's got himself stuck to the axle, and by the time I am done and stand over the body something strange has started to happen. The alley's filled with a half-dozen cats, runty little things with their ribs showing and

6

their tails worn high like they're pointing to the moon. I stand there, breathing froth into the snowflakes and watch them gather round me, soft kitty paws, and now and then a patrol car rolls past in the distance. The cats are circling us, tails cocked at the moon, their muzzles bloodied by the tail lights' glow. They are vicious bastards, let me tell you: frost on their whiskers, eyes like cut glass, a half-dozen pairs, on me and the dead man. And then they start licking. Licking at the snow I mean, the blood in the snow, they lap it up like mother's milk. And all the while from their throats, from their whole bodies, there issues this sound, you hear it with your skin, it's like an engine running under your palm. That's when I realize they are purring, man, purring as they feed on the midget's death.

'It really gave me the willies.

'Anyway, so I figure, no point sticking around, only I'm worried: that cashmere coat, man, it gives you pause. What if I nailed someone important, you know? So I bend down to have a closer look, and to check the pulse, on the neck, see, right up under the jawbone, only clearly the neck's all broke, and then I see his collar. Midget wears a pair of fucking stars, red stars, wears them through the button holes. I nearly crapped myself I got so scared. So here I am in the middle of the Russian sector, my car's all busted up, a dead midget at my feet, the cats are purring like it's Christmas and Easter all rolled into one, and the stiff is a fucking Russky apparatchik or something. I gotta think of something fast. And then it comes to me – the suitcase. It's been rolling around in my car forever; some clothes are in it, money, papers, a toothbrush, just in case, you know, only it's as big as a fucking tuba case. Plenty big for a midget. There is no time to lose. I upend the case right on the back seat of my car, and then I throw the body inside, it's a bit of a squeeze after all, but hell, he don't mind no more, and two minutes later I'm off, the cats still licking up evidence and enough snow coming down to cover my tracks inside the hour.

'Thank Christ it was a midget. Just imagine he was fully grown. Doing an ax job out in an alley.

'It doesn't bear thinking about.'

———·———

That was his story anyway, Boyd White's, the night he killed the midget, packed him away in a suitcase, and carried him up four floors to Pavel's two-bedroom in a quiet part of Charlottenburg. Boyd was California-born, a crook and grifter by vocation, a hard man grown fat in a city of starvation. For the most part he spoke like a second-rate stooge from a Chandler novel, though he had his moments of eloquence, too, like the present one in which he conjured up cats' tails taking aim at the winter moon.

You have to wonder about those cats, though, emaciated to be sure – how did they ever survive? It was the winter of '46, winter of death, people freezing while taking craps in the outhouse, you heard the spiel. Most cats in the city had long been eaten, their fur turned into gloves and collars, the black market awash with viola strings. Berlin that winter was dog-eat-dog and worse, and that night its vengeful gods had thrown a wrench into Boyd's spokes, if you will pardon my metaphors, and here he came running to the one friend he had left in the city, ran up four floors and barged through the door without so much as a knock, the middle of the night and a dead midget in his fist.

What the hell was he thinking?

———·———

When the door had opened and Boyd'd come in, Pavel had been down on his knees again, straining before the chamber pot. It had taken him a moment or two to collect himself, struggle up against his kidneys' weight. Then he had stood and studied the bulk of the trunk pulling at Boyd's arm, the crease of worry that

8

ran through the man's face; had taken in the patch of wet that had collected in one of the suitcase's brass-encrusted corners, threatening to drip.

'What's in the suitcase?' he'd asked, stiff fingers struggling to button his fly.

'You have a look,' Boyd had grunted, letting go of the trunk and shuffling over to the bed to sit down. He'd lit a cigarette, silver Zippo lighter, had inhaled. 'It's not as bad as it looks.'

It certainly didn't look good. The midget was four foot one, maybe four two, Boyd had had to bend him to make him fit. Not that he wasn't bent enough already. As far as Pavel could tell both legs were broken, and one of the arms, at elbow and wrist, and some of the head was missing, too. The body was leaking blood from all ends; it had soaked into his expensive tan suit and gave him a jellyfish slipperiness that sent a wave of nausea through Pavel's guts. Quickly, ashamed of himself, he turned the face over, but, of course, he didn't recognize it. He did not know any midgets. There was a pencil moustache and the teeth were broken. Inside lolled a serrated tongue.

Gently, getting down into a crouch to do it, Pavel closed the lid of the trunk, then limped over to the sink to scrub his hands. He had to hack a piece of ice from out of a bucket and run its jagged edge over fingernails and knuckles. It was as though he was carving away the blood stains, planing his skin like a carpenter.

As Pavel stood there, the ice pick sticking to his palm, hammering away at the ice, Boyd coughed and offered up his tale. 'I swear to God I never saw him coming,' he said. Pavel only half listened, his soul turned inward, tuned in to his breathing, his heart's anxious goose-step marching him back to the war's many corpses. God, how he hated that midget just then. And all the time he stood there, his fingers white against the sink, Boyd talking kittens, he kept wondering whether the boy could hear him through the bedroom door, and worse yet, understand.

———·———

There is no telling people. Take Pavel, for instance. By rights the midget should have broken his back, coming for a visit at a time like this; put him down like a sick dog. You picture him: a slight man, eyes like wet coals. Curved woman's lips and skin so delicate you could trace the veins. The ears almost translucent, black hair worn parted, the teeth rocking from lack of fruit. A weak man in all respects. He had bad kidneys, and that was just the start of it. Pavel suffered from that terminal disease called empathy, forever trying to exchange points of view even with the boot that kicked him. He was a quiet man, intensely sincere, often silent for hours on end though capable of passionate outbursts during which his tongue kept tripping over the edge of words and everything came out as a muddle. He'd backtrack time and again to correct himself, for above all he wished to be *sincere*. A weak man, you see, brought up for the previous century, for a world of calling cards and drawing-room courting; for chessboard gambits and the Novel; for a quiet love of life. By rights he should have been, in his time and place, a sacrificial lamb. As it was, he turned into a bloodhound the minute he took the midget's scent.

You don't believe me? I spent hours and days eye to eye with Pavel, just us in the dark, some bars between us and the scuttle of roaches. I know Pavel like the back of my hand. And yet, time and again, I was surprised by him; he threw me, more than once, and there were moments when it felt like I had to start all over again.

Boyd, by contrast, does not compare. Boyd was twentieth-century through and through: a braggart, a womanizer, a boor. Boyd talked tough and had fists to back him up. Men liked Boyd, as did women; he wore spats as an affectation and thought them a sign of originality. Forget about Boyd. I only spoke to Boyd once, and even then he had nothing of interest to say.

But we weren't talking about Boyd. We were talking about the boy, Anders, who stood ears pressed against the bedroom door, and tried his hardest to understand. What he was asking himself, in German no doubt, the word sticky in his child-mouth, was this: What the fuck is a *mit-chut*?

———·——

Whatever it was, it was dead, and Russian. The death did not bother the boy. He had seen plenty of it, had stolen from the stiff grasp of corpses more than once. Nor did he care that it was a Russian. What was there to care? One stiff was as good as another. He understood, too, why the man Boyd had not left him behind in the snow. The *mit-chut* was important, one way or another, and it was unwise to kill those who were important, even in Berlin. The boy and the crew he ran with had learned the city's rules. You robbed those who looked like they had something, and avoided those who looked like they had too much. Russkies, Tommies, Amis – they were all off limits. You sweated locals, those who had made it through the war with a bag of gold under their pillows but were too stupid or too compromised to have found protection. This the boy had learned and learned well. You didn't break the rules and walk away unbroken.

Which was to say that the man Boyd had made a mistake, and now he was sweating over it, with the thermometer at minus five. The boy had seen him around, driving his car, trading on the black market. He was a whore-man, a *Zuhälter*. He did not know the English word for it.

The conversation carried on. Anders listened, his ear at the keyhole, holding his breath so it wouldn't drown out the voices.

'What do you want to do?' Pavel asked. He sounded cool, composed, only his teeth were chattering. The boy felt a pang of pride. Pavel wasn't like the fat American. He had backbone, despite the disease.

'How the fuck do I know? If it wasn't so fucking cold, I'd drive him out to the river. Sink the little bastard.'

'You could drop him in the woods.'

'Too many guard patrols. Besides –'

'Besides?'

'He might still be useful. The midget.'

'Did he have papers?'

'Nothing. No wallet, no briefcase, not even a fucking wedding ring.'

'Okay, Boyd, I want him out of my bedroom. Let's carry him into the back room. The boy will give you a hand.'

He called him in then, but the boy had already started opening the door. He made a show of helping the man lift the trunk, but left him with all the weight. They manoeuvred it into the second bedroom and propped it up against the wall next to the window. It was surprisingly small, smaller than Anders, he measured himself out against it.

A mit-chut, thought Anders, *must be some sort of dwarf.*

When they returned to the front room, Pavel was back on his knees, trying to pee. Boyd seemed unembarrassed about the act. He sidled up next to him, frowning a little when he saw the blood. Once Pavel was finished and back on his feet there was a long silence. The boy kept away from them, trying to figure them out, the room so cold he could count his every breath.

'So you're circumcised,' Boyd said after twenty. 'You a fucking kike or something?'

Pavel smiled at that, and Boyd smiled back. The boy didn't understand the joke.

'He needs penicillin,' he said, addressing the man for the first time, and got ready to duck in case he should try to hit him.

'Oh yeah? Says who, pipsqueak?'

12

They stared at each other like gunslingers from a cowboy film. The boy knew all about cowboy films. He wished he had a gun.

'Boyd,' said Pavel, 'this is Anders. Anders, this is Boyd White. He and I used to be in the army together. He is –'

'I know what he is. He's a *Zuhälter*.'

'Yes,' said Pavel softly, 'he's a pimp.' He smiled at the word and stroked his aching back. It seemed to the boy that there had been reproach in his voice.

Boyd shrugged like it meant little to him. He peeled a pack of cigarettes from out of his shirt pocket, offered one to Pavel and then, grudgingly, one to the boy. Anders pocketed it without a word, thinking he would have it later, when Boyd was not around. The two men stood in the room, smoking, cupping their cigarettes in identical ways. It was Boyd who spoke.

'You could go back, you know, Pavel. The army. Wasn't as bad as all that, and they are desperate for interpreters. Christ, you speak all four languages. You could live like a king.'

Pavel shrugged and blew smoke. 'What are you going to do now?'

'Shove off before one of his friends runs off with my wheels.' Boyd pointed at Anders with his cigarette. 'Make some inquiries about the midget. I'll come back with some drugs, coals and cigarettes.'

'Let's swap overcoats,' he added. 'Mine is warmer and it'll drop to minus twenty over the next few days.'

Pavel accepted the charity. It irked the boy that he would accept it so easily. 'It's a kind of payment,' he said to himself, to soothe his wounded pride. 'Cheap,' he told himself, 'he's getting off cheap,' and searched for a bitter parting word.

At the door, the two men embraced like brothers, Boyd's hands careful not to press upon the kidneys.

'Belle,' he said. 'If something goes wrong, go look for Belle.'

'Who's she?' Anders found himself asking, jealous of the embrace. 'She some sort of whore?'

Boyd disentangled himself.

'You should box his ears,' he said to Pavel, but said it gently. 'She's one of my girls. She's also –'

He broke off and took the time to smile to himself.

'She's something special, Pavel. I mean *real* special.

'One day,' he said, 'I'll make her Mrs White.'

The boy thought that even his smile looked fake.

———·———

And that's how he left them, Boyd White, turned on his heel and swanned out, Pavel's thin coat too small for his frame, and a stoop in his shoulders like he was still carting it around, the midget's death, down the stairs and into his limousine that stood cold and lonely before the bomb-chewed kerb. Outside, the snow had stopped falling. It had become too cold for it.

I will say one thing for Boyd. He did a good job. I mean, for a bloody amateur, it had been one hell of a performance.

———·———

It was dawn before the boy fell asleep. Pavel waited him out patiently, reading to him from his favourite novel, trying to numb his own pain with his voice's quiet rasp. Once or twice he almost dozed off, and caught the boy trying to sneak into the back room in order to investigate its secrets. Each time Pavel called him back without anger. Somewhat to his surprise, the boy obeyed without argument.

'A *mit-chut* is some sort of dwarf?' Anders asked him once.

Pavel smiled at this.

'Yes. Something like that.'

'A dead Russian dwarf, eh?' the boy sneered. 'That God of yours has a sense of humour.'

Pavel did not rise to the bait. It was part of an ongoing theological debate they were having. He went back to the book and started reading. Eventually Anders succumbed to sleep. His breath rose above him like a plume. Pavel refrained from kissing him, lest he should wake. Now it was his turn to sneak off to see the midget. He took the bucket of ice along, and the cold shaft of the ice pick.

It took a while to wash the blood off the dead man's face. Pavel had to don gloves to prevent the ice from sticking to his fingers and they made his hands clumsy. He did not bother much with the body, but closed the mouth above the broken teeth and combed the frozen hair with a penny comb that he warmed in one armpit. When he was done, the midget stood peacefully in the leaning trunk, though try as he might Pavel could not get the eyes to close. After some thought he lifted him out once more and struggled to free his overcoat, then inspected it inch by inch. At last he set it aside with approval: the coat was too dark to tell whether it was soiled by blood or something else. There was no point taking the shirt – it was not ripped, but stained a heavy, muddy red, especially at the back. To rob him of his trousers seemed undignified; besides, they would be too short for the boy. Pavel took the boots though, after some struggle, for he did not want to cut the laces; the socks too, for they were warm and new. Once he was done, he placed the midget back in his casket and stood him up against its back. The feet stood yellow and wooden upon the trunk's lining, the nails chipped and dirty, coarse hair upon the toes. Shaken, Pavel wrapped them in an old towel, though some part or other always stuck out accusingly, the midget's feet refusing to be forgotten. At last, Pavel gave up and sat down on a stool, right in front of the corpse. He sat there, for half an hour perhaps, and watched ice crystals spread across the midget's glassy eyes, thinking to himself.

Thinking: 'Winter.'

Thinking: 'God, I hate winter.'

Trying to say a prayer for the midget, the words freezing in his mouth.

The last thing Pavel did was remove the red stars from the midget's shirt collar and place them in his pocket. Then he closed the lid on the dead man, and returned to the front room where he covered the boy with the cashmere coat. He stretched out next to him and smelled his hands. Try as he might he could not smell the blood. He shrugged and told himself it was too cold for smells. As he drifted off, towards sleep and dreams, he mumbled a name.

'Mrs Belle White.'

It sounded ridiculous to him, a thing from a fairy tale, and also beautiful. Beside him the boy, sleeping, blew plumes into the air, while the first rays of the sun began to probe the wall of ice that had grown upon their windows.

———·———

Anders woke mid-morning to find his new coat, along with the midget's socks and boots. He put them on and looked at himself in the mirror. He looked good, like he was from money, although the boots pinched a little. Pavel was still asleep, his woollen hat drawn down over his eyes. Anders snuck next door, opened the trunk. The *mit-chut* looked clean and glass-eyed, only the feet were ugly. Anders went through his trouser pockets, but found nothing apart from half a book of matches encrusted with frozen blood. He pocketed them out of habit, then went back to check on Pavel. The fever was still upon his brow, and his body shook with cold. The boy didn't trust Boyd to keep his word and come back with medicine. He tied on two of his scarves, stole a number of leather-bound volumes from the bookshelves, and went out to find some for himself.

Penicillin.

Penicillin was worth much that winter; was worth gold, worth murder in this city of the sick. The boy knew all about penicillin. It's how they had met, Pavel and he: it had brought them together, the boy thought it fate, thought penicillin some sort

16

of God, the kind you went to war for, or else the kind that got you killed. Pavel had asked for it on the black market at Zoogarten station more than a month ago, when his kidneys had first started playing up. He wasn't in uniform, wore a half-decent coat and spoke the language like a German. He looked game. Schlo' had picked him up, eleven and a half with those clear-water eyes that always put the hook in suckers. Schlo' had asked Pavel to show him how he was going to pay. Pavel had reached into a bag and unwrapped a china tea set, unchipped, along with a gold wedding ring.

'Will it do?' he'd asked as he watched the boy bite the ring. Schlo' had nodded.

'I ain't got it here,' he'd told Pavel. 'Come and follow me.'

Anders wasn't there to witness it, but he imagined Pavel noticing the tattoo upon the boy's forearm as they walked away from the station. He had a quick eye for things like that, though he was blind to so much else. Schlo' had led him on a right goose chase, deep into Charlottenburg, signalling to the boys who lingered on street corners, smoking, talking, pretending to play.

'Right over there,' he'd said, and then they had him, a dead end that finished in a pile of war rubble, twelve boys armed with clubs and stones, and Paulchen, their leader, showing off his father's Luger. Anders took position right behind Pavel, gauging his weight, the quality of his shoes, making him for a German civil servant, a little down on his luck.

'He's got china and a wedding band,' Schlo' told them triumphantly, 'and maybe some dough.'

Anders searched his pockets and found some dollars, along with his papers. He passed them over to Paulchen who took one look and started cursing.

'You fucking idiot,' he barked at Schlo'. 'He's a Yank.'

'He speaks German!'

'So what? You moron!' And to Pavel, shoving the papers into his face: 'Are these real?'

'They are real,' Pavel replied calmly.

It made him look up, Anders, the calmness of it and how he spoke without an accent. He found himself studying the man again, the slope of his shoulders, the thick dark hair. There was nothing there that prepared you for the calm.

'You in the army?' Paulchen wanted to know.

'I used to be. Not any more.'

'A civilian?'

'Yes.'

The man took a cigarette from behind his ear and quietly lit it with a match he found in his shirt pocket. The gesture reeked of army; it was there in the way he held the cigarette, in the way he took in its smoke. It was to Anders like the stranger failed to understand the situation, or else he understood it and refused to play along. He turned his attention over to Paulchen, who stood feet spread, gun in fist, the soft outline of a moustache twitching upon his upper lip.

Anders could tell Paulchen wasn't sure what he should do. The stranger didn't conform. Foreigners were off-limits; mugging them could be dangerous. Then again, this one did not look like he had any juice; if he did he wouldn't be buying penicillin on the black market. Paulchen shuffled and thought. The others waited him out. There was respect there. Rumour had it he had killed a man, in '45, with a crowbar and the heels of his boots.

Pavel helped him make up his mind.

'You can keep the tea set,' he told Paulchen. 'I get the wedding ring, the cash and the papers. That way, we both get something.'

They were preposterous terms. After all, they had him, twelve boys armed with clubs and stones, never mind the fucking Luger. He had no leverage other than being American, and Anders thought that if they burned his papers he wouldn't even have that. You had to have papers to be somebody in Berlin, papers and friends. The man did not look like he had too many friends.

18

But Paulchen bought it. Never thought twice about it. Not a word, not a threat – he just gave back the documents, threw him the ring.

'Get moving,' he said to Pavel, and Pavel walked off, smoking, a little limp to his gait from how his kidneys bothered him. Anders followed. No good reason, he just did. Something about the way he had lit up, and the terms he had bought himself. Or perhaps it was because he spoke German like that, like he had been born there, only perhaps a little softer, like he thought it a fragile tongue, one that would shatter in his mouth.

It was child's play, following him. He never once looked back. Anders gave him a head start up the stairs of his building, but stayed close enough to make sure he knew which apartment he went into. When he crept close to press his ear against the wood there was nothing but silence. Anders sat there for the better part of the afternoon, with his back against the door and enough weight in his legs to make a run for it should he have to. He sat, sucked on caramels, and listened. The only sound he heard was the metallic rattle of a typewriter that started up after perhaps an hour and continued throughout the day. At long last Anders got up and knocked. He wasn't sure why, but he knocked. The door opened a crack. Behind it, the man's tired face and a shelf laden with books.

'What do you want?' asked the man in his mealy-mouthed German.

'I can get you penicillin,' Anders found himself saying.

'You what?'

'I can get you penicillin,' Anders said again, said it in English, best he knew. 'For a price.'

'I don't have enough left to sell.'

'You have books.'

'They are not for sale,' said Pavel, also in English now, and closed the door.

Anders went away thinking that the man's English sounded much harsher than his German.

———·———

He went back. There was no reason for it, he couldn't afford to give away medicine, and besides, he didn't owe the man a thing, not a thing, but still he went back. Twice he simply sat there, listening to the typewriter through the closed door, counting the letters and typewritten lines that ended in the sounding of a bell. The fourth time he came he brought a bottle of mint liqueur which he had heard was good for when one was ill. He placed it on the step, knocked on the door and ran away. He avoided the flat for a week after that, running with his crew instead, ripping off punters and flogging wares on the market. The weather was gradually growing worse, and Anders bought himself boots and a blanket from his proceeds. The boots were second-hand army issue, three sizes too large and heavy as lead. Anders walked them proudly, and made sure they didn't carry him back to the man's door.

Then, when he almost thought he had kicked the habit, he found himself retracing his steps yet again. For an hour he stood there, one hand spread up on the door, telling himself to leave. But this time he didn't leave. Instead, he knocked, a series of quick hard raps like he had seen the police use, and went over in his mind how he would ask the man for money retrospectively, to pay for the bottle of liqueur. 'You drank it, didn't you?' he'd say without balking, and the man would have to admit that he was in his debt.

The door opened, that is to say, Pavel opened it, opened wide and without hesitation. He saw Anders, saw he was alone, outsize boots on his feet and a blanket thrown over one shoulder. There was no reaction, nothing the boy could read. Pavel simply turned, turned on his heel, and marched back over to an armchair upon which he had been sitting prior to being interrupted. He sat, threw a coat over his lap and legs, and picked up a book that lay face down by his feet, its pages spread across the wooden floor.

The book was one of hundreds. They lined the apartment's walls, standing on cheap shelves made out of pressed, unvarnished wood. Hundreds of books, bound in leather, linen and cardboard; some as fat as Anders' fist, others so thin they looked like magazines, only the size was wrong. Amongst them, a few books whose pages looked like they were made out of gold, and, in one corner, a stack with books so large they did not fit upon the shelf. Enough books so that you could smell them, the smell of paper. Anders hadn't known that paper smelled.

'Come in or stay out, but either way, please close the door.'

Anders did not react. His eyes remained riveted upon the books. He knew their worth on the market. They would have bought plenty of medicine. He stepped up to them, ran his fingers over the titles that lay embossed upon their spines.

'These are in different languages,' he said at last, impressed despite himself. 'You read all these?'

'Yes,' said Pavel.

'I speak German, English and Russian,' said Anders. And then, unaccountably moved to honesty: 'Only a little Russian. To trade, you see.'

'Do you read?' asked Pavel, and the boy shook his head.

'Reading is for pencil pushers and bureaucrats,' he explained. 'I have no time for it.'

And after some thought, looking at the book that sat in Pavel's hands: 'If you wish to read, you may read aloud, if you like. I don't mind.'

Pavel smiled at this and got up to close the door. He locked it deliberately, the sound of the lock loud in the room, reminding Anders how foolish it had been to come there. Then Pavel turned to peruse his shelves with the same quiet calm with which he had lit that cigarette in the face of Paulchen's Luger. His hand hovered over a number of books until at last he pulled out a dog-eared hardback, whose back-flap was badly torn. He settled down with it and started reading. He read:

> ' "Among other public buildings in a certain town which for many reasons it will be prudent to refrain from mentioning, and to which I will assign no fictitious name, it boasts of one which is common to most towns, great or small, to wit, a workhouse; and in this workhouse was born, on a day and date which I need not take upon myself to repeat, inasmuch as it can be of no possible consequence to the reader, in this stage of the business at all events, the item of mortality whose name is prefixed to the head of this chapter." '

Anders puffed up his cheeks and let out air, noisily. 'Gibberish,' he complained in German. 'It makes no sense at all. "I-tem of mor-tility" – it's all nonsense.'

'All it's saying is that a boy was born in a workhouse – something like an orphanage – in some town or other. Only, I forgot to tell you his name. It's Oliver Twist.'

'Oh yeah? Well it sounds like it was written two hundred years ago,' the boy said, sour-faced and dismissive. 'It's not *modern*,' he added in order to settle the issue.

'As a matter of fact it was written just one hundred years ago,' Pavel started to respond, but then he broke off, shrugged, closed the book and went back to the one he had been reading before the boy arrived.

'What's it about anyway?' Anders asked after a while, his voice feigning boredom, the feigning audible even to himself.

'Words,' said Pavel.

'Words?'

'Words. And a young orphan boy who starts living with an old Jew.'

22

'Is the Jew good to him?'

'No. He tries his best to squeeze him for every cent he's worth.'

'What's his name again?'

'The Jew? Fagin.'

'No, I mean the boy. Olliwer?'

'Oliver. Oliver Twist.'

The boy mouthed it a few times, stretching and contracting the vowels until he chanced upon a version he liked.

'You may read on,' he said magnanimously. 'Olliwer Tweest. Mind you, most likely I will fall asleep.'

———·——

He left at the end of chapter four. Night had fallen, the flat was freezing. 'Later,' he said, and wondered whether he should tell the other boys about the books. They would want to steal them.

The next day he came back with two tins of sardines and half a kilo of floury potatoes.

———·——

Thereafter the boy came time and again; dropped in after breakfast, or on his way home from work. Sometimes, though not always, he would sleep there. Mostly he came to listen to the book, or else to talk. They talked about many things, Pavel and he. It took some time for Anders to get used to this. It was strange talk, talk about thoughts one had late at night before dozing off, or perhaps on the crapper sometimes, when one's bowels made one wait and the mind started to wander. Anders had not known such thoughts were for talking. Pavel spoke of little else. When Anders asked him to tell him about normal things, say the war or his past, he declined. 'Books, beauty, and fear of the dark,' he said. 'These I will talk about. Forget about the war. There was no war. Only of course there was, but we do better in forgetting.' Whichever way he looked at it, it sounded a little *meschugge* to the boy.

Then the kidneys got worse. Anders tried to buy Pavel some medicine but there was none to be had. He couldn't tell whether Pavel was already pissing blood at that point. This was before the water had frozen in the pipes – before there was any need for the chamber pot, that is. Anders learned to gauge the disease by Pavel's walk; by the shadow that would pass across his face and force his lips into a liar's smile. The kidneys got worse, then better, then worse again. Once they gave occasion for one of those talks. Afterwards, Anders stayed away for a few nights, before he came back, wordlessly, and gestured for Pavel to get on with the book.

It happened like this. They had sat up during the night, Pavel praying in one corner, a little hat in his hair and a piece of cloth stretched taut behind his back. He was speaking foreign words. When he was done he turned, holding his kidneys, his eyes moist now with pain. 'God,' Pavel said and the word stood in the room like a lodger overdue on his rent. It wasn't the first time the subject had come up; it was in the book, here and there, and in the church bells that carried it in during their morning airing; in the prayers Pavel spoke each night and upon the covers of a dozen of his books, stars and crosses, and the slender sickle of a crescent moon. Anders thought it over and decided he should clarify the point.

'I don't believe in God,' he said. 'Don't get me wrong, I have nothing against him. He's useful, you see. Keeps the masses in place.' His hand made a dismissive gesture.

'Who taught you this?'

'Nobody taught me,' Anders said proudly. 'I taught myself. Or else the war taught me.'

He mulled it over for a minute, running his tongue through a gap in his teeth. He found he liked the sound of it.

'Yes, the war taught me. There is no God.'

He looked over to Pavel, making sure he did not look like he was looking. Pavel's face was pale, impassive. *He looks like a girl,* the boy thought to himself, *and also like a statue.*

'You disapprove?' he asked.

'And what is it to you whether I approve or disapprove?'

Pavel shrugged and picked a book from a pile that sat by his bed. He began reading it in silence, the boy sitting there, gap-toothed upon his stool. They sat like that for perhaps an hour.

'So there is a God?' Anders asked at last, and flushed because his voice sounded childish in his ears.

'I don't know,' said Pavel, upon reflection. 'There may be.'

They went back to their silence, the man reading his book, and rats scrambling in their walls.

Later, after they had shared a tin of sardines for a midnight supper, Pavel crouched to hug the boy. He lay in his arms stiff-backed and hostile.

'I am too old for this,' he said disdainfully.

'On the contrary,' said Pavel. 'You're old enough.'

The boy did not understand this and thought it a lie. Outside, in the cold, he found he was crying and bitterly berated himself for it. He swore that this time he would not go back. But then, two days later, he moved in with Pavel permanently. It was the third of December. On the sixth the cold settled upon the city. A week and a half later, Boyd came to visit. And the next morning, Anders stole four leather-bound volumes from Pavel's private library in order to get his friend some penicillin, and a lemon. He had heard it said that lemons were good when you were ill, even better than mint liqueur.

25

2

21 December 1946

Boyd did not come back that day, the nineteenth of December, nor the next, nor the one after. Nor was there any penicillin to be had on the market. In its stead, Anders bought a fungus-ridden lemon from a sallow-faced German who claimed to run a private greenhouse – a greenhouse? How could he possibly heat it? – and some Class One meat coupons that he traded in for six pounds of innards and a tin bucket to carry them in. The blood froze on the half-hour walk back to Pavel's place, and he had to chip free with the ice pick whatever pieces he wanted to use that night. The thermometer had fallen to minus thirty and made each breath hurt in his chest. It had long ceased to snow, was too cold to snow, the sky scrubbed clean of cloud and germs. The house's pipes remained frozen, of course, Anders had to fetch their water by the bucket from one of the neighbourhood pumps. On the twentieth, signs went up around the neighbourhood declaring that electricity had been limited to a few hours a day. The boy did not remember it so well, but he heard the old people grumble that it was worse than during the war. In the entranceway of the house there appeared a smeared message: '88'. It had showed up overnight and nobody moved to wipe it off. Anders asked Paulchen about it, and he told him the figures stood for the eighth letter, H. Double H: 'Heil Hitler'.

Now that he was looking, Anders found more such eights scribbled onto doorways and courtyard walls across Charlottenburg. Once, he spotted them chalked onto the green canvas of a British Army truck. That night, stretched out next to Pavel's feverish form, Anders lay awake asking himself whether there was any truth in the rumour that Hitler had survived the invasion and that his Reich would rise once more from its ashes. He got up, cut a piece of ice from out of the bucket, slipped it into his mouth. 'Heil Hitler,' he whispered past the ice's ragged edges, just to try it out, then shrugged his shoulders. It was all the same to him, just as long as Pavel made it through the night.

The fever was getting worse. Anders had no way of taking Pavel's temperature, but in the cold of the room he watched steam rise from the exposed skin of his cheeks and piled blanket after blanket on top of him. The coal oven burned night and day, but its heat lacked the strength to traverse the room. It was, to Anders, like they were burning money; coal prices soared, rumours of people freezing to death in their beds. Paulchen made Schlo' and some of the other small-framed boys creep down coal shafts at night to score a few buckets' worth, then distributed it amongst his crew. They swore unending devotion. Those who had families supplied fathers, mothers, rape-pregnant sisters. The others heated their cubbyholes and traded the excess for chocolate and smokes. Anders brought his coals home to Pavel, sat inches before the iron stove, stoking the fire and beseeching it to break through the wall of cold that grew out of the floor a mere two yards from it. Coal fumes hung so heavy in the room that the sick man's face was mucky with soot. Five times a day Anders made a point of breaking off a corner of ice, clutching it in an oven-warmed fist, and pressing it to Pavel's lips. Water revived Pavel, bade him wake. They spoke on and off, boy and man, never mentioning the midget. Pavel tried to read but had to give up. His eyeballs looked swollen in their sockets; they could not focus. Anders watched him for hours at a time and thought that surely he would die.

'Tonight,' he whispered into a soot-covered ear, mentally sorting through the contents of his bucket of meat. 'Tonight I will cook you a good dinner.

'Meat,' he whispered. 'Meat for health. It will make you good again.'

His hand crawled over Pavel's dry-hot cheek and when it crossed his lips he saw them pucker. Anders did not feel the kiss. It was parched and dry and had no strength.

———·———

Pavel dreamt. Day and night, always the same dream now. Him, naked, rolling upon a mountain of raw kidneys. Rolling in the manner of a swine, naked, the smell of kidneys strong in his nose. His naked body: writhing, and on occasion the heavens would open, more kidneys raining down on him, sticking to him, cold and clammy meat on skin. Whenever he woke, he told himself that it was nothing but the fever.

Then, early one evening, he woke yet again from his dream and found them on his dresser. He was convinced, then, that they were his own, and in truth he felt relieved. They lay upon a plate, the last of his china, at the very centre of the dresser. Lay within a circle of blood upon a plate of chipped Meissen, a pinch of dried rosemary scattered across. Pavel lay still, his eyes fastened upon the kidneys, hysterical laughter sounding in the depths of him. He tried to move and felt unbearably heavy. A pile of blankets pressed down upon his body; he had to fight to free an arm and a hand, and dug his nails into his palm to test it for sensation. Deliberately – tenderly – he reached out towards the plate. He wished to know whether they were still warm, those kidneys that had been taken from him during his sleep. He found them freezing, a coat of frost crystals clinging to their membranes. The rosemary stuck to his sweaty fingers. He brought it back to his nose and through it he smelled the tangy smell of kidney. It was then that the laughter burst free of his chest and he began to flail and kick against the blankets' leaden weight.

It went on so until the boy was there, shouting at him. The Meissen lay smashed on the floor; the blankets were bloodied. 'Meat,' the boy kept screaming at him, and at long last Pavel relented. He settled back into sleep, thinking that it did not matter now, without kidneys, thinking *I should've sold my books*, thinking *I am dead now, because I was too proud to sell them*, trying to weep for himself, asleep again before any tears would come to him, asleep upon a mountain of kidneys, writhing.

———·———

Anders woke up to his laughing, watched him kick and flail. One arm hit the dresser. The plate that he had laid out in order to cheer him up sailed down, cracked right down its middle; the meat bounced hard like a stone. The boy leapt on top of him, held him down. Marvelled at how weak he was, a grown man, his palms and cheek stained by the meat. It did not take long to calm him. Pavel slipped into sleep like a toddler, lay oblivious as Anders rearranged the blankets and cleaned his face with a moistened towel. He picked up the dinner from off the floor and went to see whether the electricity had been turned on yet. It had, and he hastily melted a piece of lard in Pavel's cast-iron pan, then patiently fried both pieces of meat until they were done. They took their while getting tender on account of being frozen, and by the time Anders was finished the outsides were scorched, the centres still bloody. He cut them into bite-sized chunks with a pen knife, shoved them into an army-issue bowl and carried it back into the sick room. The boy's entreaties woke Pavel quickly enough, but try as he might he could not get him to chew the meat. He would just lie there, a piece between his lips, and suck on its warmth. In the end Anders ate most of the kidneys himself, thinking that it had been a long time since he had tasted meat this good. Pavel had already gone back to sleep. After dinner Anders sat in the light of a candle, watching his friend die.

Anders struggled against it for the longest time. He sat on a stool by the bed clutching his knees and bravely fighting the impulse. Whenever his hands threatened to join up, or he found his eyes casting about for a towel or shawl, he would jump up and pace the room instead. The tears were in his throat but not yet on his face. When he finally relented and slipped on a cap as he had watched Pavel do, he did so with bitterness. The wood felt hard under his knees, and there was something ridiculous about the tea towel that he held stretched out behind the back of his head. Anders prayed.

'God,' he prayed, 'I think you're mean.'

'Mean, you hear. What sort of God would kill a man like this?'

'God,' he prayed, 'if he lives, I promise to believe.'

'If he dies,' he prayed, 'I will curse you.'

'Curse you, you hear.'

'My name is Anders,' he added, 'and this here is Pavel,' lest there be any mistakes.

He stopped praying then, lost for words, and grief took hold of him like a rabid dog. He sobbed and lay a cheek upon the icy floor. It took his breath, literally, and for a moment he tried to still body and blood so that he might better hear. It was to him as though, above, at the precise moment when his ear had touched the wood, he had heard a piano burst into song. He did not dare move for a whole minute and then another, sat out ten, with his breath screwed into him, biting his lip against the cold. Then he leapt up, slid a sleeve across his tear-stained face, and ran as fast as he could up the stairs to the apartment directly above.

———·———

He burst in, not bothering to knock. She must have forgotten to lock the door behind her, it gave way to his childish fist and he

30

stormed in, kicking up clouds of dust. He bolted down the corridor, she heard him crash into her suitcase, and on towards the light. The drumbeat of his feet upon her carpets – she stopped her playing in surprise, craned her neck to see, and no sooner had she done so than he, too, stopped with great suddenness, his legs still stretched for running, and stood stock still at the very centre of her living room. She picked up the candelabra from where it stood next to the piano chair and rose to inspect him.

He was an ugly boy, physically stunted, twelve, perhaps thirteen years old. In figure short and angular; a prune face above, with crooked teeth and eyes that didn't sit quite even, like he had broken a bone there some time ago and it had never been set. He opened his mouth to speak but not a word came out.

'What?' she asked, and noted how cold it sounded. 'What do you want?'

He rubbed his eyes, the dust must have got to them, his voice rasped in his throat.

'What?' she asked again, disentangling her coat from the chair, and prepared herself to use the candelabra as a weapon if need be. The boy did not answer, so she raised her left and used it to point into the black of the corridor.

'Then go,' she said, one eye on her jewelled wristwatch. 'Go, or you'll get into trouble.'

The boy would not leave. Instead, he leapt at her, or rather at her hand. Initially she thought he was after the watch, the little thief, but it was the hand itself that he grabbed and applied his weight to.

'Please,' he mouthed, just as she had resolved to hit him with the candelabra. His eyes were on the floor. 'Please.'

He smelled of street waste and burnt meat.

'What do you want?' she tried again, the boy still clinging to her hand. His prune face quivered, he was ugly like a monkey,

31

and spat when he talked, unmodulated, too loud for the room and the hour.

'Please,' he said. 'My friend, he is ill. You – you have a piano. You are rich. Please. Save him. He is dying.'

It sounded made up, a trap perhaps, and she longed to get back to her playing. It had been so long since she had enjoyed the pleasures of a piano.

'I can't help you,' she told him, and then, 'Let me go, you little beast,' only his grimy fingers were clamped upon her jacket now, pulling at it and threatening to pop its buttons. A boot-tip to his crotch got him away from her, gave her the time to sink a fist into his hair and drag him to the door. She was too fast for his flailing leg and slammed the door in his face. Then she stood, panting, and waited for him to go away.

He didn't.

Instead he drummed against the wood with feet and fists, threatening to wake up the whole house. 'Please,' he screamed, his voice breaking, and through the closed door she pictured spit flying from his crooked mouth. The fool. The Colonel would be back soon. She did not want to think what he might do to the boy. In truth she could not predict it.

'Boy,' she hissed through the wood. 'Be quiet. For your own sake, be quiet.'

The drumming stopped. She heard him shift.

'Please.' It sounded from the crack underneath the door. Half a dirty pinky squeezed its way into her apartment. 'He's sick.'

'Who?'

'My friend.'

'Your friend?'

'Downstairs. Right below. Please, he needs medicine real bad.'

She opened her mouth to answer, closed it again. Thought guiltily of the medicine chest that the Colonel had given her, that now lay inside her suitcase, wrapped in her silk nightgown and a Parisian negligee. Thought of the Colonel again, coming upon the boy like this, a German boy, dirt on his hands and a face like a prune. She pictured it, then dropped into a crouch. In one hand she still held the candelabra; on the other a jewelled watch kept ticking.

'Listen to me,' she whispered. 'I will come in two hours. Not before. If I hear another sound out of you, or see so much as your shadow, I won't show. Is that understood?'

He breathed raggedly, she thought in relief.

'I asked whether you understood what I just told you.'

'Yes, Miss,' he answered and it sounded strange and unaccustomed coming from his lips.

She waited a minute, then reopened the door. Of the boy there remained no sign; across the hall, her neighbours kept quiet. For all she knew she had none. Quickly she closed it again and wiped the corridor and living room of all signs of struggle. The place was so dusty that soon her fine cuffs and underskirts were blackened. She hoped the Colonel would not notice them in the light of the candle. Then she settled back into her chair before the piano and launched into Beethoven's piano sonata no. 17. She played it gently, her head cocked to one side, and waited for the sound of the Colonel's key in her lock.

———·———

There was every reason to be suspicious. Of the woman as much as of his heart; hope, he had learned, was an enemy. All he knew of her was that she was rich. It had rung in those piano notes that seeped through the ceiling. He had jumped up, confused yet by the prayers that his need had blackmailed out of him. Had run upstairs, found the door standing ajar upon a dusty corridor. Footprints in the dust, and the cold dance of notes – they had led him on. Anders had found her in a fur-trimmed coat. She had been seated before the piano upon a leather chair with dainty legs curved like a woman's. He'd taken in the mute tower clock, its face and pendulum long arrested. The *Volksemp-fänger* radio; the display cabinet with its cut glass and china; the carpet that showed oriental riders shooting arrows at boars and lions, and the leather armchairs that stood upon it, splay-footed and heavy. Above all he'd taken in the dust, the smell of disuse, and within it some sweet and musky fragrance that clung to the woman's skin.

She had yelled at him and bid him speak. He had felt he could not. There had been a lump in his throat, along with the certainty that she could – and must – help him. When she'd sent him away, he'd merely rounded the stairs. There he squatted down upon his haunches, his teeth in his lips, and raged at himself.

'Don't trust her,' he said. 'Don't you dare trust her.'

'Chances are she won't come.'

'If she doesn't come,' he swore, 'I'll go back and kill her.'

He ran down then, checked on Pavel, and fetched the ice pick so he'd have something to kill her with.

She received a visitor. Anders heard him walk up the stairs, a slow, deliberate tread, and fled into Pavel's apartment until he heard him unlock the woman's door. He snuck up behind and put his ear to its wood. They spoke in English, albeit a different sort of English to Pavel's. He heard him fire up the oven and boil some coffee, real coffee, you could smell it out on the landing. Then the sounds of his using her, in the manner of men. Anders listened to it red-faced, unable to picture it. He knew about sex, of course, but was ignorant of its mechanics. There were grunts, and the rhyth-mic slap of flesh upon flesh. It only lasted a few minutes.

'Good night,' said the stranger. 'Tomorrow, I shall bring you a surprise.'

His voice was genial, magnanimous. The woman said nothing, and Anders hurried up half a flight and cowered behind the corner of the stairs. Once he was sure he could hear the man descend, he dared a peek, in the darkness of the staircase, moonlight falling through the windows of the landing. He saw a man, impossibly fat, and a cascade of furs. There was no hair on the man's head; a polished dome, smooth as a grape. Above the collar, the neck folded itself into a giant, pallid slug. It seemed to Anders that his step was too soft for a man of his size.

Anders waited until he heard the door slam on the ground floor, then took up position outside the woman's door. The ice pick was in his hand. He started counting to a hundred. When he reached a hundred, he swore, he would go and ram the ice pick through her heart.

She came out somewhere in the high eighties, carrying a box marked with a cross and taking his hand as though he was a child. He did not object. Downstairs, in Pavel's place, he heard her gag at the stench, but her eyes softened when she saw the sick man.

'Pavel,' he said, weighing his weapon in his hand, 'this lady here will save your life.'

The sick man did not answer. When the woman asked him what was wrong, first in German, then in fluent English, he mouthed a single word: 'Kidneys.' She nodded and walked over to the phone to call a doctor.

'Don't worry,' Anders heard her say into the receiver, 'I have money and drugs.'

Then they sat down, one on each side of the bed, and waited for help to arrive.

———·———

There you have it: the piano sounding notes just as death comes a-knocking; a neighbour upstairs who returns after a long absence; a medicine chest draped in a negligee; and a doctor who agrees – grumpily, no doubt greedily – to come out in the middle of the night. Coincidence at the heart of our story. It has bothered me ever since I learned its facts.

It cannot be helped though, because there she was, dear Sonia, sitting on Pavel's bed and stroking his brow with a moistened handkerchief. A woman in a tweed dress, in a city where most women still wore the trousers left to them by their husbands and fathers, dead in the war. Perfume on her wrists and in those sensual valleys where collarbones grow into throat; perfume, though no lipstick. She found it whorish, which some found hypocritical, coming from her. It was not something, though, they would say to her face.

You will want a description, a study in physiognomy. We must learn to know her. I shall try, though I never met her in good daylight, and thus am liable to put too much shadow where it does not belong. Let me conjure her up for you – she is worth it. In truth she was remarkable: a remarkable face. Not by any means an everyday face, though, of course, in its own way, anonymous enough, a face you see on the tram, or in the crowds at railway stations, only this one might give you pause. You'd start studying it, and it would even seem strange to you that you should notice it amongst all the others, a little prettier perhaps, and starker; a woodcut of a face. A face with broad cheekbones, a little too Slavic for her nation and the times she had endured, though her passport made her out the purest of Aryans. The lips heavy; owlish, hooded lids; a smudge of moustache upon her upper lip, though she took care to pluck. Quite beautiful in any case, though it only became so once you had got used to it. Good teeth on her, clean breath, and a throaty voice whose moan would drive you to distraction if you were so inclined. A modern woman in a tweed dress. She wore leather gloves whenever she wasn't playing the piano.

Another thing demands mention, though once again I will be charged with stretching the limits of credulity. There was a remarkable similarity between herself and the sick man that, I believe, is not wholly in my imagination. In fact, sitting there next to Pavel and under the boy's watchful gaze, they might have seemed to him like twins – those hollow eyes and raven hair – only she wore her steel on the surface while he smothered it under layers of manners; of calm; the meekness of indecision – and yet (and yet!) the boy thought him as unbending as the times themselves. They were alike; too much alike for comfort. She saw it, too, I wager, or how else to explain the set of her mouth and the way she used her hair to shield her emotions?

But I digress, or worse, fall prey to fancy. They met in any case, Sonia and Pavel. The doctor came and stuffed him full of drugs. They made him chicken soup from an English tin she fetched from upstairs, and when the boy fell asleep, exhausted, she sat up a while, listening to his snore, and idly searched the apartment for clues about its owner.

She found one, principally, though it was quite mangled: a midget in a suitcase, his head leaking, with no socks on his wooden feet.

It gave her quite a fright.

———

The doctor was unmoved by his patient's plight. He ran long-boned, grubby hands over Pavel's body, smelled at his chamber pot and held a flashlight to its content's colour; took the temperature under the tongue and snuck a hand down to Pavel's testicles as though he were measuring them for size. Sonia studied his movements and the exposed body of the sick man. She ran her eyes along the twin rack of ribs and thought of the plaster cast of Jesus that had hung in the family living room until the day its arms fell off during an air raid. There was the birdlike ridge of collarbone and, at the nape of the neck, a twist of spine, bony like a fish carcass. In Pavel's armpit, matted black hair, clumpy with disease. She reached out to touch him but checked her movement before her glove made contact with his skin. It was hard to feel pity for something so ugly.

Throughout the examination the boy stood vigil with suspicious eye, waiting for the doctor's pronouncement over life and death.

'A mild infection,' he diagnosed. 'And a bad cold. He's already on the mend.'

He slipped Pavel's trousers down over one buttock and injected him with the contents of a little vial, then shoved two knuckle-sized pills into his patient's mouth.

'Now, as to the little matter of money.'

Sonia reached to pay him, but the boy stayed her hand.

'He almost died,' he challenged the doctor, his chin pushed forward and his hands raised into fists. For the first time Sonia heard the hoodlum in his voice. The doctor shrugged and reached for the wad of Reichsmarks and the Hungarian sausage Sonia had prepared in payment.

'As you wish.'

He left counting the money, the sausage in one grubby fist.

'You're a quack,' the boy shouted after him. 'A quack, you hear?'

It rang in the staircase and forced a reaction out of the medical man. 'Degenerate,' he shouted back. 'Filthy little *Untermensch*.'

In the building's entranceway, the doctor passed the double eight and mumbled the greeting that went with the numbers. Outside, he slipped off one of his mittens and rummaged in his pocket for the bottle of pills he had pinched from the woman's medicine chest. They would buy him his coals for the next few weeks.

———

Then a sleepless night, a trunk opened, the corpse's vacant stare. She flinched and shut the lid on him. The sick man raving a little, calling for a man named 'Boyd' who'd 'said he would come.' It made her think. She went upstairs to fetch some wine, to keep her company with her thinking.

Then, mid-morning, over some broth of beef, first chance for a conversation. She made the soup from another tin the Colonel had left; avoided mention of the corpse. Instead she wished to learn his life, knowing already that, that very night, she must betray him.

'You work as an interpreter?'

'Yes.'

'For the army?'

'Used to. Stopped. It did not suit me any more.'

'Where did you learn to speak German like this?'

'Father German. Mother Russian. French governess. Jean Pavel Richter.' He smiled thinly, like it was an old joke. 'Born in Cincinnati, 1914.'

'That's in America?'

'Ohio,' he assented. 'A rat-hole.'

She mulled over the designation, then dismissed it as the ravings of a sick man.

'Berlin is a rat-hole,' she told him.

'Well,' he said. 'It is now.'

They paused, ate soup, looked at one another. Their breaths, visible in the cold, mingled over the bed. She reminded herself that it was her duty to herself not to care.

'The boy?' she asked, in order to change the topic.

'Street loafer. A thief. Thoroughly degraded.' Again that smile, thin in his face.

'He doesn't speak as though he grew up on the street. Not always, in any case. He sounds, I don't know. Bookish.'

Pavel nodded assent, then objected: 'He does not read. I haven't figured it out yet.'

'Did you ask him?'

'That,' he explained, 'would be to break our rules.'

'You have rules?'

He took her in his eye.

'Like lovers,' he murmured. 'We like it that way.'

She left him then, thoughtful. Thinking that Pavel was a subtle man, and, as such, dangerous.

———·———

Sonia passed the day playing piano. At around six in the evening she started to drink. She drank wine and French brandy, preparing herself for the Colonel. It occurred to her that she had not washed that day but she assured herself that the Colonel would not care; that he was capable of taking pleasure even in her body's stink. She dressed in tweed, silk and furs, like an English lady; stoked the fire, cut ham upon the sideboard in case he should be hungry, and made sure her diaphragm was in place.

He came at eleven sharp and brought the promised present, grinning as she turned away in disgust.

'I got him from an old *Wehrmacht* corporal who said he used to work in the circus before the war. Isn't he a beaut?'

'It stinks,' she complained, and made him tie it to the door-knob by its lead.

The monkey screamed and clawed until he fed it some ham and sugared tea; once sated, it hunkered down to pick at its own tail. Only then did the Colonel kiss her welcome, his wet, affable lips twice the size of hers and holding her mouth in his own as though it were a sweetmeat.

'My darling,' he said. 'My sweet little strumpet. Play us something on that fabulous piano of yours.'

Sulkily, yet knowing also that he would be amused rather than offended, she chose a dreary funeral march. While she played, he undressed freely in the middle of the drawing room, oblivious to the cold. By the time he asked her to stop, he stood only in his shoes, socks and garters. The cold stretched taut his ample skin. It gave a bladder-like firmness to his girth, baby-pale and shot through with a powder-blue network of veins. He called her over and she obeyed without hesitation. The act itself she performed upon the bed, using her mouth and hands to bruise his skin in the way he liked her to. Then, in the aftermath, it became time to tell him, before he left her for his oaken desk upon which stood the photo of his wife and children, and an ashtray shaped out of a sperm-whale's ivory tooth. Still, she hesitated for another moment or two, knowing perfectly well that it was her time to talk, that she could not risk his finding out by other means. Sonia got up, crossed the room to her dressing table, and watched herself shape the words in the make-up mirror.

'There is a sick man downstairs,' she said without introduction. 'He knows Boyd White.'

She had thought that it would rattle him a little, but could spy no reaction in her mirror. He lay still upon his back, fat legs spread wide and a pillow propping up his head far enough so that his eyes could watch her across his stomach's expanse.

'You don't say,' he said. 'Downstairs?'

'We're right on top of him. Crazy, isn't it?'

He chuckled to himself good-humouredly, blew bubbles of spit from his generous lips.

'Not so crazy,' he said. 'He told us that much. Fifth floor.'

'It's the fourth, not the fifth.'

'Fifth for an American. "We are two cultures divided by a common language." I wonder who said it first.'

She watched him laugh in her mirror and thought he was taking it rather well.

'Does he know anything?' he asked.

'I don't think so. I talked to him this morning and he mentioned Boyd, for no particular reason.' There was no need, she felt, to mention the midget. Not at this stage, in any case. It would get Pavel into trouble, and she had no wish to make more trouble for him than she already had.

'He's sick?'

'Yes. Getting better, though. I called a doctor.'

41

'Wonderful. Like a Good Samaritan. I expect you can intro-
duce me in the morning.'

'What will I say?'

'Nothing,' said the Colonel. 'You will say nothing. I will do the
talking.'

He laughed to himself and used the silk of her nightgown to
wipe clean his crotch before retrieving his clothing in the living
room. Once he was dressed, he untied his present and fed it some
more ham.

'Take it away,' she begged, but he shook his heavy head.

'Just give it time. Before long, I'm sure, you will learn to love
one another.

'It's human nature,' he explained, 'two lonely souls in the
prison of their luxury. Don't worry, my dear. Before long, I
swear, you two will get on like a house on fire.'

After he was gone, promising to return before dawn, she
locked the door and went back to her drinking. She had no
stomach now to climb down the stairs and look in upon the sick
man.

3

22 December 1946

Late dawn over Berlin. The sun still in hiding behind great Russian plains, its rays giving her away, albeit feebly. In Sonia's flat, in Charlottenburg, the Colonel naked before his morning mirror. Foam in the face and upon the throat, a razor poised beneath his chin's fleshy dimple. Sonia in the kitchen, waiting, kettle in hand, for the electricity to be turned on. In the living room a frantic animal, running leathery paws over a Bösendorfer keyboard. One flight down Pavel dreams, no longer of kidneys, but of a tuba player stranded on Crusoe's island; smiles, too, for it seems absurd to him. Next door, a sleeping boy and a dead midget: the latter stiff and indifferent as befits his state, the former splayed out, luxuriously, his face screwed up in the intense concentration of the slumbering babe. Elsewhere in town, the last stirrings of bought love in a Russian-sector brothel. Across from it a young engineer, German, relieved not to wake to an officer's gun and the emphatic invitation to relocate east-wards, where Magnitogorsk has need for men with his expertise. Westward, at a Wedding butcher's, the day's first blood is drawn with bone saw and filleting knife; before the gate already his customers are waiting, food coupons buried in their mittens. Closer to home, an adolescent – Paulchen – sleeping stiff-necked upon the barrel of his Luger which protrudes from underneath his pillow; two flights down, an old woman coughing knotty phlegm into a handkerchief as stiff with cold as she is herself. Closer still – it will take them mere minutes to drive – an impromptu morgue; a steel gurney; a body curled around death in the shape of a jagged hole, a little north of the sternum, its shins split and cheekbones broken, for whoever worked on it, they knew their business. Late dawn in Berlin, and the scene set for action. A morning like this and I wake on my berth feeling old and spent like the god Odin who gave one eye so he should know past and future through the other.

Do you think he ever lived to regret his trade?

———·———

They came in without bothering to knock. The woman, Sonia, entered first, made a show of shaking hands with him with a coldness and formality new to their acquaintance, then declared that she had brought him a visitor.

'Another doctor?' Pavel asked.

'No,' she said. 'A friend.'

She started to say more but bit her lip instead. Pavel was charmed by the movement. It reminded him of the boy. He turned his attention to the visitor.

He came in like he owned the place. A most singular man. Fat, for starters, quite possibly the fattest man Pavel had ever known. It had crept into his every extremity, from the lobes of his ears to the musculature of his palms; they looked padded like a new-born's. Fat fingers made fatter by a half-dozen rings, gold and precious stones, the nails manicured and glossy. Upon his entrance, a flutter of furs. Mink, it had to be mink: a woman's coat that fell to mid-thigh, tailored at the waist and rising up to the crest of a foot-wide collar. It crouched upon his shoulders and nuzzled his neck. Underneath, an ill-fitting officer's uniform, British, brass buttons straining against his girth. His skin was the colour of dough; cakes or Kaiser rolls, not a kernel of rye. A basset's cheeks, no hair on his head. Wet lips that formed an enormous, bulging oval. The upper lip was as thick as the lower, with no furrow beneath the nose: sausages for lips, though not unbecoming. His step delicate, the tread soundless. A beautiful voice, the words shaped to perfection; his handshake dry and dexterous. Deliberately, the man placed one plump palm upon Pavel's cheek to test his fever, then wiped it on a handkerchief. A most singular man, strolling in upon a cloud of perfume. The gun on his belt holster looked oiled, and like it had never been used.

'So,' said the fat man with an air of concern. 'Sonia's sick new friend. Enchanted, I am sure.'

Pavel lay dazed, tasting perfume in his mouth, and thought that he would never be able to resist this man.

'Richter,' he said. 'My name is Richter.'

'Fosko. Colonel Stuart Melchior Fosko, at your service. I am here about a friend of yours. You know a man named Boyd White? Boyd Ferdinand White, Private, US Army, honorably discharged some nine months ago and since then active in Berlin gambling and prostitution circles? The thing is, Mr Richter, I have some bad news for you. Boyd White's dead. Dead as a dodo. I should like to figure out who made him so.'

The Colonel smiled with those wet lips of his, and Pavel found he had no choice but to return the gesture, grit his teeth and smile as he bore the news of his best friend's murder.

———·———

The Colonel gave him no time to recover from the shock. He had hardly stopped talking when the door swung open again and two British privates entered, carrying a stretcher between them and a canteen filled with French brandy. Fosko would not hear of Pavel's remonstrations that he was well enough to walk, but simply bid him roll onto the stretcher once it had been placed parallel to his narrow bed, then slipped the canteen into his hand and instructed

45

him to take a few swallows, 'against the cold'. The soldiers carried him down the stairs at a precarious angle: Pavel went head first and felt himself slide helplessly towards the frontman's buttocks. When he finally made contact the latter pushed him back unceremoniously, with a grunt and a flip of the hips. On the street the cold crept down Pavel's windpipe and assaulted his lungs. The day was clear, icy, the sky stuck in a peculiar shade of leaden blue. Gruffly the soldiers assisted Pavel into a waiting car. They promised a wheelchair at the end of the journey. The boy tried to get in next to him but the Colonel cut him off and manoeuvred his girth into the adjacent seat. His thighs bulged in his uniform and threatened to crawl up Pavel's own; he felt his shoulder disappear in his neighbour's breast and turned his face towards the window. Sonia squeezed in next to the Colonel and offered her lap to the boy. The soldiers got in at the front, lit cigarettes, rubbed warm their hands. They drove in silence through broken Berlin, the rubble frozen into jagged edifices of ice and stone.

———·———

I have often wondered what the Colonel thought about Pavel Richter on this, the first of their meetings. Naturally, I never asked him; it wasn't my place. I reckon it must have been scorn – the scorn of the silverback for the pack's ailing runt. Then again, who knows? Perhaps he saw through the disease and the habit of meekness to that stony core that took me so long to divine. If he did – for the Colonel was a fine student of character, with a novelist's eye for nuance – I wager he found it in his heart to like him. There was in the Colonel a generosity of spirit even for his enemies. In this, I never learned to follow him. I am a humble man and have a humble man's fear of those who can harm him.

'Peterson,' the Colonel would often say to me, 'you have the heart of a chicken. Stomach like a pig, deft hands, good habits, always punctual. But your heart, Peterson, your heart.'

Would say it and pinch my cheek as though I were some errand boy. I was never man enough to object.

———·———

The drive took mere minutes. They did not leave the British sector. Pavel hadn't known the Brits had their own morgue, but upon reflection he realized that they must have need for a place to accommodate those corpses not fit for Soviet eyes. The Russians ran the city police, but there was more than one law afoot in Berlin, and wide disagreement whether or not a bullet through the heart should be counted as a natural cause of death. The building's purpose was unmarked: flaking red walls, and a freezing soldier by the gate. They drove into its courtyard, parked carelessly at its centre. The driver fetched the promised wheel-chair. Once again the boy tried to take charge of Pavel's fate, but failed: the Colonel blocked his path, as though by accident, and clasped his newborn's hands around the wheelchair's handles. A door spilled them into a linoleum-lined corridor; a rickety elevator shaped like a baroque zoo cage carried them downwards in a creaky, seemingly endless journey, during which Sonia stood with her breast dug into Pavel's ear, her legs spread around the chair's cumbersome wheels. He blushed and longed to apologize for an intrusion that was not his, and a situation that lay outside his control. Only the hulking presence of the fat man kept him from doing so. After the elevator ride, another linoleum corridor; a double door on swings, like those used to separate a restaurant's kitchen from its diners, then a steel gurney ridden by a stiff-backed corpse. A sheet covered his friend, and for a moment Pavel was content to pretend to himself that there had been a mistake, that Boyd was alive and well in one of the US sector's gin joints, watching his girls hustle a soldier or one of the army of young writers who were flocking to the city in search of their muse. The hand that stuck out from under the sheet was curled into a loose fist. Its fingernails had been plucked like petals, exposing smooth, darkly bruised skin. It seemed impossible to Pavel that this should be Boyd's hand. A man in a lab coat came forward. He wore his spectacles like a shield. '*Voilà*,' he mumbled as he threw back the sheet. Underneath a broken body.

It was Boyd.

Broken.

From where he was sitting, he couldn't even tell what got him killed.

Pavel gagged and tasted bile; it leaked through his clenched lips and travelled to his chin, saliva and stomach juices warm upon his stubble. He struggled to stand and fell back into his chair; wished to shout but found no air in his lungs. *My body*, he berated himself, *conspiring against my grief.* His eyes were parched. He closed his lids to moisten them. Distractedly, as though from a distance, he heard Sonia turn on her heel and leave the room. The boy gave a low whistle and sought his side. Behind him the fat man, smelling like a bucket of roses.

———·———

The boy had never seen a corpse such as this. It had been, you know, *messed with*, though that wasn't the root of it either. Anders had seen beaten bodies before, bodies whose limbs were crushed and faces torn, and once, at a public urinal, an ex-soldier had shown him the scar left by a grenade splinter that had ripped off much of his plumbing and a goodly chunk of thigh. He had puked then, to the veteran's delight. He cringed at the memory. It had seemed weak to him even then. He did not puke now.

It was Boyd White, the *pimp* who had brought the midget. They had shot him through the throat, the wound was level with Anders' face, and at first the boy kept his eyes there, upon the star-shaped hole. The flaps of white skin looked like a three-way lip; a lip drained of blood, and sucked in over the teeth, or else *toothless* lips, lips that fell inwards, upon the darkness of a hole. He imagined the lab-coated man sticking his fingers in there in order to fish for the bullet. It boggled his mind that a man should have such a job, that he should live by sticking his hand into another man's throat, and he told himself that he would have used a tool, a pair of scissors perhaps, or something like a delicate set of pliers. The boy wondered how big it would have been, the bullet, and imagined the sound it made when it was flicked, carelessly he was sure, into one of the metal dishes that stood upon a nearby table. Not much of a sound. Anders let it echo amongst the room's tiles: a brisk little *click* like a tooth falling into the sink. Then he turned his focus back to the corpse.

There was something wrong with the face. It hung shapeless. It was as though it was being held together by the beard. Anders imagined that the cheekbones were broken – the corpse's eyes were all swollen up. He considered this fact and realized, glumly, that they must have been broken before the man was dead. It looked like they had had plenty of time to swell. The man's mouth was untouched, but there were burns upon the freckled shoulders, from cigarettes and worse. Thin welts across chest and the stomach, as though he had been whipped with a wire, the legs broken in ways that had given them trouble to put them straight again, and the left foot so swollen it looked like a black cloven hoof. It was ugly, this corpse; scrubbed, too, and shamelessly naked.

Anders wondered how Pavel saw it, the corpse of his friend, who had given him an overcoat and done nothing to help him with his sickness. He looked up at him as he struggled out of his wheelchair and stood next to the boy. Anders saw a great blankness of expression, the face of a restful night's sleep. It flooded the boy with relief, flooded him, that is, until the first of the tears started to fall. It fell past Anders onto the floor, and he covered it with the midget's fur-lined boot. A second hit his shoulder, and then they ran freely, mingled with snot, ran down

Pavel's face and pooled around the chin; stuck to his collar and chest; dangled, like threads of spit, from his buttons and his hands, which he had thrown up but then forgotten, spread out before his chest. It was silent, this weeping, and Anders stood motionless and undecided, until the fat man, the Colonel, reached over and spread a handkerchief over Pavel's features. He wiped them as one might wipe a window, or a stain upon the floor.

'My, my,' he cooed, and Pavel, in his terrible weakness, buried his face in Fosko's mink-lined shoulder and sobbed. It rather made up Anders' mind.

He made sure to kick open the door as he stormed out. It wouldn't slam – it was on swings – but the least he could do was to give it a kick. The elevator took an age to come, but he could not locate the stairs. On the way up he paced the cage, then ran out and across the yard. At the gate, the soldiers heckled him about his pallor and the wet that had collected on his own cheeks, and before he was out of sight he turned upon his heel and swung out his arm at something more than a right angle, the elbow stiff and his chin raised high into the wind.

'*Heil Hitler!*' he called back at them.

They only laughed and watched him run away.

Anders didn't have far to go. He was looking for Paulchen and his crew. He had some questions for them, about the broken corpse and the fat man. Pavel, he swore, would be sorry about that tear-stained mink.

—–·—–

Sonia walked on home alone. She knew that there would be no peace for her there. The Colonel would come and find her. He wasn't done with Pavel for the day, not by a long shot, and would want to reap the fruits of this morning's harvest; would want his pleasure, too, a lunchtime fuck, and then a smoke, running an absent-minded thumb over his manicure. She recognized herself in this, his cold relentlessness, his love for comfort. Still, if she walked fast she might garner a few minutes to herself, alone at the piano. She would play Beethoven, one of the late sonatas. She tried to focus upon Beethoven, tried to fill her head with his brooding, deaf-man's rhythms. The music would not come. Boyd White stood in the way: a hulking figure, face broken by expert fists. Boyd had had no time for Beethoven, nor knowledge of him, for that matter. He'd liked Glenn Miller and American lady crooners; had liked Goodman, Basie, and a spot of Chopin when he wanted to sound cultured. *Chopin*, he'd once explained to her as though imparting some great secret, *was Polish. Sounded French, but was, as a matter of fact, Polish.* Sonia had smiled, wide-eyed, and feigned surprise.

'Polish, eh?'

'Yeah. Want some champagne, sugar? Thatta girl.'

The body, it bothered her. She had known he would be killed, and had not cared. And, of course, he had been tortured. She had known this too, had spelled it out to herself even, so there would be no semblance of a lie. Still, the body had got to her – the broken legs, the mutilated fingers, almost black at the tips. She tried to penetrate to the root of her unease. It had to do with the violence, the capacity for inflicting such pain. It took a special sort of courage to do a thing such as that, to deafen one's ears to another's pain and set to him with rubber hose and pliers. Courage, and practice. She feared she had neither, and it struck her as weakness.

Sonia climbed the stairs to her apartment, unlocked her door and closed it behind her, savouring the sound of it, a door falling into its latch. Then: a jabbering scream, inhuman in pitch. Her body panicked, stomach, guts and rectum curling up into them-selves like hedgehogs. She had forgotten about the monkey, straining at its collar and lead, its eyes bulging and black lips distended for a clear view of teeth. It had fouled the rug; had thrown its own filth across the room and against the windowpane where it had stuck and hardened in the cold. Black islands of monkey shit, growing out of the glass like boils.

Sonia stood at the door, unclenching herself. Thinking that it was funny that fear crawled up your arse like that, shamelessly; thinking, too, that he had brought her the monkey just for this, to scare the daylights out of her in some unsuspecting moment when she thought herself safe, and him far away.

It took her a long time to prise free the animal turds from the frozen pane. She did not bother with the carpet, did not approach the animal at all. Instead she withdrew into the kitchen, lit a smoke, and checked whether the electricity was on. It was, and she boiled two pans of water, the first to heat the large ham the Colonel had brought her that morning, the second for some potatoes. When they were done she peeled them, then cut them into thin slices with a heavy kitchen knife that said 'Solingen' on the blade and sat in her hand just so. She imagined, her brows screwed up in concentration, how it might feel to slit the animal's throat; hold its chin up like a corner-store barber and cut it ear to leathery ear. Imagined the Colonel's reaction if he should return to a slaughtered animal, the carpet soaked with its blood. In the background she could hear its chattering, less aggressive now, and she realized that it wished for food. It would be child's play to poison it. There was bleach, formaldehyde and lye underneath the sink, and a tub full of sleeping pills by the bed. She filled a china cup with potato water and placed it in reach of the animal's outstretched arm. It grabbed for it and knocked it over. Up close the stench of its faeces was overpowering, even in the icy air. She walked back into the kitchen, fetched another cup. This time she slid it closer. When she saw it drink in hasty, sloppy draughts, she brought it a potato and some dried slices of apple. The monkey handled the food dexterously, using its tiny, black leather palms. Throughout it did not take its eyes off her, and she, too, crouched and watched it feed. The eyes did not seem to have any whites, and the fur around them was yellowed and encrusted with old secretions. She took a napkin from the table, wet it with her own spit, and reached to clean them away. The monkey recoiled, bared its fangs. Then Sonia heard the key in the lock, straightened, dropped the napkin mid-step, and rushed back to the kitchen.

When the door opened and the Colonel led in a stumbling Pavel, they found Sonia striding to the dining table, a steaming dish of potatoes clutched between two cheerily coloured tea towels.

———·———

Pavel sat in his chair, exhausted. The kidneys were bothering him and he wished that he could lie down on the sofa rather than sit at the dining table on a high-backed Biedermeier chair, a napkin spread across his lap, and good kitchen silver lined up before him. He watched with strange fascination as the Colonel cut the ham into half-inch slices upon a wooden cutting board, and listened to his story of how he had bought the monkey, quite cheaply, from a decommissioned *Wehrmacht* corporal after a night's carousing earlier that week. 'I know what you will say, Pavel, he stinks and he is filthy, but by God I love the little critter.' The woman, Sonia, was dishing out boiled potatoes and fetched beer for the Colonel, chamomile tea for Pavel. The food stood before him and obscured the stench of animal; it rose to his nose and seduced his body. Pavel realized that he was hungry, ravenous even, and felt ashamed. He closed his eyes to conjure up Boyd's body but already it was difficult to remember the details, the smell of gammon thick in his throat. Unable to wait any longer, he cut himself a bite and chewed on it. It tasted wonderful. He tried the potatoes and found them well salted and seasoned with chives. *Chives*, he berated himself, *you are betraying a friend over the smell of chives*. He chewed another bite and hoped the Colonel would break the silence. He didn't.

53

'Who did it?' Pavel asked after he had finished the first slice and mopped up its juice with some bread. Sonia slid another onto his plate with a meat fork. 'Who killed Boyd?'

Colonel Fosko wiped his lips with a cloth napkin, taking his time with the movement, making him wait.

'We believe it was the Russians. Cannot prove it, naturally, but it looks like their handiwork. You know about the NKVD?'

'Soviet secret police?'

'Yes. They usually handle this sort of thing. Rumour has it that Mr White killed one of their agents, and that they acted in revenge. Again, we have no firm evidence. Not even the agent's body. We are equally stumped when it comes to the motive. You see, we had no idea Mr White was involved with the NKVD. The Americans assure us they are just as much in the dark as we are. All we know for certain is that his body turned up in our sector. Which is to say that it's our problem. *My* problem, Pavel. If there is anything you can help us with, Pavel, we would be most grateful. I, personally, would be most grateful, Pavel. Most grateful indeed.'

He sat back and took a swallow of beer. His rings clinked on the glass when he set it down. In his left, the silver knife stuck out daintily from a half-closed fist. Pavel nodded wearily, and cut a bite from his second slice of gammon.

There was no earthly reason why he shouldn't just hand over his keys and tell the Colonel about the midget. Pass things over to the authorities. He had no doubt that Fosko would accept the gesture and drop any inquiry into why he should have hidden a corpse for four whole nights. There was hardly a chance, of course, that Boyd's killer would be brought to justice, not if he was a Russian operative, but at least Pavel could wash his hands of it, return to a quiet life dedicated to his books and the boy. In time, he would earn enough money to buy Boyd a gravestone and a space in the Catholic cemetery. A priest would speak and there would be closure; hookers in evening dresses paying their last respects, and a letter home to his mother whom Pavel had never met.

He made up his mind to speak, but cut himself another bite instead. Sat and chewed it with deliberate slowness. There was something about the fat man that made Pavel hold back; it was as though he begrudged him his ruddy good health. Stubbornly, half ashamed for his stubbornness, Pavel cast around for reasons to hold on to his secret. His eyes came to rest upon the woman. She sat stiff-backed, meat fork in hand, her eyes studiously avoiding his own. He took in her pallor, her cheekbones, the height of her brow. The smudge of moustache that framed her upper lip. Her face was impassive. It was foolish to expect that she would help him make up his mind.

'Are your kidneys troubling you, Mr Richter?' she asked him coolly.

'Yes,' he answered, though he had forgotten them the moment he had taken in food. 'I think I shall have to lie down.'

'Do you need help?'

'No, thank you. Much obliged.'

The words sounded false to him, as though they were acting out a long-rehearsed scene. Pavel got up and made a show of hobbling towards the door.

'Let me know about any developments,' he called over to Fosko, still with the same giddy feeling of acting out a farce. The fat man parted his meaty lips into a smile.

'Rest assured I will, Pavel. Rest assured I will.'

Pavel bowed stiffly from the waist and closed the door behind him with an acute sense of relief.

'Tomorrow,' he told himself. 'You can always tell him tomorrow. It won't make any difference.'

———.———

Anders found his crew back at Paulchen's place. They sat in a circle and were having reheated cabbage soup and smoked fish for lunch. Wordlessly, Anders joined them, wedging himself onto the sofa between the Karlson twins. The fish's meat had a green shine to it and tasted bitter, but he ate it anyway. When it was all gone, Paulchen produced a tin of sugared peaches as a special treat. He passed them out personally, and Anders noted that he gave an extra-large portion to Schlo' who looked like he had not been sleeping well recently. Anders only got a single, mangled peach – Paulchen speared it with a knife and slipped it straight into his hand. The sugar water clung to his skin long after it was gone. Anders did not complain about the unequal distribution. He had not been around much lately, and Paulchen rewarded loyalty as much as earning potential. In order to signal his good will, Anders volunteered to do the dishes. It involved fetching water from a pump two blocks over. Even so the water was half-frozen by the time he got back. Once he was done he joined the other boys in Paulchen's bedroom. Under the magazine picture of an American pin-up in black underpants and bra, they lit up smokes and talked about the day's pickings, and what they had planned for the week ahead. Word had it that another train full of refugees from the east would be rolling into the station later that day, or early the next. Paulchen commandeered a few of the boys to go and wait for its arrival. Refugees meant business: they would get off the train and require food, shelter, a kilo of firewood. Most of them were too poor to be worth much, but there would be a few valuables amongst the family possessions they carried.

'Don't rip them off too bad,' Paulchen warned them. 'They are good people who got screwed by the Russians.' Paulchen made much of the point that he was a patriot.

As casually as possible, Anders steered the conversation onto the topic of the Colonel. He told them that he had seen him come out of a building wearing a mink coat. 'A fat man in woman's furs. Man, we should rip the bastard off. That coat's worth a crapload.'

Paulchen cut in and told him the man was off-limits: 'He's a Tommy. A general or something. Besides, word has it that he's a fairy.'

'A what?'

'A fairy.'

'What's that?'

'Somebody who fucks little boys like you.'

'Fucks boys? How?'

'What do you mean, *how*? He fucks them.'

They all sat in silence, contemplating the point.

'It can't be,' Anders objected after some thought. 'He fucks this woman. I heard him do it. I swear.'

Paulchen was unimpressed.

'These *ped-i-rasts*,' he said knowledgeably, 'they fuck anything that moves.

'They should be gassed,' he told them. 'Rounded up and gassed.'

At the edge of their circle, silent young Schlo' started to cry. He was ever so much of a girl.

Anders lit another smoke and decided to stick around for the day.

———·———

In those days there were many such rumours about the Colonel. I heard them drinking in bars, always mindful, of course, to keep secret the precise nature of my association with him. The Colonel, I would hear, was a queer, a Soviet spy, a Nazi operative who had infiltrated British Intelligence back in '33 and had stayed under cover when the Reich went belly up. I was told that he was Italian royalty, part of the 'di Fosco' family who'd been expatriated by Mussolini; that he made his money in banking, in real estate, at the horses. Once, an old French journalist swore to me that he had shared a roulette table with him – along with a woman – in pre-war Monte Carlo. 'He was just back from Spain, fighting for Franco,' he confided, and would not be dissuaded otherwise. A German brothel madam told me the story of how she had had to pay the Colonel's money back, because none of her girls could satisfy his appetites, and an Irish sailor – God only knows what he was doing there – enacted for me their five dramatic rounds in the ring. 'Bare-knuckle bout, my lad,' he sang with his liquor-oiled brogue. 'That bastard's so fat, he hits the deck he bounces right back up again, like a fecking rubber ball.'

'Did you win?' I asked him, but he shrugged his shoulders.

'Now that I think of it, it was my cousin who did the fightin'.'

There is no telling where they came from, all these rumours, and I have wondered at times whether the Colonel himself was responsible for putting them in circulation, though for what purpose, other than sheer bravado, I am at a loss to say. Suffice it to state that he was the kind of man to whom legends attached themselves like lice. Every so often he would pick one out of his pelt, and pop it between his fingernails. Why not? There would always be more.

———

Pavel spent most of the afternoon in bed. By dinnertime he was hungry again and fried himself a piece of offal that the boy had left behind. The electricity ran out halfway through the cooking and some of the meat remained frozen at the centre. He found a bottle of beer in a cupboard over the sink, but was too impatient to wait for it to defrost by the oven. In the end he broke open the neck and sucked on slivers of beer ice. The alcohol went straight into his blood and muffled his feelings. He realized he was still very sick and crawled back into bed.

It was ten or eleven before he rose again and faced up to what he had wanted to do ever since lunchtime. He was ill-equipped for the task. It was hard work even to get the trunk to open. Both its hinges and copper latches were frozen and he had to work on them with the ice pick. Eventually he managed to remove the lid and slid it onto the boy's bed. When he tried to lift out the body, his kidneys rebelled and he had to sit down in front of the oven and warm them up for half an hour. He tried again, this time by turning the entire trunk upside down and waiting for the corpse to roll out. There was no sound, and when he lifted the suitcase up an inch, he saw that the midget had become glued to its lining by his own frozen blood and hung suspended halfway between trunk and wooden floor. Exasperated, too exhausted to flip the whole thing over one more time, Pavel slid a knife into the leather from above and in this manner cut enough of the lining until it finally ripped and dropped the midget onto the floor. After another break in front of the oven, Pavel pushed the trunk aside and grabbed the body's wooden feet. He'd decided to drag him over to the front room, where the light was better. The head banged the floor-board both times he cleared the doors' elevated thresholds. By the time he finally had him in front of the coal oven, Pavel was so exhausted, he slipped to the floor next to it and nearly nodded off.

The opening of the door snapped him out of his lethargy. He could not believe he had forgotten to lock it. He expected the boy, of course, but in came Sonia in her heavy tweed dress, a glass of what looked like fruit juice in one hand. When she saw him sitting there next to the body she stopped dead in her tracks. The liquids that surrounded the midget were starting to melt in the heat from the oven and a heavy, livid smell had begun to spread through the room. Pavel tried to speak, to make up some sort of explanation. His mind was a blank. All he managed to say was: 'It's a midget. Dead.' It sounded so callous to him that his cheeks flushed with shame. Any second now she would scream, and dial for the Colonel.

'You should put a blanket under him before all the blood starts running,' she said. 'Otherwise it will seep into the floorboards. Here, have some juice.'

She crouched before him and passed him the glass.

'It is important you drink a lot, now that you are on the mend.'

When she smiled some of the pallor seemed to leave her face. Pavel drank the juice greedily, and pointed out a blanket they could use.

'Wait,' she said, 'I will fetch it for you.'

Without her help, he would never have managed to cut the clothing off the midget's body. It was she who fetched the scissors from her apartment and dared the first cut. They melted some water by the oven and patiently wiped down his body, first the front and then his back. There was less bruising than he would have predicted; his skin shone youthful and white. A hand's breadth above the buttocks Pavel discovered a slender hole, a quarter-inch across. Its edges were perfectly smooth.

'He has been stabbed,' he said to Sonia. 'Boyd told me he'd run him over. With his car. Cats licking at his blood.'

'Your friend lied to you?' she asked, and he wondered whether she was teasing him for his naivety.

'Yes,' he said. 'He must have thought I would judge him.'

'Would you have? Judged him?'

He thought about it.

'Who knows,' he said. 'It's hard not to judge murder.'

She bit her lip then and for a moment he was sorely tempted to reach out and stroke her cheek. His hand, he noticed, was encrusted with blood, especially around the fingernails. He dropped it and looked for words to explain himself.

'Sonia,' he said, 'I know this isn't fair on you, but I don't want the Colonel to know. About the midget. Not yet, in any case.'

She shrugged like it wasn't much to ask. All she wanted to know was: 'Why?'

He looked down at the midget. 'The truth is, I have no idea. No idea at all.'

———·———

They decided to remove the body to the attic. In summer it was used for hanging up washing; in these temperatures it would be deserted even by rats. They wrapped a blanket around him as one would around a dead child. He tried to lift him but found he could not. In the end it was she who cradled the corpse in her arms and walked it up two flights of stairs. The attic was enormous, the space cut up by wooden posts that helped support the roof. Washing lines hung taut between these posts, empty save for a single, hole-ridden sock that balanced an icicle off its stiffened tip. Sonia wedged the body into the utmost corner of the enormous room. Pavel watched her do it, holding a candle high above her shoulder. When they turned around in the doorway, they were no longer able to make out the bundle; it had been swallowed up by shadows. On the way back they snuck past the doors of the other tenants. *This is what it must feel like*, thought Pavel, *to be a thief*. It was a lonely feeling. He felt expelled from the brotherhood of men.

Back in his apartment, they struggled to clean the floor, then cut all the remaining lining out of the trunk and stuffed it in the oven. The trunk itself Pavel pushed under his bed. It was too big to burn. The smell of the corpse lingered and Pavel felt compelled to force open a window. The cold that blew in hurt him in his teeth, his lungs, the skin of his tongue.

'Let's go to my place while it airs,' Sonia suggested. He followed her demurely, and accepted some cold coffee, along with a bread roll. She sat at the piano and played some music for him. At first he did not listen, but then the melodies drew him into themselves and he began to recognize various fragments.

'Beethoven?' he asked her when she took a break to warm her hands.

'Yes. Do you like him?'

'I always thought him melodramatic.'

She shook her head in reproach. 'Melodramatic? I just helped you hide a frozen midget.'

God, it felt good to laugh.

He stayed far too long and was conscious of doing so. Over a second cup of coffee she explained to him that the Colonel wanted her to lure him away to the doctor's the next day, so that he could search Pavel's flat.

'He doesn't trust you,' she said. 'He thinks you are hiding things.'

'It's okay,' he shrugged, 'I'm going out tomorrow anyway. Boyd told me to go look for a woman. If anything went wrong, he said, go look for Belle. One of his girls, you know. A prostitute. *"Find Belle!"* That's what I'm going to do.'

'Find a whore in Berlin?' she asked him caustically. 'Good luck.'

He fell asleep on her couch and Sonia woke him an hour before sunrise so that he could get ready before the Colonel showed up.

4

23 December 1946

Anders slept over at Paulchen's, along with a handful of the other boys. It took them until well past midnight to settle down. Before that they sat around, huddled into blankets, and swapped stories about the city and about the war. Some were old and they had all heard them before, like the one about the thirteen boys who had stood around in the schoolyard toilets late in April '45, sharing a smoke.

'Give me another week,' one of them had bragged, 'and I'll give Gretchen a good old going over.'

'One week,' he swore, 'and she'll spread them like she's a gymnast doing splits.'

'Right,' said his friends. 'And Hitler's still got us primed for the *Endsieg*.'

They all laughed. A teacher who passed by the toilets just then overheard them. It was nothing but chance, but he heard them, both the comment and the laughter. One of those hyper-loyal types who had worn his party pin from before '33. He made a phone call, and the Gestapo came right over; didn't even need a car, the headquarters were two blocks down the road. They say they rounded up the boys in the yard and marched them back into the toilets. They had to line up by the piss trough, eyes to the wall, and then they were shot, one by one, through the back of the neck. Shot for high treason and 'demoralization of the

German *Volk*'. Thirteen dead, mid-morning on the twenty-eighth of April, when bullets were already running thin, amongst the Germans that is – the Russkies had plenty, and mortars the size of God's fists. On the thirtieth of April, Hitler killed himself. Some said poison, and some said a bullet through the heart. Either way, thirteen boys dead, in the fucking toilets.

'I swear to God,' said one of the Karlsons, 'I was there when they carried out the bodies.'

There were other stories, newer ones. Stories about the Russians tracking down every German scientist and engineer in their sector. They would come into a man's home while he was away at work, pack up all his stuff in a truck, put his wife and kid inside, and then wait for him in the empty flat, with only a stool and a little wooden desk set up in the middle of the living room, and on it a piece of paper that said he kindly requested transfer of work to the esteemed Union of Soviet Socialist Republics.

'And he signs off on that?' one of the boys asked incredulously.

'His wife and child are already in the truck,' Paulchen reminded him. 'A man has to do what a man has to do.'

Then there was one about the children's hospital down the road, how every morning a van stopped at its gates to load up all the babies that had died there that night, and how they put them into cardboard boxes because there wasn't any wood to be had. It was said that they kept them in a warehouse out in Zehlendorf somewhere until the ground got soft enough again to dig them graves. Or the one about the man they called The Butcher, who took children home and promised them candy, then sold their meat by the kilo. He was said to dress in a white suit and carry a walking stick with a silver tip.

'Probably another *ped-i-rast*.'

There were stories, too, that they never told, those that were too frightening to tell, or too personal. Anders had some stories like that, and he knew most of the others did. Once, Schlo' had tried to tell him something about a giant prison out in Poland

64

where everybody looked like a corpse. Had showed him the tattoo on his forearm and told him that they burned people there. 'Smokestacks smoking night and day,' he had said, round-eyed and weepy. 'Smoking with *people*.'

Anders had thought him full of shit. 'Smokestacks smoking with people, eh?' It was important not to believe everything you heard.

The boys settled down eventually, after a final cigarette. Early in the morning Anders woke because Schlo' was crying. Making sure none of the other boys were awake to see him do it, he curled up next to him and rocked Schlo' in his arms until he fell back asleep. When dawn finally broke he helped Paulchen with breakfast, then set off to Pavel's.

He wanted to tell him that the fat man liked to fuck boys.

———·———

Sonia saw Pavel leave the building from out of her front window, a lonely figure, the body bent around his kidneys' pain, then got ready to leave herself. She did not want to run into the Colonel. At first her steps were aimless. She walked down neighbourhood streets and passed long queues of shoppers, felt their jealous glances upon her expensive coat. On Sophie-Charlotte-Platz a gaggle of schoolgirls passing around a cigarette butt; across from them two workers carting away rubble. Amongst the crowd, stolid talk of Christmas, and a man without gloves trying to sell a suitcase full of decorations. 'Please,' he said to her, 'for the celebrations.'

'I have no tree,' she fobbed him off.

'You could keep them for next year.'

She shrugged and quickly moved on.

The cold soon drove her underground. She had not been on the subway for a long time, had watched the streets from the reassuring distance of a car window. Beggars huddled in corners as she made her way down, stretched forward cups baited only with buttons. The platform itself was packed with people: Germans, British soldiers, and a pair of transport police hunting for black marketeers. When Sonia boarded the train and saw icicles growing out of its ceiling, she almost laughed out loud. A child broke off one of its tips and started sucking on it. Evidently it tasted funny: the girl made a face and dropped it. Now that the doors were closed the air in the train quickly got worse, filled by the smell of unwashed bodies – it was too cold to bathe – and something worse: the gasses of indigestion. A bent old lady broke wind next to her and glanced at her apologetically. 'You should smell the stuff I'm eating,' she murmured. Her breath stank as rancid as her fart. Sonia decided she would get off at the next station, but then she overheard a conversation between two of the Brits on the other side of the aisle.

'It rolled in this morning. More than forty dead, I heard, and a dozen amputations.'

'Amputations?'

'Yeah, they've been chopping off limbs all morning. They've frozen right off.'

'Jesus.'

'Once the Krauts get wind of it, they'll be baying for blood.'

Sonia pushed through the throng of passengers and positioned herself between them.

'*Gnee-di-guss Frow-leyn,*' they said, sizing her up. 'What is it we can do for you?'

The train jostled and she felt herself thrown against one of them. He steadied her by putting one hand on her waist.

'Forty dead?' she asked him in English. 'Where?'

'At the station. The refugee train. Would you like some cigarettes?'

'What for?'

'Company.'

She tried to muster the indignation to slap him across one cheek but found none. His face was ruddy like a choirboy's.

'Not today,' she told him, and he shrugged and let go of her waist.

'That's a bloody shame, love,' he said good-naturedly.

She turned her back on him and stayed like that until the train drew into Zoogarten station.

———-—

He marched straight in. That was the first mistake he made. He thought Pavel would still be in bed, distraught over his friend's death, or else the woman might be there, making him chicken soup from out of a tin. Instead he found the Colonel crouching on the floor like an outsized toad. His thighs bulged in his uniform trousers and even the boots seemed bloated to the boy, as though his feet had been sewn into them and were now trying to burst through the leather. Behind the fat man, Pavel's mattress stood upended, his cupboards opened, books thrown carelessly upon the floor. The oven had gone out and the room was not much warmer than the street outside.

'What are you doing here?' Anders asked, seeking refuge in German, hoping that it would startle the Tommy. That was his second mistake. He should have turned on his heel and run. Instead he decided to face the Colonel down.

'*Sie gehören hier nicht hin.*'

The fat man took no heed of his words. His eyes travelled down towards a rag that was lying on the wooden floor.

'What an idiot,' he said conversationally. 'Goes to the trouble of wiping the floor and hiding the body, but forgets to get rid of the cloth he cleaned it up with. Just look at it, it's positively soaked with blood.'

He picked up the frozen lump of cloth, then studied the boy from his cheerful button eyes. 'You understand me, don't you?'

'He's not an idiot,' Anders said, in English now.

'Ah, so you do.'

The boy stood still, gnawing his lip. He asked himself whether the Colonel had found the dead Russian dwarf yet, standing upright in his trunk in the other room. The fat man caught the movement of his eyes.

'Gone,' he said. 'Your friend left the suitcase. Spotted with blood stains. Put a hole into it – finest buckskin, a real shame. Cut the midget right out and carted him off. How did he do it, though? He's too weak to have done it all by himself, and you didn't know about it, did you now? It does make one think, doesn't it? Yes, it rather does make one think.'

He stood up, slowly, brushed off his knees with a pair of leather gloves that he held clutched in one loose fist, never letting the boy out of his sight. A glint of recognition passed through his face as he contemplated Anders' clothing, then faded away again, giving way to lazy geniality.

'When did Boyd drop him off, the corpse? You were here, weren't you?'

'I don't know what you are talking about.'

'Loyal, are we?' The sausage lips turned into a smile. 'Something else, then. Tell me, boy – how is it that a little arsewipe like you wears a fifty-pound coat?'

Anders wasn't ready for his pounce. Even if he had been, he might have been too slow for the fat man. As it was, he did not stand a chance. Before he could even so much as turn around, the Colonel's weight slammed into him, pressed him into the wall. Anders' nose got bent into a right angle, blood shot over his chin. He tried to kick, but even as he rammed a knee into the soft of the Colonel's thigh, a hand caught hold of his throat and lifted him clear off the floor. The fingers were clammy on his skin, somehow almost tender in their embrace, and yet he found himself unable to breathe. As though he were a doll, Fosko carried him over to Pavel's mirror above the sink. He turned Anders around deftly, until he could see himself upon its soap-speckled surface, chin extended, and one giant baby paw covering the whole of his throat.

'Look!' said the Colonel as he gently peeled the coat off Anders' shoulders. His voice was as cheerfully magnanimous as ever. 'Look yourself in the eye. That's right, in the eye. Watch it swell – like a slug that you squeeze between your fingers, or maybe you and your friends have blown up frogs together, stuck a length of hose in them and blown them up. That's right, it's swelling, positively bulging even. Soon now you will see it change colour – it'll yellow and curdle, you'll see, like an old man's eye, curdle, you hear, until it's the colour of butter. I have been told that, right at the end, some people start bleeding from the eyes, but maybe that's just a myth. I'd imagine it'd be quite beautiful, tears of blood running down your cherub cheek, quite a picture that, downright ravishing. Ah-ha, see your nostrils flare now. My, my, it's like a horse, a pure-bred Arab, only you have blood up yours, so there's nothing doing.'

He let go of the boy carelessly and let him fall onto the sink. Anders lay there crumpled; piss was running down his trouser leg. From the corner of his eye he saw the midget's coat. It was thrown over the Colonel's arm now, nicely folded, as though he was planning to give it a brush. Anders watched him bend down to him until he could feel his breath in his ear.

'One more thing, my little boy. If your friend Pavel hears a word about this – one word is all it takes – I will string him up with my own hands and hang him from the curtain rod. String him up, your lachrymose friend, and then we can see whether he bleeds from the eyes. Do you understand? My dear boy, I asked you whether you understood.'

Anders croaked 'Yes'.

'Then get out of here.'

He gave him a paternal clap on his backside. Of all the humiliations, this seemed the worst to the boy. He ran to the door and then down onto the street. Outside he stood doubled over, gasping for air and trying to hide his tears with his hands. Within minutes he was cold to the bone. *I must find myself a new coat*, he thought. *I will freeze to death.* His legs, shaking, would not obey. *The train station*, he told himself. *Paulchen sent some boys to the train station.* He tried a step and stumbled like a drunk; a second, a third, doubled over and blood drying on his lip. Before long he was running, heedless of all surroundings. He crashed into vendors, soldiers, lamp posts, never once looking up. Above all he avoided the glossy fronts of shop windows. It was to him like he would never again be able to look at his reflection without seeing the Colonel there, leering over one of his shoulders.

By the time he reached the train station the urine in his trousers had frozen into a stiff patch right between his legs.

———.——

Zoogarten station was in uproar. One could see the angry crowd from a long way off, standing around on the square outside the station and gesticulating. 'They are trying to kill us,' she heard a man shout. 'Because of the food shortages. They've got no bread for further mouths, so they kill us off before we even get here.' Others around him told him to shut his fucking gob.

Inside the station the chaos only increased. Soldiers stood in stiff-legged rows, bearing machine pistols and blocking off an entire platform. The crowd stood shoulder to shoulder, those who'd been drawn there by news of the catastrophe mingling with those who were trying to leave the city, bulging suitcases in their hands. A dozen dirty boys milled amongst the crowd, selling refreshments and spreading information. 'Fifty-three on the last count,' one of them told her in response to a held-out cigarette.

'Fifty-three dead?'

'Yes, and twenty-one amputations. Mostly feet, I think. You want some coffee?'

She shook her head and pushed on towards the cordon of soldiers.

It wasn't clear to Sonia what she was looking for. She half expected to see stretchers laden with people, their shins and faces burned black by frost, but of course they had all been evacuated by now. A mound of suitcases piled up on the platform floor was the only sign that any mishap had occurred. It reminded her of the days after liberation, when there had been similar mounds sprouting on the sidewalks, compiled by looting soldiers. *Perhaps*, she sneered at herself, *this is what I'm here for: a renewed sense of anger. Perhaps I've slunk along far enough on the road from victim to perpetrator that it's become attractive again to think of myself as beaten, bruised and abused.* The desire struck her as dangerously childish, and she quickly turned on her heel and made her way back to the station gates. Outside, casting her eyes over the angry crowd, she noticed Anders, running with his head drawn down into his chest and stumbling into people with every other step. He was not wearing a coat.

Her first instinct was to hide from the boy. He looked like he had run into trouble, and if this was true, it was smarter to stay away from him. But then he caught sight of her himself, and she did not have the heart to pretend she hadn't noticed him. She waved, watched him hesitate, then draw near. His nose looked swollen and there was bruising on his throat, in between collar and scarf.

'Anders,' she said, making as though to stroke his head, then thinking better of it. 'What happened to you?'

'Nothing,' he said, his lips trembling. 'It's only that I'm cold.'

She took him into a café full of foreigners and bought them two cups of hot cocoa. The boy stirred in three lumps of sugar and asked the waiter for two more. He was sulky and seemed in no mood to talk.

'Where did you go yesterday?' she asked him. 'Pavel said you ran away.'

'He shouldn't have cried,' he answered.

'Who? Pavel?'

'He cried. Like a girl.' He looked at her grimly. 'On the Colonel's shoulder.'

'I see.'

'You like him?'

'Who?'

'The Colonel.'

She hesitated. 'He lives with me,' she told him. 'Sometimes.'

'Yeah,' said the boy. 'I hate him, too.'

They sat and drank their cocoa in silence.

'Where is Pavel?' Anders asked when he had finished his. He ran his fingers along the cup's bottom, licked fragments of chocolate from filthy tips. She ordered him another, and lit a cigarette for herself.

'Gone looking for Belle.'

'Belle. That's Boyd's whore, right?'

'You shouldn't talk like that.'

'Says who?'

She scrutinized his features: those insolent eyes, the blood that sat smeared across his upper lip, the squashed little face with its crooked teeth. His chin was raised, like he expected her to slap him. She asked herself how Pavel had managed to befriend him, and why he should have wished to.

'You need a new coat. I've got something in my wardrobe I can shorten for you.'

He shook his head. 'I can't.' It was hard to be sure whether or not it was fear that stood in his eyes. 'I don't like that Colonel of yours.'

'The Colonel will be gone by now.'

'How do you know?'

'I know. He told me he's got a lunchtime meeting. If you want I'll go up and look before we go in. Make sure he's not around.'

'You promise?'

'Yes.'

72

She stretched out her gloved hand and wondered whether he would take it. He sniffed at it like a dog who's been thrown a suspicious piece of bone. It was only when he grabbed it that she realized how small his hands were. She held him gently, and he allowed himself to be led out into the street.

Outside, Anders stopped and watched the police clear the square in front of the station. A few trucks had come to the scene and inside were more police, clutching truncheons.

'What's going on?'

'The refugee train arrived,' she told him. 'From the east. Many of the passengers froze to death.'

'Okay,' he said, like it didn't matter to him. He turned his back on the scene and started walking. *God*, she thought, *we are breeding monsters*. And then, when they were almost back at their building, he made her feel ashamed for the word.

'Promise me,' he said, 'that you're not in love with him.'

'In love? With the Colonel?'

'No. Pavel. Promise me you don't love Pavel.'

She burst out laughing and stuck her key in the front door.

———

Love. No wonder she started laughing. The truth, though, is that I am not at all sure what she thought about Pavel at this point. I asked her about it later, but later is no good, of course, not when it's about something like this, an impression, a feeling, things that come and go. She maintained, in any case, that she didn't think too much of him. I reminded her that she had helped him, unprompted; had come to his rooms, closed the door behind herself, and helped him undress the midget.

'Yes,' she admitted, 'that I did.'

'You didn't care for him then?'

She shrugged her shoulders. 'He was, you know, pathetic. And – honest.'

'You care that much for honesty?'

'No,' she answered, 'I don't. Back then I thought it a disease.' She smiled without humour and checked her lipstick in a pocket mirror.

'Stop your questions,' she said. 'They'll lead you nowhere but to words.'

I didn't know what to say to that, and let it slide. Up until then it hadn't occurred to me that there could be any problems with words.

———·———

Find Belle. Pavel knew where to start looking. He'd grabbed all the remaining packs of cigarettes he still owned, along with the war photo of Boyd and himself, the two of them sitting on their helmets, eating soup. There had been no time for breakfast, and he'd bought two rolls and a cup of *Ersatzkaffee* at a baker's on the way over to the American sector. The tram at that hour of the morning was full of workers in overalls and old *Wehrmacht* coats. He got out at Kaiser-Wilhelm-Platz and noted the change of uniform amongst the privates walking along the streets: American colours and farm-boy faces. Half of Wisconsin seemed to be in Berlin just then. By the time he reached the 'Unknown Soldier' his body had started hurting from the cold. He stood panting in the entrance for a minute, then walked into the bar and looked around for Doug Priestley, a decommissioned sergeant major whom everyone called 'Tex', along with a thousand other GIs who shared his provenance or sounded like they might. Tex was working behind the bar, a leather butcher's apron wrapped around his wiry frame. He recognized Pavel at once. They shook hands, lit cigarettes and cupped them in their hands. The bar was quiet with only a handful of soldiers having a breakfast of scrambled eggs and beer. Tex poured Pavel a double shot of rye, and one for himself.

'Boyd's dead,' Pavel told Doug, his hand around the glass.

Doug wasn't surprised. 'Heard it on the grapevine,' he said. 'The Russians, they say. NKVD hatchet job. You look rough, Jay-Pee.'

Pavel had often wondered what it was about a war that made soldiers avoid one another's name. Something about the uniform seemed to suggest it.

'I had some kidney trouble. Listen, I'm looking for one of his girls.'

'A hooker?'

'Yes, and a little bit more than that. Name's Belle.'

'That's French, right?'

'I don't think it's her real name.'

'Yeah, right.'

Doug shrugged his shoulders and pulled out a leather-bound notepad that served as his address book. He leafed through its loose pages, stopping on occasion to take a drag at his cigarette. Eventually he found what he was looking for and scribbled a number on a scrap of paper.

'Best call Franzi. She used to work for Boyd. Nice girl. Big thighs.'

'She has a phone?'

Doug nodded yes. 'Boyd arranged it. He spoilt them rotten, his girls.' He lifted a heavy black telephone from behind the bar and stood it on the counter. 'Go ahead if you like.'

Pavel thanked him, then ran a finger through the dial. He let it ring a dozen times, hung up, and tried again. When she finally picked up, her voice sounded tired and hostile.

'Is this Franzi?' he asked in German, and introduced himself. 'My name's Jean Pavel Richter. I'm a friend of Boyd White's.'

'Boyd's dead. What do you want? He owe you money or something?'

'Do you mind if I come over? I need to talk to you.'

'Talk, sugar?'

'I'm willing to pay for it. I've got two packs of cigarettes here for you. More if I get what I need. Five minutes, that's all it's going to take.'

'Five minutes? That's all it ever takes.'

She gave him an address further east in the American sector, and reminded him to bring the smokes. 'If you change your mind about talking,' she said, 'make sure you bring some rubbers, too.'

Pavel thought about taking the bus but ended up walking, placing one foot before the other, oblivious to the cold. His body hurt, the lungs and the kidneys, but his mind had slipped into a strange reverie, was caught up in the joy of being alive, conscious of it, too, an animal thawing that had started during yesterday's lunch of ham and potatoes, and continued now, as yet fragile and inarticulate, but welling up in him, inexorable like a burp. Of the many people who were milling about in the street, he was the only one who was smiling.

Franzi lived in a house a half of which had been destroyed in one of the bomb raids. Some of the rubble had been cleared, and now the house stood in a gap-toothed block, cut precisely in two. If one stood a little to the side of it, one had a perfect view into the shell of half a living room, half a bathroom, and a few yards of corridor. Even the toilet in the bathroom looked like it had cracked right down its middle. In the muddy field next to it, snow had collected in soot-coloured drifts.

Pavel ran an eye over the doorbells and learned that Franzi rented the ground-floor flat. Its windows were covered by net curtains. She had hung some Christmas decorations from the curtain rail, but these were barely visible through the frost that clung to the glass. He rang the bell and Franzi opened the door for him immediately.

'Come in,' she said gruffly. 'It's freezing outside.' She did not move to take his coat, and in fact it was too cold to take it off.

Franzi was thirty going on forty, her hair dyed a henna-red and no money for make-up. A short woman with a big rump and, yes, generous thighs. These were wrapped in thick woollen tights and peeked out between her morning gown's careless gape. Puffy skin, especially around the eyes, booze on her breath and her curls still lopsided from the way she'd slept on them. Pavel shook her hand and followed her into the living room. There was a shabby divan and a table full of drinking things. The apartment stank from lack of airing.

'Have a seat.'

He sat down on the edge of a chair as she wrapped herself into a blanket upon the divan. 'There's no electricity for coffee,' she warned, and he passed over the first of the packs of cigarettes that he had promised.

'I'm looking for a woman called Belle. One of Boyd's other girls. He told me they were close.'

'Belle, huh? Guess they were. He hung around her like some puppy dog. Thought her something special, God knows why. A society girl, you know, ever such a nice accent. Airs and fucking graces. Let me tell you one thing, though: a whore's a whore. Am I right or am I right?'

'Do you know where she is?'

'Haven't seen her in a while. Four, five days, maybe a week. Some of the girls went home for Christmas, or tried to, the trains are a mess. Maybe she did, too. I know where Boyd put her up if that's any help.'

'Please.' Pavel passed over a second pack of cigarettes, and exchanged it for a hastily scribbled address.

'Second or third floor, I think, overlooking the main road. Chances are she's holed up there, crying crocodile tears.'

'You don't think she cared for him?'

'Jesus Christ and Mary. He was her pimp, and a real sleazebag, too, when he put his mind to it.'

She looked him up and down real funny, and Pavel realized he must have betrayed displeasure about her comments.

'Sorry, sugar, speakin' ill of the dead.' She made the sign of the cross, kissing her fingers lightly when she was finished. The gesture smelled of convent school.

'He wasn't all bad, never slapped us around much, you know. You two were close?'

He nodded yes.

'The army, right? Boyd wouldn't shut up about it. Made it sound like he took France all by himself. Special unit and all.' She eyed him shrewdly. 'He save your life or something?'

'Nothing like that. We sat in foxholes. Swapped jokes, shared tins of corned beef. Fired bullets across muddy fields.'

She cackled, her mouth ugly like a wound. 'Sounds real romantic.'

He glared at her sullenly.

'Sore spot, is it? Brings back bad memories, I guess. Go on, spill yer guts. We girls are used to it.'

'The war's over,' he whispered, and she wrinkled her lips like she'd tasted something sour.

'Suit yourself, sugar,' she said derisively, and got up to show him the door. 'You got a third pack for me, like you promised?'

Pavel held it out and clasped her hand for a moment as she took the pack. 'I'm sorry,' he told her earnestly, looking to reach the woman inside the tramp.

'Whatever for?' she asked him gruffly. 'You got whatever you came for, and I, well, I got my smokes.'

She closed the door in his face and he stood there for a moment longer, wishing the boy were there to tell him that the woman was talking sense. Then Pavel turned on his heel and made for the address she had given him. He never saw the one-eyed man who followed him at a discreet distance, hands buried in his pockets and his scarf hitched high enough to reach all the way up to his patch.

———·———

The boy refused to come in until she had looked into all of her apartment's rooms and proven to him that the Colonel wasn't hiding anywhere. Then he asked her to go down and look in on Pavel's flat. The door was locked and nobody answered her knocking.

'You see,' she told him, 'we are quite safe.'

The boy bit his lip and sat down uneasily on one of her sofas, his eyes on the door and his ears cocked for Fosko's agile tread. Sonia ignored him and got the monkey some water and food. It had shat itself again, and there was no way of cleaning its fur. She let it off its leash and watched it climb the living-room cupboard, rattling the cut glass and china on the way up.

She started to fix Anders and herself some bread and cold cuts, but the boy stopped her and demanded to see the coat. Wordlessly, she led him over to her wardrobe and pulled out a camel-coloured duffel coat.

'I think that will probably do best.'

He tried it on. It gaped at the shoulders and the sleeves were much too long, but it wrapped him up warm all the way down to his ankles. She led him over to the mirror to see what he made of it, but he wouldn't raise his eyes and look at himself.

'Thanks,' he said sullenly. She couldn't decide whether it was the voice of insolence, or of fear.

'Take it off,' she ordered. 'I will shorten the sleeves for you.'

She had just cut several inches off the first of the coat-sleeves when the telephone rang. It ran through the boy like a current, and drew a scream from the monkey on top of its perch. Sonia picked up, the cloth scissors still in one hand, and listened to the Colonel's voice.

'Sonia, my little dove, I'm looking for the boy. The street Arab that follows Pavel Richter around. Do you know whether he is home?'

'No.'

'Be a darling and go down and check. I'll stay on the line.'

Sonia put the phone down on the table and motioned for Anders to stay mum. She walked over to the door, opened and closed it, stood still for two or three minutes, her feet growing cold from lack of movement. Then she re-opened the door, closed it yet again, and walked back to the phone, her heels clicking on the wooden floor with every step.

'Richter's door's locked and nobody answers. What do you want with the boy?'

'Oh, he and I, we had ourselves a little talk this morning, and there's something I forgot to ask. Shouldn't have let him go, but you know how it is. Early mornings, and the brow creased with worries. We all make mistakes.'

'Yes. When are you coming back here?'

'That depends on how things develop, my darling. Did you know Pavel was out looking for Boyd White's sweet little *belle*?'

'No, I didn't. He just said he had things to do.'

'Well, he is. Don't think he will find her, but I'm having an eye kept on him just in case. Perhaps it would be a good idea for you to spend the night with him. Find out what he knows.'

She didn't respond.

'Do you think,' he asked sweetly, 'that this could be arranged?'

'Of course. Whatever you want.'

'That's my darling. I knew I could count on you.' Sonia heard him blow her a kiss down the phone line and quickly hung up. When she looked up, the boy was watching her intently.

'You can't have the coat,' she told him abruptly. 'He would recognize it and know you'd been with me.'

She turned to fetch some gold earrings from the bedroom. 'Here,' she said. 'Use these to get yourself a new coat. And stay away from here. Pavel's being watched.'

The boy nodded calmly and weighed the jewellery in his grubby fist. His eyes seemed old to her, his monkey face wrinkled.

'Eat something in the kitchen before you go, and warm yourself before the oven,' she instructed him. 'And one more thing: if the Colonel finds out you've got my earrings, I'll tell him that you must have stolen them.'

She turned her back on him then, sat down at the piano, and started playing scales. Sonia did not stop until she heard the door close behind him.

———·———

The apartment was near Potsdamer Platz, close to the centre of the city where three of the sectors ran together into a point. The building dated from around the turn of the century, like so much of Berlin's housing; five tall storeys organized around a communal courtyard. Pavel scanned the windows but it was impossible to see anything through the all-pervasive frost. He tried the front door and found it open. Before he disappeared inside, he turned around once, not knowing himself why, other than there was a faint feeling of illicitness about his snooping. He did not know what he was looking for, and hence saw nothing, just street-hawkers, going about their business, and a one-eyed man in a good coat tying his laces by the side of the road. Pavel closed the door behind himself and ran his eyes across the names on the postboxes. There were none he recognized. He had forgotten to ask Franzi about Belle's last name. Chances were she didn't know it. He shrugged and began to climb the stairs.

The soldier gave it away. Actually, he was a policeman, wearing the insignia of the Soviet-controlled police force upon collar and sleeve. He sat on a chair on the fourth-floor landing, not looking up as Pavel walked first towards, then past him. He was smoking, and the floor around his feet was dotted with literally hundreds of cigarette butts. He – and no doubt some colleagues – must have been sitting out there for days. Pavel tried to judge which door he was interested in and realized it was one floor down, visible for the sentry if he craned his neck a little over the staircase railing. Pavel tarried a while on the top-floor landing, pretending he was ringing a bell up there, then gave a sigh of frustration – far too theatrical no doubt – and walked back towards the policeman.

'Good day,' he said in German. 'Long, lonely vigil, is it?'

The man merely nodded his head.

'You must be freezing out here. No time for a coffee?'

The policeman shrugged noncommittally.

'You don't speak German, do you?' Pavel smiled, and the man answered him by blowing smoke up into his face and waving him on with his chin.

'Now what's so important that they would put a Soviet goon in a police jacket on the door?'

He raised his hand in farewell, and continued on down the stairs, examining the door with his eyes as he passed it. Its frame looked a little cracked to him, like someone had shouldered their way in not so long ago. With any luck it was no longer possible to lock the apartment. Back on the ground floor, he let the house door slam shut, took off his shoes and then snuck back up, soft socks upon the icy floor. He took position a full flight beneath the soldier, and listened to his smoking. All he required was a minute's inattention. Surely it was only a matter of time.

He waited an hour or more and nothing much happened. The soldier's smoking stank up the whole staircase, and every ten minutes Pavel could hear the flare of his match. An old woman passed him, carrying a Bavarian cuckoo clock and a large bag of cabbages. She looked at him standing in his socks upon his unlaced boots, his teeth clamped shut to keep them from chattering. He put a finger to his lips and pointed another upward, towards the sentry. 'Please,' he mouthed, from between frost-numbed lips.

'Boys will be boys,' she muttered, and moved past him. Her back was so bent it was as though her face grew out of her chest. The soldier above did not stir. The granny greeted him curtly while she unlocked the door right next to his chair.

Pavel waited another quarter-hour, stiff with the cold, and was about to give up when he heard a door open and the old woman's voice, addressing the sentry. 'Excuse me,' she said, 'I could use a strong man for a second.' And then, in bad, staccato Russian: 'Help old mother boy she short and you just sit there like furniture ready for fireplace shame on you.'

It got him his break. Pavel heard the soldier mumble something and follow granny into her flat. Flushing with gratitude, he leapt off his boots, gathered them in one hand and ran up the half-dozen stairs to the door with the broken frame. His luck held: it was unlocked, or rather, the lock was broken, just as he had hoped. Once inside, he closed the door gently behind himself and sat on the floor rubbing life back into his frozen feet.

The apartment had been searched. *Tossed*, they said in novels. Pavel walked through the debris that covered the floor, past overturned drawers and broken photo frames whose contents had been removed. The cushions of the living-room sofa had been split end to end, and a cheap tea set lay shattered next to the dining table. In the bedroom, he found a lady's wardrobe, gutted. Its door hung crooked on its hinges and evening gowns littered the floor: stoles, blouses, underwear. Pavel stooped to pick up a pair of red silk panties and once again was conscious of the shame of snooping. He had no idea what he was looking for. It surprised him a little that the clothes had not been 'confiscated'. They were of good quality and could have bought many a pleasure on the black market.

Tired, Pavel sat down upon the four-poster bed and sank deep into the well-worn mattress. Upon the comforter, the crust of dried blood. The stain was not much bigger than the palm of his hand. Pavel ran a finger over it, morbidly curious as to how it would feel. The blood was icy under his numb fingertip, as was the comforter itself. There was something about the winter's cold that obscured all difference. He sniffed at the pillow but smelled nothing. A single dark hair traversed the pillow case, too

83

long to be a man's. Next to the bed frame lay a few condoms, unused. There was no way of telling which of these things constituted a clue.

Pavel stood up again, unsure what to do. Wishing to be diligent in his search, he looked for papers: documents, a sheaf of letters, a diary. Predictably, he found none. If they had ever existed they had been taken by those who had come before him. In the bathroom, a collection of soaps and cosmetics had been dumped in the sink, and someone had scratched the Russian word *kurva* into the mirror's glass. Pavel closed his eyes and tried to imagine how the apartment had looked before it was ransacked; tried to picture a prostitute's life, her days carved up between the attentions of her customers and those of her pimp. He imagined the shame of the first tearful weeks of this existence, soon to be displaced by a fierce sort of pride; a manic delight in her own depravity that made men cower and fawn over her, whom they despised. It was no surprise to him that Boyd had fallen for a woman such as this, loved her perhaps, even as he rented out her flesh. Pavel pictured him bringing home chocolates and a bottle of champagne; smearing toffee across her pouty lips as he fed her with unwashed fingers. It made him angry with the dead man, and he opened his eyes.

He was no longer alone.

The soldier had crept up to him without his noticing. Now they stood a mere yard apart: Pavel with his hands clasped around the sink, and the Russian in the doorway, a cigarette behind his ear. Pavel could see him in the mirror. The word *kurva* cut up his features into eyes and mouth, his cheek's bony wedge. God, he looked young. His hands held a gun, its muzzle pointed at the small of Pavel's back. He didn't say anything, but just in case Pavel slowly raised his hands and placed them on either side of the mirror. They stood like that, wordless, for about fifteen minutes, until they heard heavy footsteps right outside the apartment door and the rap of knuckles upon its wood.

'Let's go,' said the soldier in Russian, and waved at him with his gun.

Out in the corridor two more soldiers awaited them, machine pistols in hand. These had not bothered to dress up in police uniforms; both were smoking furiously, blowing smoke from their nostrils. Half a flight up, the old woman was standing on the stairs, a grim smile on her wizened face.

'Now you him have,' she said in her broken Russian. 'I tell you he is doing no good.'

The soldiers nodded their thanks and walked him out to a waiting car. They shoved him into the back seat, wrapped a Russian coat around his shoulders, squeezed in on either side. Their guns' muzzles dug into Pavel's side, hurting his kidneys. The driver started the engine and they took off down the street, then turned eastward, towards the sector border.

'If he makes any trouble,' the driver instructed one of the soldiers, 'break his skull a little.'

The man nodded and grimly slipped some knuckledusters over his gloved fist.

———·———

Sonia sat upon her piano chair. Sat still enough to be conscious of the smell of her own unwashed body, and to hear the monkey on its cupboard perch, picking at its fur. She did not play. She had tried to, on and off, Haydn and then some Bach, but her mind was elsewhere. The Colonel's words were ringing in her ears: *Perhaps it would be a good idea for you to spend the night with him. Do you think that this could be arranged?*

Of course.

For a long time now she had been sitting there, upon her chair before the piano, asking herself what it would feel like to kiss Pavel. She did not think it would be pleasant. His breath might be sour, his tongue clumsy. She imagined their kissing: standing stiff-limbed, him stooping over her at an awkward angle, their hips tilted outward as they took care not to touch. She wished to get it over with, but also that it would never happen.

'What do you want to do now?' he would ask with that blank, honest look, like he'd never known duplicity.

'Brandy,' she'd say. 'I really need to get myself a glass of brandy.'

And they would drink, and one thing would lead to another, and the Colonel would get his answers.

'The thing is,' she whispered to the monkey, 'what I need to do right now is go melt some ice and wash out my crotch.'

The monkey did not answer her and she continued to sit there, at the piano, not playing any music, as the day slipped from midday to evening and, in its progress, buried the sun.

———

Pavel did not make any trouble at the border crossing. An American guard checked their papers and briefly looked over the faces in the car. The Russians had brought along someone else's passport to stand in for Pavel's. There was no way the picture could match his face, but the guard waved them through never-theless. Glancing at the men to his left and right from the corners of his eyes, Pavel realized how much he resembled them. They shared the same Slavic cheekbones and broad, high forehead. *It's almost*, he thought, *like I'm coming home*. The gun's barrel stuck uncomfortably in his side.

They hadn't gone more than a block when one of the guards pushed Pavel's hat down over his eyes. Blindfolded, he counted the minutes until he heard the engine being cut off; counted them slowly, by the measure of his breath. By his best estimate they drove for something like a quarter of an hour. That could put them pretty much anywhere in the eastern half of the city. It was even possible that they were crazy enough to have driven several times around the same five blocks, just to confuse him.

The soldiers pulled him out of the car, through a door, into a building, and down a long corridor. Pavel did not resist, concentrated on his step. He had no wish to fall. Heels clicked as two men stood to attention to his left. A door opened, then another, and he was roughly shoved down upon a wooden chair. A hand went through his coat and jacket, found his remaining packs of cigarettes, some dollars and Reichsmarks, along with his passport. All these items were placed upon a desk not far from him – Pavel heard the coins rattle on its wooden surface. He sat still, chin rolled into his chest, and cradled his hands in his lap. After an indeterminable period a voice spoke to him in lightly accented English.

'You may take off your hat, Mr Richter.'

He did so, moving his hands slowly, and blinking his eyes a few times. The room was brightly lit by a number of bulbs that dangled from the ceiling.

Pavel found himself on a chair at a few yards' remove from a heavy oaken desk, whose Nazi ornamentation had been roughly disfigured with a hatchet's help. Behind the desk, a clean-shaven man with salt-and-pepper hair and wire-rimmed glasses, trim and rather long-boned, no older perhaps than fifty. He sat in an officer's greatcoat, hands stuck in tight leather gloves, a glass of tea steaming in front of him. A tidy man, handsome even, not a hair out of place, only the skin was a little yellow, like he'd borrowed it from someone dead. Pavel's passport was in his hand. A second man stood next to Pavel's chair in uncomfortable proximity; heavy-set and hulking. He wasn't one of the soldiers who had brought him here, but rather a blond, ruddy-faced youth with eyes whose colour was drained from them by the electric light. Blue perhaps. He stood casually, one might say insolently, his thumbs hooked behind a leather belt, chewing tobacco. Pavel did not notice the third man immediately. He sat on a stool in the corner, almost in Pavel's back: a dark-haired man with a melancholy air, busy with his fingernails. He never even looked up to acknowledge Pavel.

'You smoke?' the officer behind the desk asked Pavel. A good voice, quiet and sonorous. The mouth barely moved. Quiet words from behind a borrowed face.

Pavel nodded in order to buy himself time. His mouth was dry and he wondered whether he could ask for a glass of water. The officer pushed one of Pavel's own packs of cigarettes to the desk's edge, along with a book of matches. Pavel made to get up, but the youth shoved him back into his chair and yelled at him.

'Sit, you stupid shit!' he spluttered. There were fragments of tobacco in his spit.

'You can smoke,' said the older man, 'once you've answered some questions.'

Pavel looked at him, and tried to keep all anger out of his voice.

'I won't talk,' he said meekly. He meant it.

'He won't talk,' laughed the youth, switching from English to Russian. 'We catch him red-handed in that *kurva*'s flat, and he won't talk. He's not even in the army any more, not a soul knows he's here, and he won't talk.' He wiped his mouth with the back of one hand. 'By the time I'm done with him, he'll sing bloody *Onegin*, you'll see. Everyone starts talking when the knot reaches the arse.'

His accent, Pavel noted, was Georgian, though for this he was unusually fair.

'I should tell you,' he said quietly, 'that I speak Russian. In fairness I should tell you.'

He said it slowly, taking care to shape the Russian vowels with his mouth. They stared at him dumbfounded, and for a minute or so there was total silence in the room.

Thus there commenced a strange interrogation. Throughout, Pavel remained obstinately silent. The interrogator and his young helper became strangely tongue-tied, having lost the use of any language in which they might have discussed strategy in secret. Every so often, the blond man would start in on Pavel nevertheless, hurling abuse at him and asking him questions.

'Look here, you swine. What were you doing in the flat in Lützowstrasse 92? What is your connection to Boyd Ferdinand White? Talk or you'll be sorry. You think you'll have the last laugh? Think again. We'll grind you into dust and flush you down the toilet, you wrecker.

'Prostitute! We know what you are. Confess already! Be a man and get it off your chest. What happened to Söldmann? Is he dead? Do the Americans have him? And what about the girl? Where is she? Speak, or I swear I will rip off your ears.

'Dog! Talk, or we will crush your skull and piss in it, you hear? Who's got the merchandise? Name your price. Russia is vast, Russia is rich. You can walk out of here showered in gold, or hobbling on crutches – it's all in your hands.'

For all its linguistic colour, there was a distinct lack of enthusiasm to this game. It seemed to Pavel like the man was going through the motions, performing before his superior, as it were, and earning his supper. After every outburst that saw the man stomp up and down before him with clenched fists, his face the colour of a ripe plum, there followed long minutes of silence. They stretched into half-hours as the day progressed. Rather to his surprise the youth made no move to beat him. Once or twice he seemed close, raising one fist high above his head, or pulling back a booted foot as though to kick his shin, but every time he stopped the motion, realigned his limb as though by force and carried on with his tirade. On occasion the dark-haired man on the stool would stoop to reiterate one of his colleague's questions, though never the insults that went with them. He spoke so quietly, Pavel barely understood him; slurred his words, too, as though he was the worse for drink. Throughout, the officer sat quietly behind his desk. Twice he received calls on his black office telephone and answered with a monosyllabic *'Da'*. The glass of tea standing before him had long grown cold.

Pavel kept to his silence, as he had promised. It wasn't that he wished to be impolite, let alone heroic. At first he was simply unsure what it was he was being asked to admit to; uncertain, too, as to the consequences of his words. He did not like to lie, and silence seemed to be the best strategy for gathering information and passing on none. In his mind's eye he recalled Boyd's body. Boyd's passport had not protected him. He wondered what needed to happen before the Russians started disregarding his own.

Then, as he sat there upon the hard, wooden chair, Russian breath upon his face, something else took hold of him: a sensation so sudden, he almost called out. It was as though his mind was starting to work again for the first time since he'd fallen sick. The cotton wool that had muffled his world fell away, and everything came into sharper focus, from the grain of the stool to the monotonous ticking of the big office clock above the door. Thoughts and sensations coursed through him, clamoured for a hearing. The woman, Sonia, headed off all competitors. She commanded his attention. He fell to thinking.

On her upper lip, he thought, *there are beard hairs. A dark smudge of hairs. They will grow coarse with age.*

She saved my life, he thought. *Any man would feel grateful for that. A heart filled with gratitude. There is nothing surprising in that.*

What is it then, he asked himself, *that bothers me about her? Something about the way she came in yesterday, and helped me yet again. Now why would she have done that? She wasn't the least surprised about the body. And of course she is the Colonel's mistress. He's caught up in it all somehow, the Colonel.*

And then the lout yelled at him again, interrupting his train of thought. It rather annoyed Pavel, and for the first time in the long hours of interrogation he felt his eyes flash with anger.

At long last – the clock showed it was well past ten o'clock at night – the interrogation came to an abrupt close. A woman in a

90

smart uniform entered, keeping her eyes carefully averted from the prisoner. She bent over the desk and whispered something in the officer's ear. There were several holes at the back of her tights, and the skin underneath was pink with cold. The officer listened to her, asked a question, then ran a gloved hand across his face, as though to check it was still in place. Once the woman had left he placed a quick phone call. He did not need to dial, simply pressed a button.

'What's the situation?' he asked curtly.

'How do you spell his name?'

'And the rank?'

'No, of course not. He's unharmed.'

'Five more minutes, and I'll send him out. Make arrangements.'

The man had, Pavel thought, a very pleasant telephone manner, at once precise and full of character, only it, too, seemed borrowed, along with the face. He considered commenting on it, but thought better of such a childish prank. Now that his head was working again, he didn't want it bashed in.

'You have friends in high places, Mr Richter. But I expect you know as much. We have no choice but to let you go.'

The officer paused to give a precise little bow. It was the sort of gesture that might precede a marriage proposal, or the order for execution.

'Before you leave us, how about looking at some pictures, Mr Richter? You may decide for yourself whether or not you choose to comment.'

'As you wish,' mumbled Pavel, responding to the man's courtesy, however disingenuous. The belligerent youth, he noted, turned away in disgust and spat tobacco into a corner spittoon.

The officer opened his drawer. He pulled out a number of photos, enlarged to the size of a standard letter. They had the flat, grainy look of having been taken through a long lens in bad light. Pavel recognized Boyd, and the midget. The midget was

91

wearing a beautiful tuxedo. There was a picture of an older man with a thick pair of whiskers and a lab coat, and one of a youngish tough with a handlebar moustache and a livid scar running down his cheek. There were pictures of girls in busty, low-cut gowns, playing roulette in a club, and one of two people making love on a floral-patterned settee. Pavel flicked through them slowly, trying to appear impassive. He pointed to the midget.

'Is this Söldmann?' he asked.

'Yes.'

'And this?' He pointed to the tough.

'One of his boys. Arnulf von Schramm. The right-hand man.'

'And that?' Pavel put his finger on the older man with the lab coat.

'You don't really know very much about any of this, do you, Mr Richter?'

'Quite frankly, sir, I know nothing at all.'

'Well, then I think it is time for you to go.'

He handed over Pavel's passport, though Pavel noticed that he held on to his cigarettes and money. After some thought he added a card with a handwritten name and a number. The name was Karpov. Dimitri Stepanovich. General of the Soviet Army.

'In case you remember something after all. Goodbye. – Lev!'

He waved over the Georgian youth and whispered something in his ear. The young man saluted, jumped back over to Pavel and jerked him to his feet by one armpit. His hat was pushed back over his eyes, and the Georgian marched him down the corridor and into the night. Outside, a car whisked them off across cobblestoned roads. The driver did not speak to his guard; hummed a sad folk tune. They stopped after just a few minutes' drive and stood around waiting. Pavel heard English voices.

'Now,' Lev told him. 'Get out.'

He pulled his hat back and realized he was at one of the border points to the British sector. A young soldier was waiting for him in an army jeep.

'Get in, sir, before we freeze our bums off. I have orders from Colonel Fosko to drive you home.'

'You look tired, sir,' he added as they chased down the sector's empty streets. 'The Colonel said you had a chat with them Russkies. Hope they didn't rough you up none.'

Pavel smiled absent-mindedly. He felt like he had done a good day's work. Eighteen hours earlier he had set out to find Belle. He had found her, on a grainy photograph, with Boyd's mouth clamped tight around one youthful breast. It was a frivolous thought, but Belle, she had beautiful breasts.

———·———

Back in the office, General Karpov sat alone, having dispatched both of his assistants on their respective errands. He used the phone to request a couple of files through channels, then dismissed Richter from his mind. The photos lay spread out across his desk. Karpov studied them, and ran a gloved hand over the man in the white lab coat. From afar one might have called it a caress. It's impossible to vouch for it, of course: I wasn't there to witness. And yet it happened all the same, the touch, and the name, tumbling from his tidy lips.

Haldemann.

We were all of us looking for Haldemann in the winter of '46. It was Karpov who was destined to find him in the end.

———·———

Sonia heard him climb the stairs. It was a few minutes before midnight. Of course it could have been just about anyone climbing the stairs, and yet she was sure it was Pavel. The footsteps stopped one flight down. Sonia heard his door open and close, stood still in her tracks and held her breath. It should have been quite impossible to hear anything through the floor, unless he was making a ruckus. Nevertheless she thought she could make out his quiet tread upon the floorboards, the slow, methodical motions as he fired up the stove. Pavel seemed restless. She heard him pace from wall to wall, the gait uncertain. Now he grabbed a book, read a page or two, placed it back on the shelf; sat down at the typewriter, punching out letters with no pattern or meaning. The sounds were so transparently clear to her ear that it was a shock when, all of a sudden, she heard his rap on her apartment door. She hastened over to open up for him. Pavel looked tired and excited all at once. She made a conscious effort not to interpret the tone of his voice.

'You're still up?' he asked.

'Yes, of course. Come in. Would you like some tea?'

He nodded assent and sank into one of her armchairs. She put a pan of water on the hob, lit candles and put a record on the gramophone. Sonia sat across from Pavel; sat on her piano chair, long legs crossed before her. Her fingers caressed the instrument's keys, a little yellowed with age.

'Did you find Belle?' she asked after she had poured out the tea.

'Yes.'

He looked at her with tired eyes, accusingly perhaps, and she shrugged without apologizing. 'I thought it best if you found out for yourself.'

The record player launched into a waltz, and it struck her as terribly out of place.

They sat in silence for a while. She began to think that he liked it, this silence, that he had withdrawn into it like a tortoise fed up with the weather, but then, all of a sudden, he started babbling. Well, perhaps not babbling precisely, but he started talking, a welter of words, and – this was what surprised her most – it was all utterly in earnest, this stream of words, spoken hastily but also with a shameless insistency. It was as though he had stumbled onto a secret, and now it needed out. In this, he reminded her of a schoolboy.

'All day,' he said, 'I have been thinking about Dostoevsky. It's because of the Russians, of course. They pulled me in, and the officer, he had a voice just like my grandfather. He creeps into your language, Dostoevsky does. All those *almosts* and *howevers*: they make it impossible to get a single thought straight. And the drama of it; four Russians in a room, and none of them will speak, and when one of them does – the youngest, the buffoon – all it is, is air, hot air, and secretly, on the inside so to speak, all four of them grinning because they like this, the absurdity of the mo-ment, and the buffoon screaming "swine!" My grandfather, he used to say that we were a race knit for the absurd. We're constituted for it. It brings out our passions. Hot, raging words, only a half-hour later will find us drinking, an arm round each of our enemies.

'But then they showed me the photo: Boyd's mouth clamped shut over one breast, and your neck twisted so you're looking straight into the camera. And you know what it is that I see there? Love. It's impossible, you must have hated him, down to the depth of your bowels, but on the photo, mind, what one finds is love. A smile that sits in the eyes, grainy, and enough bent to your body to imagine you are happy there, splayed out under his mouth. And at that moment, before anything else, I was happy for it. I very nearly smiled myself.

'Only, if you are in the picture, you will know how he died. And if you know how he died, and did not tell me, then Fosko knows how he died, too, and everything has been a lie, even his corpse, which, at the time, seemed like the one thing that was true. It should have made me mad, you know. Should have! – my friend dead, and you holding out on me, who looked happy in his arms, just that one second, though of course you hated him. You know, I imagined you there, in your apartment, even before I saw the photo, that is; imagined you proud, which you are, and insolent before his touch. I held your panties today. Red, silky panties. The Russians didn't steal them which means an officer

95

dealt with your flat, on order from up high. Which is to say, whatever Boyd was tied up in, it was important, or money was on the line, which I guess amounts to the same. Red panties, Sonia. Will you forgive me if I say they seemed tasteless to me?

'In any case, I tried to be angry. God help me, Sonia, I tried. Even just now, before I came in, I tried to work myself up into a frenzy. I would tear in and make a scene; strike you across one cheek perhaps. Only you wouldn't take it, would you? You would hit back, a fist to my chin, revive me with smelling salts, your brows knit, and curious as to why I insisted on this farce. "Pavel," you would say, "I never claimed to be something I was not." And I would sit up, appeased, and ask you to play the piano. And later, with your back turned, perhaps I would tell you, past the lump in my throat, that I saw you, naked, under my best friend's mouth; and that you were beautiful. Perhaps it would make you happy, just a little, you see, and things wouldn't seem so shabby to you.

'The thing is that today, from the moment I hit the street, there woke in me a strange love for life. Greed, let's call it greed, a Dostoevskian, Russian sort of greed. It's like that scene in his novel where Ivan (you have read *Karamazov*, have you not? He's the ponderous intellectual plotting rebellion against God. God, you hear!), well, Ivan is talking to his younger brother, Alyosha, and he admits to being a "greenbeak". He uses precisely that word, "greenbeak". He speaks of revolution and it's a green-beak's revolution; and faced with this, the truth of his being, he has to admit that all that matters to him – *all*, you hear – is life. There is even this bit about the "sticky buds" of spring, something sexual in any case, and for a moment it looks like youth will conquer all.

'Oh Sonia,' he said. 'Do you have any idea what I am trying to say to you here?'

He looked up earnestly, wet coals for eyes, and the faintest of smiles upon his features. Sonia just sat there, not really listening to any of this nonsense, her eyes on his lips, thinking, asking herself what it would feel like to kiss Pavel. They sat unmoving, while the monkey crouched in the corner and shat a putrid turd upon its rug. It had bowel movements like a toddler.

'Ah, well,' said Pavel, 'that's how it is.' He paused and looked her up and down. 'Do you want to tell me how Boyd died?'

'It is late, Pavel. Tomorrow.'

'Then I had better go to bed.'

He placed the mug on her coffee table, and got up stiffly.

'Don't go,' she said, and slowly unbuttoned her coat.

He flushed and stared at her blankly.

'The Colonel is having you watched. He told me to . . . spend the night with you. He will know it if you leave.'

He nodded wearily, rubbed the back of his head.

'I can sleep on the couch again.'

Sonia shook her head. 'Sleep in the bed. The Colonel will want . . . details.'

'Tell him I was too sick for it. Tell him I wanted you to hold me. He will like that.'

Sonia smiled at that, and together they cleaned up the monkey's filth. When they were done, she persuaded him to share her bed anyway; it was big enough for two, and a second night on the couch would hurt his back.

She changed into her nightgown in the bedroom, then called him in. 'Put these on,' she said, and passed over a pair of flannel pyjamas Fosko had ordered for her from England. 'You won't be cold. I have good bedding.'

He stepped back into the living room so that he could undress in peace. When he returned, they slipped under the covers together, each of them turning to arrange their pillows.

'You good and ready?' he asked, before turning off the light.

'Yes, I'm fine,' she said.

It was to her the most ridiculous of questions.

They lay next to each other on the big marital bed, taking care not to touch. In the darkness Sonia could hear the monkey clambering about, watching them; the room stank of it. Pavel's body exuded almost no heat, and she was tempted to reach over, just to make sure he was really there. His breathing was quiet and regular, and after a few minutes she heard him scratch discreetly, moving the bedding a little as he did so. She lay still, hands upon her stomach, asking herself whether she thought him a fool.

'Tell me, Sonia,' he said when she had already half dozed off. 'Did you see the boy today? Anders.'

'Yes. He's angry with you because you cried in front of Fosko.'

'I'm glad I cried. Can you understand that?'

'No,' she said. 'And neither will the boy.'

She heard him roll from his back onto his stomach. Moments later she was asleep.

———·——

Once, halfway through the night, Sonia woke and found Pavel breathing a few inches from her mouth. She reached over and put her lips on his. When she woke in the morning, she convinced herself it had just been a dream.

5

24 December 1946

Pavel woke first. Woke to darkness, an hour before dawn, and lay there guiltily for long minutes, savouring her smell: spring flowers and a touch of honey. It was her hair, he believed. She must have washed it the previous day.

He slipped out from under the coverlet and almost called out when his feet touched the icy floor. It took him some minutes to stand up. Again and again he would touch the floor with the soles of his feet, then raise them up in the air and bunch them into fists in order to get the circulation going. When he finally rose it was with the gingerly gait of the rheumatic. He stood on the outer edges of his feet and hopped along until he found a rug. It was still so dark in the room that he could see neither the bed he had left, nor the very walls that surrounded him. This circumstance gave him a delightful sense of the absence of space. Had it not been so cold, he might have stood there awhile, feeling himself lost by the world, and also at its centre.

Pavel located the bedroom door by memory, stepped through and gently closed it behind him before groping for a light switch. His fingers found it, but nothing happened. Evidently the electricity was off again. In the darkness he could hear the heavy, rhythmic breathing of the animal somewhere to his right. It sounded to him like the breath of copulation. He veered left, away from the noise, stumbled painfully over a low piece of furniture – a footrest? a coffee table? – and caught his weight upon the piano's bared teeth. The cacophony drew a screech from the monkey's throat, too close for comfort. Disoriented, Pavel sat on the floor by the piano and tried to remember where he had left coat and trousers, his kidneys already hurting with the cold. To his relief Sonia had not reacted to the noise; he was not ready to talk to her yet, wearing another man's pyjamas, the smell of her hair still thick on his tongue. He sat, arms thrown around his body, and waited for the first rays of dawn.

While he sat thus, he forced himself to think about her, this woman whose bed he had shared, and the questions he must ask. He remembered how she had invited him to spend the night with her. She had said it calmly, and the blood had poured into his face. Then the ritual of preparing for bed, always conscious of her moving around him. In the bathroom, Pavel had found Fosko's things lined up on a porcelain shelf: nail scissors, razor, a scented bar of soap. Her underwear hung half-frozen from a washing line above the tub. Standing straight, holding out the pyjama suit she bid him wear, Sonia's nightshirt had covered her to mid-thigh; white legs, curvy in the calf. Her toenails were painted a dark shade of rose, a little chipped. Upon the night table, tweezers for the plucking of eyebrows, and a forgotten cup of water. Dust on the saucer. The core of an apple. A small bottle of cologne.

Pavel had taken it all in with a strange, childlike intensity. Indeed he felt thrown back to the age of sexual awakening, and remembered a similar bedroom, many years ago, and a young aunt – a widow – who had asked him to minister to her needs one weekend when she claimed to suffer from migraine. He had laboured then under the same sense of illicit desire, and had studied with the same intensity the many paraphernalia of adult life that littered her chambers. What was absent here, however, was that strange sense of being watched by a seducer's eye; Sonia seemed to barely notice him even as she offered her bed to him.

As dawn finally broke, it seemed to Pavel that she must despise him, and for a moment he wished he had stormed in last night and taken Boyd's death out on her hide.

He got up stiffly and gathered his things, putting on trousers, sweater and coat without bothering to remove the pyjamas first. All of a sudden he was in a great hurry; he wished to leave before she should rise. There would be time to speak to her later. His cold-stiff fingers had trouble with his socks, and he took the boots in one hand to avoid any further delay. The monkey, he noticed, was playing with the gramophone, deliberately sticking the needle into its own leathery paw. When it finally drew blood it screeched yet again, and began to tug violently at the turntable and buttons. Alarmed by the noise, Pavel ran to the door and rushed out. As he walked down the flight of stairs to his own flat, he thought for a moment that he'd spied somebody lurking in the shadow of the staircase down below.

'Anders?' he called, but received no answer. Pavel stood by the landing for a few moments, the railing in one hand and his boots in the other, but was unable to ascertain whether his impression had been correct. In the end he gave up and turned to unlock his apartment door. He'd hoped that the boy would be there to greet him, but was disappointed. Inside the coal oven stood stone-cold, and he noticed some drops of dried blood on his sink that had eluded his notice the previous night.

He stood still, running a fingertip over the blood, and asking himself who had been hurt there, before his mirror's stare.

———·———

There you have it: Pavel's 'morning after'. Cold feet and adolescent reverie; a fitting harvest for a night barren of consummation. The thought of it, that he should spend a night next to a beautiful woman (for she was, in her own way, quite beautiful), a woman experienced in matters pertaining to the heart – in short, a whore – and somehow manage to walk away from it, undone. It boggles the mind.

If you ask me, the fault was all his. She must have been willing enough, if only to rid herself of all doubts that this man, Pavel, was any different from a dozen or so others whose bed she had shared, not always under any direct duress. And yet nothing had happened. Not a thing. A kiss – maybe! – in the depth of night: lips parched by the cold and briefly pressed together, too quick even to taste the other's sleep-soured breath. Ah, well. At least the monkey had some fun, tugging its Thomas late in the darkness, and smearing its own fur with the discharge. Nature will out, you see, even in this frigid age.

At the time, of course, I knew nothing of the night's chastity, and imagined (only to stay warm, mind) all manner of excess. You see, I had spent the whole of the previous morning on Pavel's coat-tails, shadowing his every step. It was me whom he saw tying my shoelaces in the street as he entered Sonia's former block of flats; and it was I who called Fosko – forcing coins down a public phone's frozen slot – when the Russians made off with Pavel. When he was returned to his flat late last night, the Colonel bid me resume my watch. I was to be relieved at dawn.

I spent a boring, freezing night, first in the stairwell armed only with a blanket and a large thermos, making quick runs out into the street when the coffee had worked its course. Out there I noticed a man slumped behind the wheel of a car and a cup of hot brew on the dash. After a few hours of sitting on the draughty stairs – I was frozen through to the bone – I decided to imitate him and got into my own car, hoping it would be warmer there. We were parked on opposite sides of the road, my fellow spy and I, the only cars in the road. I couldn't make up my mind as to who had sent him. Was he a Russian agent sent to keep an eye on Pavel? One of Söldmann's boys who had picked up Pavel's trail? Or perhaps Fosko had sent him, to keep watch on the watcher and ascertain whether I was as reliable as I claimed. To be honest, without this second lookout I might have left the post for an hour or two, driven home for some more coffee, a bottle of gin, and a fresh shirt and collar. As it was, I sat there, dreaming up ways – scenarios, positions – of how those two might be making it, and trying to keep my teeth from chattering. My windows got so steamed up and frozen over, had Pavel decided to make a run for it, there is not a chance that I'd have spotted him. Nor would my fellow watcher; once, when I got out of the car to walk up and down the street, I found him drunkenly and ineffectually scraping at his windshield with the butt of a gun. I nodded a greeting, but he ignored me. I didn't care. Chances were he was just as out of coffee and cigarettes as I was.

At dawn, I left the car and took up position two flights down from Sonia's flat. I was there, crouching in one corner, when Pavel came out, boots in hand, and hollered 'Anders' at my shadow. A half-hour later my replacement came, sporting fur mittens and a thermos full of hot grog.

'Get yourself home,' he said, after a quick shared cigarette.

'There's another watcher,' I warned him. 'Out in the street.'

He shrugged. 'Better tell the Colonel.' And added, after another rueful shrug: 'What does he want this one here watching for, anyway? We could just pull him in. Get him talking, like.'

I thought it better not to answer and made off after a quick handshake. With the Colonel, one was never sure when one was being tested. In truth, I'd had the same thought for much of the night. By this point, I think, there had awoken in me the desire to speak to Pavel face to face, and be done with these childish games of hide and seek.

———·———

Sonia woke the moment he began to stir. Long experience bid her not to speak; men, she thought, liked to wake lonely, gather their thoughts, and admire their handiwork. She listened to his sitting up, the intake of breath when his feet met the floor. He was like a child getting out of bed, reluctant to accept the fact that it was cold beyond the bedding. When he finally made his way out of the room he promptly fell onto the piano. The monkey's shriek hid her giggles. Sonia remained in bed, enjoying its comfort, and piled his half of the coverlet on top of her. Her hair smelled clean around her, and she was glad now that she had washed herself the previous afternoon.

As she lay there, her mind was thrown back to last night's scene, Pavel talking while she pondered his lips. She thought of his earnestness, how important it had seemed to him that she should believe him. It made her smile in the darkness. And all that nonsense about Dostoevsky! 'Sticky buds' indeed. A man who talked of his greed for life, and blushed when she unbuttoned her coat.

She wondered whether he had always been thus: a man carrying a schoolboy around in him, kept under buttons as it were, camou-flaged with the help of army gestures and the odd word of slang. He was worldly enough, most of the time, to keep his mouth shut and live by the rules of man; until, that is, something broke in him and it all spilled out, all kinds of blather, and all true, no doubt. Then he became like a drunk who would shoot off his mouth at an official party, knowing full well that sooner or later there would be repercussions. He wouldn't even complain about it: two ushers would come up to him and take him by the scruff of the neck, throw him out by the back door, and all the while he would apologize for putting them to all this trouble. It was hard to believe that she should fall for a man like that. It was a charming trait, no doubt, and dangerous. It stemmed from a world she had left when she had first been raped.

She heard him leave, finally, and soon got up herself to heat a pan of water over the coal oven, using some for tea and the rest to scrub her face, feet and armpits. Invigorated, she fed the monkey, then crouched upon her chamber pot. *We live in a time*, she thought, *when we bring out our waste by hand. Pellets of shit wrapped in tissue paper, up and down the sidewalk, the monkey's, mine, even the Colonel's.* How could a man like Pavel live in a time like this? Smiling, unaccountably merry, she fixed herself breakfast, then played and hummed Schubert lieder until the phone rang and brought an end to her joy. It was Fosko. His voice was full of honeyed good humour.

'Are you alone, my dear?'

'Yes.'

'Did you have a nice night?'

'He stayed over. Like you said.'

'Splendid. How much does he know?'

'The Russians got him. Last night.'

'Yes, I know. I bailed him out. But does he know about you, my dear?'

'About me?'

'Don't be dim now. About you and Boyd. That you were – what's the term – *involved?*'

'No. At least he didn't let on. I doubt he's any good at lying.'

'Is he any good at anything else?'

She hesitated. 'He – couldn't. Said his kidneys hurt. He wanted to be held.'

'Ah, well. Some other time perhaps. I have the foolish feeling that he might fall for you yet. Damsel in distress. He's the type, don't you think? Any sign of the boy, by the way?'

'No, no sign.'

'Very well, then. I will call back later, or better yet, drop by. Sonia, my dear?'

'Yes?'

'I just wouldn't know what I'd do without you.'

She set the phone down without hurry and marvelled that she would dare lie to the Colonel. She knew it was an idiocy. There was nothing she could do that would protect Pavel from his wrath, and nothing that Pavel could offer her that would have made it worth the risk. Inadvertently her gaze travelled down to the floor, and once again she found herself straining to divine what was going on in Pavel's rooms. There was no way to satisfy her curiosity. She knew him to be watched. Any move she made would find the Colonel's ear. Ill at ease, she sat down upon a kitchen stool and started to peel potatoes. They were cold and hard as stones.

Sitting there, her hands working mechanically on a tea towel spread over her lap, she asked herself – scrupulously, dutifully even – whether it could be that she was in love. She recalled the pallor of his skin and the angular cast of his bones when he had lain sick; how she had spied, below the nape of his neck, the spiky ridge of spine and thought it ugly. Nothing about him spoke to her body. She pictured them as lovers, entwined in some way she favoured, but no interest stirred in her; she could not recall the shade of his eye nor the build of his hands. Only his wedding band stuck in her mind, plain and loose upon his emaciated finger. She hadn't asked about it, had thought the question redundant. There was always a wife back home somewhere, waiting. In this he was no different. And yet she was impatient for Pavel's company, and longed to touch him, upon chin and arm. There was no happiness in her in this suspicion of love. She saw no way that it would not harm her.

When she was done with the potatoes, she put on the radio and listened to an educational programme about democracy. Democracy, the announcer explained, was the allies' gift to his listeners' ravaged land. 'Delivered from the yoke of tyranny, into an age of freedom: here lies the truth of May 1945.' Sonia turned the dial over to a radio play. She could not be sure, but she thought she recognized the voice. It had read the late-night news in the glorious days of the Thousand Year Reich.

———·———

'Fagin? That's a funny name, that. What is he, a Gypsy?'
'Something like that.'

'I didn't know there were Gypsies in England.'

'Look here, Schlo', either you want me to tell you the story or you don't.'

'Go on then, Anders. I like that other name. Olliwer Tweest. He'll probably turn out to be some kind of king or something.'

They were sitting huddled close to the oven and speaking in whispers so as not to wake the other boys. It cannot have been much past four or five in the morning. Anders had the devil of a time trying to retell Oliver Twist's adventures. His memory was sharp enough, but without the author's convoluted sentences the story fell flat somehow, disintegrated into episodes and feelings that could be related but not felt. Perhaps it was because he did not know the ending: it would be easier to tell if he had a goal in sight, some clear landmark by which to steer. Schlo' seemed to enjoy it anyway, mouthing names and events no sooner than he'd heard them, urging Anders to tell him again and again of Oliver's humble origins, the bad food and callous wardens, and his first encounter with hook-nosed Fagin.

'Hook-nosed,' he would whisper, 'just like Uncle Jakub,' and run dirty fingers over his own button nose until it was greasy like a side of bacon.

They had neither of them slept more than an hour or so. Schlo' had been troubled by dreams again, and Anders had much to think about. He lay wrapped in his new coat, a wolf-fur jacket with an outsized collar and buttons made from wooden pegs. The coat was cut for a burly man to fall mid-thigh, and Anders almost disappeared in it. He had the sleeves turned back on themselves, and there had been a rip at the back that'd taken two dozen stitches to mend. In one pocket he had found some foreign coins, in another a Viennese furrier's card decorated with the handsome drawing of a fox. Naturally, he thought it the best coat he had ever owned. When he'd come back to Paulchen's, taciturn and already troubled by his thoughts, he had much enjoyed the cat-calls and teases that greeted his new outfit. Some packs of cigarettes that he had acquired along with the coat in exchange for Sonia's earrings appeased Paulchen and cut short all questions as to where he had spent the day. Anders had eaten the lentil and ham stew in silence, and impatiently awaited the nodding off of his comrades. Then he'd sat up, his back against the oven, and begun to reason through what had to be done.

What drew his attention above all was the coat the Colonel had taken off him. Obviously, he had recognized it as the midget's, if by nothing other than its quality and gentlemanly cut. The only point in taking the coat, reasoned Anders, was that the Colonel thought some small item might be hidden in it: hidden, because otherwise he would have expected its new owner to have found it, and small, because one could hardly hide something large in a midget's coat. He would have carried it back with him, slit the lining, the collar and the lapels, in short, ruined the coat, all to no avail. Anders was pretty sure Fosko had found nothing – he had searched it himself diligently enough. It troubled him to think what the Colonel might do next. He needed to speak to Pavel, give him warning, only Sonia had said that Pavel was being watched. Schlo' was the answer.

He didn't start right in. When he noticed that the younger boy was awake, he slid over to him, stroked his hair, and told him to forget about the dreams. Anders drew him over to the oven's heat, and began to tell him stories, first a fairy tale he remembered hearing on the radio, then the book Pavel had read to him through long nights and idle mornings, until the day Boyd White had shown with his trunk and his tale of woes, and Pavel had almost died. Only when Anders was quite sure of the boy did he give him his instructions. He broke them down into easy chunks and bade Schlo' repeat them, once, and then again an hour later. By this time Schlo' had begun to fade a little, and Anders cooed over him soothingly as he settled down to get some sleep.

'Remember,' he whispered. 'If the Colonel shows, scream murder and run like the wind.'

The boy nodded, and slipped an embarrassed thumb into his mouth.

'Go on,' Anders assured him. 'I won't tell the others.'

At length he nodded off. Anders, too, felt tiredness pull at him now, but there was no time for rest. There was something he had to do, and he had to do it fast, before dawn broke and the boys' empty stomachs shook them awake. He got up noiselessly, and crept over to the room where Paulchen slept upon his own feather-mattressed bed. He slept on his stomach, the head twisted sideways and covered by a thick woollen cap. There was a patch of frozen drool right next to his face; his lip seemed glued to it, distended, the mouth gaping like a fish's. By the weak light of the oven's glow, Anders made out a watch, a sap and a pair of knuckledusters that lay side by side on his dresser. The gun, he knew, would be underneath the pillow. He imagined slipping a searching hand under Paulchen's head, but knew it was futile. There was no way of getting to it without waking its owner, and no words that would convince him to part with his prize possession.

All this Anders understood at a single glance; it was as clear and inevitable to him as a law of nature. When his fingers closed around the sap, he neither flinched nor hesitated. He hit Paulchen smartly, along the bony plane between ear and eye. There was hardly any noise, only the lip cut loose from its moorings and tore in the process. Droplets of blood soaked into the pillowcase. At the temple, a second rivulet of blood flowed downwards from under Paulchen's hat and onto his sleep-hooded lid. Here it pooled, before following the outline of his nose.

With the same quiet certainty with which he had grabbed it, Anders replaced the sap on the dresser, and pulled the Luger from its hiding place. He had held it before and was unsurprised by its weight. It fitted in his coat pocket, along with a roll and some cheese he found in the kitchen. Then he left the apartment, hoping with all his might that Schlo' would keep to his instructions after the hubbub about the theft had subsided. Out on the street he double-checked that the weapon was loaded. He tested the safety, like he had seen Paulchen do, and smelled at the old gunpowder that lined its muzzle. There was some regret in him that he would never be able to replace it and thus make things up to the lad he had sapped. He was quite sure that once they had found its bullet in Fosko, Paulchen would no longer want the gun.

———·———

Pavel stood, then paced. Sat at the typewriter, toying with the idea of writing out his questions; stiff-fingered typing drills, until the ribbon's ink ran thin. Every few minutes he made for the door, stood handle in hand and prepared himself to storm out and up. Piano notes trickled down through the ceiling, then the ring of the telephone, then silence. He wished she would resume playing, but perhaps she was busy with lunch.

His bed welcomed him. He imagined his kidneys had grown heavy again, and lay idly on his face, keen to sink back into his illness's stupor. Behind him the oven smoked and crackled, ineffectual. He rose to fix himself food, only to discover there was nothing much left; drank tea, Russian style, pouring it out from a bent old samovar, and leafed through books that offered up phrases in which to clad his confusion. The boy did not come back, and as his longing for him mounted, so did his anger, until he resolved to punish him somehow, perhaps through his silence. There was no way he could tell Anders about Belle in any case; he would denounce her a liar, and run up to spit in her face. In his loneliness, Pavel even considered creeping up into the attic, to subject the midget's body to another search, and probe his frozen eyes for answers. But he remembered Sonia's warning that he was being watched, and the shadow upon the staircase, and stayed mum, waiting for some crisis that would shake free the truth of Boyd's death without the need for confrontation. He did not want to hear her shape the words, without feeling or shame, the Colonel's razor cosy upon her sink.

At long last a knock on the door, breathless, announcing a child of eleven or so who eyed him up and down appraisingly. Pavel had met the boy before – he had cost him some china cups, and a run-in with a gun. He bid him enter and watched him place his backside against the oven until steam rose from his collar and shoulders and curled the hair that protruded from a battered sheepskin cap. The boy was staring at the books now, counting them off under his breath and releasing a finger out of his crumpled fist every time he got to ten.

'I forgot your name,' said Pavel when the boy'd run out of fingers.

'It's Schlo'.'

'That's short for Salomon, isn't it?'

The boy shrugged. 'How come you speak German like this?'

'My father was German. Jewish-German. He moved to America before I was born.'

Schlo' nodded like this made sense to him. When he took off his gloves and rolled back his sleeves to press his hands against the oven, Pavel caught a glimpse of the tattoo upon his forearm.

'Are your parents dead?' he asked softly.

The boy stood and wrinkled his nose. It wasn't clear to Pavel whether he did not know or would not say. He offered him tea.

They sat and drank. The boy gulped his down, obviously burning his tongue, and refilled his glass immediately. Pavel passed him the sugar and watched him stick a lump between his teeth. Impatiently, he waited for the boy to explain himself, but he seemed content to drink and chew his sugar, smacking his lips after every sip. After the fourth cup, Pavel put the samovar away.

'Tell me then,' he said. 'Why are you here?'

The boy made a final grab for the sugar bowl, smacked his lips one last time, and then, without the slightest hesitation, he began to talk, working his jaws into a right frenzy and piling up the words into a single breathless phrase.

'It's about the coat, see. The Colonel thought there was a secret pocket, which there was, but Anders says it was already empty which means that Boyd found it first and hid it somewhere, because if he didn't, the Colonel wouldn't be looking for nothing having already found it, you see, and if he, I mean Boyd, did hide it, he must have done so at your place, only the Colonel searched that, too, and didn't find a thing, so it must be in the other coat, Boyd's, that is yours, which the Colonel, who is a *ped-i-rast*, will figure out before long, and that's what I'm to tell you.

'Get it?' the boy asked, himself a little confused about his outburst. 'Cause that's what Anders told me to say, and the only reason I'm late is because he stole the gun, so Paulchen wouldn't let me go until I told him what's what and now he wants to meet you and have things out, American papers or no American papers, and you better bring him a new piece – loaded – or else, and he's got a bruise on his face size of an egg, only it's blue.

'You see,' said the boy, 'I'll be in trouble if I don't come back with a message, and also, I really need to pee.'

Pavel pointed him to the chamber pot and picked through the maze of his words to his water's tinkle.

'Anders stole the gun?' he asked as the boy shook off the last few drops. Schlo' looked back at Pavel like he was an idiot.

'Yes,' he nodded. 'That's what I've been saying, right?'

'I'll meet your Paulchen. Tell me when and where.'

The boy named the spot, then turned to leave, eager now to be out of there.

'Nobody calls me Salomon,' he told Pavel in parting. 'It sounds Jewish, you know.'

'Okay,' said Pavel. 'I'll try to remember that.'

Once the boy was gone, Pavel stripped off the coat Boyd had given him the night the midget had died, spread it out over the kitchen table, and calmly searched its lining for secrets. A little later he'd rummage around for his camera, a flashlight and some scissors. His was a busy afternoon full of revelations.

———·———

All day she sat and waited for a knock on the door. She found she dreaded it, no matter whom it would announce: Fosko, studying her from behind fat cheeks, his chubby hand gently combing through the monkey's pelt; or Pavel, her inept suitor, begging her for a truth he did not want, and taunting her with the possibility of love. For a while Sonia returned to the piano, trying to tease solace from its wooden guts; heard notes within notes, dark scrapings in the under-carriage that shouldn't have been there but were, and remained inexplicable to her until, opening the piano's great lid and shining a light into its workings, she found some of the monkey's waste grown hard around its strings and hammers. It seemed to her that the monkey never stopped shitting, shat more than she gave it to eat; it was as though it had been instructed to expel at all cost and thus play symbol to the absurdity of her existence. In her frustration she left the piano and sat smoking cigarettes before her mirror, one after the other, until her tongue tasted of ashes and nausea had settled in her throat. A mountain of butts, and still: no knock. She rinsed her mouth with brandy, swallowed aspirin, filed her nails.

It was late afternoon by the time Pavel showed. She was unprepared for the wave of joy that welled up in her, and immediately set to avenge herself for it. It started in her stomach, the seat of all her affects; *it must be*, she told herself spitefully, *because your heart's so meagre an organ*. She pictured it beating, empty and wrinkled like a child's scrotal sack, pumping blood so diluted it showed translucent in its vents and chambers: all this in the single moment it took him to step into the middle of the room and stand there with the stiff-waisted serenity of the drawing-room butler. In his hand he held a pair of rolled-up socks.

'You come bearing gifts?' she asked.

'After a first shared night,' she said, 'flowers are more traditional. Or champagne, if one has a touch of the cad.'

She scratched over one breast, as though to remove a stain. It brought colour to his cheek. He lowered his gaze, stepped forward, still with the same solemnity of purpose, and made to pass her the socks.

'The Colonel is looking for this. It's why Boyd died.'

She arched an eyebrow.

'Not for the socks, Sonia. For what's inside. It's what he's been after all along. Fosko.'

'You are a fool then, giving it to me.'

He shrugged and she took the socks. They were thick woollen things, well worn and dirty. She could not detect any extra weight in them. After a moment's hesitation she carried them over to a glass cabinet, took out a beautiful teapot that she no longer used because Fosko had bought her a more expensive one, and dropped the socks inside. Then she replaced it on the bottom shelf and locked up the cupboard. Pavel stood unmoved. She wished he would do something natural. Blow his nose, perhaps; hold her. His hands were on his trousers' seams, palms turned inward.

'You want some coffee?' she asked.

He shook his head. 'Sonia – what I tried to tell you last night. I have been thinking –'

'I kissed you, you know.'

This startled him, chased away the butler. He stood baffled, brows heavy knit.

'You did?'

114

'In the middle of the night. I might have dreamt it, though.' Deliberately – like a tramp – she circled him and slid up close, crushing her breast against his back. 'There is that about you,' she whispered into his ear, 'that hankers after confession.'

He tried to kiss her then, turning his head around to her, and freeing one arm from her embrace, but in his haste he somehow missed and glanced off her nose and cheekbone. His lips, she noted, were thin and pink like a girl's.

'Jesus, you are worse at this than I imagined.'

'I wish,' he said, working himself free of her embrace. 'I wish we could talk with honesty.'

Sonia giggled at that, and ran into the kitchen to make coffee after all. There were tears in her eyes. She scratched at them with her fist's knuckles, and ground coffee beans into smithereens. They spilled their odour as they were crushed.

Pavel did not follow her. He stood impassively, fingers to his lips. She watched him from the kitchen doorway, sly, furtive glances every time she turned to fetch sugar, saucers, silver spoons. Reluctantly, she admitted to herself that she wanted to touch him again.

They sat and had coffee, him pulling the chair away for her before he sat down himself. Sonia could almost picture how his governess had taught him to, or perhaps it had been his Russian mother, running well-groomed fingers through his hair when he got it right. The coffee, she realized, was far too strong. They both piled sugar into their cups without acknowledging her mistake. Halfway through the cup she rose all of a sudden, pulling him up by his elbow. He stood, ill-balanced, one foot caught under the chair legs.

'Let's try again,' she said and kissed him. She had never understood the phrase: the earth moved. Well, perhaps it did move. Her stomach heaved, too, and for a moment she thought, comically, that she might spew on him, right on his lapels. She gave a laugh, affected; held onto his elbows; shivered. He watched her passively, and allowed these things to happen. There was a quiver to his mouth.

'We still need to talk,' he said. 'About Boyd.'

She could see how it pained Pavel to say his name, especially now that his hands were balanced upon her hips. He grasped at straws: 'You don't keep a diary, do you?'

She laughed at that; a *peal* of laughter, rising out of her very throat.

'Whatever for?' she said. 'What's the point in keeping evidence against yourself?'

He heard her say it, frowned, and buried his forehead in her shoulder. They stood like this, the coffee growing cold in their cups.

Perhaps she shouldn't have been so surprised when she felt his erection against her hip. He was a man, after all. All of a sudden she felt his body's weight; felt his hands stiffen upon her. Pavel raised his head as though to kiss her again – another sort of kiss. There was what they call rapture in his eyes, a visceral sort of greed. Sonia turned her face away.

'I have never lain with a man for pleasure,' she told him stiffly.

He took it in, thoughtfully. She watched him closely, lest there be pity. There was no pity.

It was a shame, really.

Pity might have cured her.

'It's only the war,' he said.

Sonia looked back at him and mouthed the word: 'Only.'

He shrugged and smiled like he was apologizing for a joke, one that was in bad taste, yet funny. Oh, she liked this Pavel.

'I have to go,' he said. 'There is someone I promised to meet.'

His hands let go of her body; he stepped back and stuck them into his pockets, to mask his erection.

'Come back, later. We can –'

She broke off. There was no reckoning what they could or could not do.

Then, finally, he left her, smiling still, his hair sticking up where she had touched it, tugged it, torn at him. He left stiff-legged, his stride debilitated by desire.

———·———

Pavel left the building. He stopped outside the door to tighten the scarf around his neck and put on his hat. The lining of his coat was cut open along the seams, and the discrepancy between the two layers made it sit awkwardly on his narrow frame. A scarecrow, you see, stumbling down Berlin's icy streets. He would have done well to turn around now and again. He would have seen, in a dozen places where the terrain provided no possible cover, a pursuer hot on his heels. A respectable figure in a good duffel coat; middle-aged, stout and one-eyed, a patch upon the other, and lamb's wool drawn low into his eyes: in a word, yours truly. To be quite honest, I wasn't trying to be too clever about the chase. It was dark already, and bitterly cold, the kind of cold when you think your eyeball is going to freeze. The cigarette I was smoking was glowing at one end and stone cold at the other. It wasn't the weather for cleverness. I was happy just to keep moving.

There was one thing that surprised me as I hurried after Pavel down Charlottenburg's murky streets. I had expected my fellow watcher to follow us. It was still the same man, half-frozen and exhausted, no doubt, who stared back at me through his car's windshield when I left the building. Very nearly I beckoned for him to join us in our late-afternoon ramble, but of course I checked the impulse. The cold must have wormed its way into his brain by then; there was no way he was thinking straight after something like eighteen hours in that car, his bones hurting with cold and a bottle of spirits his only friend. Still, it made me think, his passivity. If he was not going to follow us, who the hell was he waiting for so patiently all these hours, and on whose orders? I tried to shake off my doubts as I ran after Pavel. There was only so much I could keep in my head at one time just then. For the moment, all that mattered was that I did not lose sight of my careless prey.

We passed a phone box, Pavel some thirty paces ahead, walking with a slouch and a tilt, coat-tails flapping in the wind. Next to it there stood a boy and a girl, hardly out of their teens, huddling in a close embrace. I remember her clutching a tin of American orange juice in an outsized mitten, no doubt a present from her darling; his hands were buried in her coat, rubbing her warm. When Pavel passed them they stopped their carousing and turned to look after him. The boy whispered something in his lover's ear. She gave a brief laugh, charmed by someone else's wretchedness, then turned back into his embrace.

I drew level with them, and wished them a Merry Christmas. '*Fro-licke Wey-nackten*,' I said in my accented German.

'And to you, Tommy,' answered the boy belligerently. Jesus, you would have thought they could forget about occupation on a night like this. Pavel and I, we walked on in darkness. All around us the city eased into the miracle of Christmas Eve.

I have often wondered how much celebrating went on that winter, the winter of '46. On the whole I am inclined to be optimistic. Had the windows not all been frozen, I am sure we would have been able to make out a tree in every living room, a little shabby perhaps and more likely than not stolen from under their occupiers' noses. On their twigs: talc candles, wooden trinkets and, amongst the wealthy, fragile glass balls, hand-painted, and a silver star to top the crooked little bugger. I gather there wouldn't have been much in the way of presents, but perhaps they managed to procure something a little special for their dinner: a roast bird perhaps, or carp and almonds, a little torte for afters and a half-shot of something lively, just to toast the Christ-child on his coming. Call me sentimental, but I like to think they kept up their spirits, the Krauts, and forgot them for a night, those pangs of defeat. Pavel, though, seemed oblivious to their merrymaking. He kept his eyes on the ground. God knows it was treacherous enough.

In the end it wasn't much of a walk, though there was plenty of time to freeze right down to the bone. No sooner had he rounded one last corner than some hoodlums set upon him from out of the shadows. They rammed him into the building wall and searched his clothes for weapons. I hung back, watched them push him over a backyard wall, and escort him through a door-way. The electricity was on, and I could watch their progress by their turning on the corridor lights one floor after another. They took him into some place just under the roof. It wasn't my job to follow him there.

I knew I was in for a long, cold wait. A little disgruntled at having been abandoned so quickly, I rushed back to the phone box we had passed in order to call for backup. Its frame was badly bent, but amazingly I got a line almost at once.

'Peterson here,' I said. 'Richter has rendezvoused with some local gang of street urchins. Schillerstrasse 48, round the back.'

'Nah, just boys from what I can see. Same place the pipsqueak ran to earlier. Richter's little friend.'

'Well, in any case, tell the Colonel. In the meantime, get me some men out here in a car, and a big flask of coffee.'

'Wonderful. I knew I could count on you.'

'And a Merry Christmas to you, Jones.'

You see, in the Colonel's employ, we were all like one big, happy family.

———·———

They handled him roughly. Pavel wouldn't have minded, but one of the boys poked him in the kidneys as he helped to lift him over the courtyard's low wall, and the pain ran through him throat to groin.

'Be careful,' he mumbled.

'What are you, some sort of girl?' said the boy. He was armed, Pavel saw, with a carpenter's hammer. He wondered whether the boy had any idea what a thing like that could do to a man's face.

They pulled him inside a doorway at the back of a filthy old building, then up several flights of stairs. 'There used to be an elevator,' one of his assailants told him proudly. The boy carried a home-made sap and something that looked like a saucepan's cast-iron lid. 'You better have something to bargain with,' he added. 'Paulchen's pissed as all hell.'

'Yes,' said Pavel, 'I will give him whatever he wants.'

They took him to an apartment on the top floor. There was no name on the door, just a rusty brass knocker. One of the boys gave it a brisk rapping. There were footsteps on the other side, and a squeaky voice asking: 'Password?'

'Open up, Hendrik, or I'll stick my foot so far up your arse I can use you for a boot.'

'Yep,' said the voice. 'That's the password.'

Pavel wondered where they had learned their humour. It may have been from the movies. It rang American, somehow.

Inside, there was a cramped two-bedroom garret, the walls lined chest-high with dark old wood. The main room's ceiling slanted down to one side and seemed to sag, yellowed and rain-damaged. It looked like the underside of some great fish that lay beached and dying; smelled, too, of cigarette smoke and unwashed child.

The latter smell came as no surprise. The room was packed with them. They lined every wall and floor-space; sat two, three rows deep on an ancient sofa livid with rot; stood huddled around the great oven or slouched in the doorway of the adjoining kitchen, unlit cigarettes behind their ears. Pavel counted something like seventeen boys, aged eight upwards. They must have come from far and wide to bear witness to his humiliation before their war leader.

He sat amongst them like a savage chieftain. Sat upon an armchair at the very centre of the room. Green corduroy gone brown and greasy along the backrest and arms; a grey army blanket to cover his legs, this in spite of the room being warmer than any Pavel had entered in weeks, heated as it was by the crush of dirty bodies. Upon Paulchen's temple, the bruise sat like a leech: black and moist and pert with his blood. In any other weather he would have iced it. The swelling had squeezed shut one eye; its darkness set off the pallor of his face. The mouth was framed by longish tufts of hair, soft as a butler's glove. A boy too young yet to know when to shave. He stared at Pavel grimly, hands folded as though in prayer. He must have studied the pose somewhere. It added years to his squint.

Paulchen gave Pavel time to have a look around. His eyes travelled from the German flag that graced one wall, to the map of Europe showing the borders of '41 and a coloured pin for every capital fallen. On a coffee table, casually displayed, there sat a shoebox filled with military insignia and honours. Pavel recognized an Iron Cross and tried to guess at its journey from some Aryan hero's breast to the pockets of a Russian looter, and onwards, until it ended up here, the cherished prize of one just young enough to have eluded service in the *Volkssturm*, that army of children and decrepits that held the city in the last desperate days and weeks. Then again, he may have served, and won his cross with a daring charge against a Russian tank, much good it did him, his city burning and deserters strung from every lamppost.

Next to the box of trinkets there stood a little tree upon a stand, decorated with red cotton bows. Its twigs hung half-wilted, the needles more brown than green. All of a sudden Pavel remembered that it was Christmas, and that it was now, in the early hours of the evening, that it would be celebrated all across Germany, just as Charlotte would celebrate it back in

Ohio, that woman he had married and whispered words to, about eternity. This was before he had made lovers of women who sold themselves for comfort; before the war and the peace and his decision to stay. The whole weight of his life settled upon him in this moment, and – briefly – he was afraid that his eyes would show tears. From the kitchen there came the smell of leek and potato soup. His stomach grumbled and washed away Christmas. He had not eaten all day.

'Can I have a bowl of soup?' he asked.

Paulchen looked at him, incredulous. He was about to flare up, then thought better of it and nodded his assent. A boy – Salomon – peeled himself from out of the pile on the sofa and ran into the kitchen. He returned with an earthenware dish of soup and a wedge of dark bread.

'Here, Herr Richter,' he said. The other boys, Pavel noticed, saw it as a collaborator's act. Young Salomon was in for a rough night.

Pavel ate greedily, gulping down soup and bread in a few quick minutes. It could have used salt, but was otherwise well prepared. The band of thieves were clearly getting by on their own wits. When he was done, Pavel placed the dish next to the little tree and returned his attention to Paulchen.

'Where is Anders?' he asked.

'You don't know?'

'No.'

'We thought you'd know.'

'Well, I don't.'

'He stole my gun.'

'So Sal – Schlo' – told me. What does he want with it?'

'How the hell would I know? Shoot someone, I guess.'

'Who?'

'He told us that someone stole his coat. Maybe he wants to shoot him.'

'Someone stole his coat?'

122

'Yeah, the pretty one you gave him, with the blood stains down the back. The thing is, some way or another he found the money to get himself an even better one. Nice little fur number with a collar this wide.' He held his hands apart theatrically. 'So really, he had nothing to complain about.'

'I see. Did he say who took the coat?'

'No.'

'Did he mention the Colonel?'

'The Colonel?'

'Fosko. Colonel Fosko. He's the big fat man who runs this neighbourhood. Surely you've run into him.'

'Ah, the fairy. Yes, Anders asked about him recently. I told him to watch his back around the man. What do you have to do with him?'

Pavel thought about this for a moment. At length, he said: 'I think he killed my friend.'

It felt good to say it out loud.

'And now you think he might snuff Anders, too, eh?'

Paulchen said it roughly, but Pavel thought he could detect concern in his one good eye. Salomon, though, had heard enough. Pavel saw him duck out, as though he no longer wanted any part of this, though surely he would have to return later for a berth, and his peers' camaraderie. Pavel would have liked to tell him to stay around, that things would turn out all right, but there was no time for it. The chieftain wasn't done with him yet.

'In any case,' he said, 'I hold you responsible for the gun.'

Pavel did not dispute the point. It was ridiculous, of course, but he understood Paulchen's logic. This way he would not have to hunt Anders down like a dog; would retain his boys' fealty without practising a cruelty that wasn't native to his soul.

'What do you want?' he asked him meekly. 'I have no gun to give.'

'Do you have money?'

Pavel thought about it. 'Yes,' he said, 'I have money.'

'"Schlo" says you live as poor as a pecker, only you got yourself shelves full of books.'

'There is a woman in my building. She will give me the money.'

He marvelled at how easy it was to say it, and dispense with Sonia's wealth before he even owned her heart. It was as though he thought them married; had convinced himself, somewhere along the line, that she was his to command. It was worse than stupid: it was treacherous.

'She will give me the money,' he repeated. 'More than a gun's worth, if I can count on your help.'

'You want to hire us for help?' Paulchen asked moodily. Pavel realized his mistake and revised his terminology.

'A job,' he said gruffly. 'Money up front for services rendered. If you boys have the pluck.'

'Don't you worry about no pluck, Mister.'

They were getting on swimmingly.

Over the next hour or two they made their arrangements. The boys in the room relaxed, broke into groups and played cards, swapped jokes and stories, competed at push-ups, squats, the wrestling of arms. Before long, Pavel was offered a second bowl of soup – it was Christmas after all – and a swig of corn schnapps from a ceramic jug. The first of the services he paid for, on credit, was the passing on of information about Söldmann, the midget who'd been stabbed in the back. Paulchen gathered what little he knew of the man and fashioned it into a yarn: grandiloquent truths grown out of unsubstantiated rumour; *pissoir* banter blown up into character study. His gang gathered at his feet to hear it all, lapping it up with no less an appetite than, in some other story expertly told, cats had been said to lap at a dead man's blood. Paulchen, too, told his story well. As he was listening, Pavel cast back his mind to how they had washed the

124

body, Sonia and he, and carried it up to the attic's darkest corner. In retrospect it seemed to him like he must have loved her even then.

———·———

But this won't do, having a boy tell Söldmann's story. It's not that Paulchen was short on wits or minced his words – quite the contrary. His horizon, though, was limited by age and lack of education. As a narrator, he was liable to render as mere biography a subject that clamoured after history. Nor was Paulchen in the best position to be free of bias, Greater Germany pining away on his wall and a box full of Nazi insignia. You do better listening to me; have I not guided you thus far, with no major hiccups? Besides, I was much better informed, having been ordered to sniff out Söldmann's story many months before, at a time when the Colonel had first taken an interest in the midget's affairs. A few deft questions to former associates and neighbours, some well-placed food parcels and the occasional threat of investigation, and the rudiments of a life began to manifest, in crude brushstrokes to be sure, though not devoid of a certain suggestiveness. The thing, of course, was that nobody knew anything for certain. Söldmann's was a war story, disarticulated and liable to distortions and falsehood. Events only become clearer towards war's end, when he turned into a crook and a fence, dealing in stolen information, primarily, with a sideline in narcotics.

In any case, people say that Ernst Rainer Söldmann was born on the eve of the Great War – the last but one, which dug itself into trenches – to a respectable greengrocer's wife somewhere on the outskirts of the beautiful city of Dresden, before, that is, it was reduced to rubble and glassy pools of molten sand. There had been no hereditary taint in the family, but a circus by the unlikely name of 'Rancini' had passed through the area some months

125

previously, so naturally there was talk when he turned out a midget and his hair much darker than Mr Söldmann's chestnut curls. Little is known about Ernst's childhood, or whether he was apprenticed and to whom. One imagines that the humiliations of school and a puberty devoid of prospects left their mark upon his fledgling soul; in any case he left home at the tender age of seventeen, a knapsack over one shoulder and a maternal kiss on his cheek.

Söldmann's itinerant years are hard to reconstruct. Once upon a time Germans had made a tradition of them – the *Wander*-years described in Goethe's *Wilhelm Meister* – but by the time young Ernst took to the road he would have been perceived as little more than a vagrant. He washed up in Berlin around the autumn of 1932, just in time to become inspired by the noxious invective of the moustachioed chancellor-to-be and his brown-shirted flock of devotees. After the *Machtergreifung* (a phrase only imperfectly rendered into English as the National Socialists' 'seizure of power'), Söldmann attempted to join their ranks. The Party wouldn't have him. It prided itself on being a racial vanguard and would not have its ranks diluted by degenerates, turncoats or opportunists. It certainly had no truck with swarthy midgets, Goebbels' pre-eminent position not withstanding. Söld-mann tried the party headquarters in Charlottenburg, then Kreuzberg, those in Wedding and finally in Berlin-Buch, on the northern outskirts of the city. Not one registrar even handed him so much as the application form. Instead they laughed in his face and made jibes familiar to Söldmann since his earliest childhood. At the Buch headquarters they sent him on, not entirely in jest, to report at the famed psychiatric clinic that had made its name by investigating homosexuals and other deviants since the middle of the previous century. Voluntary sterilization was heartily recommended.

Söldmann, with what in retrospect appears as characteristic persistency, found a tailor to fashion him his very own SA uniform cut from two and a quarter yards of coarse brown wool. The day he received it, he proudly dressed before a penny mirror that he propped up against one dirty flophouse wall and found the uniform's colour to harmonize pleasingly with his hazel eyes. All morning he stood by a window, until he finally spied a pack of brownshirts pass with boisterous swaggers, then raced down to join them. Somewhat surprisingly he was soon accepted into their ranks. He even became a particular favourite with one or two of the more amiable comrades who took to his wit and Saxonian accent, and begged Ernst, time and again, to show them his Peter, which was disproportionally large for his frame. In an attempt to improve the quality of his lodgings, Söldmann put up, with the help of deftly placed pins, a dozen newspaper photographs of his namesake, Ernst Röhm, the head of the SA, whom nature had favoured with a face like a potato, and a body like a sack of them. Little Ernst spent his nights in dialogue with his beloved leader until, on the thirtieth of June, 1934, the Night of the Long Knives put an end to their intimacy. Röhm was executed, along with some seventy-odd others, for high treason and, it was rumoured, contrary sexual instincts. The following morning, holding a magazine image of a dapper-looking Heinrich Himmler, Söldmann announced his wish to join the SS. His flophouse brethren broke out in laughter, and took to saluting him as *Obersturmgruppenführer* whenever he entered the communal kitchen. Söldmann was unabashed. He had learned long ago that all humour was – what's the word? – cruel.

It is unclear how Söldmann paid his way in these eventful years prior to the war. Spiteful tongues place him in the cabaret scene, as announcer, clown, or sexual novelty act. More charitable perhaps is the claim that he survived on the hand-me-downs of an ageing, and somewhat curmudgeonly, Jewish lover. Others still describe him as a pimp with a stable of clapped-out whores who treated him as much as their mascot as their employer. Whatever he did, he must have made the acquaintance of some well-connected people at some point or other, for by the spring of 1938 he had made real his dream. Not only had he joined the Party that had so long refused him entry, but his membership was backdated to 1926, that is, into the years of struggle before Herr Hitler's rise to respectability. As such his credentials became unimpeachable, and he soon commenced upon a remarkable transformation from flophouse *clochard* to businessman. The precise nature of his business is, unfortunately, a matter of significant dispute, though it is clear that he managed to get hold of some property and run an Aryan dancehall for some few months prior to the war, before it was shut down over a dispute (quickly hushed up) that there had taken place an illegal performance of syncopated jazz music. In the course of the war, it seems, Söldmann gradually became a supplier of rare and mislaid items: anything from banned modernist art for which some party dignitaries displayed an unfortunate taste, to the more mundane needs of what I have heard an American GI describe as 'booze and cooze'. Unfit for service on grounds of congenital smallness, he was free to make his fortune on the home front. As the years crept by, he increasingly kept himself in the background, self-conscious perhaps about his diminutive stature in this age of giants, or else because he had a former puppet's fascination for running his operation from behind the scenes.

War's end found him in a right pickle. As Hitler's Reich collapsed militarily, morally as well as financially, and new powers took over its erstwhile capital, Söldmann tried to hold on to his organization, while at the same time evading Allied scrutiny into his much advertised dedication to the Nazi cause. At the business end of things he needn't have worried. It turned out that a broken, war-ravaged city awaiting its first winter of peace had need of men like Söldmann. Occupiers and locals, they all yearned for the help of those who 'could get things done'; there was an opportunity here to become a veritable pillar of the post-war community, and Söldmann was not one to pass up the cup, as it were, when proffered.

As for his 'denazification' – issued in the form of a coveted piece of paper that the Germans took to calling their Persil-pass, after the popular washing powder manufactured by one Hugo Henkel (Party Membership No. 2266961) of Henkel & Son – well, that took some doing. Through luck and a civilian's courage to procrastinate when decisive action had been demanded, the Central Registry of the National Socialist Party had survived the order that it be summarily pulped by a Bavarian paper mill. The Seventh US Army was thus put in a position to liberate some eight and a half million membership cards, Söldmann's amongst them. In the spirit of allied co-operation we Brits, in whose sector Söldmann lived and then plied his trade, were given full access to the documents. The denazification hearings asked all Germans to fill in a preliminary questionnaire fully disclosing their involvement with Hitler's regime. The data was then compared against the Party registry. Proof of membership did not necessarily spell out the end of the denazification process. In the spirit of English fair play we accepted opportunism as a valid reason for having joined up – after all, one had to live. Having joined before Hitler's 1933 electoral victory, however, was considered a not inconsiderable faux pas, as was lying on one's questionnaire. Unfamiliar with the concept of opportunistic backdating, the officers in charge of the investigations understood the membership date found on the Central Registry's cards to represent the absolute, that is to say the bureaucratic, truth. Continuous membership from 1926, therefore, coupled with a number of letters by party functionaries testifying to one's racial value for Germany despite a certain physical malformation, was liable to be interpreted as sufficiently damning to put denazification out of the question. A formal trial, economic sanctions and, worst of all, close scrutiny of all one's activities beckoned. All this, of course, conspired to place Söldmann rather deeply in the above-mentioned pickle.

For the first time in his life his stature came to his aid, although I daresay it would not have done him much good had it not been

129

coupled with wile. Rather than waiting for the British authorities to approach him, Söldmann scoured the sector for his brethren. He found a full score and extras when he walked through the tent flap of Karli Schäfer's Circus that, with grim determination, had set down only months after the war upon a pockmarked field not far from Schloss Charlottenburg. They were practising their trampolining at the time, and as little Ernst stepped onto the arena sands some ten dwarves and midgets could be seen breathlessly suspended in mid-air. They floated in the middle distance between star-studded ceiling and the giant blue-rimmed device that lent them their wings; turned over themselves in slow, precise movements, and whooped for joy when they came crashing down again upon the canvas. There were women amongst these aeronauts: legs like potato mashers, their short skirts flaring in mid-air to reveal shiny, taut knickers in the colours of the Italian flag. Söldmann had no inkling that, due to some perversity of fate which, for the whole of the past decade, had made a mockery of the science of probability, Karli Schäfer's Circus had only recently acquired its new name. Not so long ago it had flown its brightly embossed flag under the heading of Rancini; it was, in short, the very same outfit that had passed through Dresden more than thirty years previously, and had given rise to such unflattering rumours concerning Mrs Söldmann's matrimonial virtue and baby Ernst's patrimony. Its change of name dated from that brief sliver of time when the Italian war effort was running headlong into the wall of its own ineptitude, whilst in Germany the authorities' promise of final victory – that elusive *Endsieg* – remained a tolerably believable lie. Söldmann was thus robbed of any motivation to study the faces of the assembled elder statesmen amongst the midgets for signs of family resemblance. Instead, what he saw in the flurry of leaps and turns and aerial handstands was this: tall, blonde Fräulein Persil – the iconic representation of Henkel's miracle powder, made famous on a thousand German advertising billboards – dressed in a white summer dress that only subtly suggested the firmness of her bosom, coyly proffering him her hand for the gentlest of shakes. Hell, thought he, before he was done with her, he'd give her reason to give her clothes a good scrubbing. Inadvertently, looking on at the weightless dance of the midgets, Ernst Rainer Söldmann's sizeable Peter grew erect.

From then on in it was only a matter of money and a dash of audacity. Söldmann approached the circus's director, one Mr Schäfer né Rancini, and negotiated a price. The very next day, sixteen midgets and seven dwarves made their way down to the British 'Information Services Control' at Schlüterstrasse 45, once the seat of Goebbels' *Reichskulturkammer* and as such one of the epicentres of the regime's programme of nazification. The midgets' number included a new signing, a Dresden lad with little artistic talent, whose employment papers indicated that he had been a member of their troupe ever since he'd tumbled from his mother's womb. Spirits were soaring on account of some black beer Söldmann had bought and distributed over a hearty breakfast of bread and sausage. The midgets and dwarves swarmed into the ISC's waiting area and demanded blank copies of the questionnaire in order to 'get things over and done with'. They quickly filled the few available chairs, then spread out across the carpeted floors where they lay upon their stomachs, pen in hand, answering questions on their *Wehrmacht* past and their years of service in the 'General or *Waffen* SS'. The NCOs in charge of the operation had a great time, of course, and were not opposed to being entertained by the juggling of office equipment, some routine vanishing tricks and the deft erection of a human pyramid. The completed forms were filed without a second glance and twenty-three clean slates issued virtually on the spot. It seemed inconceivable to the authorities that a bunch of degenerate clowns could be anything other than the most natural of democrats.

Within a week Söldmann had moved his operations into the US sector, brandishing his Persil-pass like a family crest. He had

131

no further dealings with Karli Schäfer's Circus, with the sole exception of a bought night of love with one of the diminutive trampoline girls. Like so many men, he just wanted to know, for once in his life, what it was like to fuck a midget. He liked it well enough, but stuck with fully grown women thereafter. There was more kudos in it, and he found he had gotten used to the dynamic possibilities that the difference in size afforded to his erotic sport. Over the months that followed he steered his business focus towards the supply of information, dealing with all four of the Allied powers. The Russians, he found, made his best customers. They had voracious needs, and Nazi coffers from which to pay for them.

In the weeks prior to his death, Söldmann was said to be working on a major business transaction concerning the sale of some highly sensitive material. The price, it was rumoured, was astronomical, and the risks involved considerable. But there is no time now to unravel that particular riddle. It slumbers, safely wrapped in a pair of Nordic socks, down a defunct teapot's gullet. Any day now it will wake, and take measures to crawl forth from its protective shell. You and I, we will be there to greet its early-morning yawn. Söldmann, on the other hand, won't have another morning. He lies, frozen solid, upon an attic's bumpy plank, and a knife-point's hole within his back.

But enough about Söldmann. Let us return to the living, those who speak and love and, consequently, can still be hurt.

———·———

The Colonel came to her not ten minutes after Pavel had left. Sonia spent the time in front of the mirror, gazing at herself in wonder. It occurred to her to open a window in order to change the air in which she was living, but the frame was frozen shut and would not budge. She lit a cigarette, resumed her position in front of the looking glass and blew smoke at herself. She found that, if she held the cigarette between the last but one joint of her middle and index fingers, and let her hand droop loosely from an upraised wrist, she very nearly looked a lady.

The Colonel was in buoyant spirits, perhaps too much so. He greeted her with a hearty kiss on the lips, lovingly picked up the monkey by the scruff of its neck, and poured himself a generous glass of brandy. Sonia thought she could detect something in his eyes other than gaiety, some mild discomfort that he was at pains to conceal. She wondered whether it had to do with Christmas; the season did funny things to people. He lowered his bulk into one of the sofa cushions and motioned for her to join him. Just then he made her gag: the roll of fat that leapt up from chest and neck to swallow the chin, and those plump infant's hands that she knew had broken bones. She drew closer gingerly, watching him undo his fly.

Taking care of his needs proved awkward. Sonia protested stomach cramps – wind – and he benevolently let her mouth do the work, a hot-water bottle spread against her abdomen. While she sat there at his feet, feeling the cold of the floor under her buttocks and his wedding ring against her scalp, Sonia studied the Colonel from under hooded lids. She was musing about what it was like to be Fosko; marvelling that, only days ago, she had thought them alike, one paw cupping her breast like a butcher weighing his meat, the other in her hair, guiding her motions. The thought crossed her mind that the war had done this to him, made him what he was. How did he behave with his wife? Had he wooed her, brought her flowers? Been shy on his wedding night, a boy of twenty, sheepishly lifting her nightdress to the glow of a blushing candle? She pictured his astonishment when the maiden wife grabbed his manhood with knowing hands. Sonia stopped herself short. She did not know this woman, and already she made her out a tramp.

When he was done he sent her away to clean herself up and had another brandy. The phone rang while she was in the bathroom. Fosko answered, and she could hear his distemper at whatever news he was receiving. Then his voice mellowed and took on a peculiar sweetness.

'He went where?' she heard him ask. 'He must be there to sell. Don't let any of them get away. Not one, you hear.'

'That's right. I want a dozen men up there with Peterson.'

'Yes, I know what day it is tomorrow. Does that pose a problem for you?'

'My good friend, I asked whether it posed a problem.'

'Ah, that's just what I've been thinking. Let me know how things turn out.'

'And a very Merry Christmas to you.'

He hung up grimly and turned to face her where she was standing in the bedroom doorway.

'Christmas,' he said with mock exasperation. 'Gold, frankincense and myrrh, and suddenly everybody wants a bloody day off.'

He poured himself yet another brandy and drank it off in one. She wondered whether the moment had come when Pavel had finally run out of luck.

Half an hour later the phone rang a second time. Sonia made to pick it up, but a quick look from Fosko banished her to the kitchen instead, and bid her close the door. Pressing her ear to its wood, she could only make out tantalising snippets. Fosko's voice dipped whenever he wanted to ensure its privacy.

'You got who?

'Ah, the boy. Splendid. He's what?

'How?

'Never mind. Here's what you do. Bring him –'

And a little later:

'No, don't. Let them go through with their business. Just go on waiting until he leaves.

'Oh, I know it is cold. Gives you a chance to practise the old "stiff upper lip", eh, Peterson? Built the Empire, remember? Think of Nelson, or Wellington, if you like.

'And Peterson – when he comes out, make sure he's clear out of sight before your men jump the others.

'Nothing. Just follow him home.

'Oh, I think he will. He's got a strumpet waiting for him here. One more thing, Peterson. About the man in the car downstairs.

'Yes, him. What you want to do is –'

She thought that there was room enough, in the gaps of his conversation, to dig graves for a half-dozen men. A spasm ran through her bladder and for a moment she thought she would piss herself. At last he rang off and called her back into the room. She ran past his watchful gaze and into the bedroom, to relieve herself on her chamber pot.

'You piss like a horse,' he called through the door, jocular. Even so, she could hear his mounting anger. She wiped herself with some paper, and swallowed the sob that had been building in her throat.

When Sonia re-entered the room, he was sitting at the piano. His fingers searched out chords, seemingly at random. The bottle of brandy sat balanced upon some of the middle keys, its neck leaning against her sheet music. Fosko played around it, delighting in assonance. Every so often he would chance upon a particularly atonal combination, and hammer it out for four, five beats at a time. Once, the monkey joined in, screeching and chattering and drumming its fists. It would only shut up when Fosko dug a sweet out of one pocket and threw it over to where it sat. Then he resumed playing.

Quietly, her feet seeking out the thick of the carpet, Sonia approached the piano. She took position behind him, not five feet from his round-shouldered back, and tried to gauge what it would take to kill him. The thought died in her no sooner than she had given it shape. Nothing in the room seemed sufficiently lethal. Had she owned a gun, she would not have dared shoot it, lest the bullet bounce off his skin and fall to the ground between them. At length he spoke.

'I wonder whether you have been lying to me, my dear. Your friend, Richter, he's not as innocent as it appeared. It looks like Boyd gave him the merchandise after all, which probably means he knows you for Belle. So the question is, is he playing you, or are you playing me?'

He turned around then, scowling at her over one shoulder.

Sonia did not react. *If he kills me now*, she thought, *Pavel will never know*.

What she felt for him. She did not put a word to the feeling. Almost immediately, Fosko's scowl softened.

'No,' he said, and ran a hand across his chin. 'You wouldn't play me. Not about something like this. There is nothing in it for you. The Yanks have a phrase for it: "seeing all the angles". That's you, my dear – look like an angel, for the most part, but on the inside it's all hard and sharp and angular. Like a broken mirror. I wonder sometimes – was it the Reich or the Russians, or were you born that way?'

He resumed playing, pressing down on the pedal to muffle the sounds. It was as though he was gagging the piano.

'Never worry, my dear. I will honour our deal. When all this is over, you'll have your passport. And the money. I wonder though – will you be happy?'

He wagged his head and hit a series of F sharps.

She was off the hook.

Sonia should have felt a sense of relief, but instead cold sweat began pouring from her armpits and the folds under her breasts. She cast around for a chair to sit on, but felt she could not move. Above all, she was sickened by the thought that he could know her so, like the calluses upon his palms. It seemed unfair to her.

Fosko played a final chord, then turned around, swivelling on his buttocks like a schoolboy. He smiled ruefully, and recommenced speaking with a changed tone of voice.

'But I forgot what I wanted to tell you all along. My wife is flying in tonight.'

'Your wife?' she blurted out, then bit her lip. 'I . . . I was just thinking about her.'

'Were you? Well, she's come for Christmas. New regulations for officers' dependants, you see. She's bringing the children, too. For all I know they are here already – I had a man pick them up from the airport.'

He dusted off specks from his uniform trousers, then wet his lips with a giant tongue. 'I got the boy a little train, and the girl one of those wooden Babushka dolls the Russians are so fond of. A garish little thing: it's built like a coffin, hollow, only there are more dolls inside, so it's as heavy as a brick. It opens up along a seam that runs the length of its side.'

His hands went through the motion, delicate despite their bulk.

'It's flawed psychology, really: you crack open the surface, and what you find is another just the same as the first, all the way down to a tiny little doll that's solid and hard and shan't be broken. I wonder what Peterson would say to that. He loves psychology. Not the book kind, mind, just good old looking people up and down, though, fact is, he only has one eye, which makes for flat viewing.'

He looked up as though he'd just woken from some reverie. 'Am I boring you?'

She shook her head no, and wondered what it was that had led him to think about breaking people. Boyd's body danced before her mind's eye; danced awkwardly, on account of its broken shins.

'I had a doll like that when I was a child,' she said, just to say something, although it was a lie.

He shrugged his shoulders as though he couldn't have cared less, and poured himself another glass.

'In any case, they are going to be in town for a few days. I thought about introducing you, but really there is no point. My wife, she takes no pleasure in the company of women, and I doubt you would take to the children.'

'I quite understand.'

'I knew you would.'

He got up to pat her cheek, then fetched a knife to peel the monkey an apple and feed it by the slice. Sonia watched him do it, and picked up the apple peel from off the ground when he was done.

They sat in silence after that, Fosko drinking further glasses of brandy, Sonia sitting on the sofa with a book spread across her lap, pretending to read. An hour passed with painful slowness, then another. She began wishing for something to happen, longing for it with all her heart. Then: a knock at her door, a familiar rhythm, and immediately she berated herself for her foolish wish. Fosko raised himself soundlessly and retreated into the bedroom, lifting up the monkey as he passed it on his way, and cradling it in the crook of his arm.

'Sonia, my dear,' he whispered. 'It appears you have a guest. Better go and open up.'

She hung her head and did as she was bidden.

———·———

The story took hours to tell, though Pavel could have picked off its facts on the fingers of one hand. Söldmann gradually drifted into its background, his life providing Paulchen with an excuse to narrate his own, and that of his parents – the mother an early convert to Nazism, the father more reluctant, a patriot, and unaccountably bitter when the order came for him to march east, and kill Bolsheviks. 'That night, they fought so hard, I thought he would beat her to death,' Paulchen confided. 'She even called him a filthy, no-good Yid.' He glanced around sternly to impress upon his brood that the charge had been devoid of grounds.

Pavel listened to it all with great attention; listened to the repetitions and asides, enjoying the vibrancy of the young man's vocabulary as it struggled manfully to keep abreast of life. At times the other boys would chirp in, providing snippets of their own tales. What united them, more than anything, were narratives of death, invariably rendered with a studied nonchalance. The Karlsons, for instance, had lost their father to Stalingrad and their mother to a German grenade, carelessly lobbed through the wrong apartment window on the penultimate day of the Battle of Berlin. She had, they said, only received a minor abdominal wound, but had never returned from hospital. 'Probably bled to death,' one brother stated matter-of-factly. 'They were running out of blood reserves just then.'

Next, a boy they called Woland told of how he had stumbled upon a ring of schoolboys climbing on each other's shoulders in order to touch – and spin – the foot of a man hanged for desertion; hanged from a lamppost in broad daylight, a paper sign around his neck that explained his misdeed. A look at his ashen face – Woland had climbed a pair of shoulders himself – and it turned out he was the boy's uncle, with whom he was living at the time. 'He didn't do no deserting,' he insisted sulkily, and repeated the phrase two or three times until Pavel conceded that 'it must have been a mistake'. The boy shook on it and his friend Hansi suggested that maybe the Russians had hanged him there, in a ploy against civilian morale. Only then was Paulchen given leave to resume his story. The upshot of which was this: Söldmann was organized crime, had been from before the peace, and dealt primarily in information, with a sideline in drugs and firearms. When Pavel asked about his headquarters, Paulchen gave him an address, a few streets over from Boyd's bordello.

'That's all I got,' said Paulchen. 'We've never done any business with Söldmann.'

'Why not?'

'He says he doesn't deal with *boys*.'

The announcement, grimly made, was met by a chorus of hisses. Pavel quickly assured them that he was no such fool.

He left shortly after, reiterating his promise of money. Outside, the cold had intensified, and he hurried home without a backward glance. His mind was on Sonia: the memory of their kiss. He wondered whether he should hold her again; there was time enough, on that walk home, to nurse the seed of a dream in which he saved her, from misfortune and her life of vice. No sooner had he thought it than he chided himself. The cold was making him light-headed.

When he reached his apartment building, Pavel walked up to Sonia's door without caring to stop at his own rooms first. He knocked, impatiently, already picturing her face. Sonia was slow to react. He was about to repeat the motion when she pulled back the latch.

'Mr Richter,' she said. 'Pavel. So good of you to come.'

He knew at once that she was not alone. Anger took hold of him, banished all prudence.

'Where is he?' he asked.

'Who?'

He walked past her and threw open first the kitchen, then the bedroom door. There, upon the edge of her bed, sat the Colonel, stroking the monkey upon his knees. He was so fat that his stomach came halfway to his thighs. The monkey clung to it like a suckling babe.

'Ah, Pavel! How do you do?'

Pavel stood in the doorway, hands clenched into fists, unsure of himself.

'A glass of brandy perhaps? You look like you are freezing. Sonia, a glass for our guest, and make it quick.'

Fosko rose, depositing the monkey on the floor. Once again Pavel marvelled at how effortlessly he moved.

'But we should go through to the living room. A lady's boudoir – it is no place for men to talk. Not amongst crumpled linen.' He waved carelessly towards where Sonia's negligee peeked out from under one pillow. 'I sense you have something important to convey.'

They returned to the living room, the Colonel leading Pavel by the elbow, Pavel allowing himself to be led. Sonia lined up two glasses, and poured from the half-empty bottle. They raised them solemnly in front of their faces; stood eye to eye like duellists; drank. Pavel's left, he noticed, remained in the guise of a fist.

'You have been out and about on business?' Fosko asked, as though innocently.

'You know I have.'

'Then perhaps it was imprudent to go. Unhealthy, even. For you and your associates.'

'You wouldn't dare.'

A flicker of amusement ran through the Colonel's face. He shaped his lips into a smile.

'It is not a phrase you should grow fond of.'

He waved for Sonia to top them up. It occurred to Pavel that Fosko might be very drunk just then.

'I should go,' he muttered, thinking that he must run back to Paulchen's, and warn the boys.

'On the contrary – you should stay awhile. It is I who has to leave. Duty calls.'

Fosko's eyes ran over Sonia's body, ignoring her face.

'She's quite something, wouldn't you say, Pavel? Good legs on her, and that husky voice. Oh-la-la. And the tits are a dream. She's morally tainted, of course, but I know what you'll say. The world has ill used her. So it has, my friend, so it has.'

'Don't you dare –'

'My mistake, forgive me. I forgot that you are delicately put together, though I daresay there's a cock on you some place. In any case, where's my coat? I have some business to attend to.'

He dressed with great rapidity, drawing his mink coat around him. At the door, he stopped himself like a man who has forgotten his umbrella.

'You enjoy yourself. My house is your house. There will be time to speak further – later.'

141

Through all this Pavel could do nothing but stand and stare. It was that, or launch himself at the man and strangle him with his bare hands. It was an unbecoming thought.

No sooner had Fosko closed the door behind him than Sonia ran past Pavel and into the bedroom. Pavel did not understand her urgency until he heard the tinkle of her urine stream, violent against the chamber pot's side. Embarrassed for her, he retreated to the far end of the room and even turned his back. She re-emerged a minute later, rubbing at her hands with a shard of ice.

'Nerves,' she shrugged, and he smiled to assure her he quite understood.

'I should go. He sounds like he's planning . . . mischief.'

She laughed at his word. Pavel sat down upon the sofa.

'I really should go,' he repeated.

'Forget it,' she whispered. 'You're finished. The minute you walk out this door.'

She stepped over to him and sat by his side. Through his anger and his fear he could smell the fragrance of her hair. He reached for her hand, not looking. By accident he touched her thigh instead. She recoiled and moved a half-foot away from him. They sat next to each other, conscious of the gap, and stared at the wall.

'What did he do to you?' he asked at length.

She shrugged, sought his eyes, then evaded them once they'd found her.

'Nothing,' she croaked. 'But he knows.'

'Knows what?'

'He knows that I – but what's the use in saying it?'

Pavel wished that, just once, she would use the word.

'I love you?' he murmured.

She got up to blow her nose. Perhaps she had not heard him. He watched her pace the room, then settle herself before the piano. Her fingers stroked the keys but did not strike them. Things would have been better had she played.

'We could just give him what he wants.' Sonia's eye travelled to the teapot in the cupboard. 'It might change things for you.'

He shook his head.

'No, we can't do that. Not if he killed Boyd we can't.'

His voice sounded stubborn to himself, like a child's, but Sonia did not argue the point.

'Fine,' she said. 'Better that way. For myself, that is.'

'Just tell me one thing,' he asked meekly.

'Yes.'

'Did you know Boyd would die?'

'I knew he was a pawn who thought himself king.'

'Yes,' she said. 'I knew he would die. I helped kill him.'

'You had no choice.'

'How do you know?'

He heard her say it and fell to thinking.

Thinking that Sonia had grown hard in the war, hardest of all on herself.

'I must go,' he said yet again, and struggled to raise himself from out of the couch. She did not stir at the announcement but sat round-shouldered upon her stool. And then, just as it seemed they would part in anger, another kiss, their third, pressed up against the piano, his hand sounding bass notes. In all his life there had been no kiss such as this.

'You taste of brandy,' she said, light-heartedly, the only time he had known her to blush.

'And you of the Colonel's cologne.'

He turned around then and walked out the door, not daring to look back and see whether or not his words had hurt her.

———·———

Pavel left her apartment, unsure what to do next. He had half expected the Colonel's men to be waiting for him there, and place him under formal arrest, but the staircase was empty of life, and dark too, with only the moon to draw its outlines. For the briefest of moments he considered whether they had misunderstood Fosko; whether the man had just been drunk, and had shuffled off to bed in order to sleep off the liquor. Pavel dismissed the notion at once. He knew better than to delude himself. His kidneys sat uncomfortably in his back and he decided that, whatever else happened, he had better take his evening medicine. As he walked towards his apartment door, he noticed that it stood ajar. There was no light on the inside.

Pavel pushed open the door, felt for the light switch, flicked it to no effect. There he stood upon the threshold, his heart beating in his throat suddenly, wedged snug against the base of his tongue. Inside, a familiar smell, of unwashed body, piss and blood. He squinted, trying to make things out. The shadows were deeper here, the moon sickly behind the double pane of frozen glass, half obscured by the curtain's swinging curve.

Only he no longer had any curtains.

He had taken them down weeks ago, to fashion blankets for the boy, leaving a bare copper rod. A dozen times or more he had used it in lieu of a drying rack, had hung up dress shirts, socks and underwear and watched the water drip upon his windowsill, until it had got too cold for washing and the sickness had made him oblivious to his stink. The rod had been empty when Pavel had left the apartment.

It was no longer empty.

He panicked, dug in his heels, stared at the shadow that must not be; took in the rod's bend, and the tautness of the rope, his hands casting around for a book of matches. He broke one against the box's gravelly side; broke another; broke a third, his fingers stiff and clumsy. On the next attempt, Pavel dropped the whole box; crouched and searched for it in the darkness of the floor. Then, finally, a match caught fire: a wild flare of light that recoiled into itself before gradually transforming into the steady flame of burning wood. Shadows danced before it, exposed, then scuttled back into the dark. At the window, one such shadow refused to budge; instead it solidified, took on features, four foot something, and skinny.

Its head stuck out of the noose at an impossible angle.

Pavel breathed and moved towards the hanging boy. He grabbed his foot – had he not been told of such a thing but two hours ago? – and spun him round. He found a death mask of a face, an angel's face, a murdered angel, young, and a little cracked on one side. Pavel spun him, faced him, placed his match so close it was as though he wished to light him up, the dead boy hanging from his curtain rod. Spun him, faced him, saw – and laughed.

Sweet mother of Jesus. He laughed! It nearly did me in, that laughter.

————·————

You must understand, of course, that I had been sitting there all along, splayed out on top of his bed, my back propped up against some pillows. He never noticed me, not until he had faced the boy, that is, and shot out that frightening bark of laughter. Only then – when I yelled at him to stop – did he turn and make my acquaintance.

I imagined I peeled out of the shadows for him, in my bulky overcoat and the eye-patch, like some divine messenger bringing news of final things. I remember his looking at my shoes, which I had placed carelessly upon his sheets, with some special sort of loathing. He had been raised better than that, and chances are he thought I should have been, too. But I was tired and cold that night, and my feet hurt from standing around outside the boys' hideaway, and besides, he wasn't going to be using his bed for a while. I suppose I could have taken them off, my shoes, but how is a man to arrest another in his stockings? It would have been absurd, particularly in combination with the gun that was in my

145

hand. Pavel looked at it with tired eyes. It did not seem to hold much meaning for him.

But events are getting the better of me, and I am in danger of unravelling this yarn from the wrong end entirely. Let me retrace the steps that served to place me within that room, upon that bed, dirty shoes soiling Pavel's sheets and the broken eye itching under its patch like something rotten. You last found me watching elsewhere, out in the street across from Paulchen's quarters, placing an anxious phone call for company in my vigil. It was a long and tiresome wait. There was a curious diversion not long after I had established myself – the other men had just come out to join me – but it was not the sort of thing liable to comfort a man's spirits. Quite the contrary. It concerns the boy, the one hanging from the rafters, dead, I am afraid, and never to wake. He showed up all of a sudden, God only knows from where. He might have been in the house, or in the courtyard behind it, or up in a tree for all I know. The first knowledge I had of him was his drawing up short, mid-step, not two yards from where I stood guard, and giving a mighty start.

'Good God!' said I, similarly startled, and thinking that the Colonel had laid a claim to this child. 'You are Pavel's little friend.'

And off he bolted.

Looked at me, a twitch of the lip – a curious sort of curling – and then he was off, flying like the wind, or rather like a nasty little gust, down the street as fast as his little legs would carry. I had no choice but to give chase, my superior limbs encumbered by my superior girth, clambering after him, shouting (like a fool, no doubt!) for him to stop. He had no intention of complying with my request.

I chased him down the empty street and was getting within perhaps five feet of him when he, nimble as a rabbit, feinted to the left and then cut to the right, down some dark alley with bomb rubble peeking out of the snow every five yards. I tried to

146

follow his motion, unaware that my bulk would not take to sudden changes of direction with the selfsame elegance the boy had just displayed, hence stumbled, hit upon a nasty patch of ice, one foot shooting to the right, the other to the left and my arms turning into a veritable windmill. In short, I fell, and fell in a rather dramatic manner that hurt my rump and brought a curse to my lips.

'Christ!' I shouted.

It was the last word the boy would hear on this earth.

Something about my invocation of our saviour compelled him. He whipped his head round, perhaps to gloat, or else to make sure there were no other pursuers (there were none, the other men being too lazy to go chasing after a street Arab, and on Christmas Eve to boot). In any case he looked back while his legs ran on. Stubbed his toe upon a bent piece of metal pipe, half lost in a snow drift. Fell forward at great velocity and broke his neck upon the sidewalk's edge, just like that, a half-inch under the base of the skull. He broke his face open a little, too, of course, and probably broke his ankle, but principally he broke his neck, so there was nothing doing, apart from picking him up and calling the Colonel. Who, in a conspiratorial whisper, instructed me to engineer that little scene in Pavel's bedroom, specifying the curtain rod and the rope, and that the light bulb be smashed, so that the man would have shadows to contend with, and the uncertainties of moonlight.

After I repeated the instructions back to the Colonel – he was particular that way – I sent a man ahead to do the hanging, it not being my line of work, and because I was uncomfortable at the thought of walking Berlin's streets on Christmas Eve with a dead child under my arm, the package's contents only rudimentarily obscured by being wrapped in a blanket. The truth is that it sickened me, this accidental death of someone so young, though I guess things would have been no better had he been killed on purpose.

Once the boy was out of sight I resumed, with heavy heart, my position outside Paulchen's flat. Our instructions were to wait for Pavel to leave. I was to follow, while the rest of the men stormed the flat and ascertained whether Pavel had been there with a view to selling the merchandise (though why he should be selling it to children, I can't say). It would call for some cracking of heads no doubt, though more like than not, not much worse than that.

As for myself, after I followed Pavel back and made sure he went to Sonia's rooms first – the Colonel had predicted this with a degree of certainty that has never ceased to astonish me – I stepped into Pavel's rooms in order to ascertain that all had been arranged, which it had. I was about to walk out, and let the man – Jeremiah Easterman, a real brute of a fellow with shoulders like a bull – make the arrest, when it occurred to me that it just wouldn't do. Having Easterman wave his gun at Pavel and mock him for his grief over the child: it felt like a betrayal of the budding kinship that I felt had sprung up between Pavel and me during the days I had dogged his steps through the streets of Berlin and tried, vainly no doubt, to divine his soul. So I sent Easterman home to his Christmas, and took up the post myself. Initially I sat on one of his chairs, but soon my aching rump and stone-cold feet compelled me to move over to the bed, and into the ill-bred sprawl Pavel later found me in.

The Colonel looked in on me, perhaps a quarter-hour before Pavel showed up. He opened the door, gave the arrangements a most cursory glance, nodded in my direction, and asked whether we had taken care of the man in the car outside.

'Yes,' I nodded, having received word about this shortly after Easterman had left. 'But we didn't know what to do with the body.'

'So?'

'So we left it there. It looks like he's sleeping. I thought no harm in it.'

The Colonel smiled at that and made to leave. 'When Richter comes down, take him home to the villa. Only make sure my wife and children don't see him. It might upset them.'

'I will, Colonel.' And added, upon consideration, and because there was a contentment in the Colonel I had only rarely noted before: 'May I ask a question?'

'But of course, my good Peterson.'

'Why this charade?' I nodded over to where the boy was swinging. 'Why not just arrest him and beat it out of him?'

The Colonel shrugged like it was an imbecilic query. 'In everything one does, Peterson, it is imperative to have a certain *je ne sais quoi*. And to be economical with one's opportunities. We have – one – a dead boy loved by a man, and – two – the man himself, who needs to be broken. I'd prefer the boy alive and the man dead, on the whole, and Söldmann's merchandise in my pocket, but we are not always free to choose our circumstances.'

'Ah,' I said, pretending I understood. And added: 'Would you have interrogated the boy? If he had lived, I mean? Would you have, you know, hurt him?'

The Colonel scoffed.

'Peterson, Peterson,' he said. 'Of course I wouldn't have.' He smiled at me sweetly. 'You would have.'

'Aye, sir, I presume I would've,' I conceded after he wouldn't let me out of his eye. He waved with his fat fingers and half closed the door behind him. I leaned back against the wall and waited for Pavel.

When he came in, finally, after what may have been twenty minutes, I sat still as a doorpost. He never noticed me, not when he was fumbling with the matches (I nearly offered to help him it was so pathetic), nor when he managed to light one, and approached the boy with solemn step. Then the laughter. I was tempted to jump up to shake him out of it, thinking he had gone hysterical, only my back hurt so. 'Why are you laughing?' I shouted instead from my perch's comfort.

'You got the wrong one,' he cried. 'You got the wrong boy.'

I couldn't understand what he meant. It was the boy who had been to visit him that afternoon. I had never met another.

'The one the Colonel is looking for, right?' I asked.

He shook his head.

'That one,' he spat, 'got away, and curse you for killing this one, who was a good boy, not twelve years old, his parents dead in the camps.'

It was the first time it occurred to me that there might be more to the man than was suggested by the unobtrusiveness of his demeanour. I remembered, then, that he had been in the war, and must know what it meant to kill. His laughter stopped, was replaced by a frown. Then: that indignant stare at my shoes, his indifference towards my gun.

'Help me take him down,' he told me, and I did, not having been instructed differently.

Once we got the boy out of his noose, Pavel cradled him in his arms. He would not deposit him on the bed, as I asked, but rather kept him there, pressed against his narrow chest, as I walked him out at gunpoint, and down the staircase's darkness. When we had rounded the first set of stairs, I could hear someone gently close a door upstairs.

Sonia had been listening.

Seconds later, I heard her starting to play. The notes ran through the building like a shiver.

———·———

Anders was having a miserable day, out alone in the cold. He'd spent his morning chasing down a black-market vendor who owed him one, and persuading him to sell him a sleeping bag on credit. The bag was Soviet Army issue, complete with a red star and Cyrillic name stencilled into its side; was not of bad quality, but stained a vivid rust colour, and smelled strongly of pickled

150

herring. Lunchtime, Anders had found himself starving, and been forced to beg food at the British Army barracks along with a horde of other boys, though none that belonged to Paulchen. He got some boiled beef and beans, and a half-bar of chocolate for which he had to fight a fifteen-year-old with a gammy leg. He settled the fight with a kick to his testicles and a flash of the Luger barrel. Then, the sun already low in the sky, he ran to take up position before Pavel's house and wait for his prey.

Taking up position was easier said than done. There was a surprisingly constant stream of pedestrians walking down the street and Anders had no wish for witnesses; there were windows, too, where it was hard to tell whether anyone might be watching through their frosty murk. The encroaching dark soon took care of that, and Christmas preparations thinned out the foot traffic, but as Anders strolled casually down the sidewalk in order to stake out a likely hiding hole, he took note of a man in a car who sat, evidently freezing, wrapped in some blankets and taking regular swigs at a bottle of schnapps. He would roll down one window whenever the windshield got so steamed up he could no longer make out a thing; that and rub at the condensation with a gloved palm, which did little to help. Once he left the car altogether, to buy cigarettes from a young woman who was walking past, pushing a pram. Anders heard him wish her a Merry Christmas.

'I'm married,' she responded and hurried off down the road.

It struck Anders that the man was engaged in something not unrelated to his own endeavour. For a moment he took comfort in the thought that he was to share his stake-out, until it occurred to him that this might be one of the Colonel's men. He was not wearing a uniform, however, and when he had asked for the ciggies, the accent had not been an English one.

There was a little mound of garbage and rotten sandbags not three yards from him by the side of a building that Anders had long identified as the most likely place for him to hide. At length, he realized he had little choice but to risk the knowledge of his co-vigilante. Anders walked towards the mound casually, then leapt on top, shifted some sandbags and in this manner dug for himself a shallow crater. Crawling into his sleeping bag, the herring smell nauseating in his nose, and lying flat on his stomach, Anders became invisible in the failing light. As an added bonus he was able to watch the street through the gap left between two sandbags. He fingered his gun and felt like a regular sniper. The man in the car, he noted, had watched his manoeuvre with a melancholy air, but made no move to speak to him, let alone chase him away. Anders saw him finish his liquor with a final, protracted swallow. His eyes were red-rimmed, tired; he needed a shave, coffee, twelve hours of sleep. The boy nodded to him curtly, and the man nodded back, and that was that. Then, shivering in his down-padded burrow, Anders set to watching, waiting for the fat man, murder on his mind.

Anders had arrived too late to witness Schlo' delivering his message to Pavel, but trusted implicitly that his friend had not failed him. Anders wondered how Pavel would react. It was hard to fathom. Pavel had not been himself recently, not since the kidneys, and that woman made a fool of him too, somehow, though Anders did not dislike her as much as he might. He hoped that whatever Pavel found in his coat lining was something that he would know how to dispose of. It might be diamonds, Anders mused, a million Reichsmarks in bold glitter, or else proof certain that Hitler was alive and plotting revenge. Either way, he was sure Pavel would figure out what to do. There had never been a man such as Pavel, even if he had cried.

Another hour or two passed before Pavel appeared in the flesh. He stepped out of the building, his hat drawn low into his brow and the coat sitting awkward on account of the cut lining. Anders restrained his impulse to call out and greet him; he studied his gait instead and felt reassured that his kidney's limp was barely noticeable now. Pavel hadn't gone twenty steps down the road

when a second man shot out of the doorway. A man in a decent
coat, middle-aged and a little heavy, with a patch over one eye
and a lively growth of brow over the other. He followed Pavel
without much of an attempt to remain unknown to him. They
were both soon out of sight. His fellow watcher gazed after them
with interest, but made no move to follow. Anders wondered
who he was watching for.

Minutes later the Colonel showed up. He parked his car just
up the road and came strolling down, walking his mink with a fat-
bellied swagger, a swing tune upon his fleshy lips. Anders
whipped out the gun and took aim. The man in the car, he
noted, slid halfway down the seat to avoid detection. It was a
difficult shot across ten yards of shadow and the watcher's bulky
hood. Thoughtful, teeth in one lip, Anders held his fire. There
would be a better moment, one when he would be sure of his
man. He stuck his arms back into the sleeping bag and rubbed
them warm against his body. The smell of herring had become
natural to his nose and no longer bothered him. It was just as
well. Had he pondered the circumstance, it might have made
him hungry.

Anders did not pay much attention when another man came
walking down the street, carrying a large bundle in both arms.
The same man would come out, a good while later, with no
bundle. It was clear to the boy that he was one of Fosko's men,
but it seemed impossible to keep an eye on all of them. All he
wanted was for Pavel to be safe, and for Fosko to make himself
available to his gun. These were small favours to ask of the day;
he considered appealing to God for them, but it was unclear
whether He would be interested. So Anders waited, without
prayer, and left religion to those with more pious needs.

It took an age for Pavel to return, unmolested, One-Eye close
at his heels. Pavel seemed happy, distracted; opened the front
door with some zest and nearly ran up the stairs. The boy
thought he was off to visit Sonia. It did not matter. Before long,

he hoped, even Pavel would see that she was little more than a tramp.

Then, a horrible thing. A man who entered the street from the other side, stealthily, and walked so softly Anders only became aware of his presence when he was almost on top of him. The man paid no heed to the mound of sandbags, however; instead, he slunk towards the car, his eyes on the mirror that stuck frozen and blind out of its side. Anders thought about whether he should warn the watcher; deliberated, hesitated, lay flat on his belly, lost of tongue. It was time enough for the stranger to carry out his purpose. Without pause or hesitation he opened the door. Out of nowhere, a knife appeared in his hand. The man in the car looked up at the intrusion; eyes red-rimmed, his motions sluggish. There was no struggle. The knife snapped forward but once, with no more violence to the movement than a man punching another in a beer-house brawl. The watcher jerked, spat steam, one final breath, red eyes gaping before the boy. Then they lost focus, froze; the man dead now, beyond any shadow of doubt. His killer closed the car door and looked casually up and down the road. A moment later, he walked across and into Pavel and Sonia's house, the knife gone out of his hand and like it had never been there at all.

'That's how easy it is,' Anders said to himself, 'to kill a man.'

He mused that there should have been more comfort to the thought.

Across from him, not five feet away, the watcher lay sprawled over his steering wheel, bloody spit slowly freezing upon his lip. For a moment Anders thought about getting out from his sleeping bag and wiping him off. Then he remembered his purpose, and squeezed the butt of the Luger.

It was just as well he hadn't got up. The killer returned after mere minutes. The same purposeful walk. He let himself into the car on the passenger side and arranged the dead man so that his head lay thrown back over the rim of the seat and the eyes lay closed under thick-veined lids. The bottle of schnapps he placed prominently upon the dash, and the blanket went over chest and belly, where the watcher had become wet with his dying. Having finished with these ministrations, the killer got out, closed the door gently and walked away. His boots, thought Anders, looked British. *You can strip off your uniform,* he thought, *but you still need warm feet.* He put the watcher down against the Colonel's account. The fat man was ripe for the sticking. All he needed to do now was reappear.

Fosko didn't make him wait too long. In fact, he made it easy for Anders. He strolled through the front door in the most casual of manners, pulling tight the mink around his shoulders. A luxurious swagger over to the watcher's car; a look through the windshield; a slow, deliberate rounding, taking note of the make, plate and tyres. Then the passenger door was opened for a second time. Huffing a little, the Colonel lowered himself into the seat. Reached over with delicate fingers to fish out the man's wallet and identification. Pocketed both without a second look, opened the glove compartment and searched it with a distracted air. Broke into song all of a sudden, a Christmas carol draped in schoolboy Latin, the voice a high tenor, dead words drifting through the air. The Colonel lit a cigar from out of his pocket, shaking out his fingers first to force enough life into them to be able to manipulate his match book. Continued humming to himself, the swine, past the cigar's soggy stump, his cheeks growing rosy in the cold that his Yuletide mood proved impotent to banish.

In short, the Colonel sat there, mere yards from the boy, and presented him with the easiest of targets: a fat man, sitting in a cloud of smoke, humming Latin. Nor was there any time constraint. He must have stayed there a full quarter-hour, smoking and humming and running a lazy hand over his scalp's massive sphere. Anders lay breathless, the Luger in his hand; the hand shaking; the other reaching forward to steady the first but adding little by way of calm; the gun barrel dancing in front of his eye;

calling upon his anger to sustain him, now, when courage was needed and the fat man must die. For perhaps twenty minutes he lay thus, taking a shaky aim upon the Colonel's breast, his finger stiff on the trigger. He would have done it, too (he told himself), if his hands had been calm, and if it hadn't been for that eerie tenor, singing the baby Jesus in a long-dead tongue. What was it to him? This man had threatened him, had strangled him; was his enemy, and Pavel's; fucked boys (somehow); sat smoking and leering next to a dead man, red-eyed and lonely and British boots on his killer.

'Shoot, you coward,' he barked at himself. 'Shoot while you can.'

He did not shoot.

Then the moment passed and the Colonel got out of the car. Across the road, Pavel appeared in the house's doorway. In his arms lay Schlo', dead, the head dangling like a wilted flower's. Behind him there was the man with the patch, holding a gun with some embarrassment and saluting the Colonel with his left.

'Get Richter to the villa,' the latter instructed, 'and make sure someone gets rid of that body.' He pointed back to where the car's door still stood open, a bloom of crystals upon the window. 'Oh – and tell my wife I'll be right home. I'll just pop up and listen to one final tune. Beethoven, Peterson. That girl loves Beethoven. I can't imagine why.'

Then they were gone – Pavel and One-Eye climbing into a car way down the road, and the Colonel mounting the stairs to see his woman – and Anders still lay there, gun in hand, taking aim at an empty space. He might have cried, but the cold had dried out his eyes and stoppered up his tear ducts.

———

He returned to her one more time that night, his big face ruddy with cold, and a cigar on his breath. He let himself in with his own key and crept up to where she was sitting at the piano.

There was no way of telling how long he had already been there when she finally noticed him. Strangely, it did not scare her. She was playing Beethoven in the dark.

Fosko lit a candle, pulled up a chair and sat next to her, attentive, listening to her play.

'We have taken him into custody now,' he said in between sonatas. 'Pavel, that is. He is wanted for questioning.'

He gave a pause.

'Did you like him, my dear?'

Sonia noted the past tense; shrugged. Only her shoulders and her fingers moved.

'Oh, I should say you liked him. Did you fuck him?'

'No.'

'You should have. If you liked him, you should have. Where is the harm in that?'

She went on playing, thinking, conceding to herself that perhaps, yes, she should have fucked him. It might have made for a memory, or a disappointment.

The Colonel got up to hover next to her. In the semi-dark she felt his girth like the weight of an executioner's axe. He was close enough to throw into shadow both her hands. His own were stroking the keyboard's lid.

'Beethoven,' he said. 'Beethoven was a romantic. A deaf man, obsessed with music. What could be more romantic than that?

'You play nicely, my dear, but you play like clockwork. No passion. It makes a mockery of him.'

'Please,' she told him, though she left her hands where they were. 'Please don't break my fingers.'

He chuckled softly, then bent low to kiss her knuckles.

'Good gosh. How melodramatic. Cold but melodramatic. That's just why I love you so.'

When he led her into the bedroom, he was as gentle as a groom on his first night of possession. He hoped, he said, that her abdominal pains had cleared up, and praised the curative powers

157

of brandy. Halfway through she realised she did not mind the act, that her body responded naturally enough. Later yet, she lay awake while he dressed and smiled at the fact that a few hours ago she should have thought of killing him. How ridiculous! She might as well take a swipe at the moon, or try to gouge out the stars. He would survive and always be there, on a night like this, sitting in the shadows behind her, making conversation.

He kissed her goodbye upon her brow, and Sonia fell asleep to the thought that he might break her back sometime. He would use a hammer, she thought, an ordinary three-pound household hammer, and break her bone for bone.

—·—

There we are, Christmas Eve drawing to a close. Across town, the good people of Berlin are bidding one another Good Night and God Bless. Children, their tummies filled for the first time in ages, rolling themselves into their blankets, content for once in this year of scarcity and hopeful for their morning's future (though there are also those who're crying themselves to sleep, poor wretches). Over at Paulchen's, yet another brood of children, some with bruises on their bodies and all of them wounded in their pride. They are sitting up late, commiserating, already busy converting events into song, in the manner of the Ancients. For these boys, all life is Epic. Their chieftain, meanwhile, is absent to their telling. He is sitting on a rickety chair, alone and exposed to the draught of a hospital's long corridor, with his arm and teeth broken and something worse, cursing Pavel, the British, and that little rat of a boy, Anders. The latter can be found not half a mile away, trussed up in his Russian sleeping bag, and berating himself over a job undone; thinking that he has flunked some test of manhood, and in a rage with himself over it, and with the Lord God, too, whose language is Latin and to whom carols were sung. Before long it gets too cold for his anger, and he runs inside, up to where Pavel's rooms stand empty and his bed is soiled with icy mud. There he goes to sleep, exhausted, though not before he has stared, pale-faced, at the empty noose swinging in front of the window, cold and stiff to the touch. Right on top of him (though he does not spare her a thought just now), there is Sonia, sleeping, alone and dreamless, while the monkey, that bundle of irrepressible vitality, sits over her pillow, petting her hair in some curious reversal of mistress and beast, before it scuffles off to sniff curiously at her chamber pot's contents of frozen urine and drills a leathery paw into its surface. Its owner, the Colonel, is in his car driving westward, towards what by convention he calls his home. In this home, in the drawing room to be precise, his wife is sitting nervously under a giant tree's shadow, framing her face for the delight she means to display upon his entrance. Upstairs her children, a girl and a boy, lie excited at the prospect of Santa's presents, and their reunion with Daddy. 'Perhaps,' confides the younger of the two, 'perhaps I shall get a new coat, the colour of poppies.' Two flights down, in the house's over-heated cellar, Pavel is receiving a perfunctory beating before he is locked up in a cage that has been pinched from a similar basement closer to the centre of town, where it had – until the recent withdrawal of favours by that most capricious of maidens, History – served a similar purpose, to wit the unofficial incarceration of enemies to a regime that flew, as its insignia, a skewed and broken cross. He does not seem to curse his fate, Pavel, though on occasion he raises an angry word about the boy, Salomon, who is dead now and had nothing to do with any of this. No questions are being asked of Pavel at the moment, the beating belonging to the sort that is to interrogation as foreplay is to sexual intercourse. Out east, in an unmarked office, an aristocratic officer in a Bolshevik greatcoat is poring over questions distinctly related to those on Pavel's interrogators' minds; poring over them in the form of a surprisingly thick secret-service file entitled 'Richter, Jean P.' while his young adjutant, Lev, stands in one corner and plays Russian folk on a well-worn fiddle. Another file lies on Greatcoat's lap, open to a page that reveals a grainy surveillance photo of the Colonel, mouth agape and a fork midway between lens and eye. On his plate, toad-in-the-hole and mash, in an *ambiance* that can only be the British officers' mess. Both reader and fiddler take occasional, furtive glances at the phone, but the man they hope will call is dead (we saw him stabbed) and is presently being mutilated on Fosko's orders: a man is carving up his face, though ignorant as he is of the means of modern forensics, he leaves in place both the ears and the teeth. Elsewhere, in a billiards hall in Dahlem, a dozen ruffians, still upset by the disappearance of their pint-sized leader, are hotly debating the rules of succession. They need not occupy us unduly, no longer having any stake in this game of buy-and-sell; it has passed on to their occupiers, though both the Americans and the French seem blissfully ignorant of its commencement. Equally ignorant, though nightly plagued by the darkest of anticipations, is an old man in Alt-Moabit; hairs on his nose and Darwinian whiskers. He's had his Christmas sausage with his hosts, whom he calls 'family' and deeply despises; for afters, they shared a song, a shot of plum brandy, and a tin of US Army orange juice. Now he's back in his cubbyhole, reading, thinking, brooding on life. It's where we will find him before the story is out. As for myself: I was tired that night and worse – weary. I turned in soon after Pavel fell asleep.

For all my exhaustion, I was gratified to locate, in the depth of my heart, the budding promise of joy. It was getting time now for Pavel and me to sit and talk. When it came to interrogation, I was the Colonel's most trusted aide.

Part Two

Pavel & I

Pavel slept and thought he must be dreaming. One cheek wet upon the concrete floor. There was a man there, standing over him, wearing a winter coat and satchel. A man with an eye-patch, who smelled like coffee. He reached a hand down through the bars but did not touch.

Pavel slept and thought: Coppelius.

Odysseus, he thought, in the cave of a giant.

Odin, Žižka, Oedipus, holding aloft his mother's spiky brooch. In the land of the blind, the one-eyed man was king.

Pavel slept and felt that there was salt upon his cheek. The salt of sweat, not blood, nor tears: his skin tingling with it, and with the heat. It was hot there, in the land of the blind. Sun setting over Thebes, dipping the world in red.

Pavel slept and thought the air was burning.

By this he knew it was but a dream.

———

He woke and I was there, crouching low beside the bars of his cage, a pack of cigarettes open towards Pavel. He started and rolled to his knees. Sweat on his brow, and bruises running the length of him; one could see it in the manner that he moved. His shirt soggy on the chest and the back, and the trousers sticking to his thighs. I watched him cast around, trying to get his bearings, his breath invisible to him, in the winter of '46. For a moment he may have thought he had lost his mind, until he remembered last night's descent and the miracle of Fosko's cellar. Its heat was generated by the giant hulk of a cast-iron stove that sat snug against the back of Pavel's cage; sat low on four stubby legs, valved and levered like something from Jules Verne. To the cage's front a plain wooden table; two chairs and a water jar, empty, and I his captor, waiting in a crouch. The smell was of dry rot; of earth and hot masonry; the copper tones of old blood.

'Have a cigarette,' I offered.

His hand barely shook as he reached for his first. I lit up myself and watched his eyes roam through the room, taking in the workbench with its wrist restraints; the tool cupboards with their straps and pipes and gardening tools; the vats of petroleum that stood piled in one corner. He took me in, too, stripped of my coat now, and my collar open to the second button, though he did not seem to notice the reassuring smile that marked my lips. The cigarette curled between his fingers. He kept scattering the ashes over himself, his drags fast and shallow, not tasting the smoke.

Oh, I know what he was so excited about. He had to be asking himself. *When the hell is he going to start?*

He ground out the cigarette, ran a hand over his face, his eyes wandering back towards the proffered pack. I remained where I was, watching him, gauging his soul.

'Go on, take another.'

He did, too, and another after that, his eyes moist with his question.

I wondered had he ever been tortured before.

———·———

When the pack was gone, I made a show of straightening up and stretching out my legs. 'I'll go upstairs and fetch us some

164

coffee,' I said. 'How do you take it?' But Pavel hadn't made up his mind yet whether or not he would talk.

———·—

Lunchtime, I brought him a portion of turkey breast, stuffing, and a large scoop of potato salad. The tray held two plates, spoons and napkins, and two pieces of lemon tart. Pavel ate cautiously, chewing each bite with extravagant care. Perhaps he feared that I might attempt to poison him. After dessert, I broke open a fresh pack of cigarettes, before exchanging Pavel's dirty plate for a toilet bucket of corrugated iron.

'You just let me know when, and I can give you some privacy,' I instructed him, but he just stared at me with his wet coal eyes. The bucket had been scrubbed with lye and emanated a pungent stink all its own that, once made conscious, routed the cellar's other smells and crowded our senses. We sat in its stench and traded glances. He waited patiently for me to ask the first question. I fetched my chessboard from the corner cupboard and set to playing a string of solitary games, sending rooks in chase of bishops, and angling for the queen. Hours passed, I switched to draughts.

And still he waited, waited for my question. But I didn't have one ready for him yet.

———·—

The wait ate away at him. Must have done, it was only natural, though little enough showed on his face. He watched me all afternoon, trying to make me out: a middle-aged man with nicotine stains in his whiskers. Square, heavy hands made ugly by life. The brow avuncular, as was the stoop. Clean white shirt, crisp handkerchief, and an eye-patch made of suede. Heavy, winter boots, scuffed from the season. I wonder what I added up

165

to for him. Not much, I wager; I was the Colonel's henchman, a second-order villain, perhaps a little rakish under my patch. His gaze kept returning to my boots. He may have wondered would I use them to break his shins.

————·——

He gave in after dinner. The silence must have grown intolerable. 'Go on,' he told me, shoving his uneaten sandwich back onto his plate. 'Put on your gloves and get it over with.' His voice, I thought, was remarkably controlled.

I rose and strolled over to his cell, formulating my first question. 'You are married?' I asked him. 'I noticed the ring.'

'So?'

'So? Is she pretty?'

'You want to know whether my wife is pretty?'

'Yes.'

He smiled at that, a bitter little smile, and shook his head. When I left him, an hour later, he was smoking again, and spinning his wedding ring around his emaciated finger.

————·——

That's how it was, our first day in the basement: a day of silence, two men puffing away at their cigarettes, and a single, inept question around dinnertime that fell on recalcitrant ears. The truth is that I was hardly as much in control as I may have made it seem, nor as calmly content with my role of silent observer. It had been a day full of surprises. I had risen early that morning and dressed with extravagant care. My apartment was stuffy with the smells of my wash-basket and troubled digestion. I might have opened a window despite the cold, but the latch was frozen shut and the glass frost-smeared even on the inside. There was no need to make breakfast – I should

166

have my morning coffee at the Colonel's – but as every morning I took the time to iron a fresh collar and handkerchief, having long cherished the belief that one could tell a man's mettle by the crispness of its crease (a foolish notion, no doubt, but one that had proven remarkably stubborn). It was not quite six when I went to pour hot water over my car's windows and hood, and not half six gone when I let myself into the Colonel's villa with my own set of keys. The drive had been uneventful enough, if cold, and punctured at one eerie intersection by the howling of wolves retreating back into the woods after their nightly excursions into the city.

I arrived at the villa and reported for work with my usual gusto, only to have the Colonel wave me away and bid me wait out of earshot. He was on the phone, a terse conversation of barked half-syllables, one jowly cheek still swathed in shaving lather. Later, when he found me sitting idly upon the living-room couch, he ignored the simple present I had prepared for him and instructed me in language more plain than was his custom not to use any form of physical coercion on Pavel until further notice. I was conscious of the absurdity of the request, of course, but did not voice any protest. Midday, when I ventured into the kitchen and saw that the Colonel was missing from the Christmas table with its half-carved turkey and seasonal decorations, his wife advised me that Fosko was receiving a Russian officer in his study, ostensibly for the exchange of gifts. Later still, the Colonel left for town in gala uniform and polished boots: I saw him drive off from the servants' bathroom window as I was taking a prolonged toilet break occasioned by my recalcitrant prostate. He had not yet returned when I knocked off from work at half six; his children sat playing under the Christmas tree without the benefit of a paternal presence, their mother thumbing idly through her husband's record collection. In other words, I had been left, for the entirety of the day, with no real instructions, and a prisoner on my hands whom I was not allowed to touch.

None of this would have made me quite as tongue-tied, being a chatty fellow by disposition, had the Colonel not made it clear that he expected answers out of Pavel Richter nevertheless. When I politely inquired how I was to do this, he merely told me that Pavel was a man 'all broken up over the loss of a boy. Just ply him with cigarettes, and he will start talking all on his own.' It was not the moment, I felt, to inform Fosko that we had hanged the wrong child.

So I went down into the basement and stood over him for what seemed like an age, my face pressed against the bars of his cage, reading his dream off his lids. He slept like an infant, his face crushed into the ground, fingers bent and his hair limp from the cellar's infernal climate. Even so he was a handsome man; a hollow-eyed beauty at once effete and masculine. Haggard, in any case. I was tempted to touch, and encourage him to claim the mattress's comforts that he had either abandoned or altogether spurned. In the end I stayed my hand, already halfway through the bars. It wasn't the time for a first touch. Instead, I straightened and patted my pockets for cigarettes.

The cellar's heat soon peeled me out of my overcoat. There must have been no other house in Berlin as well heated as the Colonel's, and no other cellar so in thrall to a furnace's pent-up fury. The wall was parched by it, a spider's web of cracks running floor to ceiling, with the exception of one corner where a water pipe leaked and bled a patch of wet onto the plaster. It was a curious detail of that winter's work that the poor souls we dragged down into the basement for interrogation or intimidation experienced, in the first few minutes and hours of their stay, the uneasy joy of finally, miraculously feeling *warm*. It was their flesh that betrayed them: after weeks of cowering, it unfurled itself and rose to meet wire, fist or knife with the moronic flush of well-being. In time, no doubt, the Colonel's visitors came to despise the heat, along with the hulking shadow of the cast-iron stove and the smell of dry brick, and began to long once again for the sterile cold of winter.

Meanwhile, my brow and underarms were running with sweat. I was loath to soil my freshly ironed handkerchief that early in the day, so I wiped my brow with my coat-sleeve instead. Still Pavel Richter would not wake. I went back into a crouch and tried to read his features. It was a mystery to me how I should get him to talk. I didn't even know what it was I could say to him.

———·———

In the end I didn't. Speak to him. The whole of that first day. There were no threats I could make and be held to, and I was unsure whether I was allowed to use techniques that left little or no mark on a man's body. Also, his face unnerved me, those dark, teary eyes that shone hard as moist granite. By the end of the afternoon, I began to fixate on his wedding ring. He did not strike me as the kind of man who would cheat on his wife (though all men did, during the war, and excused themselves by their fear of death). It came to be the only question I could formulate. What he thought about his wife. I did not do it very well and he sent me packing. I had hoped he would be polite enough to offer an answer. Then again, it was an unusual circumstance, a dead boy between us, and a lover who slept with the enemy. In any case, when I went home that evening, I earnestly hoped the Colonel would lift his restrictions upon my work. It wasn't that I had any special desire to hurt Pavel, but we needed his secret, and I for one was becoming increasingly curious to learn more about our quiet, patient friend.

———·———

I rose at half past five the next morning, and repeated my morning rituals. Then: a hasty drive, worn tyres skidding over snow-covered roads. When I entered the villa's kitchen, I surprised the Colonel's wife who, dressed in a silky morning gown with an oriental design, was preparing a family breakfast. She gave a start and dropped a butter knife, then collected herself and stooped to retrieve it. Her neckline gaped in response to her movement. I was polite enough to avert my gaze.

'Very sorry to march in on you like this. I trust the Colonel is upstairs?'

She shook her head.

'No. He called late last night and said to tell you he had to fly out to London. And to give you this.'

She wiped her fingers on her gown, picked up an envelope from the top of the breadbin and passed it over by one corner. As I accepted the letter, we exchanged a glance and shared her statement's implication. She had flown in, two days previously, to celebrate Christmas with her husband. Now she was stranded in Berlin, and acting as his messenger boy.

'Anything I can do for you?'

'Why thank you, but no. My husband said his chauffeur would fetch us whatever was needed.'

I nodded my acceptance of the arrangements and allowed her to pour me a cup of coffee.

'I understand you work in the basement.'

'Yes.'

'Feel free to join me and my children for lunch.'

'Much obliged, but I fear I will have to take my meals downstairs.'

'As you wish.'

I wondered whether her coolness came naturally to her, or at some strain. One could adduce arguments for either.

I took my coffee in the drawing room and read over the note the Colonel had left. It added little to what she had already told me. He had left for London, to report at headquarters. I should proceed as discussed. His wife was not to leave the house. He'd return as soon as possible. Kind regards, etc.

The letter seemed to confirm a budding theory of mine, that the Colonel's 'private' activities had begun to draw the attention of his superiors; he might be hard pushed to smooth things over. If so, he would certainly have no wish for the maltreated body of a United States national to surface in the villa's basement, along with a surgical bowl full of toenails and viscera. I was stranded then, with a silent prisoner and no leverage to make him talk. It was a question of breaking him, I guess: I needed to produce in him that peculiar blend of isolation and self-doubt that blossoms in detainees and makes them feel guilty before their jailers. Try as I might, the one thing that kept popping back into my head was the question of his wife.

———————

'Just a name, Mr Richter, that's all I want. A name. It's utterly useless to me. Make one up if you like.'

'Charlotte.'

'Very well, Charlotte. A beautiful name. Is she pretty?'

'It's none of your business.'

'Ah, go on. It's just a conversational question. Nothing in it. All you need to do is say yes.'

But he just stared at me with that haggard, patient face, and waited me out. His eyes, I noticed, were on my boots again. I wished there was some way of getting past his suspicion of me.

'Are you scared, Mr Richter?' I asked after some thought.

He snorted, took a drag on his cigarette, exhaled.

'I saw Boyd's body,' he said. 'I saw what you did to him. That was you, right?'

I waved away the question.

'Half of what you saw was put in place after the fact. The Colonel gave orders, you see, to make it look savage. "Make it look Russian," he told us. Our boys had never seen an NKVD corpse, so it came down to guesswork.'

Pavel gave a nod, but I could see he wasn't listening.

'It was you,' he repeated. 'Say that it was you.'

'We don't want to hurt you, Pavel,' I told him. 'You just have to start talking.'

'You are a coward,' he raged at me, and ground his cigarette into the floor. The voice no louder than if he'd asked a waiter for the bill.

———·———

I kept at him. Asked the same question over and over. The whole of that morning, cigarette after cigarette.

'Is she pretty?' I asked.

He only frowned and told me to 'leave him alone'.

I must have asked a hundred times before lunch. After lunch, I asked a hundred times more. It was mid-afternoon by the time I finally managed to make him respond.

———·———

'Is she pretty?' I asked. 'Charlotte, I mean. Your wife.'

'What is it to you?'

'I'm only asking. Is she pretty?'

He shrugged his shoulders, his brow clammy with the heat. 'Yes. She is.'

'I knew she would be. What does she look like?'

'Leave me alone.'

'All I'm asking is what does she look like? That shouldn't be so hard.'

———·———

'Short, slender. A blonde. Will that do?'

'It's not very poetic, but it'll do. I have a lively imagination. Do you miss her?'

'Leave me alone.'

'I'm just trying to figure it out, Mr Richter. You're decommissioned and there is a pretty wife waiting for you back home. No earthly reason why you wouldn't be with her. And yet you are here.'

He hung his head then, and rolled his shoulders, dark eyes turned inwards, into himself.

'One has to wonder, doesn't one? What the hell are you doing here?'

———·———

It's all I got that day. I tried again, of course, a dozen times over, targeting what I thought to be his weak points – the estranged wife, his passion for the Colonel's whore, his reticence about the midget's secret and the pain his obstinacy had precipitated. The curious thing was that I could see him being affected by my insinuations: his face would flush, with guilt or anger or shame. He never once tried to refute them, but rather listened with a certain receptive eagerness. And yet everything I said seemed to only entrench in him more deeply his refusal to co-operate. On occasion he would rouse himself to retaliate, calmly demanding that I expose myself as Boyd's tormentor and the boy's killer and thus 'accept responsibility'. He never once raised his voice, and was scrupulously polite when it came to thanking me for the food, coffee and water I handed him.

It drained me, this long day of questions. When I thought I couldn't bear it any longer, I set up my chessboard and pretended a game against my brother, who had died long ago from a familiar mixture of patriotism and mustard gas, wedged tightly into some barren furrow of French earth. For every fallen pawn, I forced myself to formulate another question; three for a bishop and a half-dozen for the queen. By the time my king fell, I knew I had to be on my way.

It was past nine o'clock. I stood, drew close to his cage, bid Pavel a good night. He nodded acceptance, sitting on the corner of his mattress, but did not reiterate the phrase. On impulse, I dropped to my haunches, looked him eye to eye.

'All I want,' I said, 'is for us to talk like men.'

He turned away then, and ran a weary hand through his hair.

I walked out without further comment and, at the top of the stairs, switched off the light to leave him in total darkness. The door locked behind me with a pleasing little click.

Upstairs, the drawing room was still alive with occupants, and I stopped at the door for a moment to watch the Colonel's young children at a game of charades: a boy and a girl in their Sunday best, whispering in some private tongue of theirs. The gramophone was spewing forth some opera, drowning out their voices, something dour and German with too much brass. I did not notice the children's mother at first. She was sitting in the shadow of the Christmas tree, stiff-backed upon the couch, with her palms in her lap and her feet aligned beneath her. It was only when she rose to greet me that I saw she was crying.

'Say good night to the gentleman,' she instructed her children. 'Mr Peterson, is it?'

'Yes, ma'am.'

The girl curtsied and the boy shook my hand, both of them doing their best not to stare at my patch.

'Good night,' said the mother.

They had all three of them the most wonderful manners.

———–———

'All I want, Pavel, is for us to talk like men.'

I'd said it lightly, on a hunch, to draw him into me and bait his heart. I wonder, though, how much truth lay in those words even then, in those early days of interrogation. In retrospect, it is hard to imagine a time when my heart was not yet heavy with the thought of him. Something about the man spoke to me: his gentleness, the calm good manners, a man dignified even when passing his water, down in his enemy's cell, and his jailer vexing him with questions.

But this is me talking now, gorged upon the illusions of hindsight. Back then, after my second day spent with Pavel, I lay exhausted, snoring, oblivious still to what lay in store. Wore a nightcap of wool and a triple layer of socks; my alarm clock ticking and a glass of water half-frozen on the dresser, eye-patch hanging off the bathroom hook. At sunup, I rose, ironed my hanky, and planned my next move. Outside, the sun hung low and sickly in the sky, barely clearing the mounds of rubble. I drove to work rehearsing words and strategies, my mind already with Pavel.

———·———

One wonders how he spent the nights, Pavel, haggard, sweating, cut off from all life. He will have searched the cage first of all; run his hands down its bars and rattled the lock. Will have kneeled in prayer, perhaps, his shirt spread out behind his head and shaping Hebrew syllables he barely understood. The conviction must have grown on him, that second night, that he would not be tortured. It may have signalled to him that the Colonel had long since secured the merchandise, and that he, Pavel, was marked for quiet execution. One can picture him coming to terms with it: a bullet to the base of his neck, or the edge of a spade, if one wanted to be quiet about it. A long, dark night, sweating into his mattress's straw; not a wink of sleep, I should have thought, and shy brittle thoughts about Sonia, spelling out words he might have said, but never did.

———·———

When I got down to the basement that morning, Pavel was on his hands and knees. He had found that, in the basement's heat, a bunch of cockroaches had decided to defy the laws of the season and come out of whatever form of hibernation their kind favours. Pavel was crouching over them with delight, watching them dart from shadow to shadow and feed on the crumbs of his previous night's dinner. 'Life,' he told me gloatingly, 'down here in your torturer's den.'

The vision of his dark, moist eyes glowering at me from the cage while insects scuttled across its concrete floor so took me aback that I forgot all about the questions I had been mentally preparing all morning. I excused myself and went upstairs to brew some coffee. The Colonel's wife was there, dressed in her morning gown. There had been no news from the Colonel, and should she butter me some rolls? We talked about the weather, the Nuremberg trials, Germany's capacity for self-pity. Half an hour later I was back in the basement with Pavel.

'Tell me more about your wife,' I said.

He turned his back on me and stared at roaches.

———·———

We said little more for the rest of the morning. I felt tired, uneasy, frustrated. Here we were, our third day in the basement, and I was not an inch closer to the information the Colonel had asked me to procure. At the same time, I was becoming aware of my mounting curiosity. I had, within those very walls, listened to perhaps a half-dozen life stories and taken careful note of them. Now I was eager to learn Pavel's, right down to his private habits and desires. You would be surprised what men part with when under duress. I cast around for something that would hurt him. Sticks and stones, I remember thinking. No words came to mind that would compare to a good old-fashioned beating. Until I chanced upon the war, that is.

'Where did you serve?' I asked.

'What?'

'In the war. Where did you serve?'

I waited while he made up his mind whether or not to answer me.

'The D-Day landing. France, then Holland, going east.'

'Did you kill any Krauts, my friend?'

'Krauts,' he echoed. 'I never liked that word.'

I repeated my question. 'Did you kill?'

'What is it to you?'

'Look who's not taking responsibility now.'

He screwed up his mouth and would not speak further, but I could see I had hit upon a nerve, blood rushing to his face and his hands curling into tidy little fists. Now it was up to me to find out what had got him so agitated about the whole affair.

———·———

I got there through sheer verbosity. Thoroughly bored of restricting myself to the same monosyllabic questions, I launched into a description of my own period of service; told anecdotes, sketched comrades, chattered about the war. I know it was hardly part of the interrogator's handbook, but I must have felt that Pavel was a special case, who would not respond to the usual rigmarole of food deprivation and bright shining lamps. It felt good, I must confess, letting go of prudent restraint. All the same, I watched him carefully, looking for a means to rouse him from his passivity and goad him into some form of self-betrayal.

Throughout my chatter he sat with his back against the bars and his eyes on the roaches, shooting me a glance, on occasion, when I was laying it on a little thick. At long last – we had just eaten our lunch – I paused and stood up from my chair and drew close to where he was sitting.

'But none of this seems to interest you very much, Mr Richter. It seems like you have no stomach for the war. It offends you. You're one of those sensitive types – it's all there in the cast of your mouth – who prefer to shut out the unpleasantries of existence. Let me tell you something, Mr Richter: I take the Colonel over you any day. Not a nice man, I will admit, but an honest one. Looks life in the eye. You walked your way from Normandy to Berlin, a gun in your hand, and now you pretend it never happened. You won't even think about it.'

I spat out a piece of gristle, and hoped to God he would take the bait.

He did in the end, though he took his sweet time making up his mind. Sat sullenly upon the mattress, his head buried in one hand, and pushed tinned vegetables around on his lunchtime plate. Surrendered his cutlery, placed the plate on the floor, and stood. Took two steps and an age to walk over towards the iron bars. His face, I saw, had taken on a peculiarly solemn cast. I remember thinking that the man wore tragedy like a lady wears her stole. It set off his eyes.

'I used to think about it,' he began. 'I worked on a list. All the bad things that happened in the war, and afterwards, in the first months of peace. The very worst of things. I wrote them down just so, unblinkingly. I distinctly recall using that word, *unblinkingly*, sitting at my typewriter late at night, the moon out across from my window –'

He broke off all of a sudden and sat back down on his mattress. I left him alone for a few minutes, his back stooped, the collar stiff with dried-in sweat.

'What was on the list?'

It took hours before he got round to giving me an answer. But then it poured out of him like prophecy.

———·———

I don't think he meant it to. You could see it in his face, those hollow cheeks and knitted brow: how he told himself to shut his trap. '*Not a word*,' he will have sworn to himself. '*Don't you say another word.'* Reminded himself about Boyd. How he got killed, and worse. *'Blue fingertips,'* he'll have told himself, *'and a cigarette burn on his scrotum.'* He took so long dithering over it, I literally fell asleep in my chair.

When I woke, though, there he was, crouching right down by the bars, so low I almost didn't see him at first. He'd already launched into it, his story. For all I know he had been speaking for the past half-hour, the voice so quiet I had to time my breaths against his rhythm.

'Item seventeen,' he whispered. 'Early May 1945. A girls' school in Schöneberg, during the last days of fighting. The teacher tells her class that once they have taken the city, the Reds will rape them. Crawl into their beds at night and rape them. She tells them, "If they rape you, there is nothing left for you but to die." By the end of that week, one third of the class have followed her orders. Dishonoured, they've jumped out of windows, hanged themselves on barn gates or drowned themselves in horse troughs. The rest of them get on with life, defiled. The teacher, too, is raped. She moves in with a Soviet corporal. Now she is married to an American GI from New Orleans. When one of her students bumps into her in the street, she asks her whatever happened. The ex-teacher shrugs. "As you can see," she tells her, "I've fallen in love." She makes the girl a present of some food coupons. They never meet again.

'Item twenty-nine. July 1945. Two children are playing out in the woods. They play a game of hide-and-seek. One of them falls down a little ditch and wakes a million flies. It stinks down there, and an arm is sticking out of the bushes. "Come out of there," cries his brother. "Just one moment." The boy in the ditch finds a boot with something in it, and a munitions belt. He picks it up and plays with it, pulls the pin out of a grenade. The explosion kills him, and busts the eardrums of his brother. He just stands there, the flash has blinded him and the world's gone silent. He stands and screams. It's how his parents find him a few hours later. Later that night the father assures his wife that things are for the best. "We could never have fed both of them through the winter." The boy doesn't hear him; his ears will never heal.

'Item thirty-one. Spring 1946. Two British soldiers in a bar. They are very drunk and hassling the barkeep in bad German. A platoon of Russians come in, three bottles of vodka between them. For no particular reason they stand up for the barkeep. Soon a fist fight breaks out. The Brits, outnumbered and already bloodied, draw their guns. The Russians do likewise, leap for cover behind the bar. Shots ring out. They are so drunk that not one of them hits the other lot. Once they've gone through their magazines, they call it a truce, and finish the last bottle of vodka together. As they step out, ten minutes later, a ring of people has formed around a woman shot through the chest. A stray bullet's hit her through the window. The Russians run for it, but one of the Brits pushes through the crowd and lifts up her sweater to have a look at the wound. There is nothing to be done – she was dead the moment she got hit. "A shame," says the soldier over breakfast the next morning. "She had a smashing pair of jugs." The others giggle, and tell him to shut his trap.

'Item forty-three. January 1946 –'

But I had heard enough. 'Okay, okay, I get your point. Life is hard. All men are greedy, fickle and ungrateful – in a word, they are bastards. Is that what's got your goat?'

He shrugged and held my stare.

'Something like that.'

'What about you?' I demanded. 'Who cares about all the rest? Deaf children and a spoilt pair of titties. Tell me about yourself, Pavel. What did you do during the war, when you weren't busy making lists?'

But he only smiled and turned, and sat himself back on his mattress. I was beginning to ask myself, then, whether I would ever learn a single truth about this man that went beyond the meekness of his smile.

For the next two hours we sat in total silence.

———·——

One wonders did he show them to Boyd, his stories. Type them out up in his room and pass them on to his comrade-in-arms, studying his face for effect. Two men smoking, and the rustle of paper. Boyd's reaction will have been much like mine.

'You're taking it too hard,' he'll have said. 'Live a little.'

The voice a little sore, because Pavel had consistently declined to visit him in his brothel.

It is hard to reconstruct what drew them together, Boyd White and Pavel Richter. I certainly never got to the bottom of their friendship. It could be that Pavel cared more for him now that he was dead. It happens. I have often noticed that the past adds a sense of clarity to affect; in the present, one too often strains to feel anything much at all.

———·——

Towards the end of the day, Pavel started picking on me. He must have been chafing about giving away too much of himself; that burst of words, it smacked of collaboration with his jailer. I could see it in his eyes, a new-found anger that peeked out of his customary serenity and hungered after confrontation.

Things started innocently enough. 'Where are you from?' he asked me late afternoon, sitting on his usual perch upon the mattress.

'London,' I told him before I could think better of it. 'The East End.'

'You don't sound English. I suppose your accent does, but your words – they come from all over.'

181

I smiled, pleased he had noticed. 'I've spent some time on the road. You pick up words, here and there. After a while I made a game of it.'

I know I shouldn't have, but I showed him my little notebook in which I had made a habit of jotting down any curious phrase or piece of slang that I came across.

'See, there's a whole section here for words from overseas. "Dope fiend." "Pussy hound." "Make whoopee." Lots of fine little phrases. I thought they might come in handy some time. For writing stories. I mean, I have seen things –'

I made an unfortunate gesture meant to encapsulate the whole of the world, though from where he was sitting he must have taken it as being directed at the room with its many paraphernalia of pain. 'Things most people wouldn't even dream of.'

He snorted and shook his head. Upon his lips the shadow of a smile, though the eyes were hard as granite. I thought he would speak, but he held on to the silence like a gun, the minutes ticking away and my underwear soggy with sweat. I could have done with a bath then, and a finger of scotch.

'What?' I asked when it was clear he would leave me hanging on his smile, and annoyed now that I had been so open with him. 'A man such as me isn't allowed to take to the pen?'

He pursed his lips like he was about to blow me a kiss. I had never before witnessed his face gird itself for mockery.

'A torturer that tells stories?' he said. 'Or is it the other way round? Are you a storyteller who's turned to torture for inspiration? Is that what you do – flail people's skin, until they stand before you naked? Stealing stories the way rapists steal kisses.

'What good can they be?' he asked. 'Secrets surrendered in order to make you stop.

'Don't lecture me on taking responsibility,' he said. 'There is a reason why I burned that list.

'Some stories,' he said, 'they pass judgement on the teller.

'Tell me what happened to Boyd.

'Tell me,' he shouted. 'Tell me how you killed him.

'Tell me,' he repeated, 'and perhaps we can *talk like men.*'

His eyes aglow like embers in a gale.

I confess I had no patience with his rant and literally ran out of the basement. I even made a point of slamming the door behind me. Mrs Fosko was in the kitchen, a pan of spotted dick steaming in her arms, and gave me the funniest of looks. I caught my breath and told her we had vermin.

She wrinkled her nose.

'Try arsenic,' she recommended and, pudding in hand, stepped through to the living room to cater to her brood. I lingered and watched for a while, soothed by the spectacle of her mother's touch.

———·———

Of course there were things I could have said in my defence. I only thought of them when I got home, rolling around on my mattress during a sleepless night. The thing was: he didn't know a thing about me. Worse than that, he didn't want to know. There he was in his prison cell, his head hung low over things that weren't his to change, and not a thought that I, his keeper, might have my own set of nags and worries, and did I go to town with them? I could have, you see: washed my linen right here in public, and pages at a time, on and on until you loved me, too, who breaks bones for a living. Did I not once have a wife (and who wants to hear about *her?*), dead from cancer, whom we buried under a rough slab of stone, the ground frozen hard and pissy out, too? And did I not hold within my breast the story of my eye, losing it that is, to a chance piece of shrapnel and a doctor's inept fumblings? The horror of easing a finger into my socket and finding it empty, save for some viscous mess which no

183

longer *felt*, let alone saw; and the morning that followed, waking up with a dull throb and an itch, thinking that all that was needed was to open my lid, and there it'd be, God's own sun, bending my eye into a squint (and how I howled when I learned the truth). Oh, yes sir, I have known my share of hardship. A father who was quick with his belt, and would use his buckle, too, if the offence warranted it; a year in service that ended in brisk dismissal and a brush with the law; first passion (a redhead named Ginny, sweet girl, udders like a bloody cow); deep pangs of hunger, like something out of Dickens, and an idiot bar fight that ended with a knife in my thigh. Then: a boat ride to America, at an age when most men had long found their station in life, my stomach heaving for a whole week, only to discover that New York was as big a dump as my native London. A year in jail, an education cobbled together from novels. Raskolnikov as my teacher, Sam Spade and Captain Hook. Rest at ease: I won't bore you with any of it. Mine is a lonely vigil, devoid of sympathy.

———·———

And still I could not sleep. Every time I closed my eyes, his face was there before me, that hollow-cheeked nobility that, once upon a time, I'd thought it my job to realign with fist and sole. It held my attention. The longer I faced his hooded stare, the more I felt my anger evaporate before it. It left something else behind I could not put a name to. As dawn began to break behind the frost-shrouded window, I slowly came to realize that I was no longer much interested in the secrets that Fosko had bid me unearth. For all I knew the Colonel was looking at dishonourable discharge, at military prison, the firing squad. No, it was the man who had begun to move my imagination. Perhaps it was our prolonged proximity that had done the trick; perhaps it had been with me all along – the deep yearning to sound his soul. This was the thought that finally lulled me to a brief hour's sleep: that I had been trying to break a man where what needed doing was more akin to seduction.

'Talk to me, Pavel,' I prayed. 'Just talk to me, and I will make sure this all ends well for you.'

As I slipped into dreams it was as though I already knew the whole of him and had made a home in his heart. I woke up in a fabulous mood.

———·———

Day four or thereabouts: early morning, and dark out. The cold tugging at my fillings, my nose bunged up, every breath a pain. The car wouldn't start and I had to go back in to fetch two additional pails of boiling water; pour them over the hood. The paint cracked under the heat, but the engine caught amidst a plume of dirty smoke. I sat pumping the gas until it'd settled into a regular rhythm, then wrestled with the frozen hand-brake. Wolves howling on my way to the villa, calling it quits on their night-time prowl. There were stories going around about the Russians shooting at them with machine pistols, for sport and for mittens; of soldiers crouching in the snow, peeling the fur off with their hunting knives and grinning like they were back on the parental farm. At the villa, no signs of portent: no news about Sonia, no word from the Colonel, Mrs Fosko uptight like a government seal, though her dressing gown was worn more carelessly with every passing day. Her boy chasing her girl around the living room, and Fosko's chauffeur dropping off groceries, including three dead rabbits for the pantry. I took my time before I climbed down into the basement, nervous now not to screw things up. Pavel greeted me with the ghost of a nod, his chin dark with stubble and rings under his eyes. I ignored him at first, cleaned out his shit bucket, made a show of setting up my chessboard. He, too, was quiet, watched me launch into a solitary game. Black won twice in a row, then a remise. The two of us waiting, wondering who would break the silence first.

—·—

'You don't seem to want to talk today.'

'You didn't ask any questions.'

'Questions or not, yesterday you could hardly shut up.'

He smiled at that, a new kind of smile, open and honest and acknowledging the truth of my words. Hoping that he, too, had decided to make a fresh start of things, I excused myself to make us coffee. I returned shortly and handed him his cup, along with a piece of chocolate still in its wrapper.

'You should try this. It's from England. The Colonel's wife brought it.'

He slipped it between his lips, pulled a face.

'It's awful.'

'Isn't it now?'

I swear to God he nearly laughed out loud.

We sat silent for a while, our tongues busy dislodging shards of sticky chocolate from our teeth and gums. This time he broke the silence.

'What's she like anyway, Frau Fosko?'

'Oh, you know. Mousy. She doesn't have an easy life.'

'I imagine not.'

'If you ask me, Mr Richter, the whole institution of marriage has to be rethought. It's somehow flawed. It isn't fair that one has to choose someone for life before one knows anything at all.'

'One could marry late.'

'That's what everybody says. And then they go and elope with their village sweethearts. Perhaps it's all those radio romances. Giving us the wrong idea.'

'Peterson,' Pavel asked. 'When are you going to stop screwing around and ask me some questions about the "merchandise"?'

There. He had to go and ruin the moment. I had just been

warming to our banter, and he had to bring us back to the squalid real, and in such coarse terms, too. Still, now that I had him talking I didn't want to anger him. The best I could do was to be honest.

'Would you tell me? If I asked.'

'No.'

'So what's the point? We'll get to all that later. There's plenty of time.'

'How much?'

'Oh, plenty.'

'Fosko is away?'

'I can't talk about that.'

'And Sonia?'

I only shrugged and shook my head.

'I wish you'd tell me more about your wife.'

———

Naturally, he sulked for a while before complying with my wish. Whenever he thought to punish me, he would get down on his hands and knees and search his cell for insects. Oh, I got the point. He preferred the company of roaches. It occurred to me that I could march in there and exterminate the lot. It might upset Pavel though, so I left him to it. Eventually, he relented.

'Why do you care?' he asked.

'Just curious,' I admitted. 'Did you get along?'

'By and large. There were disagreements, but no fights. She cried when I went off to war.'

'And then?'

Pavel sat and thought it through, closing his eyes as he did so. His eyelids were very delicate.

'I don't know.

'I hope –' he started, then corrected himself. 'Sometimes I hope she's found herself another man.'

'You don't know? About the other man, that is?'

187

'I haven't heard from her in a while.'

I knew better by now than to push him any further, so I busied myself sweeping out the basement's corners and checking on the heater.

'Are you hungry?' I asked when I was done.

'No.'

'I know what you need. A spot of brandy. Let me just run upstairs and see whether I can find us some.'

He seemed pleased when I brought down not only a half-bottle, but also two finely made goblets. I poured him several fingers' worth and handed him the glass. Our hands touched ever so briefly.

'She's okay,' I whispered. 'Sonia is okay.'

He nodded and sipped at his brandy.

———·———

That afternoon Pavel and I played our first game of chess, his hand reaching through the bars of his cage in order to move his pieces. I insisted on playing white. He must have had me eight or nine moves in – all of a sudden I was in trouble and just trying to avoid his knights. When my queen fell he allowed himself the briefest of smiles.

'Nothing's over before it's over,' I intoned, but two more moves and I had to concede.

'Better luck next time,' he offered politely. I nodded as I packed away the pieces. I like a man who's a good winner.

'Now tell me about Anders. I need to know he's okay, too.'

———·———

I tried to explain to him that I did not know. That I had never even set eyes on the boy. He wouldn't relent.

'Is the Colonel looking for him? Surely you know that much.'

'He thinks the boy's dead. Strung up to your curtain rod. The light was so glum he never noticed the mix-up.'

'You didn't tell him?'

'No. It must have slipped my mind.'

'Thank you.'

I wondered whether he might be mocking me, but his physiognomy was fixed in its habitual sincerity. I felt touched and responded with a curt bow.

'You're welcome,' I said.

I judged it too dangerous to reach out and offer him my hand.

———·———

I left early that evening, pleased with the day's work. Mrs Fosko was in the back garden, smoking a cigarette out in the cold. I waved to her, but she didn't see me. It did not matter. I would tell her in the morning. Right then, I needed to get home and start packing up my things. I had made the decision that afternoon to move in with Pavel for as long as it would take for the Colonel to come back. We should become cellmates, sharing air, food and buckets, the works. Something had begun that day, and I was keen to see it through. The first glimmer of companionship.

Oh, I know what you will say: that I was a fool. That Pavel's newfound willingness to engage with me was founded on little other than his need for information. That it was a change of strategy, for which he chastised himself before the ghosts of his friends. What of it? It gave us a chance to sit and talk and exchange our views. Time would take care of the rest. The soul is a porous thing: it leaks and betrays itself. I left for home that evening, eager for its drippings, and flattered that Pavel should be hunting for my own.

———·———

I moved in the next morning and slowly, gradually, Pavel and I started speaking with greater ease. We played game after game of chess and changed to draughts or backgammon whenever he had beaten me once too often to sit well with my pride. I made him little presents from time to time, mostly of the culinary variety: fresh rolls with butter; apricot jam; Italian coffee from the Colonel's personal stash. Used the good tableware too, English silver and cloth napkins, that I had to pilfer from the display cabinets and smuggle past a watchful Mrs Fosko who might not have approved. Pavel never made explicit his appreciation of my efforts, but I could tell he was pleased. They spoke to his breeding. We smoked a lot as the days unfolded, unhurried now, giving full attention to the rich American tobacco. To help Pavel keep order in his cell, I gave him an ashtray, though nothing heavy enough to use as a weapon. Once, he asked me for a razor, to scrape off his stubble, but this I had to refuse. I relented as far as the toothbrush was concerned, despite disquieting visions of its pointy handle buried in his throat – or mine. A man has a right to freshen his breath. Whenever one of us had to answer his bodily needs, the other turned politely away. He gave me no trouble when it came to retrieving the dishes and buckets from his cell; he'd step back a few yards and lock his hands around the bars so as to make my gun redundant, though habit still bid me draw it from its holster on these occasions. Much of the time we simply sat and talked, always keen to take the other's measure. Our talk turned on violence, more often than not. It was as though there were things in our lives that we had to first clear away before there could be any semblance of genuine understanding.

———·———

'This doesn't suit you,' he told me late one morning, his disapproving gaze upon the long workbench with its leather restraints, and the butcher's apron that hung off a hook not far away. 'How did you get mixed up in this?'

I shrugged, weary of another diatribe about the baseness of my profession. 'Same way everybody did,' I said. 'The war.'

He made to argue, then swallowed it, his face falling in on itself in an expression I could only read as grief.

'The war,' he repeated, speaking past the hand that had risen to shelter his mouth. 'It leads one down some curious paths.'

I studied him for a while with all the sympathy my single organ could afford. Imagine a cup brimming to its fill. Red-rimmed and a little greasy. But still.

'You fought and killed,' I said. 'In the war. Didn't you?'

'Oh yes.'

'It haunts you.'

He lowered his lids and turned away. 'Let's talk about something else.

'Churchill,' he said. 'We could talk about Churchill. I picture him fat and hard like your good Colonel upstairs, stroking his gut while making speeches about a battle on the beach.'

———·——

All that day we talked about the war. First we talked about strategy: soldier stuff, about the bomb in the east, and whether it might have been possible to take Fortress Europe via the Balkans; why the Canadians had failed in Dieppe in '42. Then we turned to life on the front, the coarseness of it, the company of men. 'I looked at these men and thought they were assholes,' he confided during a rare foray into vulgarity. 'I had been asked to go to war and die with assholes. It was a difficult thing to stomach.'

He kept his remarks brief and was elusive as to any specifics. The closest I got out of him to an actual war story was a narrative about sitting aboard his transport ship, approaching the English Channel, and waiting for the U-boats to sink him. Watching the sister ship go down not two hundred yards away, destroyers dropping off depth charges, a thousand seamen standing on deck, waiting to drown in black ocean and the wind so stiff one couldn't light one's cigarette. He could have made more of it

– it's a nice picture after all, but kept to a brittle skeleton of facts. It was disconcerting this, his distrust of story.

We talked about women, too, here and there; how they stood by the side of the road in France, then Holland, then Germany, watching the soldiers' march. And about the soldiers' hunger for women; the violence of their language; the way they reached into their crotches and promised copulation. It led us to atrocity, naturally enough, and from there back into more interesting waters.

'Why did you stop making lists?' I asked him. 'About the things that happened after the war, I mean. You said you stopped. Why?'

He thought about it. A closing of the eyelids, the mouth stretched into a line.

'They weren't true. Everything had happened just as I wrote it down, but they were lies nonetheless. The dead people, the children betrayed, women raped – it didn't mean anything to me.'

Pavel licked his lips and studied my face. I am sure he found in it the sobriety he was looking for. For once he was making perfect sense to me.

'It was as though,' he said, 'I'd put my pen to an outrage I never even felt. And in the war –'

'Yes?'

'I shot at people in the war. I mean I shot them. Shot them dead. I was very good at it. They gave me medals.'

'Did it bother you? The killing?'

'I remember doing it the way one remembers a scene from a book. Anna Karenina jumping under the train. God, how I sobbed when I first read it.'

'Yes,' I sighed. 'I've always loved Tolstoy.'

———

It didn't sit right with the image I had formed of him, this confession of callousness; did not befit the man I saw slumped before me, with his tousled, unkempt hair and his long fingers cupped over the stub of yet another cigarette. A man delicate down to the fibres of his bones. All through lunch I sat mulling him over, trying to make sense of him.

'You cried over Boyd,' I reminded him, my fork listless amongst the peas. 'I was told that you cried. Down in the morgue; cried like a little baby. The Colonel made a joke of it.'

'Yes,' he said, without looking up from his food. 'I cried all right. Only then, afterwards, I set to wondering whether it had just been my kidneys.'

'You don't like yourself,' I whispered.

In truth I was surprised.

He shrugged, as though what I had said was too banal for words. 'Whosoever does? One would be a fool to.'

'How about Sonia? You feel something for her, don't you? The Colonel says she's in love with you. It bothers him, I think.'

'Yes,' he said. 'I feel something for her.'

He did not say anything further. He did not need to. It was stamped into his face.

'Then tell me what I've been asked to find out. Where's the merchandise? Once we have it, I may be able to let you go.'

He shook his head.

'No. I thought I might, but now I won't.'

'Not in a thousand years?' I mocked. 'Proud words.'

He flicked a pea at me through the bars. It bounced off my forehead and plunged straight into my glass of beer, sinking, rising, swimming in a cloud of bubbles. I don't know why, but we both started laughing and didn't stop until I thought I'd bust my gut.

———·———

'You are like me,' I told him later, as we embarked on the first of the afternoon's games of chess. 'Just like me.'

'How so?'

193

'Down here,' I confided, 'we hurt people. I have seen some terrible things, let me tell you. Some of the boys, they go crazy with wire clippers. Men beaten till the bones in their faces start wandering. Burns, the smell of burned skin, it lingers in your hair for days on end. But the truth is – it doesn't really bother me. When I go home at night, I shrug it off like a coat. Inside' – I thumped my chest – 'I am unmoved.

'Besides,' I explained, 'most of these people we pick up – they're bastards. I mean *real* bastards. With some of them, I think they enjoy the torture. Christ, for them it's like a journey to the promised land.'

Pavel gazed at me thoughtfully and moved a pawn. Three moves in, and things were already looking pear-shaped for my queen.

———·———

'You are nothing like me,' he told me in the evening, just as I was settling down to share my first night with him. 'All we've got in common is this –' He used his chin to gesture at the cellar, the cage and the boiler, the cracks in the plaster. 'Other than that, we are perfect strangers.'

'Well,' I said. 'It's something, isn't it?'

'Yes,' he agreed, pensive. 'Something. It's the easiest thing in the world, you know.'

'What?'

'Identifying. It sneaks up on you like flu.'

———·———

The next day he asked me for a sponge, a bar of soap, and some lukewarm water. I brought it down for him and, from the corner of my eye, watched him strip and wash his body best he could. Not that I was queer, either then or ever; but I savoured

194

observing him in unguarded moments, searching his face and body for clues. It still felt like I only knew the half of him. The pallor surprised me, especially around the buttocks and thighs. A swarthy man shut away from the sun. There were a few scars, though nothing dramatic; too red, perhaps, to date from boyhood but all well healed and looked after. Slim hips, a birthmark on the left shoulder blade, crescent-shaped, and a fetching dark line rising out of his pubic hair to form a noose around his navel. He took his time with his wash, and stepped back into his clothes with considerable disgust, frustrated that I had been unable to find him clean replacements.

'Thank you,' he said with great formality when handing back the soap and the sponge, along with the fluffy towel I had fetched for him from the Colonel's laundry. 'And now, why don't you tell me something about the midget? I haven't the faintest idea who he is.'

———

I did, too, tell him about the midget, that is, and in return I received the story of how Boyd had brought Söldmann round in a suitcase. Not in a thousand years would I have come up with the story of the cats! I made Pavel repeat it several times, until I had it memorized.

'Incredible,' I mused. 'Boyd must have heard it somewhere.'

'It's possible,' Pavel conceded. 'But he told it well, didn't he?'

'That he did. What did you do then?' I asked. 'After Boyd left you?'

'I combed the midget.'

'You *what*? Oh Pavel, that's priceless.' And upon consideration: 'How was it?'

'Difficult. His hair had started to freeze.'

He had me in stitches, this Pavel. I could see he took pleasure in my joy, and soon he told me how he'd gone about hiding the corpse.

———·———

Pavel and I spent New Year's Eve together, down in our cellar. I had hoped we might be able to hear some of the fireworks from down there, but either the walls were too thick or the Allies kept their celebrations to a minimum. Perhaps they feared that the sound of explosions, however celestial, would bring back bad memories. I had pilfered a bottle of champagne from the Colonel's larder, and we sat together at my little table, drinking it up before it turned tepid in the cellar's heat. At midnight we shook hands and clinked glasses – proper champagne flutes, I might add, I like to do these things in style. Throughout, I felt I had to keep one hand on my gun holster in case Pavel should try anything stupid. It was the first time I'd let him out of his cage. Pavel behaved like a gentleman, however, and when the bottle was gone he got up wordlessly to return to the cell.

'Thank you for the drink,' he said courteously.

'You are very welcome.'

The bubbly gave me some funny dreams that night, including one where I combed Pavel's hair over and over, looking for lice.

'Find any yet?' he would ask, and I would answer in the negative.

'They must be here,' I insisted.

He just smiled sweetly and let me get on with the combing. He had marvellously thick hair.

———·———

The next morning, the first of January 1947, Mrs Fosko walked in on us as we were having our morning coffee. I don't know how she decided on opening the cellar door. Perhaps she had been curious about it all along. I had taken care to lock the door at night, and had thought my presence alone would discourage her and her progeny from exploring. As it turned out she had more pluck than I had given her credit for.

She had dressed for the occasion, grey flannels and a knitted patterned scarf that set off her reddish hair. Slowly, choosing her steps on the battered old staircase, she came down far enough to catch sight of us sitting on our respective sides of Pavel's cage, a Meissen cup and saucer on each of our laps, alongside some homemade cookies that I had pulled out of the oven very early that morning.

'How do you do?' she breathed, barely audible. She really did have impeccable manners. A spasm ran through her nostrils when they caught our smell. The basement lacked ventilation and no attempt at washing could dispel the odour of prolonged confinement.

I jumped up from my chair, spilled coffee from my cup into my saucer, and started walking towards her.

'Mrs Fosko,' I beamed desperately, casting around for a plausible tale with which to see her off. All I managed was a rather dangerous: 'Would you like to join us for a cup of coffee?'

Mercifully, she declined.

'That man,' she asked instead. 'Is he a prisoner of war?' Her eyes betrayed an intelligence that thus far I'd had no reason to suspect.

'In a manner of speaking,' I answered.

'My husband, he knows that he is down here?'

'Yes, ma'am, he does.'

'Does the prisoner understand English?'

'Yes.'

'Then perhaps I should speak to him.'

To my growing horror, Mrs Fosko proceeded further down the stairs and made her way towards the cage, noting in passing the various instruments of abuse that lay stacked on cheaply constructed shelves along the wall. The heat of the cellar settled on her, and I imagined I could see some perspiration gather by the side of her nose.

'You don't look German,' she said when she was within a yard or two of Pavel.

'I'm not,' he responded. 'Not altogether, that is.'

She reacted to his accent.

'American, right?'

'Yes.'

'I could alert the authorities, you know. I doubt this is legal.' She gestured vaguely at the bars and the room that surrounded them.

'You could,' he agreed. 'I rather doubt that you will.'

'Why?'

'You did not have to come snooping down here to know your husband was a swine.'

She raised her hand then, in a spontaneous gesture of reprimand, before realizing there was no easy way of slapping him short of entering his cage. Her hand, I remember, was gloriously soft and white. She stood like that for a moment, before turning on her heel to face me, the hand still raised as though in casual salute. I was reminded of newsreel images of Hitler, who'd had a similarly casual way of hailing the masses.

'He is a dangerous criminal, no doubt?'

'A threat to national security, ma'am. Half American, half German. A Nazi; unrepentant.'

'He looks it,' she sneered and then walked away, her head held high. At the top of the stairs I saw her wipe the perspiration off her face with a handkerchief she produced from out of one cuff; then she put on the gentle smile that characterized her interaction with her children, and left.

———

'You might as well have told her the truth,' Pavel complained after she had closed the door on us. 'It wouldn't have made a difference.'

'How did you know?' I asked, impressed by his instantaneous judgement of the woman. Thus far, I had been inclined to think her the perfect victim, chafing under her lot; a little cold, it is true, in her demeanour, but nursing great hurt nonetheless.

Pavel did not answer me. It was only later that the thought occurred to me that he could not bear the notion that the Colonel's wife should have been a better woman than his whore; that the one would dare challenge Fosko where the other quite literally bent over backwards to accommodate his every whim. I was about to float the idea, but dropped it. There was little point in endangering our budding friendship with such an unflattering observation. The last thing I wanted was for Pavel to revert to his early sullenness and his mongoloid fascination with his prison's insect life. Better to talk of other things. I settled on what seemed like an innocent topic.

'Did you ever want children?' I asked him casually, intending to lead the conversation to Anders and the precise nature of their relationship with one another. He shook his head, the brow creased with old regret.

'My wife was pregnant once. Before the war. She lost it in the seventh month and swore she would never have another child.'

'Christ,' I said. 'I'm sorry.'

And I was. All the same, it was becoming less of a mystery to me why Pavel was hiding out in war-weary Germany, with no forwarding address.

'Tell me more,' I pleaded.

'What do you want to know?'

'Everything.'

'Everything?' he laughed. 'The last time anybody said that to me, I ended up marrying her.'

———.———

And on we talked. Talked about family, parents and wives, and about sports; his love of books, and mine. No matter how

199

far we ranged, we always returned to the present in the end, trying to piece together events best we could. As the day slipped past, Pavel filled me in on much of what had happened to him since Boyd came to visit, from that first telephone call, to his meeting with Sonia, all the way to that final kiss they shared, though here he was coy about the details, other than stating that it had been 'very nice'. In return for his narrative, I explained to him the nature of Sonia's association with Boyd and the midget, and the parameters of her agreement with the Colonel – in short, the entire network of lies and shady dealings into which he had stumbled by accepting receipt of Boyd's mangled parcel.

How well I remember it all, this time of the telling, when we sat together and traded details, sweat-sodden hair sticking to our brows and always a game board between us, or a deck of cards. I remember his face most of all, the stillness of his face, as his lips formed beautiful, sonorous phrases. The sullen silences that would drop upon him, only to burst into animated talk minutes later: it would blurt out of him all of a sudden, the words tumbling over one another, preening themselves like cats. My own talk hardly compared: clumsy explanations of the whys and wherefores of my protagonists' actions that I tediously rehearsed until I had convinced myself of their accuracy. Pavel listened to it all with a sort of quiet intensity, never interrupting, though he would bid me repeat certain details afterwards, and point out contradictions. At night, before slipping off to sleep, I occupied myself by taking some notes, crude sketches and snippets of dialogue, along-side some vocabulary that I considered characteristic. Already the thought was growing in me of writing it all up, in the years of my retirement that is, filling in any gaps through the exercise of my imagination. Above all, I felt content, stimu-lated, happy. Nobody had ever talked to me the way Pavel did.

It was only from time to time that the feeling returned that he was having me on, which is to say that he was humouring me while his mind was animated only by the most prosaic of thoughts: escape. There were moments, when his face emerged out of the semi-dark to rest against the metal bars for a moment's solace, when all my knowledge of him cowered and fled, and left me empty-handed before the blank mirror of his stare. I would turn on him then, walk upstairs to fetch us beer, or some manner of snack, and try to shake off my doubts in the brisk air of the upper storey. Once, when I thought I had caught him staring at my gun over the backgammon board, I confronted him with my suspicion point-blank.

'You want my gun?' I asked him directly. 'If I gave it to you, what would you do? Shoot me?'

He did not answer, and his silence hurt me more than an affirmation would have.

A half-hour later, however, I had all but forgotten the incident and sunk back into the grateful contemplation of his words.

———

Don't think, then, that I was entirely fooled. Of course, he did not fall for me the way I fell for him. Of course, he faked the intimacy that I genuinely experienced; mouthed words informed by strategy rather than a will for truth. He was my prisoner. What choice did he have in the matter? Then again, the human heart is a complex thing. One can play only at so much before it starts to warm to the role. Time boils it tender, like a steak. Believe me: underneath his anger, there grew in him the seed of sympathy, fledgling at first, but fast taking root. And the words he mouthed – they, too, were true; more so, at times, than he himself acknowledged. After all, here was a man encumbered by strong notions of sincerity. Such a man finds himself continually at odds with the very idea of a lie. At best he can censor himself, starve himself of expression. But what were his options down in the heat of my basement, where we sat bartering confidences?

———

Here is what I told Pavel about the past. Söldmann, I explained, was a German entrepreneur and mobster suspected of selling information to the Russians. He sold all manner of things: the results of Nazi medical research gathered in various concentration camps; the location of underground factories and gold depots; blueprints for an early prototype of the V2. It was unclear how he had come into possession of all this information; either he had spent much of the war cultivating a network of informants, or he must have raided the offices of some very high-level officials in its immediate aftermath. Some maintained he had stumbled upon a whole archive of SS reports in an abandoned warehouse, sealed in boxes and awaiting shipment to the Argentine. More outlandish rumours placed him inside the *Führerbunker*. One Soviet report is said to mention a 'man-dwarf' rummaging around Hitler's private quarters, and making off with a three-volume diary bound in calfskin. If so, the diary has yet to surface. I should imagine it would fetch a handsome price.

Colonel Fosko got wind of Söldmann's business venture some time after commencing his quasi-colonial duties as lord and master of his particular patch of German soil, and soon nurtured a desire to learn more about its particulars. Gaining access to the inner workings of the mob-boss's organization and the precise nature of his 'product' proved remarkably difficult. While he did sell information to the British and Americans on occasion (largely details about illegal Soviet activities outside their sector, about which he seemed remarkably well informed), he had never offered them so much as a scrap of his German material. Undaunted, Fosko made a study of Söldmann's private life and discovered that he frequented a particular brothel in the American sector, owned and run by one Boyd White. As a matter of fact Söldmann had at one time thought about taking over Boyd's modest but profitable operation through a deft blend of money and intimidation. When the two met face to face, however, it quickly became obvious that they were well matched in matters of taste and temperament. Rather than taking away his livelihood, the midget quickly became Boyd's best customer. It gave the Colonel his window of opportunity. What better person to spy on a man than one of the women with whom he shares his pillow?

Now it just so happened that Fosko had recently met a desperate, hungry German girl who sold her labour for food. She had been hired by his driver and sent to clean the Colonel's private residence, which was beginning to show its want of a woman's touch. Fosko emerged from his office one afternoon, bent on the washroom, I gather, only to stumble upon a woman who was cleaning his stairs. More precisely, the woman was on her knees scrubbing the wood with a horsehair brush, her shapely (if somewhat malnourished) bottom turned upward and out, right into the Colonel's line of sight. They exchanged words, it transpired that she was handsome, spoke English, played the piano and was willing to do pretty much anything to advance her station in life. Fosko put her up in a spacious apartment in the heart of Charlottenburg, evicting a family of seven in the process, and had the place cleaned and furnished with a number of choice antiques. The piano was delivered the day after she moved in; along came a tuner, riddled with ringworm but keen to be of service. The woman made no pretence of loving the Colonel, and he asked for none. There was about him an air of mastery that set her on edge, and his corpulence was a cross to bear during their sexual exertions, but all in all I daresay she thought she had made a splendid bargain in a country where unconditional surrender had become the expected mode of life.

After two or three months of this, Fosko approached her with a proposition. He asked her whether she would accept a commission to spy for him. The task would require her to work as a prostitute for a limited period. In return for her cooperation, Fosko offered to obtain a British passport for her – or an American one, if she preferred – alongside a substantial sum of money.

'How much?' she asked.

'Enough so that you won't have to work for a long while.'

They settled on a figure that I estimate at upwards of one thousand pounds. It would not do to think of Sonia as cheap.

She went to Boyd that very same day, asking him for a position in his establishment. He fell for her directly; something about her accent, and the way she held her chin. He rented her a nice little boudoir near Potsdamer Platz and bought her a drawer's worth of silk knickers. This did not, however, keep him from selling her flesh to anyone who could afford her charms – he priced her at a premium rate.

For the first week or so, Söldmann did not seem particularly interested in her. He had formed an attachment to a well-endowed blonde who he swore could do things with her mouth he had never thought imaginable. Sonia placed a call to Fosko, and a few days later the blonde failed to show up at work. In fact she could not be found anywhere in Berlin, much to Boyd's chagrin. I have it on good authority, however, that she was spotted in Hamburg a few days after her disappearance, with a broken nose, two black eyes, and a wrist she carried in a sling. No doubt she was back on the job before the month was out.

Sonia, meanwhile, moved in on Söldmann. Before long the little man was besotted, and forbade any use of her other than his own. He will have known, in the depth of his heart, that he shared his girl with Boyd, a circumstance that put a certain amount of strain upon their friendship. The two of them showered her with presents and swore holy oaths that, very soon, they would take her out of the whoring business altogether.

It was a difficult time for Sonia. She spent her mornings cooped up in the flat Boyd had arranged for her, seeing to his needs and listening to war stories. After lunch they went down to the brothel. She was cordial with some of the other girls. They swapped stories of copulation, shared bathwater, sat around and sipped on champagne. Dinnertime on weekends a nine-piece band would show up and play for the girls as the first customers came trickling in. They played swing; Boyd had hired them in October that year, and paid them with food, drinks and flesh. The band was a big success. Söldmann never skipped a dance. He would arrive a little after nine, two strongmen in tow, and monopolize Sonia from the first. By eleven or midnight they would be off to her quarters to revisit her body's pleasures. But before that, they danced.

Oh, how they danced! You picture it – Sonia standing at the centre of the dance floor swaying her hips to syncopated beats, one leg thrust from a high-slit dress and thrown over the midget's shoulder. The midget, eye to eye with her gusset; shaven cheek smooth against her upper thigh. He'd had a tuxedo cut from maroon silk; a polka-dot bow tie and a pale, plastic rose in his lapel. One hammy fist thrust round to nestle in her buttocks' crack; the other clutching her wrist to his lips. Keeping time with his toes, waiting for the music to rouse him. Then – an explosion of movement – he would spin her from an outstretched arm and jitterbug across the floor, his feet a whirl of two-tone leather. I swear he moved like Fred Astaire. The band got a real kick out of the dancing midget, until that is, the cornet player took to calling him 'Shorty', at which point Söldmann had one of his boys cut a divot out of his lower lip. Boyd never replaced him, though he would come to miss the sound of his wa-wa mute whenever the band launched into some 1920s Ellington. In any case it was a thing of beauty, their dancing. I do not wish to picture their love-making.

While it proved easy to capture Söldmann's crooked little heart, gleaning information about his business dealings was altogether more difficult. The two shared pillow-talk, but the midget seemed more interested in parting with his past than letting Sonia in on the details of his present. Thus Söldmann confided to her, amongst other 'secrets', the sorry tale of his initial rejection by the Party, the closing of his dance hall over the playing of jazz music (an incident that still visibly riled him) and the sly trick that had obtained him his de-nazification papers. Only very gradually did he begin to let slip allusions to his present enterprise. Over time, it became clear that he was in the process of compiling, and putting on the market, some highly sensitive information of a broadly technological nature. In his dark allusions he impressed upon her that it was the sort of thing the Soviets were willing to pay a whole lot of gold for – or, alternatively, would kill for, a warning that Sonia passed on to our mutual employer.

'What is it?' Sonia would giggle over a glass of vintage Chianti that the midget had hoarded during the war and now drank by the case. 'What is this big secret you are selling? Go on, tell me.'

'People,' the midget told her gravely one night. 'I'm selling Germans. The only type of German that's still worth a damn.'

When Fosko heard this during Sonia's evening report, a smile stole across his outsized lips.

'Keep it up, my dove,' he cooed into the phone receiver. 'You're doing good work.'

I wondered sometimes whether he thought that she minded, fucking a midget for money.

The Colonel's objective was very simple: to get hold of the information without either the mob or the Soviets knowing about his involvement. A plan was taking shape that cast Sonia as a sort of double-bait, and Boyd as his frame. I was not entirely sure what motivated Fosko's interest in Söldmann's goods. Presumably he planned to sell them himself, through intermediaries, and grow rich in the process, though it is not impossible that he was genuinely concerned about national security. He and I never talked about matters of principle; I had been hired, off the books, solely to oversee the practical aspects of his various operations, most of which seemed driven by commercial interests. I wore no uniform, nor was I to be found on any official payroll. Those of Fosko's faithful who remained in regular army service treated me with quiet suspicion.

In the third week of Sonia's assignment she obtained what everybody was waiting for: the date when the transaction was to take place. December was at its halfway mark, Berlin lay paralysed with cold. Lying in bed, snug beneath two sets of down duvets and cuddled close to Sonia's fattened-up rump, Söldmann confided to her the details of his plan. She had trouble hearing it all; his mouth was pressed against the small of her back, and the voice barely carried through the layers of bedding.

'Tomorrow at midnight,' he said, 'I'll be rich. I'll retire after this. We can get out of here. I'm thinking South America, or maybe Egypt.'

She asked a few cautious questions and learned that Söldmann was meeting his Soviet contact close by, in the American sector. He said he wasn't crazy enough to venture east, where Germans disappeared every day.

'Will I see you?' she asked. 'Beforehand, I mean. I want to wish you luck.'

He giggled, slapped her arse, and promised he would drop by after ten, to pass the time.

'That,' she said, 'would be swell.'

She would be reunited with her piano very soon now.

When he was gone, Sonia called the Colonel, who told her to come out and stay in his villa the following night.

'What will happen to Söldmann?' she asked.

'Söldmann is no longer any of your concern.'

'Good,' she said. 'I never want to see him again.'

I wonder whether she meant it. It is human nature to grow fond of those we fondle, no matter the reason.

The next night, at ten, Söldmann stood outside Sonia's apartment, his hair slicked back with French pomade and a bouquet of tulips in his arms that had cost him dear. The door stood ajar for him, as it had so many times before. He won't have seen his assailant. The sap struck as soon as he was through the door. Söldmann carried a little leather pouch. Inside was the merchandise. No sooner was it found than the midget was killed. A stiletto thrust to the kidney. The killer threw the body on the bed, threaded two red stars through the holes of his collar, placed a call to Fosko and let it ring one-two-three times. Then he took off.

Don't worry – the nameless assassin, it wasn't me. The Colonel judged me too clumsy for a job such as this: blindsided, my dexterity blighted by gout. I daresay he was right.

Fosko and Sonia had been sitting in his drawing room when the phone rang. He counted off the rings, checked his wristwatch, and then gave Sonia instructions to call Boyd at the brothel. 'Tell him you are in trouble. Tell him you need him there right away. Be convincing, so he can't say no.'

She did what was asked of her. What else could she do? To her credit, she did not go as far as sobbing down the phone. All she said was: 'Boyd, it's me, Belle. I need you. At the flat. Something terrible has happened.'

That's all it took. He promised her he would 'fly like the wind' and blew her a kiss. She thanked him and put down the phone.

'Now, how long do you think it will take him to drive over to the flat?' Fosko mused. 'Three, four minutes?'

He waited for two, then placed another call. This one went out to the police station five blocks from where the midget was filling his coat with blood. The officer on duty answered. Fosko got his attention immediately.

'*Hilfe*. Help. *Mein Gott*. *Das Mann ist tot*. He killed him. A Russian officer. *Ruskie Offizier*. I saw it through my window. It was terrible. *Schrecklich*, my good man.'

He smacked his lips and waited for an answer.

He got one.

'*Ja, ja*.' The German kept repeating it. '*Ja, ja*.'

It made him sound a right idiot.

Fosko hoped it wouldn't preclude him dispatching a patrol. He passed on the address, house and flat number, asking the man to repeat it back to him.

'*Lützowstrasse*. *Neunundzwanzig*. Nine and two. *Ja, ja*.'

When the police officer asked him to pass on his personal details, Fosko hung up.

'Crikey,' he said. 'If I had known they were this dim, I wouldn't have given Boyd any head start at all.'

What happened next is subject to some conjecture, though I did my best to verify the facts. Boyd rushed over to rescue his damsel in distress. The girls at the brothel said he tried to call her back, but nobody picked up the phone. To be on the safe side, he took a gun along. He had his own set of keys, and when nobody answered the bell, he burst in without further ado, gun in hand. What he found was a dead midget: pencil moustache and blood on his cashmere. There was no sign of his beloved. A bouquet of tulips lay trampled in the hallway.

As he stood there contemplating the red stars upon Söldmann's collar, he suddenly became aware of a racket across the road. He went over to the window and looked out. The police were in the street, two, three cars that blocked off the road. Within minutes they were joined by a patrol car full of Russian soldiers. They were busy raiding house twenty-nine. Boyd was standing in house ninety-two. The Berlin street system had house numbers run up one side, and down the other. Twenty-nine and ninety-two were virtually opposite each other. '*Neun-und-zwanzig*.' Nine-and-twenty. The bloody Germans count their numbers

209

from the back. When the Colonel learned this, I thought he would never stop laughing.

Anyway, so there he was, standing in a room with a corpse on the bed and the coppers across the road. Boyd was none too stupid; he figured out where they'd been heading before a flawed translation had tripped them up. The way he saw it, he had five minutes, ten tops. If they found him with a dead man in an apartment rented in his name he was as good as done for – especially if they thought the corpse a Russian. If, on the other hand, all they found was a blood stain on a whore's fragrant sheets, he might just be able to talk his way out of it. So he picked up the body, threw it into the trunk that he had used to move Sonia's belongings, lugged it down the stairs, out the back door, across the yard and over the wall. Thankfully, he had parked his car out back in the first place, from a long habit of caution. The engine caught despite the cold. He did not turn on the headlights until he was well out of the sector.

Boyd drove to a bar, called a friend, had a drink, and shoved off. Outside the snow kept piling up. It made him think of cats, for some reason. To make things convincing he worked over the midget with a car jack in a back alley, and even gave his fender a good whopping. When we searched his car two days later, it really did look like it had been in an accident, though I doubt a midget would have made that big a dent.

Meanwhile, back in Lützowstrasse, watching the shenanigans of the German policemen and Russian Military Police who searched first one house and then – a lieutenant's superior intuition – the other, was a lone man in a car, freezing, and puzzled as to what the hell was going on. He had dropped off his diminutive boss some fifteen minutes previously, and had been instructed to wait for him until he had brought to completion his amorous errand. We have met him before, albeit briefly, on a grainy photograph in the Russian interrogator's office, where Pavel first learned Söldmann's name: a beefy young tough with a handlebar moustache and a big scar running down his cheek. He was the mobster's right-hand man, had been since the organization's earliest days, and answered to the aristocrat name of Arnulf von Schramm, though he was the most proletarian of punters, and stupid to boot. Schramm waited half the night, conscious that his boss had missed his appointment with the Russian. Söldmann never returned, nor did Schramm see the police cart out a half-sized body, which would have settled the matter, albeit grimly. Eventually he drove home, hoping against hope that the mystery would resolve itself. One should have thought he would keep an eye on the situation; track the potential re-emergence of the merchandise, dig around for Söldmann's sources. As a matter of fact, he did none of the above; went to ground instead, and got himself drunk five days running, sliding further out of our story with every swig. I don't regret it. Schramm's people had lost the war. Berlin would tolerate them only at the margins.

While Schramm was waiting in his car, the midget's killer arrived back at the villa, carrying the leather pouch like a bloody talisman. The Colonel subjected its contents to a thorough investigation, the results of which were that Söldmann had carried in his bag what in this line of business is conventionally called a 'ringer'. If he'd carried the merchandise on him at all, he still had it. For a glum few hours Fosko assumed the Russians must have it, since he expected them to have taken possession of Söldmann's body. Some hours after dawn, his informant with the Wilmersdorf police let him know that no corpse had been recovered. It is the only time I have seen the Colonel break into open jubilation. He even went so far as to offer me one of his prized cigars. We sat and smoked and had kippers for breakfast.

From here on in, things should have been easy. Boyd White had the merchandise, or at the very least he had the body. Fosko had Sonia call Boyd midday on the nineteenth of December:

211

'Someone killed Söldmann,' she whispered. 'I found him dead in my bed.'

They agreed to meet in a quiet alley that very evening.

I will keep short the details of my interrogation of Boyd. I had some others help me (the man with the knife was there, and Easterman, the big oaf) and it must be said that Boyd squealed almost at once, even before we had pulled so much as a single nail. The problem was that we did not understand his screeches, and took them for mockery. He kept giving us the same address over and over: Seelingstrasse 21, the apartment on the fourth floor. Fosko got so annoyed after a while, he put a bullet through him, right through the throat, where it made a hell of a hole. Then he instructed us to continue working on the body. He wanted it to look rough, too rough for western hands. There was a lot of racism in those days concerning the 'Asian' propensity for violence. To us, all Russians were brutes, apart from those we met in novels, for those of us who liked to read.

Seelingstrasse 21, fourth floor. We thought Boyd was giving us Sonia's address, letting us know that he knew about the Colonel's set-up. Nobody even dreamed that he might know somebody one floor down, and that Americans keep their floors in different order. I mean, Christ Almighty, it's not something you think about when you are busy sticking wires into a man's flesh.

The rest you already know. We thought we had lost the scent for a while, but then Pavel showed up on the scene, with his kidneys, and Fosko put on that show in the morgue. Now that I knew him I realized it had been naive to assume he would take fright and give up the midget. We thought he must either be a civilian who wanted no trouble, or that he was in on the game and had squirrelled away the merchandise. It turned out that he was something else altogether. *An interesting man.* I loved talking to him.

Boyd, by comparison, did not compare.

I only talked to Boyd once, and even then he had nothing interesting to say.

———·———

On the third of January the Colonel returned from his travels, a few hours after his wife and children had been driven off to the airport in Berlin-Gatow to fly back to England. He returned in the midst of our talking, and was in what can only be described as a crabby mood – a circumstance that changed when he received a telephone call a little later that day that rang like a theatre bell announcing the final act. I was dimly aware that I was partaking in tragedy, and fully expected to find the stage littered with bodies by the time the curtain fell. All I could hope (this must have been Rosencrantz's prayer, and Guildenstern's) was that I would not be one of them.

Part Three

Haldemann

1

25 December 1946

S onia woke early that morning, anticipating the sun by several hours. The room lay dark around her, its quiet punctured only by the monkey's snore. There was, in the first moment of her waking, no memory yet of the previous day's events. She stretched out an arm and stroked the pillow next to her; rubbed her eyes with the base of one palm. When her mind came into focus, she thought first of all of their kiss; held off all other thought until she had savoured it, the touch of his fingers at the nape of her neck. Then it came to her that the man who had kissed her might be dead; might be beaten, bleeding, spitting teeth. She pushed back the blankets reluctantly, found her slippers and pulled a coat over her nightdress. Outside in the corridor, all was quiet; Christmas morning and not a shadow in the stairwell. She returned to her bedroom for a moment to pull on tights and two pairs of socks. Then she climbed down the stairs and put an ear to Pavel's door.

It was his smell that drew her, though she could hardly have said why. There was a vague notion in her mind of lying down in his bed and wallowing in his smell before it dissipated in the cold. She pictured herself, supine across the mattress, sniffing at his underwear, and almost laughed.

'Oh Pavel,' she whispered. 'The things you make me do.'

Her eyes were dry when she said it. She opened the door.

Inside she found the boy, asleep and wrapped in Pavel's blankets. He was wearing a coat made of wolf's fur, much too big for him, its buttons carved out of wood. Above him, at the window, hung a frozen noose in silent invitation. On Pavel's desk Sonia noticed two camera lenses, a pair of scissors, and a military flashlight. She wondered what use they had been put to, if any. She glanced in the waste basket, but found it empty save for a crumpled page of typewritten notes.

The boy was hard to wake. She shook him twice, but he barely opened an eye. His brow was hot and clammy. Sonia gathered him up in her arms, turned to carry him downstairs, then stopped and laid him down on the bed once more. It had occurred to her that she would never return to this room. In Pavel's closet she found one of his shirts, worn and wrinkled. It had been bleached too often and was threadbare at the elbows. She wrapped it around her neck like a shawl, and picked up the boy once more. When she closed the door behind them, he nestled his head against her breast.

'Don't you get comfortable there,' she mumbled.

He was much heavier than she had anticipated.

Upstairs, she tucked Anders into her bed, along with a hot-water bottle. His hat had slipped down over his brow; she made to move it, but found herself reluctant to touch the boy more than was necessary. The boy's teeth were dug into his lips, dark with old blood. She stood for a moment, listening to him breathe through one half-clogged nostril; stooped to lay a hanky next to his grubby hand. Then, another pot of water on the cooker, Sonia stepped over to her display cupboard and retrieved the china teapot. Inside, a pair of Nordic socks. She placed them on top of the dining table, ground coffee beans in a little wooden mill, brewed up. It filled the apartment with the most wonderful smell.

He came in just as she was taking her first sip. It scalded her gums, it was so hot. She must have forgotten to lock the door behind her when she had returned with the boy. The man who entered was hardly more than a boy himself, a ruddy-faced youth in a fur-lined leather coat and similar cap. His eyes, Sonia noted, were almost transparent. It was as though they had been drawn into his face with watercolours; their blue bled into their whites. In his hand he held a gun. It was pointed at Sonia.

'You have fresh coffee?'

His German was good, but she immediately knew him for a Russian. There was not a woman in Berlin who didn't know the accent.

'You forgot your uniform,' she said.

He slid a palm over his expensive coat. 'It is Colonel's sector. Better not be noticed.'

He glanced around the apartment and whistled appreciatively when he saw the piano. 'Nice *Klavier* for *kurva*.' The way he said it, she did not think he meant it as an insult.

'What do you want?'

'Information. We want to know where is Söldmann. And merchandise.'

'Get out.'

He wagged his chin as though he was looking over a horse he was thinking of buying. In his left cheek there bulged a wad of tobacco.

'How about cup of coffee? It is cold morning.'

'I will fetch you one.'

She rose from her chair and walked over to the kitchen. As she walked, she drew her coat tight around her frame. The presence of a Russian in her living space made her uncomfortable. It brought back memories she had long thought banished.

He followed close behind her. When she reached around for a cup, he gently stopped her other hand from clasping a knife. Her eyes appraised the frying pans for their weight and heft while she poured sugar into a dish, but he caught her glance and tutted his disapproval.

'You better talk,' he urged her. 'One of our men is missing. If he's dead, we will kill you.' He shrugged like it was too bad.

'I don't know what you are talking about.'

'*I don't know what you are talking about.* You sound like movie.' He spat, tobacco discolouring his phlegm. It sat brown and viscous upon her kitchen tiles. 'These days, movies full of people who don't know what talk is about. And half hour later they shoot one another.'

He looked at her as though he expected a response; some sort of verdict on the state of cinema. Dinner-party talk in front of a loaded gun. He held it waist-high, the barrel pointing at her abdomen.

Sonia ignored him, threw a dish towel over the gob of spit at her feet. She took hold of cup and saucer, the dish full of sugar, and moved to step past him, back into the dining room. The Russian waited until she was level with him, then pushed her back into the kitchen. Her back collided with a cupboard door and slammed it shut.

'Talk, *kurva*,' he said. His eyes sat like marbles in his knotty head. 'Talk, or I'll make you. You fucked Söldmann. We have pictures.'

It might have been her fear, but she thought she saw his hands inch towards his fly.

The boy saved her. He was there, all of a sudden, pointing a gun with both of his hands. His feverish cheek burned quite as bright as the Russian's.

'Leave her be.'

The voice quivered in its childish timbre. He might have done better, she thought, not to speak.

The Russian began to turn, first one foot and then the other, shoulders bulky under his leather coat. His pistol was still in his hand. On his lips, an affable smile.

'Boy,' he said. 'You want no trouble with me. Not over her. She's no good.'

He said no more, because that's when her frying pan caught him at the back of his skull, twisting her wrist upon impact. He crumpled like a leaf.

'Help me tie him,' she ordered Anders. They strapped him to a chair with some belts and scarves. The blood ran freely from the Russian's head and dyed his blond hair ginger. Up close she could smell the tobacco on his breath and in his sweat.

Quickly, with new-found clarity, Sonia grabbed the Nordic socks from the dining table and unwrapped their content. In her rage she almost burned it: threw it in the oven, and watched it burn. Instead, she started pulling on clothes and ordered the boy to pack a bag for her.

'Take all valuables. Two pounds of coffee, my cigarettes and underwear, especially the silks. The winter coats and all the stockings you can find. The bedding, if you can fit it somewhere. Don't forget the silver cutlery.'

The boy stared at her climbing into her tweed skirt, then did as he was bidden. They were ready to go in less than half an hour.

'Will he freeze to death?' the boy asked at one point, pointing at the Russian. The monkey had climbed onto his lap and was chewing on his coat.

'I don't know.'

She paused. The boy looked at her with burning cheek. 'The monkey might eat him.'

Sonia stood and pictured it. It made up her mind.

'Stick it into a potato sack. We're taking it along. Hit it over the head if it gives you any trouble.'

Then, with their suitcases already waiting on the landing, Sonia dialled Fosko's number. He answered and immediately fell into a rage:

'I told you to leave me alone for a few days.'

'I have the microfilm,' she said.

'What?'

'The microfilm. I have it. Don't bother looking for me. I am long gone.'

He considered this for a moment.

'What do you want?'

'I want Pavel,' she said. 'Unharmed.

'Harm him,' she said, 'and I'll burn the fucking film.'

'You'll trade the film for Pavel?'

'Yes.'

'When?'

'I'll be in touch.'

'God damn it, Sonia. When?'

'When I'm ready. Unharmed, you hear me? I don't take damaged goods.'

She threw down the phone and yanked the line out of its socket.

'And now?' asked the boy.

'Now we run like hell.'

Her last glance, as they cleared the door, belonged to the piano. She would have loved to play it one last time. Inside the bag she had thrown over one shoulder the monkey started breathing deep and heavy. She prayed to God it would hold off shitting until they'd got to where they needed to go.

————

They burst out of the building in Seelingstrasse, ran down the street, rounded the corner, changed sides a half-block down and took refuge in a doorway, piling up their bags and suitcases before them. After two or three minutes' wait it seemed evident that they were not being followed. Quickly, they gathered up their things again, walked a few blocks to the main street and caught the bus in the direction of Wilmersdorf, the driver's face pockmarked and covered in Vaseline against the cold. After a twenty-minute ride they got off, doubled back on themselves on

222

the subway, then jumped onto a second bus, headed for Potsdamer Platz. The snot in Anders' nose had long since frozen and
formed a clammy slug upon his upper lip. Anders put his tongue
to it a few times, probing its dimensions and flavour, until Sonia
caught him at it and wrinkled her mouth in disgust.

'Sorry,' he mumbled.

She shrugged her shoulders and turned to stare out of the
window, her face growing hard whenever they passed a uni-
formed soldier. A grubby old man pushed between them from
behind and tried to sell them his record collection of *Volkslieder*.
They got off the bus a few blocks south of Friedrichstrasse.
Anders still had no idea where they were going. All he understood was that Sonia was trying to save Pavel. He followed her
meek as a lamb.

They walked for maybe ten minutes, their suitcases banging
against their knees, then stopped in front of a building, or rather
half of one. The other half had been bombed away with astonishing precision. The rubble still stood more than man-high,
pipes and cables sticking out of the brick. Up above, a cut-in-half
living room clad in floral wallpaper, its cut-in-half floorboards
sticking out ragged beyond the edge. Anders half expected to see
a cut-in-half maid, serving out half a Christmas lunch. His fever
was making him giddy.

Sonia chose a bell and rang it without hesitation. Anders saw a
net curtain move in one of the windows of the ground-floor
apartment. Moments later the door was opened. A fat-arsed
whore stood waiting for them on her apartment threshold. She
was wearing a dressing gown and sucking on a cigarette's soggy
stump.

'Franzi. Are you alone?'

'You? What the hell are you doing here?'

'Are you alone, Franzi? You don't have a customer in there, do
you?'

The whore shook her head.

'No. I stopped working at home a few days ago. Can't afford the heating.' She looked Sonia up and down. 'What the hell happened to you?'

'Let us in.' Sonia flashed a wad of dollar bills that she pulled from out of her breast pocket. Without another word, the fat-arsed whore opened the door and led them into her apartment.

Inside it smelled of cheap alcohol and sweat. The woman had been having her breakfast: *Ersatzkaffee*, a quarter-bottle of schnapps, and what looked like a corner of mouldy *Speck*, all laid out on a patchwork of tablecloth riddled with cigarette burns.

'Make yourselves right at home. I'd put the kettle on, but I'm out of coffee.'

Sonia got right down to business. Stood calmly at the centre of the shabby room and issued her orders. It reminded Anders of Pavel, his encounter with Paulchen's gun.

'I want you to leave town,' she said to the whore. 'Just for a few weeks. I need the apartment.'

The woman laughed. 'Oh yeah? Just for a few weeks? That's a good one.'

'I mean it, Franzi. How much will it cost?'

Sonia counted off fifty dollars and placed them next to the schnapps bottle. The bills looked crisp and tidy against the ruin of the tablecloth.

'Fifty American dollars. Well, I'll be buggered. You really do mean it, don't you?'

'Yes.'

Franzi reached out a hand and touched the money.

'I could use a vacation,' she said cautiously. 'Got an auntie just south of the city, in Trebbin. It'd be nice to be with family for Christmas. Homey, you know, bake cookies and shit. You really do mean it, don't you?'

'Yes.'

'You need a place to lie low?'

'Yes.'

'It'll cost you more than this.'

'How much?'

They set to haggling. Anders could hardly stand to watch it – the whore was taking Sonia for a ride. Within five minutes she had signed over to Franzi some six pairs of knives and forks, a pearl necklace, a silk dressing gown and sixty-five dollars in cash. Fat-arse was pleased as punch. She even gave Sonia a sisterly hug and offered her a sip of the schnapps.

'Call your aunt,' said Sonia. 'Tell her you will be on the next train out. You have ten minutes to pack. And Franzi – I will walk you to the station. Help you with your luggage.'

'No problem, darling. I quite understand. Let me just get my things together.'

'My, my,' she whistled. 'Who would have thought it? Christmas morn, and guess who comes snowing in, pretty little Belle, and her pockets full of dough.'

The boy heard it and chewed his lip. Nobody had told him that Sonia went by more than one name. He wondered whether it changed things between them.

———·———

The train to Trebbin left from Anhalter Bahnhof, not far from Franzi's flat; they walked through the cold and joined the queue for tickets. The station had no roof, the leaden sky rising out of its serrated walls. It looked like a refugee camp. People wrapped in coats and blankets sitting on suitcases; children milling, begging for scraps; the hall noisy with the impotent anger of malnutrition. Two thirds of the crowd were women, the normal ratio in Berlin's blood-let streets. They looked mannish in upturned trousers and straight-cut coats; bitter women and gentlemen's Sunday suits, the main survivors of six years of war. Sonia felt out of place in her tweed ensemble and heels.

'Where're they all going?' she wondered aloud.

'Hunting for food. There's a rumour going round that some of the villages have butter to spare.' Franzi gave a snort of derision. 'Like shite.'

A child passed them, her feet wrapped in newspapers and rags. Her toes were blackened with frostbite. She was following two smoking soldiers, waiting for them to toss their butts. Her hand was already clutching some five or six. Sonia wondered how many she would need to buy herself a pair of shoes.

At long last they reached the counter. Franzi bought a ticket, third class. First and second class had ceased to exist since the war. It was a full hour's wait before the train would leave, but Sonia refused to return home.

'I'll see you off,' she said tersely. 'The trains aren't very reliable these days.'

Franzi snorted. 'You don't trust me an inch, do you now?'

'Franzi, I know you've never liked me, and I know you can smell that there's money to be made here, one way or another. But if you tell anyone I'm in your apartment – if you so much as breathe it – then I will die, and that boy will die, and you'll be the one who's killed us. It's as simple as that. I can't keep you from taking the next train back; and I can't keep you from using the phone once you are in Trebbin. All I can do is ask that you be content with what you've already got and leave it at that.'

'You countin' on me being a Christian, Belle? That's sweet.'

'I am counting on you to stand by our deal. That's all I ask.'

'This has to do with Boyd, right? He's dead, you know. Shot, they told me.'

'I know.'

'Did Shorty kill him? The one with the maroon tux? He was real sweet on you, that one.'

'I don't know who killed Boyd.'

'Now that I'm thinking about it – there was somebody looking for you, a while back. Dark eyes, a little moist; manners like he

226

had a broomstick up his arse. He said he and Boyd had been friends in the war.'

'Did you tell him about me?'

'Just where you lived. I wouldn't have said more.'

'No? Why not?'

'Didn't like the type. He thought himself special. Airs and fucking graces. Comes calling on a woman and never even took a look at me.'

'Perhaps you two just didn't get along?'

'Oh, I don't know. I talked and he fed me ciggies. You could say we got along just fine.'

The train arrived and the two women climbed in and found Franzi a seat. The compartment was packed with a Pomeranian family; thick eastern accents and grandfather's chequered hanky bloody with TB. As Sonia stood, stuffing a suitcase into the overhead luggage rack, Franzi suddenly seized her by the waist.

'I won't tell anyone,' she said fervently. 'About you being in the apartment, I mean. I promise. Us girls, we gotta stick together.'

She squeezed and kissed her as though they had been lifelong friends.

Sonia was unsure whether to be touched by her bout of sentimentality, or see it as but another symptom of a life so very barren of tenderness, one had to invent emotion, against all the evidence. She left the train with the final whistle, and stood on the platform as it rolled out of the station. Then she made her way back to the apartment, making sure to walk to the end of the block and double back on herself before she went in. There was no sign of a pursuer. Her face and hands were so cold, it was as though they were on fire.

Inside waited the boy. He stood stiffly by the kitchen table. On the table top, close to his hands, lay the gun. Anders' eyes were ringed black with exhaustion.

'Belle,' he said. 'That woman called you Belle.'

227

'It used to be my name. For a little while.'

'You were Boyd's woman.'

'Yes, I suppose I was.'

'Did you kill him?'

'No.' She shook her head. 'But I never cared for him.'

The boy thought it over, chewing his lip.

'That's okay,' he said. 'I didn't like him either.'

He shoved the gun into one pocket, sat down on a chair and huddled deeper into his coat. Sonia could see he was running a bad fever.

'What happens now? Do we go and rescue Pavel?'

By way of an answer Sonia pulled the reel of microfilm from her coat pocket, unrolled half a foot and held it up to the kitchen lamp. They both stared at the film for several minutes, getting closer and closer until their eyes were inches from the bulb. It was impossible to make anything out.

'We need to find out what's on the film.'

'Why? Why don't we just trade it in for Pavel?'

'Because Fosko will kill us as soon as the film is in his possession. We need somebody to help us. And for that we need to know what's on the film.'

She wondered whether she believed it herself – that knowledge would point a way out of this mess. Perhaps she was being greedy. It might be that she couldn't have both: her life and Pavel. *I'd choose life*, she thought grimly. She wasn't ready yet to admit it to the boy.

'So what are we going to do?'

'We need a projector. Something to help us see.'

'Like they use at the movies?'

'Yes, but a different size.'

She thought about appealing to the Americans for help, some officer who had crossed her linens during her life at Boyd's, but decided it was too risky. The army might confiscate the film and send her packing.

'Do you think I can get something like that on the black market?' she asked.

The boy shrugged and settled back into his chair.

'I can go look,' he offered.

'You are sick.'

'I'm not sick.'

'You are sick. Tell me where to go, and I'll do it now.'

'But I'm not sick.'

He fell into a sulk and stared at her through screwed-up eyes. Minutes later he fell asleep. It was like somebody had reached into him and turned him off. He did not wake when she carried him over to the bed and piled blankets on top of him. Sonia held his hand for a while as he was sleeping, then let it go and turned her back on the boy. The monkey was watching her from underneath the sofa.

'I don't need this,' she said to herself and rummaged around for some alcohol. 'Playing nursemaid to a street urchin.' There was a half-bottle of kirsch liqueur in the kitchen cupboard. She drank it from a thimble-sized shot glass and passed the time counting the flowers on the wallpaper print. At length she fell asleep herself, and only woke when the oven had consumed the last of its fuel and the room temperature had dropped another two or three degrees. Her cheek felt as hard as the wood it rested on. Sonia cast around and found a small pile of firewood beneath the sink. It took several minutes to relight the oven. Once the wood had caught she sat with her palms pressed to the oven's metal, shivering. Wet smoke curled from its open grill and made her eyes water. Soon after she found that she was crying. This flat, it reminded her of a life she had thought to have escaped when she was taken up by the Colonel. She had become a whore since then, had paid her way with mouth and lap, but this was worse, freezing in a shabby room, cheap kirsch burning in her stomach. The indignity of poverty. The boy moaned in his dreams and she swore at him to be quiet, muffling her voice with one hand. The tears kept coming and she cried herself back to sleep, curled up next to the oven. In the shadows, the monkey came to life and chose her body's warmth for company while it examined its fur for parasites. Once, late that afternoon, it bent down low over her face and rolled back its lips to reveal yellow teeth.

Depending on how you looked at it, it was either making to kiss her, or to bite off her ear.

————

The police picked up the watcher's corpse at dawn. They found him in an alley in the American sector. He had no papers, and his face had been severely mutilated. There was no means of identifying the deceased, and they shoved him off to a morgue for holding. A call came in an hour later ordering the city police to report all recent 'incidents of violent death' to one General Karpov. Naturally, the station sergeant obeyed. By ten o'clock a Russian forensic team had transferred the body to a Friedrichshain lab, along with two other murder victims who had been discovered that morning: a corpulent youth, and a gaunt man with an SS tattoo specifying his blood group. The lab technicians compared their teeth against the information in the file Karpov had sent over, then checked the ears against a morphological chart. The man without a face was a perfect match: Sergei Semyonovich Nekhlyudov, thirty-six, special adjutant to General Dimitri Stepanovich Karpov. The photo in the file showed a melancholy man with dark hair and red-rimmed eyes. They hadn't opened him up to have a look at his liver, but judging from the tangle of veins that bloomed upon his photo's nose and cheeks, one could surmise that the man had liked his liquor.

A lab assistant called the General's office with the news. A clerk answered the phone.

'The body matches.'

230

'You mean Sergei Semyonovich is dead. How did he die?'
'Knife wound to the chest.'
'Thank you, comrade. I will inform the General.'

———·———

All this on Christmas Day, 1946. At this point, Pavel and I, we weren't yet talking – a dozen cigarettes ground into the basement tiles – and I was ignorant of Sonia's flight and the pathologists' melancholy labour. I found out after, through persistent questions and the reading of stony faces. 1947 it was by then, the smells of spring. One might have thought spring would thaw it out, our Berlin, but the city remained bitter and hard, a gut-shot Medea, crouching on her children's grave.

2

26 December 1946

The boy's fever had fallen overnight, but he remained in no condition to leave the apartment. She made it clear to him that she would go to the black market that day; he could advise her on whom to approach or choose not to, but either way she would go. He held out for half an hour during which she made sure to mention Pavel's name half a dozen times. Then he spilled.

'Paulchen,' he said. 'You could go and see Paulchen.' He gave her an address back in the English sector.

'What do I tell him?'

'Give him this, and tell him I'm sorry.' He passed over his gun. 'If anyone can find a projector, he can. On the quiet, too.'

She nodded, rummaged around for a pair of scissors, then cut off a few centimetres of microfilm so Paulchen could check the width. She put the reel back into the desk drawer and turned the key on it.

'Don't go picking the lock. We both want the same thing.'

The boy made no sign of having heard and watched her gather her things, teeth busy with his dirty nails. She was almost out the door when he stopped her.

'You promised me you wouldn't fall in love with Pavel.'

He had to say it twice: his voice broke.

'So?'

'Do you love him now?'

She wet her lips, then nodded.

He shuddered and ran a hand across his face in a terribly adult gesture of grief.

'When I last saw him he was carrying Schlo', and Schlo' was dead, and I couldn't even tell him I was there.'

'You'll see him again soon.' She forced herself to sound confident. 'I promise.'

He looked at her from between his fingers. 'You're not like him. You don't keep your promises.'

Sonia had no reply. She stepped out into the hallway and locked the apartment door behind her.

—·—

Sonia walked the long way to the boys' hideaway, hoping she would not be asked for her papers as she entered the British sector and hurrying down streets she had fled only the previous day. When she got to the building, her scarf drawn high into her face, she stood and watched it for a while to make sure it was not under observation. In the end the cold subdued her caution. She approached.

The building's door was framed by man-sized piles of rubble, snow-choked and angular. Beyond the unlocked door, a glum, battered staircase wrapped itself around an empty elevator shaft. Its banister had been stripped for firewood, along with half the steps. The walls were spotted with bullet holes and angry scrawls, chalky etchings of a thousand cocks. She climbed past them to the top floor as she had been instructed. A sentry sat planted before the attic door, shivering in a *Wehrmacht* coat. He was a boy of twelve, with filthy hair and an army knife on his belt. The left side of his face showed signs of a recent beating.

'What do you want?' he snarled.

'I need to talk to your boss.'

'He's busy.'

Sonia had no time for this, and pulled the gun out of her bag. 'I'm just returning something he mislaid.'

The gun's barrel pointed to his feet, but the boy complied without need for further threat. He opened the door.

'Some cooze to see you,' he hollered ahead, 'and she's packing.' The words sat awkward in his child-mouth. They may have been recent acquisitions.

She brushed past the boy and stepped into the attic, noted the wall with its map and Hollywood pin-ups, the rows of mats and blankets, the well-stocked coal bucket and smell of corned beef. A dozen cocktail glasses sat in a crate near the window, next to a cabbage and a cast-iron casserole all bent out of shape. Paulchen, too, was in a sorry state, the face bruised, his arm in a cast, and some teeth missing, right up front, where one took notice. He sat upon his armchair, feet up on a ragged ottoman, and an iron cross pinned to his scarf. There were no other boys around.

'Anders asked me to return this to you.' She indicated the gun, but made no move to hand it over.

'Give it here.'

'Later. I need something from you.'

'Oh yeah?'

'Yes. And I can pay for it.'

'How much?'

She placed thirty dollars onto the ottoman, along with a silver brooch.

'This, for starters. My watch, when I have what I want.'

She held it up to the window's light, so he could see the stones were real. The boy with the knife whistled in appreciation. Paulchen's face did not betray any emotion. Perhaps it hurt to move its muscles.

'What do you need?' he asked.

'Some sort of viewing device for film.' She placed the snipped-off negative next to the money. 'I brought you this so you'll know what size.'

234

He looked at it without moving in his chair. She wished she had a way of telling what he was thinking.

'Okay,' he said. 'This might take a little while. Where do I find you?'

'How long?'

'I don't know. Film like this, it's used by the military. I'll have to pull some strings. Could be a while. You think you can get it faster elsewhere, you just go ahead and try.'

She paused, then nodded her acceptance.

'Where do I find you?' he asked again.

She pointed to the telephone that was standing on the floor next to his armchair. 'Does that work?'

He nodded yes. 'Bought the line off a doctor downstairs. He said he didn't need a phone if he was going to starve.'

'I'll call every day. The faster you get it, the more I'm willing to pay. What's your number?'

Somewhat reluctantly he gave it to her. She placed the gun on the floor and turned to leave. As she was walking out, Sonia reminded herself that this was where Anders had lived for many months. It was a shabby, ugly space. No wonder some of it had rubbed off.

Sonia went shopping on the way back, making sure to leave the sector before she went looking for a butcher's shop. The queue took a good hour, and when she finally made it to the counter, the butcher was suspicious about how many ration cards she produced. He held them up against the light with bloodied fingers to check they weren't forgeries, then accepted them along with the dollar bills she'd stuck between the cards. Behind the counter sat a vat full of pig's trotters. A snout stood upright on the counter scales, blond hairs cresting the pale and puckered flesh. It reminded Sonia of the day, during the battle for Berlin, when dawn had revealed a dead horse stretched across the sidewalk just outside her building. She and her neighbours had picked it clean. Ran out of their basement hideaways with paper scissors and cut-throat razors; cut chunks out of its body until all that remained was its bones, its hoofs and a tangle of entrails. Young girls running down the street with a strip of horse flesh in each fist, happy; their arms bloodied to the elbow. Sonia hadn't entered a butcher's shop since without picturing the scene. She wondered whether she ever would.

'You want all this?'

'However much you've got. But no trotters.'

She walked home with five pounds of liver, a side of streaky bacon and a big slab of wurst. A bakery sold her a two-kilo loaf of black bread and a dozen rolls. There was a risk that they would remember such an affluent customer, but this way she would not have to leave the flat until Paulchen had found her a projector.

She could only hope that Fosko would not kill Pavel out of sheer frustration before then.

———·———

When Sonia was gone, Paulchen reached inside his coat pocket and produced a piece of paper with a telephone number. He sat staring at it for a little while, then reached down to the phone with his good arm and pulled it up onto his lap. It rang four or five times before a woman picked up.

'Margaret Fosko speaking,' she said. 'How can I help you?'

'*Ich möchte mit dem Herrn Colonel sprechen*,' Paulchen said formally.

'Oh, I'm afraid I don't speak any German. The Colonel is out.'

'*Herr Fosko?*'

'He's out. *Aus*. Won't be back for a week or so. *Eins Woche*. You understand?'

'*Ja.*'

'Can I ask who's calling?'

'*Was?*'

'Who are you? Your name?'

'*Sagen Sie ihm ich hab' seine Hure.* His woman. I has his woman.'

'Well,' said the voice, 'I'll make sure to tell him if I see him before I leave.'

'Who'd you call?' Gunnar wanted to know once he'd rung off.

'The English Colonel.'

'The ped-i-rast? Why you call him, after what they did to us?'

Paulchen closed his eyes. He remembered how they had burst into the flat, four or five men; Woland, on guard, pistol-whipped across the face. They wore no uniforms but made no effort to disguise their English voices; kicked over the Christmas tree, barked questions, slapped faces. Remembered, too, how one of them, a big bruiser, broke his arm against the corner of the windowsill. He'd lined it up and kicked it through, the way one breaks a piece of wood. The arm hanging at an angle, blood rushing into the break.

'You hear anything, you call this number,' the Brit had told him with the thickest of accents. 'You hold out on the Colonel, and I'll come back for you.'

He'd stuffed a thumb through the gap in Paulchen's front teeth and trapped his tongue underneath. 'Don't think we won't know. Berlin is our city now.'

Paulchen just lying there, trying to scream, his tongue trapped in his own mouth.

'The Colonel, he will pay us more than the woman can,' he told Gunnar.

The boy nodded appreciatively. 'Smart play, boss. Do you want me to go looking for a projector anyway?'

'Don't bother. A projector like that, that's military issue. We don't want to be messing with that.

'The last thing we want,' he said, 'is the Russians come calling too.'

237

Said it, and sat back in his chair, scratching the skin near the rim of his cast, wishing to wash his hands of the matter, and for Fosko's speedy return.

———·——

This is what it came down to then: a long wait for the Colonel. And while Pavel and I sat trading words, the city reclaimed them all, the boy and the woman and the gang of child toughs, prised them loose from the excitements of espionage, and returned them to the calmer rhythms of survival: the prerogatives of food and drink, the patient feeding of their ovens' blaze; ration cards and the constant trips to the water pump, a life by the bucket load, and always the pain of the freeze. For Paulchen and his crew it was a time of healing, and a return to the routines of the black market. Tinned sardines for butter, the butter for bicycle parts, the bicycle for a travel pass, the pass back into sardines, a profit margin of eight hundred per cent. Once daily, Sonia's phone call, a good half of them truncated by the whims of Allied electricity; a terse answer in the negative; her impotent threat that she would not wait much longer. In her flat, too, a period of calm, Anders sick and she herself ablaze with cabin fever. They sat together in silence, awkward in the roles that fate had dealt them; then turned to talk, from boredom and the need to understand the other's love for Pavel. It started over dinner one night, an awkward question and over-blown answer, range-finding on the battlefield of their relation-ship. I don't know whether they ever worked them out, their feelings for one another. In this perhaps they kept to convention: mother and son, forever held hostage by the cruelties of birthing.

———·——

They sat having dinner. She had fried two pieces of liver along with half an onion. There was bread and boiled potatoes on the

238

side. Anders did not have much of an appetite but forced himself to eat anyway. He remembered, all too vividly, the day when he had tried to feed Pavel on what he'd held to be his deathbed. It had been innards then, too. He chewed slowly and smuggled the meat past his swollen tonsils.

A record was playing, a woman singing something foreign. Franzi owned a gramophone and a few dozen records. Sonia had gone through them several times, putting aside three or four she liked. Whenever the record stopped, she got up and moved the needle back to the beginning. She did not seem to like silence.

Anders wasn't comfortable with Sonia. She kept watching him. Every time he looked up, her eye was on him. He had pieced together a few things about her: that she must have lived with Boyd, but worked for the Colonel, whom he had failed to shoot. That the *mit-chut* was involved somehow. That she sold herself for money.

'Did he force you to do it?' he asked all of a sudden. 'The Colonel, I mean.'

Her fork stopped halfway between plate and mouth. The piece of liver, seen in cross section, looked grey. There was a sliver of pink at its centre.

'Do what?'

'You know – going with Boyd and all.'

'You ask too many questions.'

'He paid you to do it, right? You could've said no.'

Sonia pushed her plate aside and stared at the tabletop. The record finished, and this time she made no move to restart it. Anders wondered whether she might be crying.

Why should she? he marvelled. *I didn't say nothing bad.*

'Did I say something bad?' he asked her after a while. 'It's not what I meant.'

She looked up then, and her eyes were dry. 'You really don't know, do you? How it is. You're too young, I guess. Good God, the way you sit there, dangling snot into your dinner – who would ever believe that a few years down the road you'll be one of them.'

'One of who?'

'Men. We'd all be better off without them.'

'Why?'

The question shot out before he had time to swallow it. He felt it gave him away somehow, made him look childish. Still, it slipped out, and he was keen for an answer. 'Why?'

She sighed and took a deep breath.

———

It wasn't something she could explain. She took refuge in platitudes, launching into a speech about men controlling women's lives: second-hand truths inherited from her suffragette mother and her claque of liberal friends. She told him that as a woman she could not rent an apartment or buy a car without a father or a husband signing for her; that she could not cross a border without papers that were issued by men. 'A man decided whether I was a Nazi or not,' she told him, 'while he shot glances at my breasts across his narrow desk.'

She stopped herself short and studied the boy. He sat, untouched by her ramblings. She wanted to drop the conversation, but found herself asking a question instead.

'Do you know what sex is?' she asked. 'Love-making?'

He nodded. His teeth were in his lip.

'It's like a disease. It takes hold of them and won't let go. When a woman steps near, you understand, and there is a curve to her body, just so' – she stroked her flank where torso gradually widened into buttock and hip – 'Christ, it well near eats them up.'

Sonia pulled a face, then smiled.

'But I'm telling you fairy tales. Ghost stories, is what I am telling. Here, let me put on a new record. It's Glenn Miller, who plays trombone. My grandmother used to say it sounds like a god breaking wind.'

They sat and listened to Miller for a while. Every time the trombone set in, the boy shifted to one buttock and made as though to fart.

———·———

Later, over tea and milk, he told her he wouldn't get mixed up with sex.

'I won't,' he said sulkily. It made her laugh.

'Won't what?'

He sat in silence, searching for words.

'I won't be mastered like that.'

She swallowed her laugh and watched him spoon sugar into his tea. He used so much of it she would have to get another packet soon.

———·———

'Where did you learn to speak like that?' she asked him as she stood doing the dishes in Franzi's cramped little sink. '*Mastered.* It's a bookish word. But you don't read.'

He sat there chewing his tongue. 'Should I say it different?' he asked.

She shook her head.

'No,' she said. 'I think it's one of the reasons why Pavel loves you so.'

He looked away at that, and she pretended not to see the tears that sprang into his eyes. He might have accepted some comfort then, a hug or a brush of the cheek, but she didn't find it in her heart to reach over and touch him. She poured more tea instead, and made him drink it. When it was all gone, she went out to fetch more water from the pump and suggested he wash, despite

241

the fever. The boy smelled to high heaven. Anders acquiesced when she promised that she would not come into the bathroom while he was in there getting clean.

'God knows,' she murmured to herself, 'I have seen enough peckers in my life.'

He surprised her by singing as he stood naked in his wash bowl, sponging himself with Franzi's lavender soap. He could barely hold a melody. The monkey joined in, and between them they made a right racket. While they were thus occupied, Sonia went through Franzi's wardrobe and found a pair of men's briefs that she laid out for the boy to wear. His own underwear was soiled beyond repair. She threw it out along with the undershirt, then washed her hands with soap. If Pavel had been there, he might have taken care of such domestic duties. She tried to picture him, to remember his hand on hers, but all she could conjure was the myth of their love. It was devoid of content: three brief kisses and some half-hearted admissions; the pressure of his erection against her body. It did not suffice for mourning. Moodily she searched the apartment for booze, but all she found were empty bottles. She tried smoking instead and noticed she was running out of cigarettes. There was no piano to play, nor any books to read. She sat around on Franzi's well-worn couch and asked herself what she would do once Paulchen found her a projector.

The boy came out of the bathroom and got into bed. She put a hand to his forehead an hour later and noticed his fever had risen again. Sleeping, his face looked particularly ugly, screwed up and wrinkled like the monkey's. It might have been easier to care for a handsome child.

Sonia left the apartment to go for a walk. The cold taut on her skin and in her joints, forcing itself on her body. She entered a bar, charmed cigarettes off an American journalist and drank chocolate liqueur, the only alcohol on offer. When the barman suggested she might want to go home with him and warm his bed, she called him names and stormed out. It wasn't that she was upset about his offer. She had simply learned that one needed to be emphatic in one's refusals, lest one be misunderstood.

———·———

Early the next morning, Sonia called Paulchen to see whether he had got hold of a projector for her yet. He hadn't and sounded annoyed.

'It'll take a few days. Maybe a week.'

She rang off and wondered whether Pavel had that long. It might be best to forget about it; burn the microfilm, run for cover. Only then she would never know what she had sold her body for, and whether there could be such a thing as love.

Tomorrow, she told herself. *You can always burn it tomorrow*.

The boy woke, and she put out some rolls. They ate breakfast in silence. He remained feverish, and visibly preoccupied by last night's talk. As the morning stretched into midday she watched him strain to formulate a question. He would curl his lip around the first syllable or so, then abandon the effort.

'What is it?' she asked, irritated.

Anders flushed and dug himself into his blankets.

'You were like Franzi, right? One of Boyd's girls. Did you' – he hesitated – 'did you ever do it with the *mit-chut*?'

She nodded yes, amused at his choice of verb. He sat with his forehead creased in thought.

'Was it any different?' he asked.

'No different.'

'But he was shorter than you.'

'Yes,' she agreed. 'That much is certainly true.'

'I shouldn't have asked.'

'No,' she agreed. 'You shouldn't have.'

'Pavel wouldn't have.'

She considered this. 'No, he wouldn't have. But I'm sure he must have thought it.'

She could see he didn't understand her and refused to say anything more. There were things in her past about which she would not talk.

'Tell me about your family,' she asked instead. 'How come you don't know how to read?'

'I didn't go to school,' he answered. 'My uncle didn't want me to.'

'Why?'

'Don't know. Something to do with politics.'

'You're Jewish?'

'No.'

'How do you know?'

'Schlo' said that if you are Jewish you have a number on your arm.'

He showed her his wrists.

'Look,' he said. 'I'm clean.'

———

She got his story out of him bit by bit. Best she could tell his family really wasn't Jewish. It sounded like Anders' father disappeared in '33, shortly after Anders' birth, which probably meant he was a socialist. Reds were rounded up first. Jews didn't start disappearing until later, along with Gypsies, Jehovah's Witnesses and men who had a taste for men. Anders didn't know the slightest thing about his father. All he had was a name – Herbert. Nor did the boy remember a mother, other than a photo in a bedside frame that showed a dimpled beauty. He grew up with Uncle Richard in his two-room flat in Wedding.

The war started when Anders was six. School curricula had long been revised to reflect Aryan values, and a new law made membership of the Hitler Youth compulsory for all Germans from the age of ten. It would seem that Uncle Richard had no wish to see his nephew indoctrinated by Nazi ideologues. They moved out of their apartment and found shelter in a decrepit old mansion by the Müggelsee, in the far east of Berlin. Its owner was Richard's eccentric mother-in-law, Marlene. Richard's wife had left him years earlier and emigrated to the Argentine. She sent money on occasion, and once, in a well-padded parcel, an authentic *bola*, the three-limbed throwing device that local *gauchos* used to lasso their cattle's feet. Anders could describe it in considerable detail.

Mutter Marlene was what they call 'a character'. She lived in the inflated memory of a theatre career on the stages of Munich, Bayreuth and Vienna. Richard had bestowed upon her the sacred trust of Anders' education. She taught him how to roll cigarettes, play (and cheat at) cards, and how to rouge one's cheeks. They sat in front of the wireless most of the day, pink-of-cheek, aces up their sleeves, puffing on hand-rolled smokes. She liked cultural programmes, especially radio plays. Sometimes they would recite entire monologues together; she went first, and Anders imitated her every inflection. They were both inordinately fond of history plays. Their absolute favourite was Goethe's *Iphigenie auf Tauris*: Marlene did a mean fury, and Anders could still remember snatches of Orestes. For lunch they would slice a loaf of bread and toast it on their cooker's hotplate until it was black and covered in soot. Then: a spoonful of butter that would slowly soak into the burned slice, and the energetic rubbing of a peeled garlic clove along its rim. Sometimes there was also some soup – pea or lentil, ennobled by pieces of smoked ham or sausage. When the radio got to be monotonous, Anders would play in the overgrown garden at the back of the house. He was forbidden to leave the premises, but took off anyway, on select afternoons, to explore the neighbourhood. Richard came home late every evening, dead beat from factory work with two bottles of beer under one arm. Anders did not know what he did for a living, but said he smelled of machine grease and petrol. On summer weekends they would ride a bus out to the woods and collect mushrooms in a wicker basket. In winter they built snowmen back in the yard, stones for buttons and a smile made of brittle twigs.

Towards the end of the war – the radio said that victory was imminent – Richard had to report to the front. Until then he had been considered too old. He wrote letters for a while which Marlene read out to the boy in fast declamatory snatches. Then the letters stopped and Uncle Richard dropped out of Anders' life.

The old lady was soon to follow. One afternoon in early March '45, Anders returned from an excursion into Berlin proper to find the house in flames. Perhaps Marlene had forgotten to shut off the cooker after making her lunchtime toasties, or else the building's rotten cabling had outwitted the fuse and sparked a flame. The house was so filled with papers and knick-knacks that it burned like kindling. No body was recovered from its smoking foundations. The old lady had just rolled up into herself and turned to ashes.

Anders lived in streets and doorways in the months that followed. The war was ending, and nobody paid much attention to a child vagrant roaming the city. Before long he had hundreds of companions, and the Soviet Army ruled the city. He met Paulchen and the Karlsons in May that year; together they laid the foundations for what was to be a criminal organization, a brotherhood, a society *en miniature*. They had been inseparable until very recently. In his heart, no doubt, he was yearning for a surrogate father who would read him Dickens at bedtime, and share his lot in life. He had found one in Pavel, on account of his kidneys and a certain way of holding his own. Now he was living with Sonia, sharing her breakfast and asking awkward questions about men and the midget, using words that he had snatched from a thousand radio broadcasts. They had rolled so easily from the old actress's lips.

She heard him tell his story, nodded, and put on a record. If he was waiting for consolation, she had none to give. It was a war story amongst many others. She had her own, and a taste for brandy, urgent just then, when there wasn't a drop to be found.

He fell asleep after his telling, and she – she paced the flat in silence, humming swing tunes under her breath.

3

27 December 1946

December twenty-seven by the Gregorian calendar, and ten days to Russian Christmas, for those of his nation's comrades who flouted the law and remained addicted to the homely fumes of the people's opium. A cold day, though there had been colder days in Moscow. Dimitri Stepanovich Karpov, General of the Red Army, was standing before a freshly dug grave. The earth stank of gasoline. His aides had had to burn the frozen ground in order to make it malleable to their spades' sharpened edges. Even so, their best efforts had only yielded a shallow grave, barely deep enough to admit the coffin. It was made from ragged plywood, hastily painted to give it a veneer of dignity. There was a dearth of man-sized boxes in Berlin just then.

Inside the coffin lay Karpov's assistant, Comrade Sergei Semyonovich Nekhlyudov, age thirty-six. An ex-wife in Leningrad, and a new one in Smolensk; three children, Anton, Evgeny and Masha. Sergei had been found in an alley, without his face. Dimitri Stepanovich had yet to write his letters of condolence. He placed a piece of shrubbery on the coffin in lieu of flowers, and called to mind some Pushkin. The men took it as a sign to start shovelling back the dirt.

The General was a clean-shaven man with salt-and-pepper hair and wire-rimmed glasses. Trim and rather long-boned; wore his face like a mask. He had asked Sergei to follow Jean Pavel

Richter after his interrogation. Richter had seemed genuinely ignorant about Söldmann's whereabouts, but the fact that he had shown up in Söldmann's woman's flat could not entirely be ignored. To be on the safe side, Karpov put in a request with headquarters to inquire whether the agency held a file on the man.

Sergei had telephoned in after midnight to report that he had taken position outside a house on Seelingstrasse. He sounded cold. Karpov told him that his efforts were appreciated.

'The Union of Soviet Socialist States is grateful,' he told him.

Sergei replied that he was proud to serve.

He called a second time at six-thirty the next morning. He'd gone to get bread rolls and tea at the corner bakery, along with information. The baker had identified the woman on the surveillance photos as a resident of Richter's house. She had been away for a while but had recently returned, had more than her share of ration cards, liked poppy-seed rolls and kept bothering him for doughnuts.

'I asked him what was the problem with doughnuts. He told me they used up too much frying oil, and that he was short on sugar.'

Karpov instructed Sergei to arrest the woman. Sergei demurred. 'There are too many people around. I think they're keeping an eye on her. A guy with an eye-patch and a gun bulging under his coat. There may be others.'

'Do you know who he works for?'

'Not sure. No uniform. But he looks English to me.'

'So the English are involved. Or maybe just the Colonel, the one who made us release Richter.'

'What do you want me to do?'

Karpov thought it over.

'Wait until she comes out, then arrest her on the quiet. If there's trouble, call the police. I would rather this did not become an incident.'

Sergei told him not to worry. The truth was that Karpov did not think the lead would amount to much. If the woman knew anything, the Brits would have pulled her in long ago. The fact that they were watching her meant they had no more knowledge of Söldmann's whereabouts than the NKVD. They had to be hoping the midget would contact her. It was like believing in Father Christmas.

Then, late on the night of the twenty-fourth, Karpov received Richter's file and his assessment of the situation changed dramatically. His first instinct was to take a whole squad car over to Seelingstrasse and arrest anyone he found. But little would be served by a diplomatic incident that would alert the American and French authorities; the British, too, if he was right in assuming that Colonel Fosko was playing a private game. Sergei's call was long overdue. He was either pursuing the woman and unable to contact the General, or else something had happened to him. When he had still not called by five a.m., Karpov sent Lev over to find out which. He instructed him to move carefully and scout the area first. The house was being watched.

Lev took his time. He identified the house, walked around the block several times. There was no sign of Sergei, or anyone else for that matter. He studied the nameplates next to the doorbells, trying to figure out which flat the woman lived in, without success; all he knew of her was that she had worked under the name of 'Belle'. The front door was locked and not one of the windows lit. Patiently, Lev waited for Seelingstrasse to wake to Christmas morn, spitting tobacco juice into the snow drifts, and rubbing his gloves over his face whenever the cold had robbed it of sensation. Nobody approached or left the building. At around six-twenty a window lit up on the second floor. Half an hour later a man emerged, his face and hands hidden in an enormous coat.

'*Wo wohnt diese Frau?*' Lev asked him in his staccato German as he shouldered past and into the hallway. He held a surveillance picture to the man's nose. The other answered without hesitation.

'*Vierter Stock, Vorderhaus links. Schon wieder Herrenbesuch?*'

Lev grinned at that. '*Another gentleman caller?*' This was Belle all right.

He found her, made small talk, fell prey to her frying pan. Around ten, Karpov, concerned for his young adjutant, sent over three further men, armed to the teeth. They came back an hour later saying they had found Lev tied to a chair with a bloody lump frozen to his head; the doctor was having a look at him now. By then his office had received a phone call that Sergei's body had been found and identified. The General allowed himself a modicum of anger.

He acted without hesitation. Called British Army headquarters and demanded to be given Fosko's private address. He sent a formal complaint to the British Military Police urging an immediate investigation, then drove over to Fosko's villa in order to confront him personally. In the flesh, he had to admit that the Colonel was imposing. Fat. Composed. Unhurried. The General told him point blank that he knew Fosko was trying to acquire Söldmann's microfilm.

'Do you have it?' he asked.

'It's the first I hear about it.'

The Colonel pointed to a tray of biscuits he had lined up in front of his visitor. 'You should try those. My wife made them herself.'

'Hand it over,' Karpov ordered. 'The microfilm is Soviet property. We will not tolerate interference.'

'Are you threatening me?'

'There will be an investigation. By your own people. I have already sent in the report.'

'Ah. I'd better call by headquarters. Smooth things over.'

He was perfectly self-possessed. His fat lips were smiling.

'Where is Richter?'

251

'I haven't the foggiest. My advice, though, is to leave him well alone.' The Colonel scratched his head ruefully. 'That man is nothing but trouble.'

There was nothing else Karpov could do, apart from shoot him, so he left and ordered his agents to search the city for Richter, Söldmann and his *kurva*. Thus far they had not turned up anything, not even a body.

They buried Sergei on the morning of the twenty-seventh. Karpov had a plaque engraved that named him a hero of the Great Patriotic War. When the planned memorial was completed, near Treptower Park, he would have the body transferred, there to bask in history's glory.

Later that day, the General sat in his office, sipped on scalding hot tea, and wondered whether it was worth the risk to have the Colonel killed. It might precipitate a diplomatic fuss, but if he was reading the British correctly, they had no stomach for another war.

For the time being, he settled for having the Colonel's house watched around the clock.

———·———

Three days into the wait, and Sonia's patience was wearing thin. She needed to know whether Pavel was still alive. If he was dead, there was no point in staying in Franzi's apartment any longer; she would clear out, attempt to leave the city. Head west, or maybe southwest, into the American zone. Far away from all this.

She waited until Anders fell asleep after lunch, and dialled Fosko's number. The electricity remained unreliable and the line went dead a number of times. Eventually she got through, counted the rings. A woman picked up after the fifth.

'Margaret Fosko speaking,' she said.

Sonia had forgotten about the Colonel's wife.

'Is the Colonel in?' she asked in English.

'No, he's away. Can I take a message?'

'When will he be back?'

'Not for a few days, I'm afraid. Who am I talking to?'

'Have you seen a man in the house. An American?'

'Who are you?'

'Dark hair. Slender. Have you seen him?'

The woman mulled it over. Sonia could hear her thinking down the line.

'You are German, aren't you?' she asked. 'Could you help me with a word? Somebody used it in a conversation with me recently, and I just cannot work out what it means. He was saying something about "Fosko's *Hu-re*". Do you have any idea what that means?'

Sonia hung up. She scrambled for her cigarettes, then for a book of matches. At last: smoke in her lungs. She kept it there for as long as she could stand it.

'*Fosko's hoor.*'

She wondered who had described her to the Colonel's wife like that.

The rest of the day she spent stretched out next to the boy's sickness, thinking about the past. It was the final months of the war that stayed with her. She remembered the air-raid sirens, sounding all hours of the night. The weary calm with which one collected the pre-packed suitcase; one's mattress and blanket; the bottle of water to moisten one's lips. She had hated the shelter, that forced community of neighbours, always a *Blockwart* amongst them, the party's spy, egging on their conversation. People eating, talking, farting in the dark, fear playing havoc with their bowels; half-whispered apologies and the giggling of girls. Sonia would sit alone in her corner, unloved for her pride and her family's supposed wealth, and patiently await the all-clear.

She remembered ascending the stairs afterwards, dust motes dancing in the morning sun. It might have been April by then, the Russians drawing closer every day. Long queues at the butcher's, casting jealous glances at those who had finished their shopping before it was disrupted by yet another air raid. People falling into a hush whenever they spotted someone with a party pin ahead, or a patrol of coppers. Picking through their words to determine whether they had said something they had not meant to say. Their shadows shrinking in the late-morning sun.

Sonia remembered, too, the propaganda flyers outlining what the Russians did to the women along the moving front. She found them posted on advertising pillars and lampposts; tore them off sometimes and took them home to peruse them at her leisure. The flyers were fond of facts: the age, whether the woman had been married or not, and how many times – it all boiled down to numbers. Three in one night for a virgin of sixteen. Seven in an hour for a mother of two, the last one a Mongol who had the daughter next. A war widow endured twenty-three before slitting her own throat, the Führer's name upon her lips. A girl of fourteen, a girl of twelve. A girl of seven. There was, to Sonia, a strange fascination about the flyers; they brought the war home somehow, and mixed it with the mystery of sex. Sonia remembered hunting for them on her city strolls. She read them and broke into goose bumps; blushed at the thought of bodies exposed.

This was before Berlin was taken. This much she could articulate to herself, and with something like nostalgia. She stopped short when it came to picturing what happened next.

The boy beside her groaned in his sleep. She rose and wiped his brow with a dampened cloth.

———·———

She never spoke about the rapes. Who could blame her? It had been a trying time. Her reticence was not caused by a failure of memory, or by what psychiatrists call repression. Her first, in any case, she remembered quite vividly. He took time to close the door, secured the latch with great care, and proceeded to undress before he had so much as laid a hand on her. In this he was different from many others who took their women standing up against some kitchen table, trousers around their ankles. Whole queues formed like this, man standing after man with a loosened belt. Sonia's first scorned such rush, found time even to roll up his socks and stick them into his boots' grease-slick shaft. He had spindly white legs, skinny white buttocks, untouched by the sun, save for the feet which showed signs of some tanning. Out of this meagre carriage grew a solid body the colour of dried earth, sunburned and knotty like a bulbous root. She had never seen anything quite so grotesque.

Afterwards, when he stepped back into his underwear, she looked on in wonder as he carefully pulled away the elastic and reached in to arrange himself to the best of his comfort. Only then did he step into his trousers and pull his soldier's shirt over his head. His face, as she lay there and bled, was serenely peaceful and he rubbed his neck and cheeks with his palms, delighted at his good health. Is it a wonder then that she came to hate men – all, that is, apart from Pavel who 'snuck into her heart' (a fine phrase that, for is not all love thievery?) while her hatred lay slumbering, huddled inward perhaps from too much cold.

There you have it, her story. She hated, she loved, and of the rapes she would not speak. Myself, I have no such compunction. After all, you have a right to know.

———·———

Sonia did one more thing that day. Idly, sitting over the remains of their dinner, she unrolled the first few metres of the reel of microfilm, where it was wound a little sloppily. She soon found out why. A metre and a half in, the film came loose in

255

her hand where it had been cut in half. Sonia sat and studied the cut at either end and came to the conclusion that they did not match up. Someone had removed part of the film, literally cut it out of its middle. It wasn't clear to her what difference it made. She wound the film back onto the reel as tightly as she could manage, and fastened it with a rubber band. Then she leaned over the sleeping boy, and fed the monkey. Outside it had warmed up enough to snow a little, though soon the skies would be clear again, and a thin crust of ice would form upon the powdery lightness of virgin snow.

4

3 January 1947

Midday on the third of January, precisely ten days after his somewhat hasty departure, Colonel Stuart Melchior Fosko pulled into the driveway of his Berlin villa in a newly requisitioned Volkswagen Beetle whose cramped space pinned him awkwardly against the curve of its wooden wheel. He got out, walked over to the front door, unlocked it, and stood in his hallway, a carpet bag in one hand, and the stump of a cigar in the other. There was no answer to his call of greeting. His wife had left for England after breakfast, the driver had taken the rest of the day off, the men were busy with their routine duties, and I was too preoccupied with Pavel to take notice of the somewhat crabby 'Hello' that rang through the upstairs of the house. In fact, I only became aware of Fosko's return when I went up to fetch some beers a quarter of an hour later, and stumbled over the overcoat that he had carelessly thrown on the floor. As I searched the downstairs rooms for a sign of my master, I chanced upon a trail of discarded clothes that led me up the stairs and down the hallway to the main bathroom. The door stood ajar, and I found the Colonel, buck naked, testing the water with one chubby toe. His penis cringed in the relative cold of the upstairs rooms. I was impressed that water pipes and boiler were working impeccably.

'Ah, Peterson,' he sang out. I felt immediately that he was somehow very angry. 'How good of you to come.'

He eased one leg into the bath, then the other, went down into a crouch and stood for a while, his buttocks a half-inch from the steaming water.

'I'm sorry, Colonel. I was down in the basement.'

He finally settled in the bath. The tub was not made for a man his size, and his stomach and hips stuck to its sides. The combination of electric lighting and white tiles brought out his flesh's clammy pallor. He reminded me of a cuttlefish.

'So, how is our guest? Well, I trust.'

'Yes. As instructed.'

'Did he spill the beans yet?'

'Beans, sir?'

'Don't play dim now, Peterson. Did he tell you what he knows?'

'Some of it.'

'Some? What have you been doing?'

'You told me not to hurt him.'

'I told you I didn't want any visible damage.'

'Ah. I must have misunderstood.'

'Perhaps I should see to him myself. Light me a cigar, will you? There's a darling.'

I walked over to the cigar box next to the sink, selected one and cut off its end, keeping my back turned towards the Colonel to hide my agitation. My heart was pounding with the realization that, very soon now, Pavel would be lost to me forever.

'All I need is one more night, sir,' I told him as I passed over cigar and matches. 'I'll have something for you in the morning.'

Fosko studied me attentively, blowing out a plume of blue smoke.

'One more night, Peterson. After that, he's mine. It's time we stopped mollycoddling the bastard.'

He asked me to stay around until he was done with his bath, and help him dry off. I was working on his left leg when the phone rang in the study next door. Naked as he was, Fosko walked over to it. I followed, towel in hand, like a faithful valet. Truth be told, I had a premonition about the call: it rang to the final act. The Colonel answered with his usual air of self-possession.

'Colonel Fosko speaking.'

'*Endlich. Sie sind zurück.*'

'Who is this? *Wer da?*'

'Paulchen.'

'The head of the arsewipes? *Kinder-Gauner-Chef?*'

'Yes, sir.'

'Hold on, I'll put my man on the line. *Warten.*' The Colonel waved me over and handed me the phone. 'Your German's better than mine. It's Paulchen. The boy mobster. Ask him what he wants.'

I held the phone to my ear and introduced myself formally. A strange three-way conversation ensued.

'*Peterson hier. Was wollen Sie?*'

'*Ich weiß wo der Film ist.*'

'He says he knows where the film is.'

'Well, where is it?'

'*Wo ist er?*'

'*Die Frau hat ihn. Sonia.*'

'He says Sonia has it.'

'Dear Lord. I know that myself. But where's Sonia?'

'*Wissen Sie wo Sonia ist?*'

'*Nein. Aber ich kann sie Ihnen besorgen.*'

'He says he can get her for us.'

'When? Tell the nitwit to spit it out, or we'll pay him another visit.'

'*Wie schnell?*'

'*Heute noch. Ist aber nicht umsonst.*'

'Today. He says they can get her today. He says they want something in return.'

'Money? How much?'

'*Wieviel?*'

'*Dreihundert Dollar. In bar.*'

'Three hundred dollars in cash.'

The Colonel sneered. 'Tell him no problem. I'll send someone over to stuff it up his tight little rump. He just make sure he gets Sonia. And the film. Tell him if next time he calls he doesn't have either, he might as well save us the trouble and jump out the window. It'll be easier that way.'

I translated this best I could. I couldn't remember the word for 'jump', nor the one for 'rump', but the boy assured me he understood perfectly and rang off. I replaced the receiver with great care and turned back to the Colonel. He stood there in the centre of the room, stood naked, the cigar in his hand and smoke curling from between fat lips. I had rarely seen him this pleased.

'Well, what do you know? One goes, breaks a few bones, not thinking twice about it, and a few days later life throws you a line. Must be what those Hindus mean by Karma. What goes around, etcetera.'

He scratched his stomach and shook water off one leg.

'Make yourself useful, Peterson, and lay out some fresh clothes for me. And fix me some sandwiches. With mustard. I'm starving. You wouldn't believe the pigswill they serve up back home.'

———–—

'Paulchen here.'

'Do you have it?'

'Fräulein Sonia?'

'Yes.'

'I'm so glad you called. Right on cue, too. Yeah, we got it. Pricey, but it'll do just fine.'

'It's the right size?'

260

'You gave us some film, remember? Yeah, it's the right size. Where do I drop it off?'

'I'll come and fetch it. It better not be garbage.'

'We'll be here. Come as soon as you can.'

Sonia hung up and ran a hand over her face. The past few days had not been easy. The boy's fever had refused to surrender entirely. Every few hours it would flare up and bathe his cheeks crimson. Whenever he felt better, he whined to be let out into the street and hatched childish plans of how they would go rescue Pavel, 'infiltrate' the Colonel's 'compound', 'take out' Fosko's 'stooges'. Then he'd go back to shivers, drenching the sheets in sweat. She wondered where she'd heard it said that a child's sweat did not smell. The boy's reeked like gone-off milk. She wrapped cold compresses around his ankles and played him Glenn Miller. He asked her once whether she prayed; folded his hands together when she looked at him uncomprehendingly, and mimed devotion. Perhaps he worried for his life in his childish way.

She said she didn't. Pray.

'I don't either,' he told her. 'All it is, is superstition.'

For some reason he seemed disappointed when she made no move to disagree.

Twice she considered leaving him. Leaving Pavel, too, and disappearing into the western outskirts of the American sector. She would pay somebody to share their flat until she had arranged for a travel pass out of the city. With luck she might make it to Munich. She'd never been, but she'd seen postcards. Munich looked nice. Full of GIs, of course, but nice.

The second time around, she went so far as to pack a bag while the boy was asleep. She packed money, whatever was left, and her underwear. As she stood there, zipping shut her small suitcase, it came to her that she packed like a prostitute: cash and work clothes. She slipped out without leaving a note and climbed on a tram headed for Teltow. For two hours she walked around the suburb, looking for a friendly face she might ask for lodgings; found one in the elderly owner of a corner shop, who sold chocolates under the counter, and inner tubes for bicycles. She made up her mind to ask her; queued for some fifteen minutes, her question on her tongue, then bought chocolates instead, and pre-war cocoa powder for the boy. When she returned to Franzi's place, he hadn't even woken; lay senseless upon the bed, the blankets in a pile around his feet. She pulled them back up and told herself she should have stayed out longer; long enough for him to miss her. The monkey, by contrast, seemed ecstatic to see her. It even took a break from its methodical destruction of the living-room sofa and clambered over to sniff at her ankles. She pushed it aside with one tired heel.

Sonia unpacked the bag, fetched water from the pump and set to scrubbing the floor. The water half frozen in the bucket; hands numb to the wrist. Afterwards the floorboards proved as slippery as sheet ice. When the boy finally woke around nightfall, he demanded to go out for a walk. It was the only time she cursed him to his face. It had darkened then, turned savage in his anger.

Now, it was looking at her expectantly.

'Paulchen has found one?' Anders asked.

'Yes. Finally.'

'How's Pavel doing?'

'I have no idea. As far as I know Fosko's still out of town. I made inquiries. I doubt they would hurt him while he's away.'

'What happens now?'

'I go over there and pick up the projector. Then, we have a look at the film and figure out what all this fuss has been about. And then –'

'What?'

'I don't know. I'll think of something.'

She gathered up her coat and handbag, made sure she had all the money and jewellery she'd promised Paulchen. The monkey

262

was chattering, and she stroked it absent-mindedly, noting how matted its fur was, crusted with food and worse.

'I'll go,' the boy blurted out all of a sudden.

'No.'

'I'll go.'

'You're sick.'

'I feel better. And I want to see Paulchen. Make it up with him.'

'Then we both go.'

'What if it's a trap?'

'What do you mean, a trap?'

'What if Paulchen tries to hold you. Sell you out to Fosko or something. He wouldn't sell me out.'

'Why not? You stole his gun, didn't you?'

'Thieves' honour,' he said and winked at her theatrically. 'I'll pay up and bring back the projector. And then we go get Pavel.'

They squabbled a while longer, but in the end she agreed. She gave him the money and valuables, made him repeat how much they owed Paulchen. Wrote out Franzi's phone number on a piece of paper and stuffed it into his pocket in case he got into trouble. She cautioned him to try the projector on the inch of film she had already passed on to Paulchen, and not to disclose their whereabouts.

'Above all, keep warm. It's murder out there.'

The boy promised and she draped an extra shawl around his neck and head. His ugly little mug was alive with excitement as he ran out the door. 'Good luck!' she called after him and watched him run down the length of street until he was swallowed up by the dark of late afternoon.

Then Sonia sat down and picked through the motives of why she had let him go instead of herself.

'It might be a trap,' she mused aloud.

'If it's a trap, better him than me.'

She said it twice, to see how it sat with her, said it to the dresser's mirror, her mouth shaping words that ran afoul of her stomach.

———·———

I served the Colonel a late lunch up in his office, tying a starched napkin around his thick throat and pouring him a glass of mineral water. He peeled the boiled egg with great fastidiousness, depositing its shell in an ashtray, then sprinkled it with salt; buttered three slices of toast and covered them with corned beef and mustard. At any other time it might have been a pleasure to watch him at his table. That afternoon, however, I could barely stand the thousand details of his culinary ritual, and winced whenever he smacked his lips over some titbit or other. I stuck around long enough to ascertain that he did not want for any ingredient, then quickly excused myself, and returned to the basement.

As I climbed down the stairs and slipped out of my coat, my agitation must have been ill concealed. I moved my desk next to the cage, set up the chessboard, but rather than taking his customary place across from me on the corner of his mattress, Pavel stood and faced me squarely.

'He's come back, hasn't he?'

'Who?'

'Fosko. He's been away, and now he's back. Don't look at me so surprised. I can tell he's back. It's written all over your face.'

'Pavel,' I said, and inched closer to his cage. 'You have to tell me what you know about the microfilm. If you don't –'

'I understand.'

We stood not a foot apart, my eye in his. Once again I remarked how delicate his features were.

'Where is Sonia?'

'She's been hiding. Ever since we picked you up. I think she has the film.'

'Does Fosko know where she is?'

'No.'

'You swear?'

'I swear.'

'If he finds her, you will tell me, won't you, Peterson?'

I was silent.

'Promise me, Peterson. Promise you'll tell.'

'Okay,' I said. 'Now, how about you play white for a change? Play for pennies? We can settle up when you're out and flush.'

We played without enthusiasm. I promised him some hot buttered rolls for his tea.

———·———

It can't have been easy for him. Nine days gone and no news about Sonia or the boy, just the two of us talking, and a chessboard full of slaughtered pawns. Time had stopped as far as he was concerned; he could count off the days or measure their passing by the length of his stubble, but these acts did not reference any reality beyond the cellar's walls. All he could do with time was pass it. Talk took care of that: the pleasure of making speeches. Even this was soured by the constant fear of giving away too much of himself. Just about anything might have slipped out somewhere along the line; slipped out not because it had to, the irrepressible cry of the heart, but simply because it was there. Words feeding away at his memory, like carrion birds, leaving him with the mere bones of things, skeletal outlines of a past he no longer recognised as his own. All traded for a handful of truths, about Sonia and Boyd and the crooked Herr Söldmann, that answered to his curiosity but were powerless to change the fact of his imprisonment.

All this changed that day. Fosko returned, and time started anew. It energised him; a jolt of fear, and he looked to me for help. A savage look, half plea, half threat, though his voice remained level.

For the time being I resolved to keep his door securely locked.

———·———

Anders did not walk to Paulchen's. He skipped. Spurned bus and tram, choosing to brave the winter chill; wiped snot across his jacket's fur at every other intersection; felt his heart pound at being outside again, the afternoon moon hanging low in the sky. He was certain now that Sonia would come through for Pavel, that soon – perhaps that very night – he would be reunited with his bookish friend. He pictured them shaking hands in acknowledgement of what they both had suffered, then sitting down at the kitchen table to share a cigarette. Blowing smoke in the air, while Pavel outlined the means by which they should take their revenge on the Colonel.

'I'm not a vengeful man,' he would explain, 'but the Colonel's got to go.'

'I'll help,' Anders would answer. 'You just say the word.'

At the corner of Paulchen's apartment building, he bumped into one of the Karlsons. He must have run into trouble. His nose was swollen to twice its normal size and both eyes were ringed purple.

'What happened to you, Mannie?' Anders called over to him. 'You look like a house fell on you.'

Mannie pulled a face but didn't answer. Anders drew level with him and spat.

'Haven't you heard?' he said. 'I brought back the gun. Paulchen and I, we're on the up-and-up.'

The boy stared at him sullenly, then turned on his heel and walked away. They weren't a bad lot, those Karlson twins, but boy, did they hold a grudge.

Next, Anders met Woland. He was sitting on the stairs right outside headquarters, laying a hand of solitaire on the step below. He, too, had been in some sort of fight, his lower lip split and clotted, and a nasty bruise running across his cheek from eye to mouth to chin. All of a sudden, Anders was worried.

'Woland?' he called out.

'Anders? I thought the woman was coming over.'

'I came instead. Is everything all right?'

The boy didn't answer.

'Is it a trap? You would tell me, wouldn't you? If it was a trap? I brought back the gun, didn't I?'

Woland turned over a card, the ten of clubs, then another, the queen of diamonds.

'It's okay,' he said. 'You gotta go in.'

He wouldn't say more. Anders watched him a while longer, preparing words of apology. It was evident that Paulchen remained angry with him. Anders would offer him to go ahead and sock him one. A free shot so that they were even, in the face or in the body, wherever he liked.

'Go on,' he would say, 'I deserve it,' and afterwards they would hug and be friends once again.

Anders walked over to the door and knocked. It swung open almost at once.

——·——

Paulchen had picked Georg to administer the beating. He was new to the gang, and didn't know Anders all that well. A big bruiser, too, for a kid of fourteen, who hung out at the boxing gym in the evenings and laced up fighters' gloves in exchange for tuition. He went about it professionally; taped up his fingers, stuck penny rolls into the hollows of both his fists, and gave Anders a wordless beating, the nasty sort that seeks out the short end of the ribs and the soft parts next to the spine. Anders would be pissing blood all week. Thus far they hadn't asked him any questions.

The beating took place at the very centre of the room. They'd had to make space for it: had moved the armchair and the table, cleared away ashtrays and milk bottles, a drying rack full of socks. Anders had watched these preparations, his hands on his hips and waiting for an explanation. Thus far, Paulchen hadn't said a word to him. The boys had expected the woman to come, but it had been the boy who'd shown up, babbling about the Luger and how Paulchen should 'sock him one', only he seemed to have broken his arm, so maybe he could save it for later, when it was healed. He fell silent when Georg sidled up to him, on his leader's command, and grabbed Anders roughly by the collar.

Paulchen had understood right away what needed to be done. No sooner had he seen Anders than he knew they'd have to hurt him. They were in it up to their necks. He didn't even consider asking him nicely. He'd lived with Anders since the end of the war. He knew him the way a man might know his wife. This one, he didn't like to do things the easy way. Paulchen told Georg not to pull any punches.

When the beating started, the other boys formed a ring around the two combatants; flinched whenever the elder boy hit home. At first it had looked to them like any other afternoon fight – an uneven pairing perhaps, but whoever said life was fair? When Anders went to the ground for a third time, they started to become uneasy, looked over to their leader, an unspoken question on their lips. Paulchen ignored their stares. They were nothing but children. They hadn't really understood yet what was at stake.

Anders hit the floor a fourth time. He hit face first, his arms too tired to catch his weight. One of his teeth broke. You could hear it crack. The boy lying there with an arched hip, crumpled like a pack of ciggies.

'That's enough.'

Georg held off a kick that was already mid-swing; lost his balance and stumbled, trampling on Anders' hand as he did so, leaving behind a dirty print. Paulchen crouched down next to his friend and whispered in one ear.

'Where is Sonia? You tell me, or the Colonel will massacre the lot of us.'

'Screw you,' said the boy, and blood came pouring over his chin.

'Have it your way.'

This time, Anders went down with the very first punch. He lay senseless, his eyes rolled over to display their whites. One of the boys tried to bring him around with water but all it did was soak his hair and clothes. His skin felt hot and clammy. There was nothing to do but wait. Paulchen had not counted on the boy passing out. *Scheiße,*' he said, and lit himself a cigarette.

'You want me to go through his pockets?' Georg asked. He was icing his knuckles with some snow he'd scraped off the sill. 'He might have cash on him or something.'

'Sure,' Paulchen said. 'Go through his pockets. Anything you find, put it on the table. Maybe we can figure out where the fucking woman's at.'

———·———

I was back with the Colonel when he received the call. We were both in his study where he stood, clad only in underpants and vest, ironing his shirt. I had offered to do it for him, of course, but the Colonel was particular about his linens. 'I have seen your shirtfronts,' he muttered caustically, and bid me take a seat by the smoking table. 'Watch and learn,' he said. Thus far he had spent five whole minutes on the left sleeve.

The phone rang. He let it ring three times, tutted, then walked over to his desk with no especial hurry.

'Yes? . . . Ah, our friend Paulchen. Hold on, I will put on my expert in Krautspeak.'

He waved me over, and strolled back to the ironing board.

'He says they don't have the woman yet, but they have her phone number.'

'Her number?'

'Yes.'

'It's in Berlin?'

'Yes, sir, a Berlin number.'

'Excellent. Write it up, Peterson. Anything else?'

I hesitated. It should have been easy to lie.

'Spit it out, Peterson.'

'He says he has the boy.'

'Which boy?'

'Pavel Richter's boy.'

'Oh. I thought we had killed that one.'

I stood embarrassed.

'Perhaps, sir,' I said, 'we made a mistake. He asks what they should do with him.'

'Hold on to him, naturally. I'll come and pick him up once I have a moment. Tell them to guard him with their lives. Boys like dramatic language like that.'

I translated Fosko's message, and listened to Paulchen's glum assent. The line went dead.

'Do you want me to dial Sonia's number?'

'Good heavens, no. Call the police. The Tiergarten station. Ask for Wachtmeister Studer. Tell him I need to know which address belongs to this number, and I need to know fast.'

He smiled in obvious self-satisfaction, and turned his attention over to the right sleeve.

'Let's just hope Studer doesn't also report to the Russians. Last thing I want is that Russian General on my case now that I'm so close. What's his name again?'

'Karpov.'

'Carp-off, yes. A tiresome fellow, though he has splendid English for a Bolshevik.'

———·———

I saw him off. He finished ironing his shirt, dressed with elaborate care, then collected his coat and car keys.

'What are my orders?' I mumbled as he squeezed himself into his Volkswagen.

'Orders? I don't know. The house could use a hoover, I guess. And put some fresh sheets on my bed; my wife sweats like a pig.' He turned the ignition, pumped the accelerator a few times until the engine warmed up.

'If Karpov calls, tell him as far as you know I'm still in London getting scolded for exceeding my authority. Use precisely that phrase. It'll please him no end.' Then he tore away down the driveway and onto the icy road towards the city.

Morosely, I climbed the stairs back up to his study and sat down behind the Colonel's desk. He had forgotten to unplug the iron, the only clue to the fact that he must have been uncommonly excited. It sat steaming on the ironing board; a slender, steel pyramid, pink at the tip, the colour of broiled salmon. I should have switched it off, I know, but I left it steaming, staring at it across the room. Mentally I was with my employer, hurtling along pockmarked roads. I will admit, it sat uncomfortably with me, this cloud of unhappiness that was gathering over Sonia. I wish I knew what the Colonel was thinking.

Thus far I have resisted the temptation to slip into the Colonel's mind, out of docility, you might say, mixed with the fear that any amount of exposure would beget sympathy, however reluctant. Perhaps, though, such scruples are misplaced, or even unfair. After all, it is not inconceivable that there lurked a heart somewhere in his fleshy bosom. A scene

271

comes to mind, of the Colonel playing with his son (I forget his name, or never knew it): the two of them sitting on the villa's floor, mid-morning on Christmas day, six feet apart and pushing a wooden train back and forth between them. Where did he take it from, the Colonel, that artless laugh, whenever he launched the train across the gap? All this in the shadow of the Christmas tree, his wife knitting to Caruso.

It is hard to know what to conclude from a moment such as that. Now that he sat in his car, his mind intent upon his prey, one searched his face in vain for traces of Christmas morn. From the way he clutched the wheel, it is tempting to infer that his hands were already rehearsing their impact upon Sonia's flesh, and though the depth of shadow within the car won't allow us to be certain, there seemed to be an ominous bulge by the side of his crotch that gave this imaginary beating a particularly unsavoury edge. Another story comes to mind, from the early days of Fosko's stint in Berlin: November '45, or thereabouts. In those days the Colonel kept a tiny, naked dog, not much bigger than a rat, that he claimed was Mexican, until one morning, in a fit of temper (it had peed on some important papers), he broke its back over one knee and watched it crawl under his desk in order to die. He did it in sight of the cleaner, who spread the story. I daresay he meant her to. He wasn't one to waste grand gestures of cruelty. Once the cleaning lady, an elderly German, had done her work and spread the tale, Fosko had her sacked on suspicion of espionage. She was investigated for several months and could find no work in the meantime. Finally, she admitted to everything, in the hope, not entirely misplaced, that she would be better fed in prison. And so it goes. For all the use she is for my narrative, I might have buried her in silence. In any case, as a vignette, the Mexican dog might serve to balance Christmas day; together they offer something akin to truth.

Whatever his mindset – and his worth as a man – the Colonel drove the few miles to the city centre in record time and parked the car a good block away from Franzi's ground-floor apartment.

It would be wrong to say that he *slunk* down the sidewalk towards the house's door; he certainly did not run. He walked up, in slow, girthy self-assurance, past the half-house's rubble, and rang the bell same as any visitor would have done. There was no gun in his pocket, and he clutched neither truncheon nor sap. All he had with him was his smile, fat on those lips, and the fury of having been betrayed.

Sonia opened the door at once. Afterwards, she reasoned that it was because the monkey gave a chatter of joy as though it had recognized the coming of a friend, and also because she was glad that the boy had made it back from his errand. Fosko slipped through the entrance and pushed his bulk past the apartment door with astonishing speed. There was no time for Sonia to cry out. The door slammed into its lock behind him.

———·———

Pavel stood in his cell shouting for his captor. Stood, brow knit, jaw raised, a vagrant's stubble on the stretched-out throat.

'Peterson!' he yelled up towards the ceiling. 'Come back.

'Come back, Peterson!' he yelled. 'Tell me what's going on.'

It would have been difficult for him to explain his agitation. He had been alone for perhaps an hour. There was no indication that anything was amiss: no sounds that had travelled down the stairs, nothing to go by other than his knowledge that Fosko was back, and was hunting for Sonia. And yet he was certain that she was in danger while he clamoured helplessly behind bars. He yelled again and felt himself getting hoarse.

There was no answer.

———·———

She had forgotten how fat he was, and how quick. Sonia had been packing when the bell rang, arranging her possessions by importance, one suitcase full of essentials, the second for her luxuries. Folding and re-folding her blouses, nervous for the boy's return. Then the bell. Mechanically, she'd folded over one more collar, then stepped out from behind the kitchen table and opened the door. Her hand was still on the doorknob when Fosko burst in; stood looming in her living room.

Good God, he was fat.

Dripping in mink and jewellery.

The monkey gave a cry of delight and scrambled over to hug his leg. The Colonel bent to pick it up by the scruff.

'You haven't been feeding him,' he complained. 'He looks scrawny.'

She'd forgotten about his voice, too, the wet of his lips; his hands chubby like a choirboy's. Sonia backed away from him. She wished he'd skip the talking and start hitting. It would be easier that way.

'My, my, the trouble you've caused me. You and your dreamy-eyed lover. First Söldmann, then Boyd; the whole long dance to see who's got the merchandise. Now I've got a Russian general up my arse over a dead soldier, and a Yank in my basement who's eating me out of house and home.'

He dropped the monkey onto her bed, and took another step towards her.

'Is he still alive?' she chanced. 'Tell me. Is Pavel alive?'

He smiled; fat lips smiling. There was spit in their corners.

'Alive and well. Making eyes at my dear Peterson. Another week or so, and they'll go and elope. Of course, now they won't have a week. Romance cut short. The year, it starts in tragedy.'

'What will you do with him?'

He shrugged and stepped closer. 'You have other things to worry about.'

He was almost touching her now. She stood pressed against the kitchen table. There should have been a knife on the table.

There wasn't a knife. There was a pair of panties, Parisian lace; mending in the gusset. She noticed him noticing.

'The film, Sonia,' he whispered. 'Give me the microfilm.' He stretched out one hand. His fingernails were filed and painted with a subtle gloss. 'Please.'

She handed it over. What the hell else was she going to do? Got it out of the cupboard drawer, and placed it into his fat-fingered palm: not a word of protest, resigned to it now, her skin crawling with his presence. He reached up and stroked her cheek with the other hand.

'There. That wasn't so hard.'

All of a sudden she felt dizzy. She stumbled, and he had to steady her by the armpit to keep her from falling over. Up close he smelled of talcum powder. They stood like this for long minutes while the monkey played under her skirts.

When she had regained her balance, he helped her close the suitcases and tied a piece of string around the animal's throat. The Colonel stuffed both cases under one arm, and wrapped the leash around his wrist. 'Let's go home,' he said. He did not bother to wait for her as he stepped out the door.

Sonia followed him out and over to his car. Somewhere along the line her nose had started bleeding and she dabbed at it with a tissue until the blood clotted and dried.

———————

Anders woke upon a hardwood floor. He fought to open his eyes. The left one wouldn't obey. Something pressed down on it, from the general direction of his brow. His legs hurt, and it was difficult to breathe. When he tried to move his arms, he realized they were bound. He had no feeling in his hands.

'He's awake,' a voice announced. The blood was pounding in Anders' ears, and it was hard to be sure who had spoken. Nor could he see much of anything. Anders lay on his side, the good eye close to the floorboards, a broken tooth rising jaggedly out of its grain. He tried to turn his head but was stopped by a jabbing pain that ran from crotch to gut. He wondered whether he'd been stabbed.

'Go on,' he croaked, struggling to get the words out of his swollen mouth. 'Hit me again. I won't say nothing.'

'It's over, Anders. We found the phone number. Now, it's all up to the Colonel.'

Anders retched. Something was wrong with his stomach. It felt lumpy and bloated, like a sack of mouldy spuds.

'You gave it to Fosko?'

'Yeah.'

'Why?'

He didn't receive an answer. Instead, he felt someone crouch next to him; felt a hand in his hair. Anders couldn't tell whether the gesture was meant to appease him, or announced another beating.

'Forget about it,' the voice said, not unkindly. 'It's out of your hands.' The boy thought it might be Paulchen.

'I have to go warn her. We were going to rescue Pavel.'

He tried crawling, pushing his body along the floor with the strength of his knees. The hand in his hair turned into a fist. It shoved him back into the floor, right on top of the broken-off tooth.

'You're staying here.'

A blanket was thrown over him, and someone – Gunnar? – pushed the corner of a pillow under one cheek.

'There's water if you want some.'

'Fuck you,' said Anders, searching his vocabulary for terms of abuse. 'Arsehole-sackrat-bastard-pig. I fucking hate the lot of you.'

Not one of them bothered to answer his curse. He listened to them lounge about, smoking, drinking, playing marbles, arguing about whose turn it was to cook dinner. It was as though Anders was eavesdropping on his own past. In his mind he went around and stuck a knife in each of their chests; watched them bleed. It made his gall rise within him, and he lay there coughing, choking on its juice.

———·———

The Colonel drove a Beetle. At another time she might have laughed about it, the way he sat, his stomach trapped behind the wheel, and the gear stick snug against his thigh. It was a clear night, inky, the moon so low in the sky it seemed to balance on the treetops. Berlin was a glow at their backs. It was the sort of night Pavel might have liked. She grimaced and opened the glove compartment to look for a cigarette. The monkey jabbered behind her and clambered over the Colonel's shoulder down onto his stomach's ledge. It hadn't been able to keep its paws off him ever since he'd returned into its life.

'What are you looking for?'

'Cigarette.'

'There's a pack in my coat pocket. I can't get to it in this sardine tin.'

She reached over and ran her fingers through the mink until she found his pocket. His elbow brushed her face as he shifted gears.

'Excuse me.'

She straightened up, opened the packet and lit a smoke. The monkey wrinkled its nose in disgust.

'I talked to your wife,' she said abruptly.

'When?'

'I don't know. A week back. She called me your *"hoor"*.'

'Did she? What a splendid word. She must have it from a novel. It's shocking what women will read these days.'

'Is she still in the house?'

'No. She left before I got back. I hardly saw her at all.'

277

He turned to her then with half an eye. Let go of the gear stick and placed his hand upon her thigh, gently, almost shyly, one chubby hand, and the monkey jeering in his lap.

'I missed you, Sonia,' he whispered. 'It's been ten long days and I haven't had a single fuck.'

Here we go, she thought and didn't move.

'I won't,' she said, her voice level.

He removed his hand, put it back on the stick.

'We'll see.'

It was hard to tell whether or not he was angry.

'I haven't seen Pavel since I got back. We should say hello to him later. Peterson tells me he's taken to my wife's cooking.'

She didn't reply, and he gently steered the car off the road and down his villa's driveway.

'Quite frankly, I can't believe you fell for him. I thought you were immune to such folly. Counted on it, to be frank.' He got out, cradling the monkey, and walked around the car to open the door for her. 'It's been ever so disappointing.'

Sonia didn't respond. He walked her to the front door, then up to his study. His words turned in her. The thing was, the disappointment was not altogether his. Once upon a time she had thought she was immune to folly as well.

———·———

No sooner had the two figures disappeared inside the house than an engine was coaxed into a coughing start behind a wall of bushes some thirty yards down the road. A car soon emerged, leaving behind a pile of loose shrubbery and an empty bottle of vodka. It did not turn on its lights until it had made it past the first bend, then went roaring towards the nearest public phone, located in a hotel lobby a good mile down the road. There, surrounded by British officers who had requisitioned the hotel for the evening in order to celebrate a subaltern's twenty-first, the driver stood in one of a row of booths, trying to dial the number. He had trouble with it because his fingers were well and truly frozen. It had been a long wait. After six or seven attempts he finally succeeded. The voice that answered was Russian. 'Yes?' it asked.

'It's the Colonel. He's back from his outing. And he brought the woman.'

'Good. We'll be right over.'

———·———

When I heard the Colonel's car pull up in the villa's driveway, I beat a hasty retreat. I jumped out of Fosko's chair, nearly knocking over the glass of brandy I had poured myself but did not have the heart to consume. As I stood, stamping life into my cold feet, I noticed that I'd left the warm imprint of my buttocks on the chair's buckskin seat. At the room's centre the clothes iron was still smoking on its perch, the whole of its surface gleaming bright pink now. I rushed to unplug it; wished there was time to hide the glass and drum my arse out of the Colonel's leather; open the window and freshen the air. By then I could already hear his key in the door; heard her cross the threshold with the double click of woman's heels. It was all I could do to race down the stairs and hide out in the kitchen while they traversed the living room. Then, another two steps and I was back in the basement, at the top of the stairs, that is, resting my back against the door. I don't really know why I was so reluctant to run into the Colonel; I doubt he would've begrudged my being a witness to his evening's triumph. You might say it was a loss of nerve. Whatever was going to happen was to some small degree my fault. Perhaps Pavel had rubbed off on me and I was growing 'a conscience'. Had he known, it might well have pleased him. I was about to voice the thought when I caught sight of him. Good God, he looked forlorn: a bearded Monte Cristo, grubby hands buried in his hair. The electric light stood mirrored in his eyes, making them impossible to read.

'Is she safe?' he called to me as I made my way down the stairs. His voice was hoarse. I wondered had he been shouting.

'Who?'

'Don't play with me, Peterson. Is she safe?'

I sat down at my table and rubbed the back of my neck.

'How the hell would I know?'

'You promised, Peterson. Remember that you promised.'

He spoke so agitatedly, flecks of spittle carried all the way over to my desk.

I counted the minutes. Literally counted them out, my eyes fixed on my wristwatch. Pavel was talking, howling in the background, but I ignored him. I almost got up after three, but then settled back and counted out a further five. With every second it became clearer to me what I would do. By the end, it seemed inevitable to me, the feeling that sneaks over you just as you lean into your first kiss. Man does not get closer to providence than that.

'Pavel,' I said, and got up to unlock his cage. 'You must understand that I cannot let you go. You must understand this.'

I stepped into his cage to explain myself.

'Where is Sonia?' he croaked at me.

'Upstairs. With the Colonel.'

'Is she alive?'

'I think,' I said, and laid a hand upon his shoulder, 'I think we should play some chess now. A nice game of chess, I think. Let's see whether I've got any better.'

I turned my face for a moment, to locate the board.

This was when he threw himself at me, and rammed a fist into the side of my throat.

———·———

But I didn't tell it right. I didn't tell you how we stood, my hand on his shoulder, sweat on our brows, coming to terms with the moment. I remember shifting my weight just before he lashed out at me, treading a cockroach underfoot. It made a popping sound. I might have missed it, but Pavel noticed; started, one eye on my boot. Pavel, hoarse from howling, his hand already crumpled in a fist, and yet he noticed. It was almost shameful.

We both knew what would happen next. It was as though it was written into the moment. In truth, I hardly felt the punch. I went down, a little too easily perhaps, and lay limp while he wrestled gun and keys from my belt. He locked me in the cage, took the safety off the gun, and ran up the stairs. Somewhere, upstairs, Sonia was fighting for her life. I wonder whether this meant he expected to find her rutting, or dead.

Pavel closed the door behind him, and I closed my eye, struggling to follow the sound of his tread as he entered the house.

———

The house was larger than he had imagined. He forced himself to search it slowly, methodically, telling himself that nothing would be worse than to fail her now, be caught by a chance guard or a dog trained to maul. It cost him, this patience; he bit his cheeks bloody under its gag. Already, he was shivering. The upstairs was much colder than the cellar, and Pavel'd gone prowling in his undershirt. The air, to him, smelled impossibly sweet. It spelled out to him that, nine days into captivity, and despite his attempts at getting clean, he must stink to high heaven.

Pavel stepped out of the basement and found the kitchen and larder, some stew on the stove, ready to be re-heated. The two doors at either end gave on to hallways, one leading to the front door, the other deeper into the house. He chose the latter, turned left into a drawing room. It held a leather sofa, an armchair and footrest, the leather's brown clashing with a red paisley-patterned blanket. To one side stood a cabinet loaded with an old-fashioned gramophone and a sizeable collection of classical music. Vivaldi, Bach, Pachelbel; tokens of a love for the baroque. A corner ashtray cradled the butt of a single half-smoked cigar. Next door, to the right, a library of sorts; German law books, dusty, and a corner devoted to Agatha Christie in translation. On the wall, the study of a dark-skinned nude, somewhat sub-Gauguin, her nipples red against a tranquil sea. Underfoot, a Persian carpet, well worn. Another door down, the family dining room. A polished oak table, set for a lonely diner and abandoned. A fresh napkin made of starched cotton. Walnut cupboards lined the wall, and a display cabinet with china. Through the bay window there was a view of the garden, smothered in snow; pines around the fringes, reaching for the moon. A rectangle of light was shining down from an upstairs window. Upon this gleaming stage, a shadow of movement, impossibly enlarged. Pavel, shivering now, chewing bloody patience.

He backtracked, found the staircase off a door in the drawing room. Got confused about where he had seen the light, and stumbled into the upstairs bathroom; patches of water on the floor. Soap shavings and pubic hairs ringed the plughole. Next to it, the master bedroom. It had been slept in, though only one half of the bed showed signs of use: a slender imprint, long, dark hairs upon the pillow. In the guest room to its right the mattress stood stripped and showed the dark ring of a pee stain, moist where someone had tried to wash it out. Another cot stood close by, still clad in its linen. At the end of the corridor yet another door – closed. A sliver of light underneath, and the stench of old tobacco. Pavel put his ear to it. The door was padded in leather. It cradled his lonely cheek.

Pavel stood, caressing the door, and heard precisely nothing.

———·———

She watched it as though it was happening to someone else, impressed by its colours and sense of the absurd. Fosko had walked her up to his study without comment. Had turned on the lights and let loose the monkey. It sat on the ground for a moment, sniffing the air, its nostrils dilating as it sorted through its flavours. It clambered up the ironing board, drawn by the residual heat; sat chattering, paws grabbing at the column of steam. The next moment, it leapt to the ground, interposed a cartwheel, took hold of the curtain and pulled itself up to the windowsill, before returning to the Colonel, fawning at his feet. Both Fosko and Sonia stood and watched its shenanigans. When it wrapped the Colonel's boot into a tight embrace they almost smiled.

Fosko walked over to the window and opened it an inch; stooped to straighten a corner of carpet, then returned to the table and picked up a glass of brandy that had been poured but left undrunk. Sonia studied him intently. She used the wall mirror, half-veiled in condensation. The Colonel stood framed in ornamental gilt, from chubby chest to placid chin. There was no hurry to his movement, no sign of urgency at all, nothing that would divulge his plans for her. Sonia called to her mind the words he'd spoken in the car; the hand upon her thigh. He had made her an offer. She had answered it. 'I won't,' she had told him. She wondered whether it was true.

He seemed to guess her thoughts. Stood with his back turned to her, pouring the brandy into a plant pot, the plant yellow and sickly, and launched into speech.

'You know, Sonia,' he said, and stroked a withered leaf between thumb and finger. 'I have always thought of you as the perfect mate. I'm not just talking physically, though you have a rare gift there, too. Angular yet supple, and an arse-cleft like a painting.'

He tore off the leaf and watched it sail to the ground.

'It's more than that, though. Something in your attitude towards the act. A rare enthusiasm. Your face, of course, says you hate it, and most likely you genuinely do. But your body,

283

Sonia. Your body loves the touch. It gives itself over, shamelessly. I have never had anything quite like it.'

He bent to one knee, opened the door of a corner wardrobe with a little golden key, and reached into it with both hands.

'I've always wondered whether you owned up to it. Being born for love. My wife, by comparison, is as frigid as a floor plank, though she tries, the darling. Good God, how she tries. It is ever so grotesque.'

He straightened up, lifting a large metal box, and carried it over to the table. A lens and a set of reels protruded from its angularity. A plaque marked it as army issue. Fosko lined up the machine with the wall behind the desk, placing its front feet on a book to elevate them slightly. The monkey launched itself at the projector and began dismantling one of its reels. Fosko swept it off the table with a disapproving tut.

'Behave.'

Then he turned his attention back to Sonia.

'You must be pining to see Pavel,' he said. 'Perhaps we can get to that later tonight.' His hand reached into his coat pocket and fished out the reel of microfilm. 'Really, it's just a matter of finding an accommodation.'

He licked his fingertips, caught hold of the end of the film and slowly, methodically, began unreeling its first yard.

'We are, after all, reasonable people, you and I.'

She long saw it coming. The moment the film would come apart in his hands and he'd realize it had been cut in half. For a second he was simply undone: puzzled, slack-jawed, ribbons of film trailing from each of his hands. All the colour drained from his face. He hunched as though in seizure, the mink riding him like a bitch. Sonia made a mistake then.

She smiled.

A proper smile, teeth and all. She imagined she even broke into dimples. He saw it, saw her happy, here upon the ashes of her defeat, and threw back his shoulders.

'Where?' he barked. 'Who?'

Her joy dissolved in fear. She swallowed the smile; cast off the dimples.

Shook her head.

Retreated.

'I don't know.'

'You don't know? *The film's in pieces and you don't bloody know?* Sonia,' he whispered. 'One of these days you'll break my fucking heart.'

Said it and launched himself at her, a whale of a man, skin so pale you'd swear he'd died underwater.

She jumped to the side, desperate to avoid him, looking for shelter behind the ironing board's flimsy frame. He did not bother going round it. Instead he took hold of its wood and threw it to the side, ramming one corner into the wall. The iron went flying. She remembered watching it, following its arc with her eyes – a lifetime of fear of fire taking hold of her. Sonia stood paralysed. The fat man, he lunged again.

She almost felt him slamming into her; the hurt of her spine as it caught the windowpane. Fat fingers tight around her windpipe, a knee parting her crotch; his big mouth chewing her up, literally.

He never made it, though. Something caught him short. The monkey. It had watched their dance with mounting excitement and chose that moment to make a run for its master's boots; had a good mind to mate with them, in fact, judging by its erect manhood, a pink little worm that had screwed itself out of its fur. A twenty-pound monkey latching itself onto polished leather, a whale growing out of its shaft. It should hardly have been enough to slow him down.

It cost Fosko his balance, though. A fat man in motion, and a monkey on his boot; his arms missing the woman and running headlong for the window now, snow crystals livid upon its panes. Trying to avoid collision, he threw his weight to the left.

Slipped on a corner of carpet, fine Persian silk.

Overbalanced.

And fell.

For a fat man, he hardly made a sound at all.

It took her a while to realize he was not getting up again. She stood still and counted the seconds. The only movement in the room was the monkey, screwing Fosko's boot for all it was worth. Then, in the total icy quiet, there issued a moan. Sonia cast around, found a paperweight on the desk, and walked over to the fallen giant. Out of the side of his skull, a good inch above the ear, grew the pyramidal body of his clothes iron. The blood poured from the wound and congealed upon its steaming surface. It stank of sausage.

The fat man wasn't dead. His eyes stood open, his lips were moving, then one hand, searching his body for hurt.

'Please,' he mumbled. 'Please.'

Sonia retched and was violently sick down the front of the silk blouse the Colonel had bought for her the day she'd agreed to be his whore.

———·———

Pavel eavesdropped and heard precisely nothing. It was clear to him that whatever had happened, he'd arrived late. The knowledge of it sickened him. He reached for the doorknob and slowly swung open the door. All of a sudden, the gun in his hand felt out of place. It made as little sense as if he'd come carrying roses.

Behind the door, the Colonel's study. An icy draught issuing from an open window. On Pavel's right, a desk and chair; a projector set up to illuminate the wall; a reel of film unravelled across the ground. On his left, the Colonel. Lying prone on one side; his legs moving, slowly, sluggishly, walking his body in a circle around his head's pivot. It was as though it had been nailed to the floor. The floorboards slick with fast-cooling blood, and steaming. Crouching to one side, high heels planted in the Colonel's effluvia, jacket and blouse torn off, and greenish bile discolouring her skirt's chequered front: Sonia; crouching in a black lace bra, her hands and arms smeared with blood, tears in her mascara, and a rhythm to her body as though she was rocking it asleep. She, too, was steaming in the cold of the room. Steaming from her mouth and from the blood on her arms; from her armpits and the sweat upon her brow. It clung to her like a shroud.

'Sonia,' he said.

She didn't seem to hear him. Instead she started screaming.

He dropped the gun, sat down next to her, and shushed her like a frightened dog. Meanwhile, next to them, the Colonel kept on making his rounds.

Already Pavel had begun to ask himself what they should do with his corpse.

———·———

Of course, she'd taken notice of his entrance. Taken notice of his greeting, too, and the idiotic cooing that issued from his lips. She wasn't ready to acknowledge him yet. Fosko was still alive. Just now, he had pulled his skull out of the iron, and begun to drag himself towards what he had to be mistaking for the door. He disgusted her. Vomit caked the inside of her mouth.

Slowly, Sonia reached over to where Pavel had dropped his gun; wrapped her hand around its butt. She stood up, walked stiffly over to the Colonel, the floorboards dark with blood. Pulling the trigger was a small thing.

She wondered what stayed her hand. Was it that killing was wrong? Of all the men in the world, surely this one deserved it. The gun in her hand would not stop shaking. She looked up and found herself in Fosko's gilt-framed mirror, a slip of a girl, half-naked and freezing. Her body was shivering so hard that her breasts jiggled, white against the black lace bra. Behind her, Pavel looked on with distracted disapproval. It was impossible to love him just then. She slung her arms around her frame and sought to suppress her shivers.

In the mirror, all one could see of the Colonel was one shiny boot. The monkey clung to it as though it were its long-lost twin.

She pointed the gun again, this time in earnest. Steadied it, with the palm of her left hand.

'Don't,' said Pavel.

'Why not?'

'I need to think it through first.'

He sat down behind Fosko's desk and threw his brow in creases. God damn him, this Pavel. He sat and thought like he was Newton, inventing gravity. All this, just to figure out whether or not to kill a man who was already dead.

'What do you want me to do?'

'Give me the gun. Go to his wardrobe and find us some coats. We are both freezing to death. And some cigarettes.'

She nodded yes and left the room, wondering where it had come from, his ability to treat her like a servant, or a wife.

———·———

While Sonia was away, Pavel picked up the gun from where she had placed it on the desk and walked over to the Colonel. He bent down to him, searched out his eye, placed the muzzle to his neck. They fell into each other's rhythm of breathing. The Colonel whispered something.

Perhaps he was just trying to breathe.

Pavel reached down and wiped off blood to better see the Colonel's wound. It was a messy crater of viscous matter. There was no way of telling how much time he had left.

When he heard her return, Pavel straightened up and hurried back to the desk. Sonia passed him a woolly sweater and a tweed jacket, both much too large. She was wearing a double-breasted fox-fur coat, knee-length, and a cotton scarf in the colours of an Oxford college, complete with crest.

'Did you kill him yet?' she asked. Her nonchalance was skin-deep. One could see the quiver underneath.

'No,' he said. 'I'm still thinking.'

'What's there to think about? Put a bullet in him.'

'And have him found here, with your number in his pocket book? What do you think will happen when the police show up? I doubt they will rule it an accident.'

She frowned, ran a hand over her cheek. The hand was beautiful. It struck him that he hadn't touched her yet.

'So what are we going to do?'

But he just shook his head and sat, unmoving. Behind them, amongst the clutter of knocked-over furniture, the monkey clambered over to squat on the Colonel's face, and drilled a leathery finger into his skull, the Colonel watching it out of the corner of one fatty eye.

———·———

And thus they sat idle while the minutes ticked away. I would not have thought he had it in him, this cold rationality in the face of another man's suffering. Sonia, too, could not make head nor tail of it. She thought it unworthy of him, the man she had built up in her dreams. That, and he was filthy: a beard on his face, the stink of prison. She had waited for this moment. Now she felt cheated.

One can relate to her frustration. Pavel had returned from the dead and walked in five minutes too late, dressed like a bum. Came to save her, no doubt, but came late nonetheless, the gun drooping in his hand. He did not touch her, kiss her, stroke her cheek. Stank. Sat puzzling. The same old voice, gentle like a girl's, awkward in his bearded face. The beard obscuring the cast of his mouth; his cheeks and forehead covered with grime.

She will have clutched at straws. *Maybe*, she will have thought, *maybe all he needs is a good wash. One good scrub, and he'll go back to being soulful.* Dribbled spit on one finger and ran it down his mucky temple. Trying to find the man underneath.

———·———

They should have been heading for the road. Left the house, no matter where. Pavel's indecision struck her as crazy. Worse than crazy. Constipated. Hamlet whispering to graveyard skulls.

'Let's go,' she urged, and ran a toe over the reel of microfilm on the floor. He didn't seem to hear her. She wondered briefly would he react if she crushed it with her heel.

'What's on it anyway?' she asked.

This time she got an answer.

'Scientific papers,' he said. 'Curricula Vitae. A number of addresses.'

'It's incomplete.'

'Yes.'

'You cut out a part. That's why there was a photographic lens on your desk, and a flashlight. You looked at the film and cut some of it out before you brought it up to me.'

'Yes.'

'I tried to figure it out. Why you did it. Then it became clear. You didn't trust me with the whole of the film.'

'No. I didn't. Couldn't risk it.'

'What's on the missing part?'

'Another address. Photos of a man entering and leaving a building. Details about his activities during the war. I only read scraps and pieces. My projection didn't work very well, and I had to work fast.'

'So you were clever then, too. Worked fast. And thought fast. Faster than now.'

290

'You're angry with me,' he whispered.

'I haven't the faintest idea what sort of man you are.'

She said it and the phone started ringing. It was hard to tell whether it had been her words or the phone that had made him flinch.

———·——

The phone rang. He was in the midst of it, making up his mind, and the phone rang. It was a heavy black phone that sat at one end of the desk, next to the cigar box. A cigar cutter lay by its side. Pavel remembered that he still hadn't had a cigarette. Sonia hadn't brought him any. He could have lit a cigar but felt too self-conscious to do so. One did not steal from the dead. He slipped a hand into the tweed jacket and searched it for cigarettes. He found a shilling piece and a rusty screw.

The phone rang a second time.

It might be best to just make a run for it. Take Sonia by the hand, climb into the Colonel's car and drive as far as they could before the morning, when Fosko's corpse would be discovered, alongside an agitated Peterson, and the Brits would declare a manhunt. She might forgive him then, after a bath and a shave, at least until such a time as they got caught. It seemed impossible that they would not get caught. This was occupied Germany, a roadblock every few miles. He didn't even carry a passport. It might buy him a few days with her. And nights. He wondered whether he was willing to throw away both of their lives for those few nights.

The phone rang a third time.

Pavel could shoot the Colonel. That part didn't make much of a difference to anyone, only in court they might say it was murder. It would be an act of mercy. He could shoot him with Peterson's gun, which might help hide their tracks, assuming that Peterson was nowhere to be found. Unlike Fosko, one *could* get

291

rid of Peterson; march him out of here; make him disappear. Why not? The man deserved it. He was a torturer. Boyd had been under his fist and knife. Others would be. Over time, it would seem like justice, killing Peterson.

The phone rang a fourth time.

Assuming they did get away; collected their money and his papers, and got out of the city. A few days' head start was all they needed. Where would they go? Back to the US, where he had a wife, and a mother who loved him? Russia might have him, but Sonia wouldn't come. France might do for a while, though they'd treat her as an enemy. He pictured her telling her story over there to a bunch of resistance fighters. How she went to bed with a midget, on His Majesty's service. Much could be forgiven for that, especially in France. The one person who wouldn't forgive was Anders. He had never fallen for her tattered smile.

The phone rang a fifth time.

'Where is the boy?' he asked all of a sudden.

'Shit,' she said. 'The boy.'

Her eyes fastened on the phone. Pavel saw it and made a grab for the receiver. By the time he got to it, the caller had already rung off. He tapped down on the fork, but the connection was gone. He tried to speak; his mouth was dry, his tongue looking for spit to speak by.

'Where the hell is Anders?'

Sonia reached over and dialled Franzi's number. There was no answer. She tried again, but the line went dead halfway through the second ring. She could not even get the operator.

'He's at Paulchen's. He was meant to pick up a projector. But he never came back. Something must have happened.'

They both turned to stare at the Colonel. It dawned on them how he'd gone about finding Sonia.

'Is he alive?' she screamed at him, and the Colonel blew a bubble. Pavel got up and stood over him with the gun, the second time that evening.

'You bastard,' he said.

It wasn't clear to Pavel whether he was answered by a cough, or laughter.

Surely, he thought to himself, *I'm going to shoot him now*.

Sonia gathered momentum and kicked the Colonel right in the crotch. It little changed the sounds he was making.

———·———

While Sonia kicked and Pavel wavered – while Fosko bled and spoke through bubbles – while Anders sat, broken-nosed and broken-hearted, a leering Georg looming large on his horizon – while I stood waiting in one much mended stocking, boot in hand and a host of roaches crushed upon its heel – while Söldmann slowly rotted, up in his attic's grave, and Franzi, long forgotten, stamped star shapes into rolled-out dough for cookies – while Berlin sat at cards, sat in blankets and mittens, trumping clubs with hearts, or boiled up ice upon the cooker in order to soak dinner-stained crockery – just then, at that very moment, General Dimitri Stepanovich Karpov's long-boned finger pressed down upon the front doorbell of Colonel Fosko's private residence in western Berlin. It had a celebratory air, that ringing; he'd even shed the kid glove for its pleasure. A moment before, at Karpov's signal, his adjutant, Georgian Lev, had cut the phone cable where it led into the house; cut it deftly and spat tobacco at its shower of sparks. Karpov's men had long since surrounded the villa, a little surprised that nobody was about to guard the compound. The General had not yet decided whether or not to deal civilly with Fosko. As it turned out, he would be spared this particular decision; the Colonel, he was soon to learn, was indisposed. The bell rang through the house for a full minute. Karpov had the good sense to stand somewhat to the side of the door and only present his profile. With a man like Fosko, he mused, it was hard to predict when exactly he would start shooting.

He was not greeted by bullets, however. Rather Pavel Richter opened the door, pale and tweed-coated, an English firearm slack in his hand. The women from the surveillance photos was by his side. Underneath her fox fur, Karpov noted, she seemed to be wearing nothing but a black lace bra. He cocked a brow and took the time to make a formal bow before he placed them under arrest. Sensibly, neither of them attempted to resist. He requested to see the Colonel, and with what struck him as something akin to mirth, they led him up the stairs to meet him. Karpov's men, meanwhile, searched the house for hidden dangers. They found me on my bug hunt and warmed their hands against the boiler. I did not speak any Russian and could not even ask them what the hell was going on. You imagine it: a storyteller locked out of his own tale. It turns one into a historian, that retrospective scrounger of fact. I cannot think of a more sordid occupation.

3 January 1947 (cont.)

The bell rang downstairs. It reminded her of something she had heard on the radio once, before the war. An American writer of crime fiction fielding a question about the paroxysms of his plot. 'When I don't know what happens next, I have someone come through the door with a gun.' Dead bodies littering his prose. It had all seemed frivolous to her. Before the war.

Pavel accepted it first. 'We better open.' There was no fight in his voice. They walked down together, like a couple expecting dinner guests. At the bottom of the stairs, Sonia reached out to grab his hand. She found it holding a gun; recoiled and wondered whether he had noticed the motion. They passed a window and saw movement in the garden. 'The Russians,' Pavel said flatly. It amazed her that he could tell from so casual a glance.

The General was tall and polite. He was accompanied by the man she had hit with a frying pan: those watercolour eyes, they ran with recognition.

'Take me to the Colonel,' Karpov instructed after disarming Pavel. He had a man pat Pavel down, but searched Sonia for weapons himself. She had to unbutton the fur for this, endure an embrace. His hands did not linger. He was a gentleman, or else he liked boys. When they were done, they led him up the stairs and towards the Colonel's study. The youth with the water-eyes left the procession to go to the bathroom and piss. He left the door open, leaned his rifle against the wall; stooped and spat chewing tobacco past his own jet of urine. In a single gesture he became everything Pavel was not.

The first thing Karpov did, upon entering the study, was shoot the monkey. He shot it casually, pulling a handgun from his coat pocket and putting it back as soon as the barrel had cooled. He bent briefly to examine Fosko's wound, then walked over to pick up the two parts of the microfilm off the floor. Lev rejoined the group, still buttoning his trousers. Two of the Russians were briskly ordered to search the rest of the house.

'This film has been damaged.'

Karpov's voice was perfectly composed. In his efficient leanness he cut a sharp contrast to the dying man. The General rounded the desk and sat in Fosko's chair.

'Where is the rest?'

Pavel shot Sonia a glance. 'We don't know. That's how we found it. On Söldmann.'

Karpov considered this, pursed his lips, then barked something at the blond youth. He spoke in Russian.

Pavel paled, stuck to English. 'But we don't know anything.'

'I believe you have said this before, Mr Richter.'

'She doesn't know anything.'

'We'll see.'

'We can't. Go. Not right away.'

'And why not?'

Sonia watched Pavel run his hands through his hair. She liked the gesture. It spoke of exasperation. It was suicidal, she knew, but she liked a Pavel who was finally out of his depth.

He did not stay like this. The hands dropped, and the tongue took a turn; switched alphabets in fact, spoke the language of rape. It held Karpov's attention. He gestured to his subordinate and had him fetch a chair so that Pavel and he could have a civilized conversation. Soldier to soldier, man to man. Sonia spoke no Russian and felt left out. All she understood was a name, oft repeated.

Haldemann.

She stood, trying to remember where she had heard it before.

———·———

Pavel tried to explain about the boy. That he was being held, in all likelihood, by a gang of German hoodlums. 'A good boy,' he explained. 'From the streets of Berlin.'

Karpov made a gesture to indicate that he was not impervious to the plight of a minor; that he was a cultured man, a sentimentalist even, despite the world.

'Alas,' he said, 'the times are bad.' He softened his mockery with the hint of a smile, right around the eyes. 'What can you offer me, Mr Richter?'

'I know where Haldemann is hiding.'

'Yes?'

'You can take a few days to beat it out of me and hope he's still there when you're done. Or I can just tell you.'

'If I rescue the boy.'

'If you rescue the boy.'

'It's a generous offer.' Again, that hint of an ocular smile, though the lips did not move. It was as though he could cut his face in two.

'A phone call might do it.'

'To say what?'

'That the Colonel is dead. It might do it. Just as long as Anders is alive.'

Karpov shook his head. 'It'll be better if we all go. Pick him up. Move on to Haldemann. I assume he's hiding in the city?'

'Yes, in the city.'

'I'll tell my men to get ready. You tell the woman. And get your coat.'

'You'll let us go when you have Haldemann?'

'If everything goes to my satisfaction.'

'You will let us go?'

'Your coat, Mr Richter. And the woman.'

When Pavel got up from the chair and turned, he found Sonia crouching next to Fosko's body, one hand in the monkey's fur. It was smoking from its chest.

'We never even gave it a name,' she complained.

Pavel reached down and put a hand on her shoulder.

'I thought you hated that monkey.'

'So did I.'

He couldn't see her face but thought she might be smiling. Sonia bent her neck towards her shoulder and placed one cheek upon the back of his hand.

'What happens now?' she asked.

'First I get my coat, then we all go get Anders.'

'And then?'

'There's this man they are looking for. From the microfilm.'

'Haldemann.'

'Yes, Haldemann.'

'Who's he?'

'He's who everybody keeps dying for.'

'Someone special then?'

'A Nazi.' He looked over to Karpov. 'We have to go.' He held out his hand and helped her up. For a moment they stood face to face.

'The last time,' she said. 'The last time we stood like this, you leaned forward to kiss me.'

'Yes, I did.'

She shrugged, blushing, her hand in his. 'You'd better get your coat, Pavel Richter. You might freeze.'

———·———

The Russians walked them both out into the corridor, then down the stairs and into the cellar. Underground, the air was hot and rotten; two Russians on guard, their shirts open to the navel, and a one-eyed Englishman under lock and key. They found me sitting on the ground inside the cage, cradling one boot by its heel. Around my woolly stocking there lay scattered the carcasses of insects. Pavel ignored me at first; searched the basement shelves for his coat. It had been taken off him when he had first been dragged down there. He found it and shook off the dust. Lev kept his eye on him, making sure he didn't pocket anything that could be used as a weapon. As he dressed, Pavel approached the cage.

'Where are they taking you?' I asked him.

'To Anders. I'm trading him for Haldemann.'

'And the Colonel?'

Pavel shook his head. I took it to mean that the Colonel was dead, or getting there. It was sobering to think that he had outlived his role in our lives; that all he should leave us with was a picture: a fat man with fat lips, and a *faible* for mink.

'What will happen to me?'

'I don't know.' He turned to Karpov who stood at the top of the stairs.

'What happens to him?' he called.

'We take him along.'

'They take you along,' Pavel translated. I think we both broke into a smile at the news. Behind Pavel, watching our easy interaction, stood Sonia, sweat running into her fox fur.

I fetched my coat and we moved out, five Soviet soldiers in civilian clothing and three prisoners, bracing ourselves for the cold. Outside, the moon stood ripe and heavy, and the air so raw that one rationed one's breath. We got into the General's limousine. Karpov drove. Lev sat at his side, covering us prisoners with his gun. The other Russians jumped into a second car, its ignition coughing until it finally caught.

'Where to?' Karpov asked Pavel.

'Charlottenburg. Schillerstrasse.'

Sitting beside him, Sonia slowly, shyly, stole her hand back into Pavel's.

———·———

And so we left the Colonel's house, squeezed together on the back seat of a requisitioned German limousine, a Georgian gun in our faces. Pavel sat next to me, his eyes on the road. To his left, Sonia was holding his hand. A tender gesture, regretful of the time she had wasted on anger, only his wedding ring kept catching on her knuckle. I wondered briefly what Pavel would have done had I made to hold his other hand, my fingers laced with his. All I wanted was for him to know that I did not begrudge him his violence towards me. In the end I decided against it. It would have been too ridiculous. In all things one must answer the call of dignity.

We raced towards Berlin. The Grünewald woods soon gave way to the city's outskirts, and country road turned into thoroughfare. It never ceased to take my breath: those majestic roads lined by a landscape of rubble. Here and there a wall stood up out of the debris, five storeys high, its windows shattered, the roof collapsed, leaning into the moon like a drunk picking a fight. At the next corner, two lampposts, bent at the waist as though in curtsy. The car hurtled on and came upon a street where buildings stood plentiful; a little chipped, it is true, but defiantly beautiful with their twelve-foot doorways and *Jugendstil* balconies. Drawn curtains at the windows, the streets too cold for foot traffic, and too poor to afford more than a handful of cars. One could drive through Berlin on nights such as this and feel like there was not a living soul beyond those headlights; the city dead and one's every breath a smoke signal, sent into the air in the vain hope of an answer.

Another corner, a change of gear, and the car rolled to a halt.

'There,' said Pavel. 'Towards the end of the block. They might have posted sentries.'

Karpov cut the engine and got out of the car. Sonia sat shivering while Lev passed around cigarettes, then a match, one hand always on the gun, eyeing them for movement. We sat smoking, aware of Sonia's mute shiver, waiting for what would happen next.

Outside, Karpov sent two soldiers to circle the building, then wrenched open the gate to Paulchen's backyard, and disappeared within.

———·———

The door burst open, amidst a shower of splinters. Whoever had been on guard must have been asleep or had been taken without a chance to call out. They wore civilian coats over their uniforms, but Anders recognized them for Russians immediately. You could always tell by their boots. The trim man with the wire glasses was their leader. Unlike the others, he wasn't holding a rifle.

'Which one is Paulchen?' he asked into the mass of boys who sat rooted to their various corners, chess piece or marble in hand, or a spoonful of soup arrested midway between bowl and mouth. His German was open-vowelled, the rhythms wrong. He had to ask again.

'Which one is Paulchen?'

The boys' eyes turned to the armchair where Paulchen had been brooding by the phone. His Luger was stuffed down the seat-cushion's side, along with a half-bar of chocolate.

'You?'

A glum nod.

The Russian shot him. There was no haste to the act. He threw back the coat, unbuttoned his gun from its leather holster, took it out, levelled it, and shot Paulchen in the face. The bullet whistled through the backrest and shattered the window behind. It wasn't as loud as Anders would have imagined. As the blood squirted from the hole underneath Paulchen's eye, he remem-

301

bered his vow to set to his comrades with a knife. It threw him into hot anger with a God who answered prayers willy-nilly, and made an angel of this silver-haired Russian who now bent down to him and ran a probing hand over his injuries.

'Are you Anders?' he asked.

Anders nodded, just as Paulchen had done a moment earlier. He had no fear of being shot.

'Can you walk?'

Another nod.

'Then stand.'

As Anders staggered to his feet, the man scooped up the telephone, dialled a number and spoke briefly in Russian. Before he hung up, he passed on the address, injecting something like a 'j' before the 'i' of Schillerstrasse. Then he walked back over to Anders, took hold of his hand, and marched him out like a schoolboy. The other Russians stayed behind. Anders wondered what would happen to his comrades of old.

Downstairs, another Russian joined them, also armed with a rifle. They walked through the yard, out the open gate and towards a jeep and a limousine. Pavel and Sonia were in the back of the limousine, along with the one-eyed man who worked for the Colonel. Anders had last seen him when they'd carted off Schlo', his neck bent double like a fish hook. The three figures sat together like they were sharing a taxi. The boy stood rooted, confused as to what to feel, until he made out the gun that was pointed at them from the front. It reconciled him, and he allowed himself joy at seeing his friends alive.

'Move,' said the Russian. 'Get in the car.'

He was not sure how to greet Pavel, so he hugged Sonia first, stuck his face into her furs then withdrew embarrassed when he encountered bare skin.

'I didn't squeal,' he started to say, but she shushed him, passed him over to his grave and bearded friend. They shook hands. Pavel's thumb soft upon his knuckles.

302

'You're hurt,' he murmured. 'What happened up there?'

'The Russians shot Paulchen.' He tried to keep it in, but it tumbled out nevertheless. It was that or burst into tears. 'How come you're both sitting in a car with them?' he asked, and was embarrassed when he saw they did not know how to respond.

———

Karpov opened the car door briefly to get his cigarette case which he had left on the dash. It was made of ornamented silver, and bore three monogrammed initials, СИК. The cigarettes inside were American. He offered one to Pavel. Pavel accepted. 'Your father?' he asked in Russian, pointing to the monogram.

'Yes. Stepan Ivanovich. May he rest in peace.'

'Why are we stopping?'

'We are waiting for some of my men to come with a truck.'

'Whatever for?'

'To transport all those boys. The Soviet Union needs workers for its mines.'

Pavel tried to read Karpov's face. He failed. The moon rendered it lifeless and wooden.

'You don't have to do this,' he said. 'All those boys. Just to teach me manners.'

The General shrugged. 'It's nothing. In the greater scheme of things. You'll forget about them before the week is out.'

He inhaled and blew smoke into one gloved fist. 'Trust me, Mr Richter. Very soon you will find yourself getting sentimental over something, something quite small really, a kitten on a garden wall, and it will be like those boys never even existed. Yesterday's news. A line you read in the paper and used for kindling.'

'You're cold, Karpov. You have a dead soul.'

'I forgot that you're a poet, Mr Richter. They left it out of your file. It's a serious oversight.'

'My file?'

'Your file, Mr Richter. Your military record. We got it through channels. And here you are judging other men's souls.'

Karpov smiled and closed the door on Pavel; Pavel sitting there, asking himself how many others would be made to suffer for his mistakes.

'What did he say?' Sonia wanted to know.

'They're taking the boys away with them.'

'Why?'

'Because they are witnesses. This is the British sector. The Soviets have no right to be here.'

'What a bastard.'

'Yes,' said Pavel. 'That's precisely what he is.'

He turned to her then, and to the boy who sat sprawled across her lap, and wondered what needed to be said before he went and found Haldemann for Karpov, and all their lives hung in the balance.

He spoke to the boy first. It was difficult to know where to start. Anders looked over to him; the boy was cooling one cheek against the window's glass, running a cautious hand over his twice-broken nose. Pavel thought about touching him, on the knee perhaps, or at the crook of his elbow, but was unsure of himself.

'We never finished *Oliver Twist*,' he said at last. 'Made sure he comes out all right.'

The boy waved away the attempt at banter.

'I was mad at you,' he told Pavel, teeth in his lip. 'On account of you cried. On the Colonel's shoulder. Back when we saw Boyd White. When he was dead.'

'Are you still mad at me now?'

'No, I'm not. The Colonel – he's dead, too, right? That's why you're here, with the Russians.'

Pavel had trouble controlling his voice.

'Yes,' he said. 'The Colonel's dead. An ugly death.'

'Aren't you glad?'

304

'Yes, of course.'

The boy looked up at him to see whether he meant it. He reached out a hand and stroked Pavel's cheek. They stayed like that for a while, the boy's hand growing cosy in his beard.

'What's going to happen next?' Anders asked eventually.

'We give them what they want.'

'And then?'

Pavel hesitated, looked over to Lev and the gun that was pointed at his face.

'I don't know, Anders,' he said and the boy accepted this without a murmur. He let go of Pavel's cheek and leaned back into the door.

———·———

The truck arrived and they sat waiting while two Russians in civilian garb got out, climbed the stairs and returned with a procession of boys, pale-faced and underdressed. They walked in an orderly line. Sonia wondered where they had learned it. Perhaps they had been born to it, the soldier's march, and the prisoner's. Things might have been different with a procession of girls. Surely one of them would have twirled a lock of her hair, or stuck out a hip; bent clumsily from her waist to pick up a handkerchief, or stopped to smooth out her skirts. She counted thirteen boys, all different sizes, all of them mucky. The last soldier carried the body, wrapped in a sheet. There was no mistaking the shape, nor the red stain that stuck skin to cotton and made recognizable the cut of the chin, the low, boyish brow. The soldiers worked slowly, loading up the boys one by one, unperturbed by the many lighted windows and their owners' watchful eyes. Paulchen was loaded up last. They lay him right at his companions' feet. For a moment, she tried to guess where they'd cart the dead boy. Chances were they would simply drive him over to police headquarters and instruct the medical examiner to diagnose him with terminal TB. Dead bodies did not strike her as a problem for a man like Karpov. At most they amounted to paperwork, a nuisance. She wondered whether, if he had stood where Fosko had stood, she would have attended to his needs with the same mercenary docility.

But it was Pavel who crowded her thinking, always Pavel, with his wild man's stubble and the gall to sacrifice a dozen boys' lives to buy slack for another. As she leaned against his shoulder and warmed his hand between her own, she watched him surreptitiously, from behind lowered lids. It was hard at this point to understand how they had got there, sitting thigh to thigh under a Russian's gaze. She wondered whether either of them would live through the night.

Karpov ordered two of his men to climb into the back of the truck and guard the boys. He stood watching it drive down the moonlit street until it turned at the corner. Then he got back in the car and asked Pavel where to go next.

'It's time you keep to your part of the bargain.'

Pavel hesitated. 'You can let the boy go now,' he said. 'And the woman.'

The General flashed a mirthless smile. 'You know very well I can't. Where to now?'

'Alt-Moabit. Near the park.'

'Good.'

He started the engine and pulled the car into the road.

———

Pavel was running out of time. They were almost there: another few blocks and he'd have to tell Karpov to stop the car. If he was going to speak it needed to be now, three men listening in, and Haldemann already crowding his mind. Pavel gestured to the boy to inch closer.

'How are you feeling?' he asked softly.

'Okay.'

'When we are done here, you need to go to a hospital.'

'I'm okay.'

'There could be something wrong. Internal bleeding. You need to have it looked at.'

The boy nodded consent, but suspicion was beginning to cloud his eyes.

'What's happening?' he asked.

'I'm going to get someone for the General. Someone he wants. You'll wait here with Sonia. You'll be all right, won't you?'

'Sure.' And then: 'There isn't any choice, right?'

Pavel smiled ruefully. 'Come closer, Anders. Come real close.'

The boy leaned over, wincing as he moved his ribcage. His mouth was a swollen mess of dried blood and shreds of skin; the nose a dislocated lump. Gently, Pavel reached out, grabbed his face on either side and planted his own lips upon the boy's. He held him like that for two or three moments, then let go, amidst the taste of blood.

'Euhh,' said the boy. 'What was that about?'

'It's a Russian thing. It means there is no anger between us.'

'Are you going to give Sonia one, too?'

But Pavel had no answer to this.

He gave Karpov a sign to stop the car and cut the engine. All this was done without the need to utter a single word; a tap on the shoulder and a look was all it took. The two Russians got out and waited for Pavel to follow suit. He leaned forward a little, to unwedge himself, but Sonia stopped him with a tug at the arm. Pavel looked at her then, looked at her from up close. The moonlight reflected off her chin's down; a thousand silky hairs that clung to the planes of her cheeks like ivy. The mouth a tight line; furrows on the brow. Pavel thought it anger. He was surprised when she reached out and gently stroked his cheek.

'I know,' he mumbled. 'I ought to shave.'

The brow unfolded. 'I was beginning to forget about that.' And quietly: 'You'll come back?'

He smiled weakly. 'What choice do I have?'

'Oh, Pavel. You really know how to cheer a girl.'

They parted without a kiss. Outside, Karpov offered him another cigarette and asked him to point out where Haldemann was hiding.

———

'Which one is it?'

'That one over there.' Pavel pointed to a brown brick building. There had been a photo on the microfilm, and a close-up of the doorway. He took a long drag on his cigarette, held down the smoke, exhaled. It gave him the illusion of patience. The next moment he shattered it with a question.

'What do we do now?'

The General hesitated. His eyes wandered over to Lev, then to the driver of the second car. He had lost all his other soldiers to a truckload of boys. His attention reverted to Pavel; studied him with a peculiar intensity.

'I should call for backup. I could use another three or four men. Somebody to guard the exits, in case he makes a run for it.'

Pavel nodded. 'It could take a while, though. Finding a working telephone and all. And then, of course, he might still throw himself out the window. When he learns you are Russian, I mean.'

They stood smoking, looking at the building. Pavel watched Karpov clench and unclench his fist as he was trying to make up his mind. His fingers had to be freezing in their thin leather gloves. Minutes passed before he spoke.

'Are you a chess player, Mr Richter?'

Pavel shook his head. 'I don't know the first thing about chess.'

'Really? I would have thought you did.'

'I'm sorry to disappoint.'

Pavel held his stare, blew white smoke into the night. His teeth ached with the cold. 'Why don't we go in and finish it? You and I, General. We'll pick up Haldemann. Convince him to come quietly. And then we can all go home. Warm up over a glass of hot tea.'

Karpov stood, pursed his lips. He took his time making up his mind. 'Lev will go with you,' he said at length. 'He's younger than I am. Stronger. A better shot, too. You understand what I'm saying?'

'Perfectly.'

'Just get the man out of there. Tell him it's for the best. You're good with words, aren't you, Mr Richter?'

As though on cue they both turned to look at Sonia who sat huddled together with the boy on the back seat of the limousine. Karpov's voice took on an unpleasant edge.

'She is quite beautiful, you know. A German Grushenka. Only not as plump. The fox suits her.'

'There is no need to threaten me.'

'Who is threatening you?'

'You'll let her go afterwards?'

'She holds no value for the Soviet Union. Don't do anything stupid, Mr Richter, and everything will go as agreed.'

Pavel threw his cigarette into a mound of snow and gestured to Lev. Together they crossed the road and approached the brown brick building.

———·———

And so they went inside. Woke up the caretaker in the ground-floor flat with a rap on his window, bade him unlock the front door, and vanished inside. Karpov sent the other Russian in after, to keep guard at the bottom of the stairs, then positioned himself near the door, always keeping his eye on us, the hostages. A working-class neighbourhood, two blocks north of the Tiergarten; a horse butcher's on the corner next to a derelict beer cellar with no glass in the windows. Nobody spoke. Sonia sat stone-faced, her hands drawn back into ample sleeves; shoulders squared, feet planted, fast, shallow breaths through a half-open mouth. To her left sat Anders. He kept glowering at me, mistaking me for young Salomon's killer, then cocked his head to listen for internal seepage. Pavel's talk about internal bleeding must have got to him: a twelve-year-old boy, face to face with his own mortality. His hands searched his belly, to test it for swelling, defiant eyes turning to fear. As for myself, I kept my eye on the General, six foot tall and sleek in his greatcoat. He took a gamble when he sent Pavel up to act as his mouthpiece, a strategy aimed at defusing those first few seconds of shock in which a man might do something foolish, before the realities hit home and accommodation replaced rebellion as the motive force of action. It wasn't much of a gamble – Lev's gun made sure of that – but a gamble nonetheless. I thought I knew its origin. Karpov *liked* Pavel. The way they had stood together, sharing a smoke, their faces lighting up with every puff. While Lev paced and awaited orders, they shared a moment's peace: time enough to discuss procedure, and to comment on a woman's beauty. We in the car witnessed it all with stoic resignation; slaughterhouse cattle on the threshold of the knacker's barn. All we could do was watch and wait. I remember that, despite the cold, sweat kept gathering on the inside of my eye-patch until I was forced to mop it up with a corner of my handkerchief.

———·———

The caretaker held the door open for them, then quickly disappeared back into his apartment; he had long since learned to display no curiosity. Pavel mounted the stairs, reading the nameplates off doors whenever they got to a new landing. Lev

310

was right behind him, his eyes transparent in the staircase light. Here and there he would stop to spit tobacco from one corner of the mouth. They stopped on the fourth floor, in front of a door marked 'Braun'. A sliver of light bled from under its wood.

'He's pretending he's Braun?' Lev asked.

'No. He's hiding with the Brauns. Now, not another word. I do the talking.'

Pavel reached out a hand and twice rapped the door. A shadow moved inside the apartment's hallway, then the silence of indecision.

'Who is it?' sounded through the door.

'Herr Braun? We need to talk to you. Open up, please.' His German gentle and educated; a doctor making a house call. The door opened a crack.

'Who are you?'

'Please,' said Pavel. 'Don't do anything stupid. All we want is to talk to the Professor.'

The man started to say something, a denial of knowledge, and close the door on them. Then he saw Lev's gun. It wasn't pointed at anything in particular but he got the point.

'Russians?' he asked.

'I'm American. Please. We just want to talk.'

The man hung his head and let them in. Chez Braun: a room, a kitchen, and the toilet out on the landing. In the living room the marital bed stood squeezed right next to the sofa. A cracked mirror adorned the wall. The place smelled of cabbage and burned wood varnish. One kitchen cupboard lay dismantled to serve as firewood. Braun's wife turned at the cooker, wearing her coat indoors against the cold. She saw the gun and started crossing herself. Pavel nodded to her in greeting, then put a finger to his lips.

'Where is he?' he asked, the voice reassuring even in whisper.

By way of an answer Braun pushed to one side the sagging sofa. It slid with ease, the floor long worn smooth by the motion. The backboard hid a half-sized door, visible only by its wooden knob and hinges. Pavel bent to open it, but Lev shouldered him aside. He took a deep breath, flaring his nostrils, then tore the door open and leapt inside.

Behind the door lay a closet big enough for a cot and a writing desk, minus the chair; one would have to work from bed. On the cot sat the Professor: an elderly man wearing a dressing gown over his sweater and slacks; the eyes overlarge behind thick slabs of glass; Prussian whiskers and an unkempt air of genius. There was no window from which he could have thrown himself, but even so Lev took no chances. He jumped on the old man and pushed him into the wall; tied his wrists with a length of wire, then stuck two fingers inside his mouth to search his gums for cyanide. It was a well-executed, methodical arrest. He even confiscated the man's glasses for purposes of disorientation. Pavel watched it all through the open door. He only stepped through once Lev had straightened up, pleased with his handiwork. There was a bloom of colour on the Georgian's cheek, from the exercise. The Professor, by contrast, was deathly pale.

'Manfred! Wilma!' he called out past the two men who filled his closet. 'Who is this? Are they Russians?'

'The dark one says he is American. He speaks German, though.'

A glimmer of hope woke in the Professor's myopic eye. Lev yanked him up by the crook of his arm, then dropped him back on the cot when he saw Pavel moving to intervene. The gun rose and perched itself in the soft of Pavel's neck.

'Easy now.'

'I just wanted to ask him to collect his papers.'

He gestured to the stacks layered upon desk and floor; page upon page of equations and notes, all in the same fastidious hand. 'Karpov will want them.'

Lev considered this. 'You do it. Haldemann can give you instructions.'

Pavel bent to follow the command, but there was hardly enough space to move. Grudgingly, Lev backed out of the doorway in order to make space. He sat crouching in the exit, his eyes alert to each of their movements. The Brauns stood behind him, holding hands. Bent low, picking up papers, all Pavel could see of them were their legs and those hands, folded in companionship. To his side, still lying on his cot, the Professor quietly began to weep.

'You need to tell me which of the papers are the most important, Professor. We can't take them all.' Pavel located a leather satchel and opened it up. 'How about this folder here? Will you need this?'

'What will you do to me?'

'You are a famous man, Professor. These people' – he pointed to Lev – 'they just want to talk.'

'He's a Russian?'

'Yes, he is.'

'Oh God.'

Haldemann lost control of himself then: broke into sobs that shook his whole body, until Pavel laid a hand on his cheek and shushed him like a little girl. Abruptly, in between sobs, the man told him about his modest little dream. It was as though he had rehearsed it. All he'd ever wanted, he told Pavel, was a cottage by the sea. The Ostsee, if he had any choice, though any sea would do, he loved the smell of it, the brine and the sand; it reminded him of childhood. And in this cottage he would devote himself to the breeding of snails. Pavel thought he had misunderstood at first; mixed up the word, or simply misheard. Then it dawned on him.

'For eating, you mean?' he asked him, still busy stroking Haldemann's hand.

'Ja, ja,' the man nodded. 'For eating.' He mimed the act of sinking his fork in a shell and eating its contents, his cheeks dry now, though still salty with tears.

'Professor,' Pavel told him politely, 'you need to tell me which papers to pack.'

Behind them, in the doorway, Lev barked at them to hurry the fuck up.

———.——

There may have been time, in that closet, to smuggle a question past Lev's vigilance. A moment was all Pavel needed. Surely he will have wanted to know how much Karpov's prize was really worth. I know that I have lost sleep over it for a good twenty years. He must have asked him, then. Surely he will have asked. About the German bomb. How close they had got, Haldemann and his colleagues, down in their underground lab. Perhaps it hadn't been so much a question as an exchange of glances while he tended to the Professor's tears: a touch, a gesture, a twitch of the mouth. Enough to constitute a question and an answer, and perhaps just a little bit more: an agreement about their mutual future.

I know it must have happened, back in the Brauns' closet, in that half moment when Lev patted his pockets for a fresh twist of tobacco, or when the *Hausfrau* distracted him with her confused offer of a cup of *Ersatzkaffee*. It eludes me, however, the precise nature of their secret communication. Try as I might, I have never been able to put it down on paper. It is a hole at the centre of the story. It isn't the only one.

———.——

His dream divulged, Haldemann calmed down sufficiently to assist in the selection of his papers. Pavel filled up the satchel, then helped the old man step through the half-sized doorway and into Lev's custody. The wire cuffs were biting into the Professor's wrists and cutting off the circulation; his hands looked grey and lifeless. He may never have felt Pavel's furtive squeeze designed to wish him good fortitude. Without another look at the Brauns, Lev marched them out into the corridor, Haldemann walking first, and the Russian last, his gun in Pavel's back. Short-sighted and unable to support himself against the banister, the Professor moved very slowly, probing for the stairs with his feet before every step. He stopped to catch his breath on the third-floor landing, Lev skittish and snarling at him to keep moving.

'I really thought you would try something,' he said to Pavel as they resumed their descent. 'Karpov said you'd be the kind of man to try something. He said he read it in your file.'

Pavel just shook his head.

'That mysterious file,' he complained. 'I don't know where you got it from, but someone's been telling you stories.'

Lev grinned and spat tobacco on the floor.

———·———

On the second-floor landing, Pavel missed a step and stumbled forward. He fell into Haldemann's back, then reached out with his arms, to catch him lest he fall. His pale, fine-fingered hands missed the old man's shoulder and grabbed his neck and chin instead.

They used to slaughter chickens like this.

When it was done, Pavel eased him gently to the floor. He turned to face Lev, his features calm and composed. Between them, in the staircase, the bark of broken bone. The Georgian stood, wide-eyed, choking on his twist of tobacco.

———·———

There you have it: Professor Dr Joseph Haldemann, rocket scientist, dead as a doornail. All this time my story has been about him, and no sooner does he take the stage than he dies, his neck broken, the taste of imaginary snail still fresh on his palate. He didn't know a thing about Fosko, Söldmann, and all the rest; had spent his days in ignorance, hiding out with the Brauns, his proletarian relatives by marriage, and slinking back into his shelter behind the sofa whenever someone thought to ring the bell. Oh, he had heard them, the stories of scientists who were being rounded up by the Russians and shipped eastward, to serve his namesake in the fortification of Socialism in One Country. The past two years had not been easy for the good Professor. First the Reich fell apart, and with it his hopes of unlocking the atom's secret. Then he found he had little hope of denazification on account of his distinguished record of service for yesterday's *Heimat*. As a potential war criminal, he was eligible only for the lowest category of ration card and consequently starved. But at least he was in the western half of the city, safe – or so he thought – from the Bolsheviks and their voracious appetite for German science.

As soon as he heard that the Soviets had no compunction about venturing into their allies' sectors for ill-masked abductions, and had compiled lists of preferential targets, he went into hiding. Cousin Manfred had a secret room. In the years of the Reich it had briefly housed a nephew who Witnessed to Jehova but saw this as no reason to share the burdens of camp life alongside Yids and Queers. Back then, Haldemann had known and kept his mouth shut; now he came looking for shelter himself. Manfred Braun wasn't enthusiastic, either about the Professor as a person, or at the prospect of having another mouth to feed, but the stamp collection the disgraced Nazi handed over to him did much to sweeten that particular pill. Not that Manfred gave a monkey's about stamps but he soon learned that he could get five pounds of fresh steak for a single pre-Napoleonic Thurn-und-Taxis, and that was good enough for him.

But there's no point in dwelling on Haldemann much longer. He was a scared old man, with crimes on his conscience, and a brain full of formulas that could scorch the earth. More to the point, he was dead; died mid-step, his hands numb and feet probing to escape a fall.

There can't have been much pain. The execution had been too professional for that. It is the executioner one should pity. There he stood, moist of eye, before Lev's loaded gun, asking himself whether he was visiting death upon those he loved most dearly.

———·———

Anders was restless. Pavel and the blond Russian had been gone for a quarter-hour. How long did it take to pick up one man? Sonia said he was called Haldemann. The name rang a bell somehow; perhaps he had heard it on the radio.

'Is he important?' he asked.

'Fosko was willing to pay thousands of pounds for him.'

The boy whistled. He had never met anyone quite as important as that.

His body hurt, and he was sure now that his insides were leaking, filling him up with his own blood. Even his hands and feet felt bloated, and he did not seem to be able to get enough breath. He wondered whether one could drown from bleeding on the inside. If so, he hoped Pavel would return to be with him when it happened. Perhaps they would kiss again, never mind it being yucky.

Beside him, Sonia sat as stiff as a doll. She did not react when he reached over and squeezed her hand, nor when he raised a hand to remove a strand of hair that had fallen to mask her face.

'No need to worry,' he whispered to her. 'They'll be right out.' There was no telling whether or not she had heard him. Anders sat and wondered how she could be so aloof.

At long last Pavel emerged. He was carrying an old man in his arms, staggering under his weight. A bruise showed in his face, narrow and oblong, from ear to mouth. Anders heard Karpov

317

curse in Russian. Sonia did not move, only her lip started to tremble. Anders wished she would get a hold on herself and tell him what the hell was going on.

———·———

She saw it and knew he was lost to her. Perhaps she had already known it when he'd left her in the car. He hadn't kissed her. She hadn't asked him to. It had violated their mutual sense of decorum. Now he was carrying a corpse.

It was clear to her that he must have killed the man. It was there in his face, and in Water-Eye's angry gesture. The thought chilled her: that her Pavel was a killer. Everything ended here. The only question left to her was whether she would live through the night. Suddenly, in her chest, there unfolded an enormous need to live. It took her by surprise. She watched Karpov run over to Pavel, furious. The third Russian emerged from the building and saw they had been left unguarded. He rushed over to the car, waving his gun. Not one of them had made a move to escape.

Sonia watched them talking, Pavel and Karpov. At first, the Russian was agitated, but within a few moments he had calmed. The cigarette case appeared in his hand, took the place of his gun. The two men strolled the street, smoked and talked. They would be negotiating about Anders' life, and her own. It angered her that it was this way: two men smoking, figuring out whether or not she should live. Pavel looked like he had done this all his life. God only knew what he had left to offer; she would have thought he'd long run out of trumps. He had put the corpse down, and the old whiskered man was lying on the cobblestones, his head loose upon its trunk. The neck was broken. She looked back up, to Pavel's hands, and found no trace of violence there. An hour earlier those very hands had held her own; had touched her cheek, and the rim of one ear. She hammered on the car window, but he was too far away to hear it. Eventually, they concluded their talk. Both men looked impassive, as though little enough had happened. Pavel stepped towards the car and, despite Lev's hiss, she rolled down the window. Pavel bent forward a little, gazed in. His eyes were veiled in shadow. ·

'They'll let you go. All three of you. Peterson – your job is to explain Fosko's death to the British. Without mentioning Karpov and his men. I gave him my word you could do it. On my life, you understand.'

'Yes, of course.'

'Bring the boy to a hospital. And give her the money. Anything you can find at Fosko's. It belongs to her. Can you do this for me?'

Only then did he deign to turn to her. He looked as he always had. Eyes like moist pebbles, and a voice to charm killers.

'Sonia?'

Tears blinded her. She lifted her hands into fists, then buried her face in them.

'Who the fuck are you?' she started to ask, but never got past the first word. There was no hope for an answer.

A moment later she heard the boy call out and knew Pavel was gone. She did not see whether he'd just turned around or had been ushered away. Then Lev's bark: 'Get out, all of you!' Anders made her leave the car. He opened the door and lifted her ankles out onto the street. The click of high heels on cobbles. She stood up mechanically, braced herself against the cold. Behind them, car doors closed and engines started. Wheels turning upon the icy road. Then silence. When she finally turned she was relieved to find the street empty.

They had even remembered to take along their corpse.

6

3–4 January 1947

Our first stop was a hospital. I had thought that Sonia would refuse to come with me, but she trudged along obediently enough, holding the boy by one hand. Perhaps she was keen to get her hands on the money. Silently, walking shoulder to shoulder down Berlin's empty roads, we headed for the Virchow clinic. Inside, there was a line of people waiting to see the night doctor, but when they saw that we had brought an injured child a few of them waved us ahead, content to sweeten their pain with the knowledge of their own nobility. The doctor who welcomed us looked like he should have been pensioned off a decade earlier. He wore a Tolstoyan beard and pulled up the right shoulder in a manner that suggested he suffered from rheumatism. He examined Anders gruffly, frowning over the bruises that clustered around the back of his spine, and straightening the nose between his practised thumbs. Upon his muttered suggestion, I slipped him some money, and he found the boy a shot of morphine.

'Who did this to him?' he asked while the boy got dressed.

Sonia and I exchanged a long glance.

'He fell down the stairs,' she said at last.

The old man nodded, and helped Anders with his shoes.

'If this happens again,' he whispered to him, though none too quietly, 'you should move somewhere where there aren't any stairs.'

We left in a hurry, walking down the hospital's long, draughty corridors and flattening ourselves against the wall whenever a nurse passed with a gurney. Outside, I bribed and bullied an ambulance driver to run us back to the Colonel's villa. He pocketed the money and we squeezed into the driver's cabin next to him.

'Grünewald,' he said testily, his face close to the dash so he could see out of the one corner of windshield that he'd scrubbed free of frost. 'Long fucking way.'

'Just get us there, my friend,' I told him, my thoughts alive to other issues.

———·—

I watched them while we sat in the ambulance, the boy and the woman. They looked shell-shocked; huddled together in silence, in their eyes a look of total incomprehension. I sympathized with their feelings of betrayal, but something else busied my heart: Pavel's commission, so emphatically given, to look after his loved ones. He had forgiven me, had trusted me with their lives. It felt as though our friendship had finally been consummated.

Mine was a muted celebration. It only lasted until the car swung into the Colonel's driveway. The villa looked gloomy, like something out of a Gothic painting, magpies on the gables and a light burning in the study upstairs.

'Here you go,' said the driver.

I noticed that neither Anders nor Sonia were in any rush to get out.

———·—

We crept into the house like thieves. Initially, I guess, we were hushed by the question of whether or not Fosko was still alive.

We stood stock-still in the dining room, near the corner where the good china lay stacked in a glass cabinet, and listened for a sound of his movement. None was audible. Not one of us ventured to go up the stairs just then.

His pain assuaged by the morphine, the boy soon fell asleep. After a moment's hesitation, I carried him downstairs into the cellar, and laid him on the mattress that had been Pavel's. The warmth would do him good. I guarded him for half an hour or so, but he never stirred, let alone woke. Reassured by his regular breathing, I went back up and joined Sonia, who was sitting on the living-room sofa and had put on a record to keep her company. I took a seat at the sofa's far end, careful not to crowd her. Bach was playing, the Cello Suites. The Colonel had been very fond of Bach. Perhaps he still was.

We sat a long time before she asked me.

'Why did they let us go?' she asked. 'The Russians?'

I thought it over, formulating various theories to myself.

'Perhaps,' I said at last, 'Karpov isn't that bad a sort.'

She smiled at that and stood to turn over the record.

'You said you wanted to give me money?'

'Yes. The Colonel has a safe in his office.'

'Get it then.'

I did as I was bidden: walked up to the study and opened the door, keeping my face averted from the spectacle of Fosko until I had opened the wall safe and counted out some three hundred pounds for Sonia. Then I turned and chanced a glance. It wasn't a pretty sight. The man just wouldn't die. He lay on his back, slick as a seal with his own blood; spoke from time to time, bubbles of spit rising from his sausage lips, or moved an arm in a half-circle, writing red crescents into the wood. The worst of it was the monkey. In the cold that had seeped in through the half-open window it had become frozen to the Colonel's shirt. It stuck to him like another limb, a hole in its chest, filthy, a dour witness to his dying.

'I'll be back,' I told him, and quickly returned to the living room.

Sonia counted the money and stuffed it into her pocket, then instructed me to get her some blankets from upstairs, and wake the boy.

'We are going. I'm taking Fosko's car. I'll leave it somewhere in Charlottenburg. You can find it there if you care to.'

I followed her instructions without a murmur. The boy would not wake, so I just carried him up as he was, and then out to the Beetle.

'Don't come near me,' she said as she started the car. 'Don't even think about it.'

I promised I wouldn't, and waved as she made her way down the driveway. Then I went back inside, brewed up a big pot of coffee, and went upstairs.

Do you know what I did?

I sat and watched Fosko die.

I swear to God it took him all night.

When he was finished, I wrenched the monkey from his shirt, stuffed it down the old outhouse toilet, then called the British Military Police to report a terrible accident.

'What sort of accident?' asked the chap over the phone.

'Domestic,' I said. 'I just reported to work and found the Colonel dead in his office. He seems to have fallen on his iron.'

'You stay where you are and we'll be over with an ambulance right away.'

I did just that and braced myself for a hundred indiscreet questions.

Part Four

After Pavel

1

Spring 1947

Winter did not break until the fourteenth of March, when the temperature suddenly rose by twenty-five degrees in a matter of hours. There was a moment when the air was already warmer than the frozen ground, and water collected in the streets and hardened into black ice. It cost a few lives, and of all those lost to this winter, they may have been the most tragic, tripped up on the verge of spring. Berlin's streets were full that day, and even more so the next: people staring up into the sun, and breathing air that no longer stung their lungs. All of a sudden the city was alive with the smell of grass and dog shit. By the end of the week, Berlin stood in the fullest of blooms. I am no sentimentalist, but I bought myself a big bunch of flowers as soon as they became available. They gave a little beauty to my poky little room.

The investigation into Fosko's death had taken me out of circulation for a few weeks. I was suspect because I was a civilian whose services to the Colonel had been strictly off the record. In fact, I passed myself off as a butler-cum-housekeeper, and to my relief the other chaps in Fosko's employ, headed by the chauffeur and burly Easterman, backed me up on this. In the end the Colonel's death was judged an accident. Rumour had it that headquarters was pleased to see the back of him and quickly shut down any further investigation. As for me, I found myself stranded in Berlin without an income, living frugally off my meagre savings. It was from the marginal vantage point of a middle-aged pauper that I watched history unfold. Berlin was in the eye of the world in the spring of 1947.

As the new year got going, the relationship between the western Allies and the Soviets slowly dipped from bad to worse, and it was beginning to smell like another conflict. By March, the Americans had declared the 'Truman Doctrine', vowing to 'contain' the spread of Communism throughout the world. The Soviets reacted by sabotaging Berlin's electricity and water supply at random intervals and by filling the streets with violence. Incidences of murder spiralled out of control, and there was talk of German prisoners of war dying in Russian uranium mines. Scientists and engineers continued to disappear at alarming rates. New rumours made the rounds day after day, growing more outlandish with every passage from tongue to tongue, and feeding a mounting economic panic. Berliners talked food stamps, talked currency, talked glorious Hitler.

Against this rich canvas of history, my prime interest, of course, lay with the life paths that had so recently intersected with my own. About Pavel I was unable to ascertain a single fact, not even whether he was dead or alive. I tried writing to his family in Cincinnati, but could not locate any Richters who were missing either a son or a husband. Former comrades told me a story or two about his past, but not even a Russian drinking buddy (a major, no less) could procure any information about what had happened to him after Karpov had whisked him off.

Sonia was easier to keep an eye on. Against my expectations she did not leave Berlin immediately. Instead, she moved flats, to a two-room maisonette in Wilmersdorf, and had the Bösendorfer grand transferred there from her old quarters. I made the acquaintance of the lady who lived across from her, Frau Walkowitz, a war widow of a well-preserved forty, and met her once a week for coffee and cake in order to sound her out about her

328

neighbour. She must have thought I was courting her, and after our last meeting in September, when I announced that I was leaving Germany for good, I left her with tears in her eyes. She told me that Fräulein Sonia Drechsler lived frugally with her teenage son. She was teaching the boy to play the piano and to read; for some reason he was not enrolled in school. In early April she confided that she thought the young *Fräulein* might be pregnant; two weeks later she was sure of it. I would have loved to learn who was the father, and also why she hadn't taken any precautions. Even if I had allowed myself the liberty of sending her a letter, however, there was no easy way to phrase such a question to a perfect stranger. The only time we had spoken was in Fosko's villa, to the rumblings of a cello. In May there was another shocking piece of news. Despite her pregnancy, Sonia had 'made the acquaintance' of an American serviceman who had agreed to marry her without much ado. His name was Skinner, rank of lieutenant. They would leave Berlin in October, taking the newborn and Anders along. The boy, I was told, never referred to Skinner by anything but his last name. The Lieutenant did not seem to mind and treated him well once he'd heard that his father had been a socialist. 'He has sympathies in that direction,' the widow Walkowitz confided. Trust Sonia to find the one card-carrying pinko in the whole of the American occupation army.

Once I heard of Sonia's plans to emigrate, I too decided to leave the city before things could deteriorate any further. In the event, I anticipated her departure by a week and a half: packed my bags, put a parting tear in the widow's eye, and returned to old Blighty where the economy was shot to pieces and people eked out miserable little livings without a shadow of a hope for improvement. After some months I found work as a night watchman and went about my life guarding a chemical factory with the assistance of an Alsatian by the name of Fritz. We had a close relationship until he developed testicular cancer and had to be put down.

One detail that busied my mind for many weeks before I left Berlin was the fact that the midget had disappeared. He should have been found up in the attic when spring stole over the city, but he was not – I looked for news of his discovery in the papers every day, and, one morning in April, I went over to the house in Seelingstrasse in order to find out for myself. I asked all the tenants, but nobody had the slightest idea what I was talking about; searched the attic, but found nothing apart from a row of bloomers that one of the tenants had hung up to dry. Of Söldmann there was not a sign. Who is to tell who took him? If I were to hazard a guess, I would say one of Pavel's former neighbours had stumbled upon him and snuck him down into their basement larder. Stuffed him next to the pickle barrel, perhaps, where they'd complement one another in their smells. To what purpose, you will ask. Ah, well, there you have me stumped. For food or barter? To add to the assemblage of skeletons in one's closet? Because they knew he'd once been notorious, and now was dead? With the hope, perchance, of selling him to the authorities, for a shovelful of coals? In any case, Söldmann disappeared and it is unknown where he met his final thaw.

The day I left Berlin, at the end of September 1947, I clutched to my breast a little suitcase filled with notebooks. In these, I had put down all that I knew and remembered, clumsily to be sure, with many repetitions and in the order of memory rather than that of event. The guard on the train had trouble convincing me to store it in the luggage net overhead, and even after I did, I kept my eye on it all the way to Calais. I remember falling asleep near the Belgian border, my head thrown back upon my shoulders. I woke with a flailing motion, afraid that my memories were gone. There they sat, though, heavy in their case, and all that had happened was that I'd got myself a crick in the neck, sticking fast like a bloody burr. It took me days to shake it off entirely.

2

May 1964

I couldn't leave it at that. Wanted to, I'll admit, but curiosity got the better of me. I had to see them again, one of them, or all three, whatever could be arranged. I failed with Pavel. There was no way of locating him. I had extended my inquiries into his past as much as my meagre income permitted, and had learned some disquieting facts. His present was lost to me, the Soviet Union a sealed box. If he had got out since his 'arrest' (and there was some reason to believe that he did get out), he was now living under a different name, in Washington DC most likely, or perhaps in Bonn, in the service of a government or two.

Sonia I did find without too many problems. After their wedding, the Skinners had moved to Lexington, Virginia. He was in carpets (a Communist in carpets – ridiculous, I know), she gave piano lessons. Anders had left the house as soon as he had come of age and returned to Germany. The younger child, a daughter by the name of Jean, was a 'junior' in high school and working hard on becoming next year's prom queen. I saved up for a flight to the United States, wrote Sonia a letter and requested a meeting. 'You may not remember me,' I wrote, 'but I had the pleasure once of passing on to you some money that you were owed. I was Pavel's friend,' I added, thinking it might help. She wrote back a week later, suggested meeting in a downtown coffee shop, and showed up in a flower-patterned summer dress and sunglasses. Her hair was very Jackie Kennedy. It had been seventeen years since I'd last seen her, and she was still beautiful, if a little thicker of waist.

'I almost forgot you had an eye-patch,' she said after we shook hands. I grinned like a fool and ordered a cup of coffee. We sat in a booth at the back near the jukebox. Fortunately the place was as good as empty.

We talked, and at first Sonia proved a little monosyllabic. I asked her about her life, and she answered in short, precise phrases that she was doing very well, thank you very much. The coolness of her response surprised me; the speed with which she had responded to my request for a meeting had convinced me that she would be keen to talk herself out. I had even toyed with the idea of asking her in advance to put pen to paper, and supply me with her own version of our story. In my confusion I started babbling, explaining to her again who I was and how I knew Pavel, skirting over some of the more unsavoury details, perhaps, and going easy on the parts that outlined her sexual conduct back then. There was no point in insulting the woman. What I ended up dwelling on, I'm afraid, was the time Pavel and I had spent down in the Colonel's basement, talking. The thing is, when does one ever get to do that? To talk of the essential things, all those thoughts and experiences a man shuts up in his chest and gags on for half his life? They don't spill out but once or twice in a lifetime – and very often not at all. Pavel and I, we had spoken as one might to a priest, only better than to a priest, for even there all talk is strategic, and especially that portion of it that is self-accusatory. It's filled my life, this talking. Only sometimes I feared we had never really talked at all.

'Sometimes,' I explained to Sonia (and I'm afraid I was gesticulating a lot at this time, threatening to knock over our cups of coffee time and again), 'sometimes, in retrospect, you see, it's like he was just having me on, leading me further and further into the maze of some personality he'd constructed on

332

the spot, and all with but a single aim – to knock me senseless and escape.'

I stopped, exhausted.

'So?' she asked.

'So?!'

'You spent a few nights together, like boys at camp, and he had you on. Are you asking for my sympathy?'

It was then I realized that she had never forgiven him for what he did.

I might have gone at that point, cut short my interview and left her without a second glance. I had a good mind to do just that, but the truth is I was too needy. There were things I wanted to know, and I was willing to pay the price of her rudeness. I finally got round to what was on my mind when she made noises to leave. I reached over to where she was fumbling with her purse and laid a hand on hers. What I needed to hear was whether she knew more than she was letting on.

'Did he ever contact you?' I asked.

'You mean show up on my front lawn one afternoon, while I was giving a lesson, and ring the bell?' She pulled a face and sipped at the remnants of her coffee. 'No, he didn't. For a while I thought he might, but then I realised that it wasn't the way things would work out.'

'How did they work out?'

'I have a good life,' she said. 'And you?'

'Respectable.'

'Well, be happy. It's more than a lot of other people got.'

She said it with utmost sincerity. It must have been the same tone of voice with which she'd given her marriage vows. I couldn't accept that she would lie to herself like this.

'You loved him once, didn't you?' I asked her. 'I need to know that you loved him.'

She pursed her lips in a manner that suggested displeasure. Her lipstick did not go with her *teint*.

'You can convince yourself of all sorts of things,' she began. 'That you have never loved. That you have always loved, loved undyingly, and could not but love. Once you get some practice at it, there comes the time when you experience an epiphany every other day of the week. And the worst of it is, you really feel it: your body feels it, the truth of your life has finally been revealed. Only by Wednesday it's another truth and your body feels that one, too. Down to the bones.'

It was the longest I ever heard her speak. Nothing I knew of her had prepared me for such loquaciousness.

'You're bitter things didn't pan out,' I told her.

'You haven't been listening, Peterson. You like telling stories, but you don't listen for shit.'

She waved for the check. The waitress came over, slipped a piece of paper under my saucer. I kept my eyes on Sonia.

'I know things you don't,' I told her.

'Like what?'

'I know what he traded your lives for. Yours and Anders'.'

She held my stare for a moment, then shook her head.

'Keep it,' she said. 'I know all I need to.'

We exchanged two or three more words about trifles. Then we were both off on our separate ways. I think she despised me because I insisted on going Dutch.

———·———

I did not tell her, then. The things I had found out. That I had inquired into his service file, and found it was classified. Had talked to fellow servicemen who had served with Pavel in 'Intelligence and Infiltration': tight-lipped veterans with the habit of caution, even after a bottle of Irish. That I tried to track down his wife and learned he had no wife. No parents in Cincinnati, nor a baptismal record. It was easy to guess what Sonia would have said to all this. 'So he lied to you,' she would have said. Or, perhaps, it could have goaded her into making excuses. 'You must have mixed up the city,' she might have said. 'After all, it was seventeen years ago. You are liable to have mixed up all sorts of things.'

Either way, I would have persevered. I would have told her that I'd met an American officer in London, in August 1953, just after the Union of Socialist Soviet Republics had developed their own atomic bomb and half the world blamed it on the Rosenbergs. His name was Finnigan, James Arthur Finnigan. As a favour to me, Finnigan had looked into Pavel's service record and learned that, if the paperwork was correct, the man had never been decommissioned. Of course it could have been an administrative error.

'It just doesn't make any sense,' I would have told her. 'Killing Haldemann. We talked for nine days and he never even mentioned politics. Or loyalty to his nation. National security. He mentioned his wife, and the boy. Once he told me he had kissed you. "On the mouth," he said, eyes downcast. He was so delicate about it you'd think he'd crap himself.'

But what would have been the use? She would have heard me out and walked away, a shrug to her shoulders and no way of telling what she was really thinking. I had spent half my life with her memory, and when I met her again I finally stumbled on what she was: inscrutable. There was nothing I could do that would move her to help me assemble the facts.

I tried the boy next. Anders Skinner. I half expected he would have changed his last name, to 'Richter' if in doubt, but he was living under his adoptive father's name, working as a second-rate journalist for a Düsseldorf daily. I made tentative contact via letter, sending along a few pages from my notebooks that outlined some of the events of his past. There was no answer. I had no money just then to fly out to Germany, so I got hold of Anders' phone number instead and called him collect. To my relief he accepted the charges.

'Who's this?' he asked, and I introduced myself. 'Yes,' he said. 'The man with the eye-patch. You sent me a letter.'

I gave him a brisk summary of all the things that bothered me about the events of the past, then hit him with my question as quickly as I could. There was no way of telling how much money he was willing to spend on this, and the tone of his initial response pointed to some modicum of hostility.

'Why do you think he did it?' I asked.

'Did what?'

'Kill Haldemann. With practised hands. Snapped his neck like a Christmas turkey.'

'You don't know that,' he said. 'You were in the car, waiting for them to come down. For all you know the old man slipped on the stairs. Broke his neck on the way down.'

He said more, much in the same vein, recommending that I should shave my memories of all their romance and boil them down to the facts. 'And I mean actions,' he said, 'not some passing observations. You put too much faith in shrugs and frowns, build whole castles on a smile. Just write down the things he did and leave it at that. Like Hemingway. It makes for better copy.'

I was hurt by this critique and quickly switched to accusation.

'You never even loved him,' I said.

'Mr Peterson, I was twelve years old. Now I am thirty. All I remember with any clarity is that he read me Dickens.'

'You're lying.'

He hung up on me. Perhaps he figured he did not have to stand around and pay for my insults. I tried him again a week later, but he was away. I lost heart after that and ripped up his phone number.

Don't think I did not take Anders' warnings seriously. Of course I was plagued by the possibility that I had misperceived or misremembered. It is a terrible thing to distort the past. All the same, I came to realize that I simply could not remember it

336

otherwise, down to the last little frown. At long last I accepted my commission and brandished the pen; sat and wrote him out, my Pavel, belabouring each comma and word. I thought it would put him to rest in some poetic sort of way, but that was to prove an illusion. He haunts me at night; not quite every night, but often, especially in winter. Oh, I have dreamed him many times since I finished, dreamed them all, dreamed them through their own words, will you believe it, Pavel's blushing confessions through the bars of his cell, Sonia's acidity, even the boy (whom I barely met) mouthing man-words with his crooked mouth. In my dreams I become what Thomas Mann calls the 'rasping conjurer of the past', only the German indicates the grammatical tense, not the past as such, which through some irony all its own bears the title 'imperfect'. The rasping conjurer of the imperfect. The imperfect's rasping conjurer.

There you are, shaking your head: your guide's read his Mann. You don't like it, I sense. It does not befit a torturer.

Feel free to doubt me, then. I don't really mind: it is part of the story, built into it from the first word I wrote. Just one thing you have to believe. I loved that man, loved him like a brother. The thing is, he wasn't born for this, a story about microfilms, but this is what he got, and he damn near broke his heart over it. Broke mine too, and the boy's, and chipped away at Sonia's best he could. I wish I could talk to him again, just one more time, and ask him what he paid with to save our lives.

He'd give me the briefest of smiles.

'I simply asked,' he would say.

'Asked politely, without pleading. Karpov had said it himself. You had no value for the Soviet Union.'

And he'd kiss me, right on the mouth, five whole seconds, to let me know we did not part in anger.

The End

Acknowledgements

This is a work of fiction. While many facts about living conditions in Berlin during the winter of 1946–47 have been rendered with a good degree of accuracy, the events and characters that populate this novel are pure invention. There was no such person as Colonel Fosko. The administration of occupied Germany was performed by some surprisingly flamboyant figures, some of whom may have strayed beyond the strict confines of their legal mandates, but none that I know of wore mink. Elsewhere, I have bent or disregarded historical fact to accommodate novelistic needs. It is highly unlikely, for instance, that a refugee train would have pulled into Bahnhof Zoologischer Garten (Zoogarten station) rather than one of the city's other stations during the period under discussion; there are significant inaccuracies in the depiction of the command structure within British and Russian forces, and some minor inconsistencies in the description of border procedures as well as of those governing food acquisition via ration cards; the number of functional telephone extensions was smaller than the novel may seem to imply, and so on. In a book interested in the question of how many of our personal needs and desires we inject into narrations of the past, such inaccuracies may perhaps be excused.

For readers wishing to learn more about the period there exist some excellent books dedicated to the primacy of historical fact.

For a general overview, deftly told, one may confidently turn to *Faust's Metropolis: A History of Berlin* by Alexandra Richie, and Douglas Botting's *In the Ruins of the Reich*, both of which are rich in anecdotal accounts of the hardship experienced during the post-war years, and proved invaluable to me as reference works on anything from the exchange value of a cigarette on the Berlin black market, to the occupation armies' policies towards the German civilian population. For a visual impression of what Berlin looked like in the immediate aftermath of the war, Roberto Rossellini's *Germania anno zero* makes for sombre viewing.

Many of the anecdotes told by various characters in the novel are adapted from true-life events as narrated by a number of eyewitnesses. The most astonishing of these accounts, perhaps, is Ruth Andreas-Friedrich's diary of the period 1945–48, published in German under the title *Schauplatz Berlin*. Here one may find the story of starving Berliners cutting a dead ox to shreds during the battle for Berlin; of a schoolteacher's reprimand to her female students to choose death over the ignominy of rape; an account of the execution of a dozen schoolboys at the Markusschule just days before the collapse of the Reich in reaction to their 'unpatriotic' remarks. Andreas-Friedrich also recorded the vagaries of the weather in the long winter of 1946–47 with great specificity, and was punctilious in her descriptions of the toll exacted by this extended freeze. For a version of the story of the denazification of Karli Schäfer's circus – complete with 'Lilliputians' – one must turn to George Clare's memoir, *Before the Wall: Berlin Days 1946–1948*; for a harrowing yet level-headed account of the mass rapes that followed the city's liberation by Soviet soldiers (complete with some psychologically remarkable observations about the fascination of rape propaganda as disseminated by the Nazis) the anonymously published memoir *A Woman in Berlin* is without peer. Annett Gröschner's edited collection of Berlin school essays from 1946, *Ich schlug meiner*

Mutter die brennenden Funken ab, provides fascinating insights into how teenagers experienced the first year of peace; Vladimir Sevruk's collection of eyewitness accounts entitled *How Wars End*, and the final volume of Konstantin Simonov's war diaries offer powerful descriptions of the city in the immediate aftermath of the war as well as of the attitudes prevailing amongst Allied soldiers and German civilians. All these books have provided me with a thousand little details that facilitated my creation of a version of post-war Berlin which, though fictitious, makes close reference to a glum piece of reality just sixty years old.

Like all stories, and perhaps more so than some, Peterson's wild yarn also draws on those told by a host of fellow fabulists, many of whom far outstrip his own modest literary talents. These have contrived to wriggle into his memory, shape his vocabulary, and fuel his imagination. Unlike many storytellers, ours seems sufficiently indiscreet to pay overt homage to at least some of his heroes – above all to Dostoevsky and Dickens, both of whom may have wished to protest such imposition. In the spirit of Peterson's indiscretion one should nonetheless add a few names, equally referenced in his tale, though perhaps less openly. These include Wilkie Collins, whose fat Count finds himself reincarnated in an officer's garb to plot new villainy, and Günter Grass, that post-war poet who holds a near monopoly on clever midgets, and whose sense of line and grammar proved irresistible at times. It may be thought disconcerting that fiction throws as deep a shadow over this novel as the sombre realities of historical fact, but this, alas, cannot be helped.

I would also like to take this occasion to thank those people who have helped me in writing the novel, either by providing first-hand information about the period, or through their careful responses to, and corrections of, my manuscript. These include: Simon Lipskar at Writers House, Kathy Belden and Mike Jones at Bloomsbury; Richard Lapidus, Kristin Semmens, Aya Soika,

Bernhard Fulda, Eckhard Leberl, Ivan and Anna Crozier, and Johanna Greenwood. I would also like to thank my family for putting up with a son who has taken it into his head to write in a foreign tongue, James Boyd White for lending me his name, and my wife, Chantal Wright, whose editorial pen marks every page of this book. Your efforts were greatly appreciated.

A NOTE ON THE AUTHOR

Dan Vyleta is the son of Czech refugees who emigrated to Germany in the late 1960s. He has a Phd in history from the University of Cambridge. He lives and works in Edmonton, Canada. This is his first novel.

A NOTE ON THE TYPE

The text of this book is set in Berling roman. A
modern face designed by K. E. Forsberg between
1951 and 1958. In spite of its youth it does carry the
characteristics of an old face. The serifs are inclined
and blunt, and the g has a straight ear.